# BRISTLECONE PEAK

BY
## DAVE BROWN

*To Dennis Johnson*

BRISTLECONE PEAK
A Golden Feather Press book / February 1998

February 1998

Published by:          Golden Feather Press
                       PO Box 481374
                       Denver, CO 80248

First Edition

Library of Congress Number 97-78165

ISBN 1-878406-13-2

Printed in the United States of America

# AUTHOR'S NOTE

This book is pure fantasy in a real setting. Its purpose is to take any level of reader on an adventure fraught with love, laughter and excitement so that one might, for a time, escape the colossal horrors of the present day, especially AIDS.

All the characters, except one, are fictional and a product of my own imagination. James McParland actually was the head investigator for the Pinkerton Detective Agency in Denver in 1886, and his office was located in the Tabor Opera House on 16th Street. Sam Hartsel, who is not a character but merely mentioned, owned one of the largest ranches in Colorado in the late 1800s and built a hotel with a hot springs pool. The town of Hartsel still thrives in South Park, Colorado, and a few ruins of the hotel remain. Father Dyer, also mentioned, was an itinerant preacher who trekked the South Park and Leadville areas for years carrying mail through blizzards, delivering babies, helping to build homes, caring for the sick and spreading God's word to those who cared to listen.

To protect the citizens of South Park, Colorado, the names of some mountains, canyons and rivers have been changed as well as a few locations, but the landscape remains vast and awe inspiring.

Alma, Colorado, vying with Leadville as the highest town in the U.S., actually had an Alma Hotel. Both the Silver Heels Bar--closed in the mid-1980s but now a fine bakery--and Mount Silverheels were named after Girda Bechtel, a dance hall girl who wore silver shoes and acted as a Florence Nightingale for many smallpox victims in the town of Buckskin Joe in 1861, then disappeared without a trace.

The Espinosa brothers, originally from New Mexico, went on a killing rampage through South Park in 1863. A man named Baxter was mistakenly hanged for the brothers' crimes by a vigilante mob in Fairplay. Jose and Vivian Espinosa were eventually killed separately in the general areas described in the book. The Hanson murders, however, are fictitious.

In 1880, the residents of South Park did throw rocks and bottles at the Ute Indians as the army led them out of their land, forever.

# ACKNOWLEDGMENTS

In 1986, my good friend, Dennis, suddenly said from his hospital bed, "Dave, I wish I could read a western with a gay hero." I agreed but found none for him in any book store. One week later, Dennis succumbed to AIDS.

I pondered the idea of writing such a story myself and finally gained the initiative when my Aunt Helen, also on her deathbed, exclaimed, "David, do it, now!"

This book was completed (except for my continuous editing) in January 1992. The story and dialog came so fast and furious, I'm convinced Dennis and Helen collaborated with Jake and Wiley.

Jim, my partner for 25 years, has given me more love, understanding and encouragement than I thought humanly possible. Quietly and apologetically, he served as my vital devil's advocate. Jim continually urged me to keep writing while he tirelessly counseled drug users and alcoholics or found homes and food money for persons with AIDS. In his "off hours" Jim almost single-handedly remodeled our entire home. This book could not have been written without Jim, and we love each other more every single day.

Don Carter has been our friend for ages and has listened patiently to every blabbering word I've said about "my book and Jake and Wiley." He mostly kept silent, which always made me feel like I could write better. He's an excellent photographer and took my picture for the back cover. It has to be an art making "Thunder Joe" look good.

Mo Olson did the final edit, got the manuscript camera-ready, and has given me much insight into writing, editing and keeping on track. Mo took Dennis' place. We solve the world's problems.

Special thanks goes to Windy Newcastle for her close friendship and her PHD-inspired literary flair and dynamic, creative writing course; to Mike Daniels, Don Hamm, Tom Bohnsack, Dan Conroy, David Stevenson and Tim Plofkin for endless encouragement; to my brother Mark in the land "down under" for his straight, right-on-the-mark ideas and enthusiastic support; to my brother Leo for completely overhauling my computer three times; to my co-workers, Mary, Bundy, Laura,

Dusty, Jo Anne and Peggy for their encouragement and interest in all phases of this endeavor; to Raul Tapia, Native American artist, for capturing Jake and Wiley so perfectly on the cover even though he hadn't yet read the book or knew Wiley was ambidextrous with his gun, and to Ken Krenz, who has stuck by me through disasterous times and joyous times--someday he should head Scotland Yard.

Dave Brown

PS: If anyone finds Jake and Wiley smooching in the bushes, please tell them to get back here. We have more work to do. ·

# INTRODUCTION

"You're obsessing, David," my partner Jim said after my thirtieth edit, and again after each of the next twenty or so edits.

I realize he's probably right, but I wanted this to be a comfortable book. A book you can pick up at any time and read. Open it anywhere and be instantly sucked in! That was my plan.

"I like the idea," Jim said when I told him, "But don't you think that's a pretty tall order?"

Was it? How was I to know? I'd never written anything before except letters to editors griping about something or other. Every newspaper in Denver had a wastebasket with my name on it.

After our friend Dennis died in 1986, I started reading Westerns just to see what he liked about them. Working at the time in a hospital billing office crammed with desks, computers, printers and thirty-nine women, I started reading on my lunch break. In the next five years, I read over 400 westerns by well known authors, and authors who wrote only one or two books. I became hooked because of the masculinity of the main characters and the wide-open spaces the authors took me to. But, after all that reading, I realized western authors seem compelled to get the hero hitched to a woman at the end of the book. And nearly always that woman was the only female within a hundred miles of anywhere, and so what if the hero had traveled with the same male partner for fifteen years. What I (and Dennis) wanted to know was: what happened to all the other guys working on the ranch now that the only woman had ridden away with her prince charming? And what happened to the male partner of fifteen years? Victorianism and prudishness don't want us to even consider that part of life.

After Bristlecone Peak was written, one of my straight brothers read it, then said, "Dave, I liked the book but had to skip over all the men-kissing-men parts and some of the other parts too. They made me feel very uncomfortable."

I chuckled and said, "Now you know how I've had to read most novels my entire life."

# CHAPTER 1

"Jake Brady, get yer ass out here like a man!"

Horses galloping into the yard had startled Jake out of a sound sleep, then Seth's angry voice outside forced its way into the remnants of a lingering dream. The Harrises. It sounded like all six of them. What did they want? Jake raised his head from the knife-scarred table. Had his cows gotten into their barley again? If Zeke had come, he'd take his side, then stay and help with the cows.

Jake listened for the riders to dismount. When they didn't, he sighed and dropped his head back on the table. Barely able to move his arms, he stretched them as far as he could. All his muscles ached, and the skin on his entire body stung and itched from scratches he'd gotten during the last two days of plowing brambles down by the Kentucky River. Even his grandparents had struggled with brambles down there, and they seemed to fight back harder each year. He swore the damn things grew even in the dead of winter.

Jake raised his head and squinted across the L-shaped room at the position of the sun's rays on the floor. It was two o'clock. He'd slept for two hours. Jake yawned and relaxed his heavily muscled body back to the table. He just wanted to sleep. It was noon when he'd stripped off the protective leather skirts from his tuckered mule, and he vaguely remembered forking fresh hay for Smiley and the milk cows before staggering to the house and collapsing at the kitchen table.

"Jake Brady!" Seth yelled from outside. "I know yer in there! Get out here! Now!"

Jake sighed. He raised up and slowly scooted back the chair. After smoothing down his wild blond hair, he pushed against the table and rose to his feet. He rubbed his hand across his short, darker beard and focused on the front window above his sleeping cot to see how many of his neighbors were outside. He couldn't tell. The lace curtains, yellowed and fuzzy with dust, masked all but vague outlines of the skittish horses. Jake shrugged and ambled to the door.

"Took yer damn sweet time," Jed Harris sneered as Jake stepped out to the porch.

Jake looked at Jed and remembered the drawing of a flamingo he'd seen in school years ago. He wondered why Jed still felt important being Seth's oldest son. Seth treated everyone like a dog.

"What do you all want?" Jake asked. "I ain't done nothin'." He looked for Zeke among the milling riders but didn't see him. If Zeke hadn't come, it meant real trouble. "Where's Zeke?"

"Zeke didn't wanna come," Jed sneered. "Said he don't like what you've done to Sara Jean, and he ain't never comin' here no more. Most likely thinks Sara Jean'll get more use outta your whanger than he will, now." He threw his bony head back and laughed.

"Shut yer mouth, boy!" Seth snapped. The tall, gaunt, gray-haired man in his fifties, with a long gray beard and no moustache sneered from under his battered leather hat when Jed cowered. Seth yanked on the reins to steady his horse, then glared down at Jake. "What do you mean by gettin' my Sara Jean all knocked up with child? This here's eighteen eighty-six now, and it ain't right what you've done. You never said nothin' about marryin' her, but you're gonna marry her now. You hear me, boy?"

Jake's gut tightened. Sara Jean had told him the same thing earlier in the day, and she was crying when she'd left.

"I never done nothin' like that to Sara Jean," Jake said. "Why're you sayin' I done it?"

"I'm her pa, and she said you done it, boy," Seth snarled. "You're gonna marry her tomorrow mornin'. I'm leavin' Clem here to make sure you don't try runnin'. And you better not even think a-runnin' or I'll hunt you down and hang you from a tree 'til you're dead. Even if it takes the rest of my days. You hear me, boy?"

Seth jabbed his heels into the sides of his horse and galloped toward the road. Jed, Aaron and Abe followed after their father. Each man flung a hateful glance at Clem. He'd gotten picked over the three oldest to guard Jake, only because of his nervous trigger finger.

Shocked by the threat, Jake stared at the four men as they rode past the barn, out the gate and disappeared around the bend in the road.

Marry Sara Jean? Tomorrow? Jake walked stiffly to Clem's horse and grabbed the hackamore.

"Why'd Sara Jean say I done it?" Jake hoped for a civil answer, even though their friendship had ended years ago after he'd refused to help Clem tip over Mr. Benson's outhouse, door side down. He wouldn't have helped even if Mr. Benson hadn't been using it at the time.

The stocky man with the long Harris nose and filthy brown hair slid out of the saddle and shoved his rifle barrel into Jake's stomach. "Get in the house! I'd like to roast you over a fire jest to hear you scream and holler fer doin' that to Sara Jean."

Being two years older and a great deal bigger, Jake wasn't afraid of Clem, but didn't trust him with a gun. He turned, stuck his hands in the air and ambled toward the two-room room house. He felt Clem's rifle jab his back to hurry him along.

Once inside, Jake stopped and glanced at the closed door of his parents' bedroom. He wished it would open and Ma would come out. She'd tell Seth he wasn't the one that got Sara Jean all banged up. Even Pa would laugh the Harrises to scorn. But it had been two years since that door had been opened, and even longer since he'd been in the room. After Ma had died, Pa wouldn't let him within three feet of the door. But, even though Pa was dead, too, he had no intention of ever going in there again.

Clem shoved Jake farther into the house and slammed the door.

Deciding to ignore Clem, Jake ambled to the part of the main room used as the kitchen. He stuffed the stove firebox with kindling and lit it. When the flames began to roar, he pumped water into a pan, then lifted off the round, iron plate on the top of the stove. After tossing in a few wrist-size logs, he set the pan directly over the flames.

Jake needed to think and wanted Seth and the others far away before he tried anything. But, try what? He didn't have an inkling. Wandering slowly around the room, Jake collected the dirty dishes on the mantle, the coffee cups on the floor next to the matching rockers his grandparents had brought from Ireland, and the dusty plates strewn under his cot, then ambled to the sink and piled the dishes into a basin.

Jake knew Clem was getting angry and, like all the Harrises, went kinda crazy when upset. He just might pull the trigger, whether he intended to or not.

"Zeke's perty rankled at what you done to Sara Jean," Clem sneered.

Jake busied himself with his dirty dish hunt and didn't even look at Clem.

"I'm talkin' to you!" Clem hollered.

Jake could feel his gut churn like it used to when Pa had yelled at him. He tried to put on a stony face, but found it hard moments before his possible death.

"I said, I'm talkin' to you, dammit!" Clem's left eye started twitching. "I've a mind to plug you here and now." He jabbed the barrel of the rifle into Jake's back, jarring a spoon off the dishes Jake carried. It fell to the floor and bounced.

Jake looked down at the spoon but couldn't pick it up without dropping the other dishes. Suddenly, he had an idea and figured it must have come from his friend, Jesus.

After sliding the dishes into the basin, Jake pulled out a dirty cup and filled it with coffee left over from that morning. He dipped out a glob of honey from the sticky, red pot on the window sill, dumped the honey spoon into his cup and sat down at the end of the table farthest from the stove.

Clem jerked the chair out opposite Jake, plopped into it and slid the rifle onto the table, aiming it at Jake's massive chest.

Jake stared at the swirling liquid as he stirred the coffee. He could tell Clem had nearly reached his breaking point the way he squirmed in his chair and grabbed at his twitching eye.

Jake took the spoon out of the cup and dropped it on the floor. It bounced halfway under the table.

"Damn!" Jake crouched to pick up the spoon, but instead, grabbed the edge of the table, jerked it above his head and shoved it into Clem.

The rifle boomed. A bullet plowed high into the wall. Jake's shove and the force of the blast flung Clem backwards, and he bashed his head on the edge of the stove. The rifle clattered to the floor and Jake's coffee cup slid into Clem's lap, drenching him with the liquid.

Jake dropped the table and lunged at Clem. He yanked Clem out of the chair and slugged him in the face. Clem flew sideways, rolled across the floor and slammed into the closest rocking chair. Jake rushed to him, pulled him to his feet and threw his mule-kick punch to Clem's jaw. A bloody tooth skittered across the bare floor and hit the wall by the front door. Holding the unconscious man up by his shirt, Jake stared at the tooth. He hadn't meant to hit Clem that hard.

Jake easily slung Clem over his shoulder and walked outside. Slowly, he glanced around the small yard, used only for tying horses at the rail or hitching them to wagons. The front of the barn faced at an angle on his right and was sheltered by the branches of the huge old oak. Should he climb the tree and stash Clem in the tree house he'd built years ago? Thinking Clem might struggle when he came to, fall to the ground and break his neck, he decided against it. He could hide Clem in the thick brush surrounding the yard, but what if it rained? Jake sighed and headed to the gray, weathered barn. He stopped at a pile of hay just inside the door and dropped Clem like a sack of grain. Once Clem's hands and feet were tied, Jake stuffed a rag in his mouth, then pulled down some hay to keep him warm and partly conceal him. They'd find him tomorrow.

Worried that Seth and the others might have heard the rifle shot, Jake hunkered down in the shadows across from Clem and leaned against the wall. His guns were in the house, but if they came back, he'd be safer near his horse. No one in Jessamine or Mercer County could catch him on Mac.

Marry Sara Jean? Jake suddenly felt faint. He'd never kissed a girl his whole life, except his mother, and figured everybody knew it by now. He shuddered when he remembered how his Pa had always moaned to everyone that his only son was "one of them damn sissies."

But, no matter what his Pa had said, Jake knew he couldn't help getting all fluttery inside whenever he saw a handsome man. He couldn't remember ever wanting to make love to a woman, and getting hitched to one never entered his mind, except when Pa used to yell that he damn well better. But now his life had suddenly turned around to heck and gone.

Marry Sara Jean? Jake buried his face in his hands and sobbed. Jed's scornful words about Zeke hurt deeply. He thought Zeke knew he'd never do anything like that to Sara Jean. Or to any woman.

He'd fooled around with Zeke for over a year before he finally figured out Zeke was in love with him…at least before all this happened. But Zeke was only eighteen, and he longed for someone his own age. Yesterday he'd turned twenty-four and felt old enough to be Zeke's father. Besides, he ached to hold a man at least as big as himself.

Jake closed his eyes and wished Sergeant Moss were here. He'd know what to do. Next month it would be six years since the handsome soldier, traveling through Kentucky, had ridden into the yard and asked to stay a night in their barn.

That evening, bringing the soldier a meal he'd cooked himself, Jake remembered walking into the barn as the man washed up at the water barrel. The soldier had been naked. To this day, Jake couldn't recall what he'd done with the food, but he'd never forgotten how the Sergeant smiled and held out his arms to him. He could still feel the man's strong arms around him as they had rolled in the hay, their naked bodies crushed together. And, even after all this time, the musty, sour-sweet odor of the big soldier's sweaty body seemed to linger. Jake breathed deeply. Tingling all over, he remembered how every ounce of strength had drained from him when their lovemaking reached a climax he'd never experienced before, or since. He idolized Sergeant Moss, and even now the big man invaded his dreams.

Jake could still hear himself the following morning, pleading with the bare-chested soldier to show him how to get bigger muscles, and how shocked he'd been at the patient, almost loving way the sergeant taught him the Union Army's rigid training program. No other man had ever treated him that way. Since then, he'd rarely let a day go by without doing at least fifty push-ups, and often wondered if Sergeant Moss would be proud of his now powerful body.

A small part of the haystack slid onto Clem. Jake stared at him. Should he run? That's why he knocked Clem out, wasn't it? He searched his mind for regrets about leaving the farm, possibly forever, but couldn't think of any. Since he'd buried both his parents, he had no ties here. Alone for the past two years, he'd stayed on only because he didn't know what else to do.

Jake glanced around the barn. The deep shadows in the stalls seemed to move closer, as though wanting to grab him. A beam of sunlight fell on a coil of rope hanging on the far wall. It looked like a noose! Jake cringed. He jumped to his feet and glanced at the door. The Harrises weren't coming back, not after this long. He grabbed two sets of saddle bags and ran to the house. Quickly, he stuffed his clothes and a few belongings into one set of bags.

After Jake packed dried meat and a few stale biscuits into the other bag, he pried loose the floor boards in the corner of the kitchen and lifted out the cloth sack of money he'd been saving for two years. After selling eight pigs and four cows at the town fair last fall, he had two hundred and fourteen dollars. With that much, he hoped he could take the train somewhere and still be able to eat for awhile. But where could he go so the Harrises wouldn't find him, and what would he do when he got there? He shuddered, then crammed the money bag into his pocket.

Jake grabbed the pan of boiling water, dumped it into the stove firebox and slammed the lid. Steam billowed into the room, and filthy black water poured from the bottom of the stove. If he ever came back, he'd clean up the mess. After closing two windows, he put on his hat and hauled his bedroll and saddlebags to the barn.

In the stall by the rear door, Jake stroked the neck of his sleek, sorrel quarter horse.

"We gotta get outta here, Mac. It's just you an' me, an' we gotta long way to go. An' I don't rightly know where we're goin', neither."

Mac nudged Jake's hat off his head.

"Now, don't you be doin' that!" Jake yelled. "An' don't you go swellin' yourself up when I'm tightnin' the saddle!"

Mac did, and showed his teeth.

As Jake led the horse through the barn, he glanced briefly at Clem. The unconscious man's jaw had already swelled up and a trickle of blood leaked out the side of his mouth.

Without slowing his stride, Jake crossed the yard and tied Mac to the front rail. Unmindful of puddles, he plodded down the path to the birch grove in back of the house and stood before two weathered crosses inside a picket fence and surrounded by tall, brown grass. One cross tilted crazily, but Jake made no attempt to straighten it. He pulled off his hat and bowed his head.

"Bye, Ma. Don't know if I'll be back. I ain't never gonna marry Sara Jean, an' know you won't be fussin' at me up there. Lookin' down, you know I ain't the one that got her banged up."

Jake's eyes teared, and he wiped them with the sides of his thumbs. "Well, I gotta be goin'." He glanced at the tilted cross, then turned his back on it. If Pa were alive, he wouldn't care what happened to him.

Halfway to his horse, Jake stopped and shut his eyes. "Jesus, I know you're my friend an' you're always with me. But I can't see you or hold you. Can I find me a friend sometime...one that'll like me, too?" He swiped at his eyes again and whispered, "Wish I had me one, now."

After one last look through the house, Jake strapped on his gun belt and struggled into his heavy coat. The wool made the bramble scratches on his arms and back sting even more. He grabbed his Ballard rifle, gently closed the door and mounted up. After a final glance around the yard, he rode off toward Mr. Pritcher's farm, his closest neighbor to the west.

\* \* \*

"Land sakes!" Ruth Pritcher said. "You can't be marrying that Harris girl, Jake. Why, you'd go just as crazy as the rest of them. Dan, give Jake some bullets. He's gonna be needing them."

The heavy-set woman, with graying hair tied back in a bun, bustled about her kitchen packing food for Jake. She loved Jake as a son, but didn't ask him where he was going, convinced her nagging had caused her own sons to leave years ago and never come back.

Dan Pritcher grabbed Jake's shoulders. The tall, lanky man with an angular face, softened by his concern, peered into Jake's eyes. "Don't you worry about your place, Jake. We'll take care of everything. I'll bring Smiley and the pigs over here, and turn the cows loose in your pasture next to me. If I have time, I'll even plant your upper plot. And if you don't come back by harvest, I'll sell the barley and corn and save half the money for you." Dan shook his head. "But I ain't tangling with that land by the river. It's cursed, I tell you! Them brambles are like the hands of the Devil."

"But I just finished plowin' it today."

"Why were you plowing so early?" Dan Pritcher asked. "It's only the fifth of March. Well, no matter, I ain't gonna plant that piece."

Dan hugged Jake. "Take care of yourself, son. And you be sure to watch your back trail. I'll try and send the Harrises on a wild chase, but don't expect they'll believe a word I say."

After hugs good-bye, Jake mounted up, walked Mac to the crest of the hill, then reined to a stop. He turned in the saddle and looked back at Ruth and Dan Pritcher standing outside their front gate. He saw Ruth's apron wrapped tightly around her hands. Tears welled up in Jake's eyes when he realized they were the only ones in the world who cared if he lived or died, and he might never see them again.

Quickly, he turned away and spurred Mac into a gallop, allowing his horse to choose the way west. All he could see through his watery eyes was the streaked blur of the rapidly setting sun.

# CHAPTER 2

Jake pushed Mac harder than he'd ever pushed him in the five years he'd raised him. Now that they were miles from Wilmore, Mac was the only friend he had in the world and didn't want to hurt him, but he was scared.

Since he'd run, Seth would never stop until he tracked him down and hung him. Once Seth got something in his craw, he never gave up, and he'd most likely bring all his sons with him. There'd be six of them chasing after him.

But he had to run. He couldn't marry Sara Jean. Jesus didn't want him to marry a woman. He'd known that as long as he'd known Jesus and couldn't remember when he hadn't known Jesus. Somewhere he'd find a friend to help him. Maybe Sergeant Moss?

At midnight, Jake rode into Bloomfield and realized he'd traveled close to forty miles. He knew the town well since he'd raced Mac there on occasion.

Jake headed toward the livery. Samuel, the hostler, would still be up. The kind old man would fix him something to eat and let him sleep in a haystack. He'd also give Mac a bucket of oats and rub him down.

He walked Mac to the barn and dismounted. Before he could grab the door, it opened from the inside. A round, puffy face smiled at him from the soft lamp light inside.

"Jake! What're you doin' here? Ain't no races 'til next month!" The old man opened the door wide, patted Jake on the arm, then grabbed Mac's reins. "Y'all come in here where it's warm."

Jake tried to talk, but his jaws seemed frozen in a clench. He realized he was shivering. Walking stiffly, he could barely keep up with Samuel, who hobbled to the potbelly stove in the center of the room. The barn seemed warm and cheery, not filled with shadows of dread like his own barn had been before he'd left.

Samuel eyed the big man closely, puckered his lips, then shook his head. "You sit yerself down in my chair an' let me take care of Mac. Maybe you'll thaw out some so's you can tell me what you're up to."

Jake shoved the rocker closer to the stove, sat stiffly on the edge of the seat and leaned toward the warmth. He didn't have much time. It was thirty-five miles to Louisville and a train west. In six hours Seth would find Clem in the barn. No matter how fast he went, Seth would be only a day, maybe two, behind him. Wondering why his life had become so mixed up all of a sudden, Jake relaxed into the chair and stared at the flames licking out three sides of the stove door. Samuel must have just added wood.

Jake's head bobbed, then dropped to his chest.

Waking with a start, Jake discovered he was lying in a pile of hay and wrapped in a blanket. Sunlight streamed through the livery door into his eyes. He wrestled out of the blanket and jumped to his feet.

"Damn! What time is it?"

"Time fer you to be eatin' and gettin' on yer way...if somebody's after you." Samuel grinned at him from his rocking chair. "Got your food ready." The old man leaned forward, slid a tin plate off the top of the potbelly stove and handed it to Jake. "Now, you tell me who's after you."

Jake juggled the hot plate piled with bacon, eggs and grits and quickly set it on the ground. "It's neighbors of mine. Them Harrises. They're sayin' I got Sara Jean all banged up with child." He hunkered down on the blanket, grabbed the fork sticking out of the grits and mashed the runny eggs into them.

Samuel watched Jake fork food into his mouth. He smiled slightly as he handed Jake a cup of steaming coffee. He'd never noticed until now that Jake reminded him of his sister's boy, Otis.

"Well, did you do it to her?" Samuel asked, after a long silence.

"Hell, no!" Jake yelled through a mouthful of grits.

"How much head start you got?" Samuel asked.

Jake washed the food down with coffee. "About now, Seth's most likely findin' out I ran." He shifted the position of his plate for the third time and, between huge, egg-runny bites, told the events that lead up to the present.

Saddled and snorting to go, Mac walked up to Jake from behind and nudged his back, upsetting the delicately balanced coffee cup on Jake's knee. Grabbing for it, Jake dropped his nearly empty plate, food side down.

Samuel chuckled. "Guess that means it's time to go."

After picking the old man off the ground in a bear hug of thanks, Jake leaped into his saddle and rode out to the street. The rising sun felt warm on his face. He patted the horse. "We got a long way to go, Mac."

"There he is!" a man shouted. "After him!"

Jake snapped his head around. The Harrises! They're already here! He jabbed his heels into Mac's sides, and the horse quickly became a red-brown streak as he galloped through town.

Tightly grouped, the five Harrises spurred after him, causing early risers to gawk as they galloped down the street.

In his racing tuck, Jake suddenly had to pee. Damn! It always happened when he drank coffee. He glanced back and couldn't see anyone behind him, but knew they were there. Knowing Mac's long-strided gallop ate up the miles, Jake ran him for ten minutes, then glanced back. Not seeing anyone behind him, he slowed the horse and led him into the woods beside the road. He leaped out of the saddle and sighed as he watered the tangled underbrush. Looking back at the road, he could barely see it through the thick growth.

Before he'd even finished, Jake heard the galloping of horses. The riders passed by the place Jake had pulled off, and the sound of many hooves faded quickly, then died out completely. Had the riders gone on, or only slowed down?

Jake remained frozen where he was, not making a sound. If the riders were the Harrises, he hoped they'd kept going and he'd lose them. Jake knew Mac wouldn't move or blow. He'd trained the horse not to so his pa couldn't find them.

After waiting several minutes, Jake carefully led Mac deeper into the woods. To his left, he heard a noise and stopped dead.

Scarcely able to breathe, Jake peered into the leafless brush. Everything looked dead and twisted, and the bare branches seemed like brown claws reaching for him.

Another noise, closer! Suddenly, the brush in front of Jake parted and Zeke Harris's face appeared.

Jake let out a gasp and backed up a step.

Zeke struggled through a tangle of vines and stood in front of Jake. Not saying anything, the lean, muscular man, lacking the long Harris nose, lovingly searched Jake's face. Suddenly, the handsome man's expression became pained and his soft, gray-blue eyes turned the color of hardened steel.

Zeke pointed toward the road. "Pa saw where you turned off. We're mostly all around you now." He lowered his eyes for a moment, then looked straight at Jake. "Had to get some from my older sister, didn't you? When Sara Jean said you was the one that got her all blowed up, I knew you never had no feelin's for me."

Jake reached out and grabbed Zeke's shoulder. "I ain't never done nothin' to Sara Jean, Zeke. I ain't never even kissed her. You gotta believe me."

Zeke pulled away. "Now you hafta marry her! Then all you'll have time for is just *her*! I hate you, Jake!" He spun around and shouted, "He's here, Pa! I found him!"

Jake panicked. He grabbed Zeke, jerked him around and popped him on the jaw, then gently lowered him to the ground. He heard shouts as the other Harrises scrambled through the brush all around him. They were closing in.

Jake flew into the saddle, turned Mac toward the road and nudged him through the trees. Suddenly, Clem leaped out of the brush and leveled his rifle at Jake. As he rode by, Jake kicked Clem's gun as hard as he could. A bullet blasted the sky before the rifle sailed out of the man's hands.

Another shot. The slug whizzed above Jake's head. Abe Harris rushed toward him on the left, ready to shoot again. Jake spurred Mac, and the horse leaped over a cluster of bushes, narrowly missing a downed log, and galloped through the trees. As he turned onto the road, Jake heard cursing behind him, then the deafening blast of Seth's old buffalo gun.

After traveling a half mile, Jake glanced back. No one was behind him, but they would be soon. Where had the Harrises come from? How did they know he'd run? Zeke? Zeke must have gone to see him last night and found Clem. He gently nudged Mac to go faster.

* * *

Seth slapped Zeke's face, leaving a red mark. "Get up, boy! Jake's given us the slip!" He started to slap his son again, but Zeke raised his arm to fend off the blow.

"I'm awake, Pa! Jake didn't hit me that hard." Zeke shook his head and felt his jaw.

"Well, get your horse, and let's get after him!" Seth pulled Zeke to his feet. "Get your horses!" he yelled at his other three sons.

It took only a few minutes for the Harrises to resume the chase. But, having traveled all night, their horses began frothing after a few miles. Reaching the head of a long, straight stretch of road and not seeing the dust of Jake's horse, Seth raised his arm, then slowed his mount to a stop. The others reined in beside him.

After dismounting, Seth walked to Aaron's horse, pulled his second oldest son out of the saddle and backhanded him across the face. Aaron's long, greasy hair flew out as his head snapped to the side. The tall bony man dropped to the ground. Stunned for a moment, he looked up at his father, then felt his bloody lip.

"You damn fool!" Seth screamed. "That'll teach you to go yellin' a warnin' to Jake when we was in town! You let him get away!"

Aaron hung his head. "Didn't mean to, Pa."

"That ain't no excuse! I should'a left you home instead of Jed. But, since you went and done that, *you* gotta find us fresh horses. Ours is foamin' at the mouth. If we run them any more, they won't be worth tradin'." The old man pointed up the road in the direction Jake had disappeared. "Now, start walkin'! You hear me, boy?"

Aaron struggled to his feet, briefly glanced at his father's scowling face and headed up the road.

"After we water the horses at that crick over there, we'll be tailin' your be-hind," Seth yelled to him.

Zeke looked at his father. "We can't trade our horses, Pa. We've named them all." He folded his arms defiantly, but hung his head. "I ain't tradin' Shot. Jake gived him to me, an' he's pretty near as fast as Mac."

Seth spun around and glared at Zeke. "That's the horse we're tradin' *first*!"

* * *

Jake galloped Mac for twenty minutes, then slowed him to a trot. Nearing the end of a long stretch of straight road, he glanced over his shoulder. Seeing no one behind him, he pointed the horse into the brush, dropped from his saddle and watered the ground again, sighing.

Mac nudged him, and Jake peed on his boots.

"Don't you be doin' that," Jake growled softly. "This ain't no time to be funnin'."

Allowing the horse to rest and drink often, Jake kept Mac in a strong canter. The miles slipped by, and soon he saw the smoke of Louisville ahead.

"Where's the train station?" Jake asked a man on the side of the road. "I ain't never been here before."

"Stay on this road," the man said. "Keep going on it and you'll ride in the front door."

As Jake neared the station, he couldn't help staring. It had to be the biggest building in the world. He tied Mac to the water trough and timidly went inside. After asking directions from a man wearing a railroad hat, he took his place in the ticket line and began gawking at the high ceiling, huge arched windows and scores of milling people.

"Where's ever'body goin'?" he asked out loud to himself.

"They're going to all parts of the country, son," a man behind him said.

Jake spun around. "What?" He saw an older man in a brown suit and vest. His graying hair and beard were neatly trimmed.

The man smiled. "I said, they're going to all parts of the country."

"Who?" Jake asked. The man's smile made him feel edgy. "You laughin' at me?"

"Of course not," the man said. "You asked where all the people were going. I merely answered you." He extended his hand. "My name is Clyde Balmont."

As Jake shook Balmont's hand, he remembered Sergeant Moss warning him to always be cautious of strangers.

"Er...I'm Jake. Jake Brady."

"Glad to make your acquaintance, Jake." Balmont cleared his throat. "I think you need to move along in line. You're next."

"Oh!" Jake spun around, closed the gap and stared straight ahead.

Suddenly, it became his turn in line. He hesitated for a moment, then moved to the counter.

"Where to?" asked the balding man behind the grille.

"Uh...west," Jake stammered.

"Where, west?" the ticket agent asked, sharply.

Jake glanced around. "The next train west. I don't care where."

The clerk eyed him with suspicion, then scanned a chart for a moment. "The next train west leaves in two hours for Saint Louis, Dodge City and then on to Denver."

"I'll go there," Jake said, quickly.

"*Where*?" the agent snapped. "Young man, I don't have all day. There are other people waiting."

"That last place. Denver. I'll go to Denver."

"That will be sixty-two dollars."

"Sixty-two dollars!" Jake shouted. "Hell, that's most all my money!"

Clyde Balmont moved beside Jake. "Allow me to pay for the gentleman's fare." He looked into Jake's astonished face. "Are you taking a horse?"

"Hell, yes. I couldn't leave Mac. He's the only friend I've got."

"It's twenty-four dollars extra to take a horse," the agent said.

Balmont slid a hundred dollar bill under the grate. "Take it all out of this."

Jake's eyes grew wide seeing the money, but said nothing.

The clerk raised an eyebrow, then snatched the bill and stuffed it into the cash drawer beside him. After handing Balmont his change, he prepared the ticket and shoved it toward Jake. "Bring your horse to the livery on the right side of the building. Show your ticket, and they'll take care of it." He rubbed his eyes. "Next?"

As Jake moved away, Balmont grabbed his arm. "Wait for me in the center seating area. I'd like to offer you a job in Denver."

Holding his ticket, Clyde Balmont approached Jake from behind and watched him gawk at the huge chandelier hanging from the center of the room. He chuckled, then sat beside the big man.

"Are you running from the law, Jake?" he asked softly.

Remembering Sergeant Moss saying, "Don't tell strangers anything about yourself," Jake fidgeted before he answered. He couldn't lie. "Uh...I'm hankerin' to get away from home is all."

Balmont smiled. "A woman?"

"How'd you know?"

The older man laughed. "It's common."

Jake glanced at the huge clock over the door to the trains, then at Balmont. "Thanks for buyin' my ticket. I only got two hunnert dollars."

"Think nothing of it," Balmont said. He looked Jake over carefully. "How would you like to help build houses in Denver? I recently got a contract in the part of town called Highland, and I have to build thirty homes before the end of the year. There aren't many men there as muscular as you, and I need hod carriers. I'll pay you two dollars a day."

"What the hell's a hod carrier?" Jake asked.

Balmont smiled. "You'd carry bricks up a ladder to the men building the walls. It's hard work, but you look like you're used to it."

"Hell, that don't sound hard. Back home, I can toss them hay bales to the upstairs door of the barn." Jake eyed him suspiciously. "Why're you here if you're buildin' them houses?"

Clyde Balmont laughed. "Good question, Jake. I'm on my way to New York to get more financing from my partner." He glanced at the clock. "I have a few more hours to wait for my train east."

The two men talked for over an hour. Balmont wrote out a note of hire for Jake to his foreman in Denver, walked with Jake as he led Mac to the livery for boarding, wished him luck and then departed. Once Jake saw that Mac was safely on the train, he boarded and found a window seat.

A thrill of excitement flooded Jake's veins as the train lurched, then began to move. His first train ride! He chuckled. He'd gotten away from the Harrises and even had a job in Denver. "You sure gotta be helpin' me some, Jesus," he whispered.

Staring out the window as the train slowly pulled out of the station, Jake saw a group of riders approach out of nowhere and dismount a short distance from the tracks. The Harrises! Before Jake could duck out of sight, Clem and Abe spotted him. They shouted to the others and pointed. Zeke ran toward the train, but it was already moving too fast and within seconds the men were out of sight.

Jake did little during the long train ride except watch out the window while the countryside, towns and cities slipped by. In Saint Louis and again in Dodge City, the train stopped for several hours. He wandered to the stock car and checked on Mac, reassuring him they would be safe once they reached Denver. At least, he hoped they'd be safe. Once again, Jake shuddered when he remembered Zeke's angry face as he'd run for the train and, again, shoved it out of his mind that the Harrises now knew where he was going. Maybe if he was working, they'd never find him.

On the morning of the fourth day, the sun glistened on the snow-capped peaks of the Rockies as the couplers slammed together down the line when the train came to a complete stop. The jolt woke Jake from an uncomfortable sleep. Opening his eyes, he saw a wide expanse of train tracks, a river on the far side of the rail yard and, beyond that, a snow-covered bluff dotted with a few houses and even fewer trees. Stiffly, he sat up straight and looked around inside the car. Everyone excitedly gathered their belongings.

"Where are we?" Jake asked a passing man.

"Denver!" the man shouted joyously. He stopped suddenly, breathed deeply and smiled. "Can't you smell the gold in the air?" He nodded to Jake and headed for the door.

Jake glanced out the window again. His traveling was over. He'd arrived in Denver. Excitement, mixed with terror, gripped him. This was a new place, and he didn't know anybody. He pulled out the piece of paper Balmont had given him. After unfolding the note, Jake scanned the writing but couldn't read a word of it. How would he ever find Balmont's foreman?

# CHAPTER 3

Jake walked Mac down Seventeenth Street and surveyed the bustling city. Wet snow clung to window ledges and capped ornate trim at the tops of the buildings, some five stories high, that lined both sides of the streets in every direction. Shopkeepers swept snow from doorsteps into the sloppy, mud streets. Jake rode in the sunlight as much as he could, wondering why the temperature dropped when he ventured into the shade.

He turned up Holladay Street, hoping to find a saloon. Maybe a bartender could read the note Clyde Balmont gave him. As he passed Nineteenth Street, traffic thinned and he noticed many of the buildings looked shabby. He saw women standing in doorways or leaning out second-story windows. A few called out to him.

"New in town, sugar?" one yelled. "How about a little fun?"

From the opposite side of the street, a woman waved from a red-curtained window. "We serve iced drinks, honey."

Jake panicked. Quickly turning Mac around in the middle of the street, he galloped the opposite way until he reached Fifteenth Street where heavy traffic forced him to slow his horse to a walk.

Delivery wagons and buggies seemed to appear out of nowhere from around corners and out of narrow gaps between buildings. Many were parked, some even double parked, as vendors unloaded their wares. Trollies pulled by horses along mud-covered tracks had the right-of-way, and the clanging of their bells never ceased.

Jake traveled one block over to Blake and spotted the Palace Theater, a two-story building with nine arched doors on the ground floor. A wooden porch had been built out to the street over the center three doors, and he saw several men standing on top leaning against the railing. They all had beer mugs in their hands and were laughing. Jake knew it had to be a saloon. After tying Mac to the front rail, he eyed the toughs loitering in the street and felt relieved when none seemed to notice him enter.

After his eyes got used to the darkened interior, Jake glanced around. Across from him, a stage curved out into the large room, and a red velvet curtain hung in the background. Similar drapes closed in viewing boxes that surrounded the room on the second level. Tables and chairs filled the main floor, and scattered groups of people sat at them eating or only drinking. The delicious aroma of food made Jake remember that to save his hard earned money, he hadn't eaten much on the train. After hearing the price of the train ticket, he'd realized two hundred dollars wasn't much outside of Wilmore.

Carefully, Jake wove through the tables to the bar and stood close to a red-haired, bearded man standing by himself. Jake took in the man's handsome features, then ordered a beer.

"That'll be two bits," the bartender said.

Jake pulled out his bag of money, fished in it for a quarter and paid. As he stuffed the bag into his pocket, he felt a hand on his shoulder.

"Shouldn't be showing everybody your money bag," the red-haired man said. "Somebody's apt to jump you when your back's turned."

"I gotta get to it somehow," Jake said.

"When you come in here, put loose change in your pocket and only pull out what you need." The man glanced around the room, then whispered, "There's a lot of thieves that hang out here just waiting for people like you." He grinned and held out his hand. "I'm Donny Murphy."

Jake shook Donny's hand. "Uh...Jake Brady."

"You're Irish, too?" Donny eyed Jake up and down. "And *big*. What do you do, box or wrestle?" He laughed.

"I'm gonna be carryin' bricks." Jake reached into his shirt pocket, pulled out the folded piece of paper and handed it to Donny. "This here's what I'm gonna be doin'."

Donny opened it, then snickered. "Don't ask me to read this. I can't. Never learned how."

"You can't read neither? Thought I was the only one." Jake frowned. "How am I gonna find out who I'm workin' for?"

Donny scanned the room, smiled, then grabbed Jake by the arm. "Sid can read." He pointed to a table where three men sat. "He'll tell you what this says."

As they approached the table, Jake gasped when he saw one of the biggest men he'd ever seen in his life. The man's huge frame wasn't firm like his own, but this giant didn't have any fat on him. He had a thick black beard, bushy hair, and took up one complete side of the rectangular table. Sitting to his right, a tall gray-haired gent wearing a brown derby grinned at Jake behind his beer mug, then took a swig. The third man, small with slicked back hair and shifty eyes, reminded Jake of a rat.

Donny secured two chairs and shoved them up to the table across from the giant. He motioned for Jake to sit.

"This is Jake Brady," Donny said. "He's an Irishman, too." He turned to Jake. "The big fellow across from you is Sid Thompson." Nodding to the man wearing the derby, he said, "Clayton Tate." Seeing the scowl on the third man's face, Donny quipped, "And this bad-tempered, little scoundrel is Arnie Stuck."

Jake shook hands with Sid and Clayton, but when he extended his hand to Arnie, the man shoved his hands under the table. Jake wondered why Arnie did that. And why was he glaring at him? He hadn't done anything.

"Sid," Donny said, "Jake has something he'd like you read. He asked me to read it."

Clayton chuckled.

Jake hesitantly gave the note to Sid, glanced again at Arnie's frowning face, then lowered his eyes to his beer.

Sid squinted as he read the hand-written note. After clearing his throat, he looked across the table at Jake. "This is written to a man named Eric Bokin. It says he's to make you a hod carrier and general laborer. You can start at once, and you're to be paid two dollars a day." Sid grinned at Jake and raised his thick eyebrows a few times. "What did you do for him to get such a good wage?"

Jake blushed. "He helped get my train ticket in Louieville, then offered me the job." He decided not to tell them Balmont paid for his ticket, especially since Arnie still scowled at him. "Don't know how I'm gonna find that there Bokin. I just got here an' don't know nobody but you."

Sid glanced at his two companions. "We'll ask around." He handed the note back to Jake.

"You've just arrived?" Donny asked.

"Sure have. Just this mornin'. I ain't even ate nothin'..."

"Eat here," Sid interrupted. "The Palace serves some of the best food in town. You can get quail, turkey, pork, antelope, oysters...and, of course, beef."

"My favorite is breast of prairie chicken," Clayton said, kissing the tips of his fingers. "But, it'll cost you day's wage no matter what you order."

Jake grinned. "Hell, I ain't never had no antelope my whole life. Guess I'll have that."

"Hail, ah ain't never had no antee-lope my whooole life!" Arnie mocked. "Now, ain't that cute!"

"Shut up, Arnie!" Donny scolded. He turned to Jake. "Don't pay any attention to that rat-faced midget. He hates anyone bigger than himself." He glared at Arnie and shouted, "And that's most of the world!"

When Donny decided to eat with Jake, Sid motioned to the others and they shoved their chairs back, excused themselves and left. Halfway to the door, Arnie turned and scowled at Jake one last time.

Since it was almost noon, the room began filling up with men in suits. Donny shifted across from Jake so no one would ask to share their table. They ate leisurely, but said little until their plates were empty.

Jake leaned back in his chair and patted his gut. "Damn, that was the best meal I ever ate my whole life!"

"Where you staying, Jake?" Donny asked.

"Ain't stayin' nowhere, yet."

"Why don't you stay with me tonight? I've got a double bed in my room. I'm leaving tomorrow to go back to Alma. If you like the room, you can rent it after I'm gone. It costs four bits a day."

"I gotta have some place for Mac. He's my horse."

"There's a stable in the back, and the hostler will treat him well." Donny looked into Jake's eyes and grinned. "Well, how about it? Will you stay with me tonight?"

"Uh...sure thing." Jake felt a flutter in his gut when Donny smiled at him. He hadn't felt that way since he'd first seen Sergeant Moss, years ago. Nothing like Sergeant Moss, Donny was a head shorter than himself, stocky, and had a handsome face. Was he the one Jesus had picked to be his friend?

After getting Mac situated in the livery of the Graystone Hotel and stashing Jake's saddle bags in his room, Donny took Jake on a walking tour of the main part of Denver. Jake wore his coat, but ended up carrying it.

"Damn," Jake said, glancing at the cloudless sky. "There was snow all over this mornin', but now it's almost *hot*."

"Denver's like that. One minute it's snowing, and the next...well, it's like now. But, it'll be cold tonight." Donny shrugged. "Alma's not like this. It's in the mountains at ten thousand feet. Everything's frozen until May, and even after that it can snow. The nights are real cold, especially when you're alone."

Jake's heart leaped thinking of spending the night with Donny, but suddenly felt a stab of loss. "Why're you goin' to Alma?"

"I work there. At the Bancroft mine. I've been in Denver for three days on a supply-buying trip. I'm here with Sid and the other two you met. We finished loading the rail car today. The train leaves at seven in the morning."

They walked a full block in silence.

Turning onto Blake Street, Jake suddenly collided head-on with Sid, slipped in a patch of mud and nearly fell to the ground. Sid grabbed Jake with his bear-like arms to keep him on his feet, then squeezed him to his body.

"You're a comfortable feeling man, Jake." The huge man laughed when he saw Donny's frown.

Sid let go of Jake. "I found Eric Bokin for you. He's got an office down on Wazee. I can take you there. It's in the next block."

"That's mighty nice of you," Jake said, straightening his shirt. "An' thanks for catchin' me." He scraped his muddy boot against a lamp post. "Donny an' me was just walkin' around. We got time."

As the three men headed toward Wazee Street, Donny asked, "Where's Clayton and Arnie?"

"Clayton took Arnie to the hospital. Denver General. He mouthed off to a railroad man in the Arcade and got his nose bashed in. Serves him right, but if my last name was Stuck, I'd be an asshole, too."

"You'd be stuck *in* one, that's for sure," Donny quipped.

Jake quietly opened the heavy oak door to the second-floor, Wazee office and peered into the room. It was bright inside. The green and white striped walls seemed like grass against a cloudy sky. He'd never seen curtains like the ones hanging in the two sets of windows. They weren't lace, but he could see *through* them. Jake carefully stepped on the thick rug, turned and closed the door. It clicked loudly.

"Oh!" a woman's voice said.

Jake spun to his right and saw a blond woman push herself out of the arms of an older man that looked like Mr. Pritcher's bloodhound, but bald as a plucked chicken.

"I...I'm sorry," Jake stammered as he backed toward the door. "I'll come back. I...I was lookin' for Mr. Bokin."

"I'm Bokin," the man snapped. He waved his hand to the woman, and she slipped past Jake and out the door. "This better be important." He folded his arms and scowled at Jake.

"Uh...I'm Jake Brady. Mr. Balmont gave me a job with you." He pulled out the paper, shuffled a few steps closer and held it out to the man.

"Balmont, eh." Bokin snatched the paper, read it, stared long and hard at Jake, then asked, "Did he tell you what you'd be doing for me?"

"He said I'd be carryin' bricks."

"You ever carry a hod?"

"I ain't never even seen one."

Bokin sighed. "Well, you've got the body for it." He read the note from Balmont again, crumpled it and tossed it into a brass bucket beside his desk. "Report to the job site tomorrow morning at seven-thirty sharp. It's in Highland. Our tool shack is at the corner of Seventeenth and Erie."

"Where's that? I just got off the train this mornin' and don't know nothin' about this here town."

Bokin sighed again. He pointed to his left. "Stay on Fifteenth Street, toward the bluff to the northwest. Once you cross the Platte River, take the right fork. We're near the top of the hill." He turned abruptly and stared out the window. "On your way out, send that girl back in."

Outside, Jake found Donny and Sid leaning against the building. He was glad they'd waited for him.

"Well, how'd it go?" Donny asked.

"I start workin' tomorrow." Jake shrugged. "He was messin' around with a woman when I went in. It got him kinda rankled an' he tossed my note away."

"He what?" Sid shouted. He clenched his teeth and pushed his way into the building. A few minutes later, Sid came out, smoothing out the wrinkles of Balmont's note. He handed it to Jake.

"You won't have any trouble with him," Sid growled. "I put him straight. You keep that note in a safe place. And make sure he pays you two dollars a day."

Later that evening in Donny's room, Jake stripped off his shirt and was about to venture down the hall to the washroom when Donny grabbed him by the arm.

"I...uh, shouldn't say this, Jake, but...you're a fine looking man. If you're not careful, some woman will snatch you up, then keep you locked up."

Jake blushed at the compliment, but anger screwed his face an instant later. "Ain't no woman gonna snatch me *nowhere*. Jesus an' his Pa didn't make me for no woman. He's gonna find me a partner."

"*Jesus*? Jesus is going to find you a partner?" Donny pulled back and stared at Jake. "How do you know that?"

"Hell, Jesus tells me lotsa stuff. He don't talk, but tells me stuff soft-like, inside. We been friends my whole life."

Donny sat on the edge of the bed and stared into space. "I've never heard anything like that." Slowly, his eyes focused on Jake. "Do you think Jesus would let me be your partner?"

Instantly, Jake thought of Sergeant Moss. "Jake," Moss had said, "I've got things to take care of, but one day I'll be back. It may take years, but I'll be back."

"Uh...I don't know," Jake stammered. "You reckon we can be friends first? I don't know about us bein' partners, cuz you're leavin'." Seeing Donny's hurt expression, Jake pulled him to his feet and squeezed him in a bear hug. Donny grabbed Jake around the waist, and the two men stayed locked in each others arms for several minutes.

Suddenly, Jake pulled away. "I gotta pee somethin' terrible. I'll be back." He quickly disappeared down the hall.

After closing the door, Jake found himself alone in the washroom. Earlier, Donny had told him the guests pee in the bowl, then pull the chain when finished. Jake did, but was mesmerized by the flushing water. Where did it go? He searched the floor. No water anywhere. Wanting to see it work again, this time with something in the bowl, he grabbed a wash rag and tossed it in, then pulled the chain. The water swirled around, and the cloth disappeared. Jake heard a gurgling sound, and he laughed. After a few minutes, he pulled the chain again, but something seemed different. The bowl began filling up, then water spilled out on the floor. Standing close, his boots got drenched.

"Damn!" Jake yelled as he jumped back. "I *hate* wet boots!" He stamped his feet and splattered water on the walls.

"This damn thing's broke," Jake said out loud. He pulled the chain a few more times, hoping it would fix the commode, but each time more water gushed over the side of the bowl.

Suddenly, the door opened and a man looked in. He saw the water on the floor and yelled, "What's happening in here? Water's pouring on the desk downstairs!"

"This damn thing's broke," Jake said calmly. "I kept pullin' the chain to fix it, but it just keeps throwin' up."

"It's *plugged* up! Any fool can see that. What did you do, shit a week's worth?"

"I didn't shit nothin', but I put one'a them rags in there to watch it go down. Maybe that broke it."

"You're damn right it broke it," the man snapped. "Who *are* you anyway?"

"I'm Jake Brady. I'm stayin' with Donny in room 204."

"You're not staying there any longer! I want you out of this hotel! And I mean, *now!*" The man grabbed Jake by the arm and pulled him into the hall. "Get your things and get out!"

Jake hung his head as he walked down the hall. Several doors stood open as guests, wondering about the shouting, watched him pass. Jake ignored them. What would he do now?

He slipped into Donny's room and shut the door.

Donny sat on the edge of the bed with his long johns unbuttoned halfway down. "What happened down the hall?"

"I gotta leave. I broke that thing you pee in an' got water all over. Some man throwed me out."

Donny jumped up and grabbed Jake around the waist. You *can't* leave. I'm all worked up about you being in my bed tonight."

"But..."

A loud banging on the door startled them.

"Open up in there! I'm here to escort that man out the back door. Now, open up!"

Donny let go of Jake and opened the door. A different man from the one in the washroom barged in, grabbed Jake and started yanking him out the door.

Jake pulled his arm free. "I ain't leavin' without my saddle bags an' stuff."

"Well, get them!"

Donny shoved himself between Jake and the hotel manager. "Can't he stay the night? He just got in town and doesn't have anywhere else to go."

"No. There's plenty of other hotels in town."

Quickly, Jake put on his shirt and coat and grabbed his saddle bags. He grinned at Donny and said, "Hope I see you again, sometime."

"Come to Alma. Sid and I can get you a job there."

Before Jake could say anything else, the manager shoved him out the door and down the hall to the rear stairs.

As the hotel door slammed behind him, Jake felt the cold night air sink to his bones. Slowly, he saddled Mac and rode down the frozen mud street. Finding the Victory Hotel a few blocks away, he checked in, got Mac taken care of and went to his room.

Lying in bed in the dark, Jake wiped away a few tears from the sides of his face. Strange sounds and voices in the hall outside his door made him long for home and the stillness at night. He suddenly missed the hoot owl that used his old tree house as a perch. What was he doing here? Where were the Harrises? Would they follow him this far? Maybe he should go to Alma? At least, up there, he'd know Donny and Sid. But Mr. Balmont paid for his train ticket. It wouldn't be right not to carry his bricks. Trying to imagine Sergeant Moss's strong arms around him, protecting him, Jake fell into a fitful sleep.

# CHAPTER 4

For the next five weeks, Jake worked hard carrying his hod of bricks up a ladder. Sometimes he'd help plant trees or shrubs in the yards of the completed homes. Whatever his job, he continually watched for the Harrises, but never saw them.

After work, Jake occasionally rode Mac up and down the streets until he could find his way around town without any trouble. Twice, he ventured into the Palace Theater, but both times he arrived during a stage performance. Finding the house packed with rowdy people terrified him, and he quickly left without even getting a beer. He missed Donny and Sid and wondered if he should go to Alma, but the thought of working in a dark mine kept him in Denver. He loved being outside, and the growing strength he felt in his body from carrying bricks made Sergeant Moss seem closer.

On his job, realizing Jake didn't want to talk about women, few of his fellow workers spoke to him. It was only his size and strength that kept them from making insulting remarks.

Dorsey Coburn, nearly as big as Jake, and Elliot Ramsey, his handsome partner, became Jake's only friends. Usually nooning together, the three men sat in the sun and chatted.

"You still haven't seen your neighbors?" Dorsey asked Jake.

"No. I'm hopin' they went home. But the look in Zeke's eyes when he seen me on the train makes me think they kept comin'." Jake cleared his throat. "Why don't the rest of the men talk to me? What'd I do?"

Elliot put his hand on Jake's shoulder. "They're afraid of you, Jake."

"But, I ain't done nothin'."

"Try thinking of it this way...they're all married. Maybe you remind them of things they've enjoyed doing in the past with other men. And, just maybe, they'd like to do those things with you. But they wouldn't dare let anyone know. Even if they talk to you, the others will accuse them of being like you. They act like girls." Eliott chuckled. "But I watch them. They can't keep their eyes off you, Jake. Especially when you work without your shirt."

"Along that same line," Dorsey broke in, "have you seen your friend Donny since he left for Alma? Maybe the two of you could become partners. You seem so lonely, Jake."

In his mind, Jake saw Sergeant Moss's face smiling at him. "Uh...no, I ain't seen him since I got throwed outta his hotel." He glanced at Dorsey. "Where's Alma?"

"It's in the mountains about a hundred miles southwest of here. The fastest way is to take the South Park train. Or you can ride the stage road. The train costs eleven dollars one way. Are you thinking of going?"

"Hell, I been here over a month an' never seen the mountains yet. If I take the train to Alma, can I get there an' back in one day?"

"No," said a man behind them. "It takes six hours to get there. You'd have to stay all night and come back the next day. *If* you're still alive. They eat sissies for breakfast up there."

The three men turned their heads and saw one of the bricklayers standing over them from behind.

"Ed, you were eavesdroping!" Dorsey snapped. "That's not polite."

Ed snickered and walked toward a group of men standing together. After Ed whispered something to them, they all looked back at the trio and laughed.

Jake thought of the girls in third grade, his last year of schooling, and how they'd snickered and pointed at him because he wouldn't kiss them.

\* \* \*

Several days later on a Saturday, after working only until noon, Jake sat in a barber chair and watched people milling about on Blake Street. Suddenly, he saw a tight group of four men, all dressed in black coats and wide-brimmed black hats, walk past the shop. The Harrises!

The same instant that one of the Harrises peered through the window, the barber thrust a mirror in front of Jake's face, unaware he'd saved Jake from being recognized.

"How does it look?" the barber asked. Seeing Jake's horrified expression, he added, "Well, I don't think it looks *that* bad."

Jake leaped out of the chair and pulled away the apron around his neck. "How much?" he asked, breathlessly.

"Two bits, but if you don't like it, I'll..."

Jake slapped a quarter into the man's hand, grabbed his hat off the rack and pushed it on his head. When he reached the door, he turned back to the barber.

"Thanks kindly."

Jake opened the door, then slowly slipped outside. He looked down the street and saw the backs of the four men halfway down the block. Why only four? He distinctly remembered five in Louisville. He quickly untied Mac from the rail, swung into the saddle and galloped down the street in the opposite direction.

* * *

"Where you been, boy!" Seth snapped. "This here's a big town. I don't want you traipsin' around by yourself. It'd cause me all kinds a trouble if you was to get killed. You hear me, boy?"

"Pa, I know where Jake is," Clem said.

"Well, why didn't you say so, boy? Where is he?"

Clem glanced at each of his brothers. He saw envy on their faces for his discovery and would enjoy telling the story even more now.

"While you was walkin' down the street after makin' me stay with the horses, I seen Jake come outta one'a them stores with a candy pole out front. He looked at yer backs and jumped on Mac. Well, I jumped on my horse and took out after him. I seen where he's stayin', Pa."

Seth screwed up his face. "You sure it was Jake?"

"I'm sure, Pa," Clem said. "And he looked scared."

Seth rubbed his jaw. "We won't get him yet. He ain't goin' nowhere. We watch him, see what he does. We'll get him when he's alone."

* * *

Jake paced in his hotel room after he'd seen the Harrises. One of them had looked in the window of the barber shop. It had been either Aaron or Abe. Had the man recognized him? Where did they get the matching hats and coats? And why were there only four?

Jake walked to his window and peered out through the slit between the curtains, but couldn't see anything except the building next door. He trembled, wishing Sergeant Moss or Donny and Sid were with him. They'd know what to do.

Jake had promised to meet Dorsey and Eliott for drinks later at the Palace, but spent the rest of the night in his room. On Sunday afternoon, he ate in the hotel dining room and used that evening to catch up on the exercises Sergeant Moss had taught him. Before he went to bed, he propped a chair under the door knob.

* * *

At four o'clock Monday morning, Abe kicked Clem awake. "Pa said fer me to sit here. He wants you. He's back by them stables with Aaron an' Zeke."

Clem struggled to his feet and stretched. He'd been sitting in a cluster of bushes across from Jake's hotel since yesterday. Without saying a word to Abe, he staggered across the street and slipped down the dark alley toward the corral.

Suddenly, a hand reached out from between two buildings and grabbed him by the collar. Startled, Clem fought back.

"Don't you be fightin' me, boy. It's yer pa. I want to know what you seen."

"I didn't see nothin', Pa," Clem whimpered, still stunned from being grabbed in the dark.

Seth backhanded Clem across the face. "You was most likely sleepin'!"

"I weren't sleepin', Pa," Clem whimpered. "I didn't see Jake no time." He gently touched his lip. "I'm cold, Pa. Can't we use somma that money you found and get somethin' to eat?"

Seth spat. "You'll eat when I'm good and ready."

"Where'd you find that money, Pa?" Zeke asked. "It must'a been a heap. You bought all these hats and coats to match."

"Never you mind where I found that money, boy. Whoever lost it won't miss it." Seth chuckled to himself. He could still pick pockets as slick as when he was young. "We'll eat after it gets light."

As dawn brightened the east, the four men, crouched in a small space between two buildings, heard the back door of the Victory Hotel open. It closed softly.

Seth crept toward the alley and peered across at the stable. Still too dark to see clearly, he saw the black figure of a man saddling a horse. Not sure who it was, he crept back to the others.

"That might be Jake. I'm gonna follow him. He'll likely head down the alley to keep out of sight. Aaron, you wait 'til I get to the end of this here alley, then you start out. Clem, once Aaron gets to the end, you come on. Keep each other in sight. Zeke and Abe can stay here." He slipped out of the space and headed toward the bushes where they'd tied their horses.

* * *

Jake woke up earlier than usual. Had he even slept? In his long johns, he crept to the washroom, sponged under his arms and his crotch, then wet and smoothed down his hair. Looking at himself in the mirror, he knew he'd have to be careful going to work. The Harrises could be anywhere. Seth always said he could smell the man he was tracking a mile away.

After deciding to take everything he owned with him from now on, just in case, Jake dressed, strapped on his Double Action Colt pistol, then packed his things in the saddle bags.

He turned down the gas light, then carefully slipped down the stairs and out the back door. Mac seemed jittery as he saddled him. Once Jake thought he heard the rustle of bushes and figured he'd be safer traveling by the streets and not alleys. He slid his rifle in the boot and secured the bags, then walked Mac through the gate and shut it behind him. He leaped into the saddle and turned the horse toward the street. At the end of the alley, he spurred Mac into a gallop down Larimer.

Barely light enough to see, he kept Mac running as fast as he dared in town, even though few people were up at that hour. As he approached Fifteenth Street, he glanced back and saw another rider two blocks behind, galloping toward him. Was the rider after him? As the rider passed a gas lamp, Jake saw a flapping black coat trailing behind. It looked like one of the Harrises!

Jake spurred Mac down Fifteenth Street toward the river. At Wazee, he turned left and rode the half block to the Elephant Corral knowing it was the livestock exchange for the city. At the gate, he dismounted. It seemed deserted at this early hour. Quickly, he led Mac into the yard, closed the gate and found an obscure pen in the back by a building. He hunkered down in the stall and pulled his gun. It wasn't loaded, but it made him feel safer.

A few moments later, a lone rider slowly walked his horse past the corral, then trotted to the edge of Cherry Creek, came back and stopped at the gate. A thick silence fell over the area. Jake broke into a cold sweat and shuddered.

After a few minutes, the rider outside the gate turned his horse toward Fifteenth Street. Soon, the soft clops faded into silence.

"What are you doing here?" a loud voice asked.

Jake leaped to his feet and, without thinking, pointed his gun at a stocky man with a full head of white hair and a white beard.

"I...I'm hidin'."

Seeing the gun, the man put his hands up and backed away.

Jake looked down at his pistol and quickly holstered it. "That weren't meant for you. Somebody was chasin' me, an' I hid out in here." He glanced at the main gate. "Guess he's gone." Jake grabbed Mac's reins and led him out of the stall. "Guess I'll be goin'."

A horse galloped down Wazee toward the corral gate, and Jake ducked back into the stall.

"Whoever was chasing you sure scared the pants off you, son," the white-haired man said, lowering his arms. "That's only Ralph. He works here and, as usual, he's late. Why don't you get a cup of hot coffee? The Palace across the alley is already open." The old man ran his hand down Mac's neck and shoulder. "This is top horseflesh you have here, son. Ever think of selling him?"

"No! I couldn't never sell Mac!" Jake turned away. "I better be goin'. Mighty obliged for lettin' me...er, hide here." He hesitated a moment, then led Mac through the gate.

Cautiously, Jake rode back to Fifteenth Street and glanced around. Even though more people were about, he didn't see anyone wearing a long black coat. Where was the rider? It must have been one of the Harrises. Probably Seth or Aaron. Jake peered down the street the way he had to go. It sloped to the river, then climbed up the bluff for several blocks before splitting into a Y. Could he make it? It was almost a mile to the work-site.

"We gotta make it, Mac," Jake whispered to the horse. He got into his racing tuck and said, "Let's go, Mac!"

Mac responded instantly, reaching his full gallop two blocks before his hooves clapped on the wood-surfaced bridge that spanned the Platte River, then he stretched himself out up the long hill. Reaching the Y in the road, Mac kicked up dust in the turn, but steadily climbed the slope with ease.

Jake glanced around. On the bluff, only scatterings of homes or trees would conceal him until he got to the row of houses they were working on. He looked back into the brightening sky, but couldn't see anyone following him. Maybe Dorsey and Eliott would be early.

Reaching the building site, Jake slowed Mac to a walk, led him to the far side of the house he'd been helping with and dismounted. The house was third from the end, and he hoped it would make a difference if someone came looking for him from town. He glanced around at the thick shadows. Where was everyone? Realizing he was an hour early, he wished he'd stayed in town for coffee.

Standing in Mac's shadow, Jake waited fifteen, then twenty minutes. Still, none of the other workers came. Darkness slowly lost its grip except inside the half-built houses scattered down the street.

Suddenly, Mac perked up his ears and Jake heard a footfall in the tangle of bushes behind him. He spun around and gasped as he saw Seth ten feet away with his Sharps pointed at his gut.

"Found you, boy!" Seth snarled. "Figgered you hid so I hid too, an' waited 'til you come out. We been all over this town an' been up here, too. Now, you're comin' with me. We're gonna hang you proper, like we should'a done that night before you ran."

"But, I didn't do nothin' to Sara Jean."

"You ran! That proves you done it!" Seth pointed toward town. "Now get your ass a-goin'. We gotta find them others."

Jake slowly led Mac between the houses to the street. Now what would he do? He barely knew anyone, and Donny and Sid were in the mountains. Tears came to his eyes. Why was this happening? He hadn't done anything to anyone. Especially not to Sara Jean. Where was the friend he'd asked Jesus for?

Seth followed behind with his rifle shoved into Jake's back. When they reached Seth's horse, tied to the sapling Jake had planted last week, the old man grabbed Jake's arm.

"Now, get on yer horse an' let's get goin'. Ain't no way yer gonna get outta this."

"I wouldn't be too sure of that," Dorsey said from behind. "Drop your gun, and get your hands up."

"There's two guns on you," Eliott chimed in.

Seth jerked his head around. "This ain't none'a your affair! You leave us be!"

Quicker than he thought he could, Jake spun around, grabbed Seth's rifle barrel, yanked the Sharps out of the old man's hands and flung it over the top of a house. They heard it hit, far down the hill.

"You get to riding, Jake," Dorsey said. "We'll keep this ugly cuss here until you get out of sight."

Without a backward glance, Jake leaped on Mac and galloped along the top of the ridge, heading south and away from town. He'd thank Dorsey and Eliott later. Right now, he wanted to get to Alma, wherever the hell it was.

The three men watched Jake until the ridge took a dip a mile away, and he disappeared from view.

Seth glared at the partners. "I'll find him. I've tracked him this far. An' once I kill him, I'm comin' back and kill you, too."

They kept Seth prisoner at gunpoint until the other men began showing up for work.

As Seth searched the hill for his rifle, Ed the bricklayer ambled through the weeds toward him. He held up his hand to Seth. "Mister, I saw what happened back there. If you want to find that sissy and hang him, try Alma. I'll even draw you a map."

## CHAPTER 5

The Union Pacific train sped along in the dark, fifty miles west of St. Louis. At one end of the parlor car, Wiley studied the hand-drawn map that Mike McGelvy had given him. The town of Alma nestled in the middle of the Colorado Rockies. He glanced at the ceiling of the rail car and mentally practiced his alias. Wiley...Gray. Wiley Gray. He'd combined his nickname from college with the first part of his mother's maiden name. He couldn't use his real name. It was too well known, especially out West, even though he'd never been there.

Wiley slid his hand inside his jacket to the breast pocket and felt the brown envelope containing the five hundred dollars Mike had given him to do this job. He'd never been paid that much before. Any living expenses would also be taken care of.

He folded the map and slipped it into the pocket beside the money, then opened his favorite book, Walt Whitman's Leaves of Grass and read. Since he'd eaten a big meal in a restaurant near the St. Louis train station, then topped off his dinner with a double shot of bourbon, the gentle rocking of the car and the effects of the alcohol soon lulled him to sleep.

A woman's scream from the far end of the car startled Wiley awake, and his book fell to the floor. He snapped his head in that direction and saw a man wearing a huge brown hat and a red bandana tied over his nose and mouth. The man slammed the door and bolted it, then pointed his gun at the passengers.

"Get your hands up!" the outlaw yelled. He waved his pistol from side to side. "I want your money and jewelry!" He took off his ten-gallon hat, flipped it over and handed it to the first woman on his left. "Put that necklace and those earrings in there, then pass it down. Everybody else put their money and jewelry in there, too." He cocked his gun. "Anybody that thinks he's a hero will get it between the eyes. I'm a dead shot."

The woman nervously removed her jewelry and dropped it into the hat. As she started to pass it to the gentleman beside her, the outlaw yelled, "Dump the stuff in your handbag into the hat, lady, then pass it on!"

The hat was passed from one to the other down the left side of the car. After the last man stuffed in his wallet, not sure what to do, he glanced at the gunman.

"Get up slow and pass it across," the outlaw said. "Then, everybody pass it up that side." He glanced through the window in the door behind him. "And hurry it up!"

The passenger's hand trembled as he stood up and passed the hat across the aisle.

Wiley took it, glanced inside, then set the hat on the floor beside him. He sat up straight, shoved his jacket back, rested his right hand near his belt then stared at the outlaw with cold brown eyes. He was glad he'd worn his right-handed holster since his draw was faster and more accurate with that hand.

"What do you think you're doing?" the gunman yelled. "I told you to put your wallet in the hat and pass it on!"

Slowly and deliberately, Wiley said, "This is as far as the hat goes. If you want it, come get it." Finally, he was seeing some action. Having gone a month without a gun pointed at him had slowed his reflexes, but now they were razor sharp.

The outlaw laughed. "Trying to impress the ladies by being a hero? I told you, I'm a dead shot." He took a couple steps toward Wiley, but stopped. The big man's cold stare and self-assurance unnerved him.

An older woman, who had just given up several strands of pearls, leaned forward. "Pass the hat, sonny. None of us want to get killed." Several other passengers chimed in the same.

"Listen to them, Mr. Hero," the outlaw said. "They're not impressed, either. Now, like I *said*, dump in your wallet and pass the damn hat!"

One corner of Wiley's mouth raised in a sneer. "I don't give my money to some two-bit tinhorn who thinks he's good with a gun." He liked 'two-bit tinhorn.' He'd learned it from a dime novel.

By observing the outlaw, Wiley could tell the man understood what he'd implied about his own ability with a gun. Now the masked man's eyes should show a flicker of fear the instant before he pulled the trigger. The flicker of fear he knew so well that he might not be fast enough and get himself killed.

The gunman tauntingly waved his pistol at Wiley. "I'm going to have to shoot you, Mr. Hero, in front of all these people." He laughed. "Mr. Handsome Hero's going to have a bullet hole in his forehead."

"I doubt it," Wiley said, never taking his eyes off the outlaw's. "But you're going to end up with a bloody stump where your gun-hand is now."

Wiley read hate in the man's squint as the outlaw leveled his gun at Wiley's head. The squint changed to wide open eyes as the gunman finally noticed the scar on Wiley's right cheek. Then, suddenly, Wiley saw the flicker of fear in his eyes.

So fast no one saw him do it, Wiley drew his gun, aimed and fired, putting the bullet slightly lower than down the barrel of the outlaw's gun, where he'd intended. Wiley's slug hit the underside of the man's pistol just as he fired, deflecting the shot into the wall four inches above Wiley's head. Wiley's bullet smashed through the cylinder of the gunman's pistol and detonated two of the shells. The outlaw's gun, and his hand, exploded into a red splattered mass.

Women screamed. The outlaw looked down at the bloody stump where his hand had been, opened his mouth wide, then fainted.

Amid screaming and yelling from the passengers, Wiley removed his jacket and rushed to the man on the floor. He slid the handkerchief off the gunman's head, untied the knot and wrapped it tightly around the man's bloody arm just below the elbow. The gushing of blood slowed to a trickle.

Wiley glanced up at the passengers standing around in a tight circle. "Everyone fan out and see if there's a doctor on the train!"

"You *shot* him!" a woman screamed.

Wiley stood up. His muscles bulged under his shirt as he towered over nearly everyone. With a bloodstained hand, he pointed to the far wall where he'd been sitting. "His bullet missed me by three or four inches, Ma'am. Go see for yourself." He glared at everyone. "But *first*, get a doctor! This man could bleed to death!"

Two doctors were found on the train, which everyone agreed was highly unusual so far west. The physicians worked for an hour on the outlaw in a private compartment. Finally, one of them emerged from the room and dodged curious onlookers and one irritating reporter as he made his way to the parlor car where Wiley sat by himself reading. The doctor stopped in front of the powerfully built man with coal black hair and a dime-size crescent scar high on his right cheek.

"The bone was splintered, and we had to amputate his arm just below the elbow," the doctor said. "But he should make it through. His days as a gunslinger are over, unless he learns to shoot with his left hand."

Wiley shrugged. "He probably will. Then, he'll come looking for me. Men like that never learn."

The reporter walked over to the two men. He tried to shove the doctor aside, but the portly physician shoved back and glared at the unkempt man holding a pad and pencil.

Undaunted, the reporter leaned over and stared into Wiley's face. "I'm going to ask you once more. Are you William Deluce, a man who has a reputation of being one of the fastest guns alive? You have a scar on your cheek like Deluce is suppose to have."

Wiley grabbed the man's shirt and pulled him forward until their noses were inches apart. "And I'm telling you, *once more*, it's none of your damn business! I told the conductor what happened and it's *finished*. If you keep pestering me, you could easily lose a big toe, or a *hand*." Wiley shoved the reporter away. "Now, get out of here, and leave me alone!"

After the man scurried out the door, the doctor grinned at Wiley and pointed at the book in his lap. "Leaves of Grass. That's one of my favorites, also. I'm dammed sorry I didn't heed its message." With a nod, he turned and walked toward the door.

Wiley stared at the cover of the book. The message, as he understood it, had something to do with being glad who you were. He didn't know if he was or not. Finding women sexually unattractive and usually annoying, made his social life almost nonexistent. Not that he cared, but it would be nice to have a few more friends who felt as he did. Real men, not flittering sissies.

For some reason, Grandpa Gray Feather felt close. He missed his Iroquois grandfather and tried to visualize his regal face. He wished he could talk over his trip West with him like he'd always done when he was young. A thrill went through him as he thought of being part Indian, but then cringed when he wondered what his grandfather would say about his present line of work.

Grandpa Gray Feather had been the only one he'd ever told about his desire for men, and the old man had only nodded and smiled. Why had he done that? Something stirred in the depths of his mind about the moment of his grandfather's death. Why did he think of that now? But the memory slipped away too quickly.

Wiley shook his head. "If it hadn't been for Grandpa, I wouldn't know how to track, wrestle, or even shoot," he said softly. "And he taught me dignity and courage."

Footsteps approached him. "Would you like a drink, Suh?" a black porter asked. "Boss says it's on the house."

Wiley straightened up in his chair. "Yes, I would. But just two fingers."

The porter handed Wiley a glass, poured the bourbon, smiled and bowed, then left the car.

Wiley held up his drink and stared at it. How often had he and his college teammates gotten drunk after a wrestling match? He chuckled. He might have been the top wrestler for three years in a row and a decent boxer, but he couldn't drink as much as the others. He could still hear them laughing as he'd throw up in the bushes.

Wiley's body tingled when he remembered Max Gordon helping him home after he'd gotten sick at one of their parties. Max had been so gentle that night, not like the brute he usually was in the ring. Max had been the only one to beat him at wrestling in two years, and that had happened only because he'd gotten so aroused by Max he couldn't think clearly. Wiley always wondered if that match had anything to do with Max kissing him goodnight after he'd helped him into bed. But all his attempts to get close to Max after that were met with a cold shoulder.

Wiley sipped his drink and thought of Mory and the other derelicts he'd taught wrestling and boxing to in Philadelphia's skid row called Little Russia. He realized he only had one friend who was like himself, and Burt was always hungry for his body. But Burt talked constantly and made jokes about his tracking ability. That didn't measure up to his idea of how a partner should act. Wiley sighed. He might be too picky.

Would he ever find a partner? Max came closest to looking like the man he'd always visualized in his head. The almost perfect partner. He fantasized wrestling with Max, both of them naked and covered with oil.

Wiley shrugged. "Dream on," he said under his breath. He glanced at the two porters with wet rags still cleaning up spots of blood, then left the car.

In his compartment, Wiley stripped naked and slowly slid his hands over his massive, hairy chest. Too bad they weren't Max's hands. He sighed and got into bed.

All night, Wiley dreamed of Grandpa Gray Feather on his deathbed, but he could never hear what the dying Iroquois brave kept whispering to him.

# CHAPTER 6

Not wanting to call attention to himself, Wiley stayed in his compartment for the remainder of the trip, hoping the chatter about the shooting would run its course.

Long after the train pulled into Denver, Wiley read in his cabin and ventured out only when he thought the rail car had emptied. Carrying his leather bag with his rifle tucked under the same arm, he strode through the station, ignoring excited whispers as he passed. He quickly left the building and headed up Seventeenth Street.

So this was Denver. He glanced around. It seemed bigger than he'd imagined. And filthy! Mud streets in the heart of the city? And the stench of a smelter seemed to follow him everywhere. He felt a twinge of remorse for leaving Philadelphia.

Out of habit, he began searching for a hotel. When he turned down Curtis Street, Wiley saw the sign for the St. James. Liking the name, he decided to stay there.

Finding the respectable hotel catered to businessmen, he felt more at ease, preferring the quiet atmosphere, and hoped the upper-class guests would be less likely to recognize him. In his room on the top floor of the five-story building, he gazed out the window. In the distance, the white-capped Rockies glistened like teeth in the setting sun. Alma lay somewhere up in that frozen landscape. Would he find the man he was looking for there? He tingled with excitement at finally being in the West, but couldn't shake the nagging loneliness inside. He'd always worked alone, but he wasn't always working.

Deciding to eat in the hotel, Wiley unrolled his suit and shook out the wrinkles. He hated suits, but didn't want to appear conspicuous, and hoped he wouldn't have to wear it in Alma.

After shaving and giving himself a sponge-bath, he blackened his boots, then dressed meticulously in front of the floor-length oval mirror.

In the dining room, he chose a table against the wall with a view of most of the room. While he studied the clientele, Wiley spotted a man staring at him.

Instantly, Wiley recognized the solidly-built man, sporting a moustache and wearing spectacles as James McParland, the head of the Denver branch of the Pinkertons.

McParland got up from his table and approached Wiley. He sat down opposite him and raised one eyebrow.

"What are you doing in town?" McParland asked.

"I'm just passing through. I'm on my way to California." Wiley wondered if he'd been convincing.

McParland leaned over the table. In a hushed voice he asked, "Were you involved in a shooting on a train from St. Louis? We had reports of a man resembling you blowing the hand off a thief."

Wiley cleared his throat and glanced around. "What makes you think it was me?" He casually rubbed his right cheek, covering his scar with the tips of his fingers.

"Well, if it *was* you, you'd better not stick around here," McParland said. "Somebody will probably be gunning for you. The story's been in the newspapers for two days running."

"I'm leaving the day after tomorrow."

"Make sure you do."

McParland got to his feet and returned to his table, tossed money next to his empty plate and left the dining room.

Wiley watched the Pinkerton agent walk out the door and wondered if the man really didn't know why he was here...or was he a good actor?

The next morning, Wiley walked the block and a half to the Daniels and Fisher department store on the corner of Sixteenth and Lawrence. The moment he entered, a handsome clerk in his early twenties dropped what he was doing and approached Wiley before anyone else had a chance.

"My name is Nathan. May I assist you, sir?" His eyes took in every inch of Wiley's handsome face and solid body.

Liking Nathan's looks, Wiley smiled and said, "Tell me, Nathan, have you ever been to a mining town in the mountains?"

"Yes, I have. What would you like to know?"

"What does one wear in a town like that? You know, to blend in."

Nathan chuckled. "If you *really* want to blend in, knock a wino over the head and wear his clothes. If you merely want people to leave you alone, dress in Levis or leather. We carry both. We also carry Levis that we've washed so you can get the proper fit. Can I show you something?"

Wiley grinned. "I'm counting on it."

As Nathan led Wiley to the Levis, he asked, "What size do you wear?"

"Measure me. Especially the inseam."

After trying on six pair of pants and an equal number of shirts, Wiley chose two pair of pre-washed Levis, liking their tight fit in the crotch and seat. He also bought a rawhide shirt and one Nathan picked out for him in white, billowy cotton. Both had open fronts.

"With a chest like yours," Nathan said, laughing, "you should wear open-front shirts...for the rest of us."

Spying knee-high moccasins, Wiley bought a pair, having worn his last ones out years ago, and picked out a western-style leather hat.

After he paid the bill and gathered up his packages, Wiley thanked Nathan for his help and headed for the door. Before he left, he turned and glanced back. Nathan stood behind the counter watching him. Wiley smiled and nodded, then walked outside. Had he noticed longing in Nathan's eyes? Why hadn't he asked the man to have dinner with him tonight? He shrugged. It would be too risky. Especially now that the shooting on the train had been in the papers.

Later that evening, wearing his new Levis, the white shirt Nathan had picked out and his knee-high moccasins, Wiley strapped on his gun, concealed it under his jacket, and left his hotel room. With his hat pulled low, he wandered the streets of Denver, finally deciding to eat at Pell's Fish House and Oyster Bar on Arapahoe Street.

Spying a small table near the front window, he grabbed it and sat with his back to the wall. After he ordered, he relaxed and watched the people in the street. Everyone seemed in such a hurry. Maybe it was the chilly air? Or could Denver, barely thirty years old, still be a wild western town? Philadelphia was two hundred years old, and things seemed to happen more sedately.

Suddenly, two men across the street caught his eye. One of them was Nathan. He watched as the pair laughed at something, then the other man put his arm over Nathan's shoulders. They smiled at each other as they turned the corner and disappeared from his view.

Wiley barely remembered when his food arrived, or much about it. Try as he did, he couldn't shake the overpowering sense of loss that had gripped him after seeing Nathan and his friend. After twenty-five years, why didn't he have a companion? Maybe he needed a different profession, one that didn't require him to travel alone and keep his gun well oiled. He had a college degree, but knew his present reputation would prevent him from following any other line of work. Besides, the money was good.

Wiley thought of holding Nathan all night. As much as he liked the looks of the man, one encounter would have been enough. He could snap the salesclerk in two like a twig. The man he wanted would have to match his strength, and the likelihood of finding someone like that seemed slim.

After paying for his meal, Wiley walked the block to his hotel, thankful he'd be leaving for Alma in the morning. He needed to keep moving and was anxious to visit a real mining town high up in the Rockies.

# CHAPTER 7

At London Junction, the Denver and South Park train veered west toward the London and Bancroft mines, bypassing Alma. Having heard passengers talk of terrifying train rides over some of the high passes, Wiley was thankful he wouldn't have to experience one. During the trip from Denver, he realized he didn't care for sheer drop-offs, especially when they were on his side of the train. Nothing he'd ever seen in the East could compare to this ruggedness. He loved this country, its wildness awed him.

"Sorry, sonny," the London Junction ticket agent cackled. "Ain't no tracks laid yet to Alma. Yer best bet's the stage out front. Two bits fer the ride, but you'd best light yer fuse. She's runnin' a mite late."

"Thanks." Wiley slapped down a quarter, grabbed his bag and rifle, and rushed out the door.

"Wait!" he yelled to the driver.

"Toss your rifle up first," the driver said. He strapped both items securely on the top of the coach. "I'm full. Luck to you in finding a seat."

Wiley heard gasps from the already cramped passengers as he opened the stagecoach door. A blond woman in the center seat giggled and shoved the old man next to her into the side of the coach, trying to make room for Wiley.

Wiley glared at her and squeezed between two portly men in the back. The coach started with a lurch and after it hit the first bump, he realized the dilapidated Concord mud-wagon didn't have any springs.

Someone mentioned the trip to Alma took fifteen minutes, but Wiley felt it lasted longer than the six-hour train ride from

Denver. His side ached from being elbowed with every bump, and his tailbone had gone numb.

As the stagecoach lurched to a stop in the middle of town, the passengers groaned as they received one final bruise. Wiley waited until everyone left the carriage before escaping the tight quarters.

Planting his moccasined feet squarely on the frozen mud, he stretched the kinks out of his back, flipped up the collar of his heavy jacket to ward off the icy wind and pulled down the brim of his hat. Despite the cold and the reason he was here, his heart leaped as he gazed around the bustling main street of Alma, Colorado. At long last, he'd arrived in the heart of the West.

His bag sailed past his head and landed in the street with a loud smack.

"Welcome to Alma, Bud. Yer ten thousand feet high."

Wiley glanced up and saw the grizzled face of the stage driver peering from behind a frost-covered woolen scarf with his hat pulled down to his eyebrows. Broken icicles gracefully swept backward from his moustache and mingled with those in his long hair. Wiley chuckled. He could pass as Old Man Winter.

Wiley nodded thanks as the driver handed down his Winchester rifle. After stretching his shoulders once more, he picked up his bag and started across the street.

"Get the hell out of the way!" a wagon driver yelled.

Wiley jumped back as a massive ore wagon pulled by a team of four oxen nearly ran him down. It clearly had the right-of-way as it lumbered through town on its way to the smelter. Others followed, all spaced a block apart. Wiley watched as the crowd in the street unconsciously made way for the wagons. After one passed, the empty space behind it quickly filled until the next one came.

Glancing around in the twilight, Wiley realized Main Street, nearly six blocks long, was lined with wooden buildings, every one different. Some looked ready to collapse, and he wondered if they'd ever seen a coat of paint since they'd been built. One stately, whitewashed building a few blocks down stood out like a white spot on the rump of a black horse. Bold letters across its side spelled out "Alma Hotel." He headed for it.

Wiley dodged wagons and large groups of miners and made it to the other side of the street. He realized the throngs were mostly men and wondered if Victorianism, which he felt had dehumanized the East, dictated the men's actions here.

A fleeting whiff of fried meat caused a sharp pain in his gut, and he remembered the roast beef sandwich he'd ordered on the train. It had been delicious, and he would have eaten three of them, but the kitchen had run out. He shrugged and kept on toward the hotel.

Wiley gasped as he opened the front door of the Alma Hotel. Nothing he'd seen in town so far had prepared him for the lobby's elegance. He gently closed the heavy door and gazed around the spacious room. It reminded him of the Wellington Hotel in Boston where he'd stayed on occasion.

His moccasined feet made no sound as he walked around the scattered Moquette rugs, tightly woven in pastel shades of gold and green. He thought they looked like furry islands floating on the polished hardwood floor. As he approached the desk, he noticed the brilliant crystal sconces on the walls made lacy patterns of light on emerald wall coverings and matching drapes. When he reached the black, parlor stove overlaid with silver trim, he extended his hands to the warmth.

No one was around. Wiley glanced through a doorway beside the registry counter. It opened into a hallway lined with doors and stretched to the back of the building.

He ambled toward the adjoining room and spotted another stove surrounded by a grouping of gold high-back chairs.

"Is anyone here?" he asked loudly.

A newspaper rustled. As Wiley approached, he saw a young man huddled in front of the stove with his feet propped on the edge of a low table.

The man jerked his head around the wing of his chair and gasped, "You startled me!" As he struggled to his feet, his shoes hit the floor with a bang. "What can I do for you?"

"I need a room," Wiley said. "Preferably on the second floor, with a good view of the street."

"I've got just the one for you." The thin, red-haired clerk dumped the newspaper into the chair, hustled into the main room and slipped behind the counter. After checking the register, he looked up at Wiley. "Room 201 is empty. It's at top of the stairs, first room on the left." He examined the big stranger and noticed the finger-nail size, crescent scar on his right cheekbone.

After Wiley signed the book, the clerk spun it around. "Oh, you're from Vermont. Nice place. I have a sister living there, but I've only visited her once. That was on my way out here." He extended his hand. "My name's Miller."

Wiley shook it. "Glad to meet you, Miller." Usually claiming Vermont as his home while away from Philadelphia, he added, "Yes, it is nice in Vermont."

Wiley checked out the lobby and realized the hotel didn't have a dining room. "Where's the best place in town for a good meal?"

Miller grinned and Wiley noticed a gap between his two front teeth. It was an asset to the man's perky, freckled face.

"Definitely the Regal," Miller said. "If you came in from London Junction by stage, you stopped right in front of the place. Best food in the whole area, but you'd better get over there soon. The place fills up mighty fast this time of day with the miners getting off work and all. By the way, how long you staying?"

"At least a few days." Wiley grabbed his key. "Beyond that, I don't have any idea." He picked up his bag and rifle, nodded to Miller and started toward the stairs, then stopped and turned back to the clerk. "If you sit so you can see the door, you wouldn't get startled when someone comes in." He smiled and nodded, then silently climbed the stairs to the second floor.

Wiley quietly shut the door to his room and tossed his bag on the floor. He propped his rifle against the dresser, turned up the gas lamp on the wall, glanced around briefly, then ambled to the window.

While scanning the street below, he realized Alma wasn't quite what he'd expected, but much of his knowledge of the West had come from dime novels. Occasionally he'd listened to the exaggerated adventures of someone who'd been out here, but he didn't remember any novel or traveler mentioning the smell. The town reeked of wood smoke, and the stench of processed ore made him feel slightly queasy, but the deepening night and rosy glow of street lamps seemed to soften the bleakness. He tried to quell the growing excitement of finally being in the West. For his own safety, a clear head was vital right now.

Two drunken miners came into view on the street below. As they staggered arm-in-arm, laughing, Wiley felt the pang of loneliness creep back. The train ride had caused him to forget. Suddenly, a chill gripped his gut as he realized working alone had another drawback, especially in a town like this. There wouldn't be anyone to cover his back if things got rough. If he wasn't careful, the five hundred dollars Mike had given him could easily be used to bury him.

Shoving that thought out of his head, Wiley glanced up and down Alma's main street once more before turning from the window. He slowly took off his heavy leather jacket and hung it on one of the tall bedposts. After unbuckling his gun belt, he carefully placed it on the bed and pulled the Navy Colt out of its well-oiled holster and checked the cylinder. The ends of five brass bullets glistened in the soft light. He slid the gun back into his right-handed holster.

Wiley stripped naked and glanced at his reflection in the tilted mirror above the dresser. His two-hundred-thirty pounds were as well defined as any of the men he'd wrestled, maybe more so, and he knew how to use each muscle to its fullest. He smiled as he ran his finger through the black hair on his chest. His father had jokingly called him a burly French trapper. Grandpa Grey Feather had named him Great Running Bear. But that was so long ago.

Wiley cupped his hand over his balls and squeezed the way Bert sometimes did to him when they found a place to be alone. He missed grappling naked with Bert, but not his incessant talking.

He used the pitcher and bowl to wash up as best he could, amazed the water was still liquid in the unheated room. He could see his breath.

Wiley dressed quickly in Levis and his rawhide shirt, then laced up his knee-high moccasins and buckled on his gun belt. He grabbed his jacket and started to put it on, but decided to brave the cold without it. He needed to toughen up for the job ahead.

After Wiley opened the window a few inches to air out the room's musty smell, he turned the lamp flame low, then out of habit listened at the door before opening it. The hallway was empty, but his moccasins made no sound on the hardwood floor. He cautiously opened the fire door and descended the L-shaped staircase.

When he reached the bottom step, Wiley glanced into the adjoining room and grinned. Miller had switched chairs so he could see the front door.

When the clerk looked up from his newspaper, Wiley said, "Thanks for the tip on the food."

"Sure thing, Mr. Gray."

As Wiley stepped out the front door, the frigid air stung his face like someone had slapped him with a wet glove. It was May eighth, for God's sake! He looked around and couldn't believe it when he saw ice crystals sparkling in the air near the street lamps. He remembered that the trees had already leafed out in Philadelphia before he'd left over a week ago.

Wiley tensed his muscles and strode up the frost-covered boardwalk.

# CHAPTER 8

Outside the Regal Cafe, Wiley glanced back through the window of the restaurant and shook his head. Wonderful food, but the clientele would take getting used to. Didn't anyone take a bath here? Nathan was right about wearing a wino's clothing to fit in with everyone else. He'd seen everything from ragged sailor uniforms to high-water pants with a split seam in the seat, and that particular gentleman had a nice butt to show the world.

Wiley diverted his eyes to the street. The ore wagons must never stop their lumbering procession through town. He hunched his shoulders against the cold and felt sorry for the oxen, steam billowing from their nostrils, as they strained against the ponderous weight behind them. The earth trembled each time a wagon passed.

The din of the town astonished him. Nothing like Philadelphia's prim and proper streets, Alma seemed more like a circus in the middle of nowhere.

For some reason, he thought of Buffalo Bill's Wild West Show. He'd come across it two years ago in Fitchburg, Massachusetts, and had only caught the last stagecoach act, but he'd stayed for the cleanup. Somehow, that had seemed more real. He'd never forget Buck Taylor, the King of the Cowboys. The cowboy had a magnetic smile and carried himself like a man. Wiley had watched Buck hand his horse's reins to a boy, then run to help force an ornery buffalo into a trailer. Wiley chuckled. The boy holding the reins of his hero's horse had been in shock and hadn't noticed that his friends had pleaded to let them help.

Wiley shivered from the cold. He spotted the Silver Heels Bar across the street and decided to have one drink before returning to the hotel. He glanced up and down the street at the teeming humanity. Where was everyone going? Didn't anyone own a coat? Most of the men were mere skeletons and seemed half starved.

A man hurrying down the boardwalk plowed into Wiley and knocked him into three miners going the other way. All five men groaned from the impact.

One of the trio grabbed Wiley, shoved him away and yelled, "Mister, get your thumb outta yer ass or get off the damn boardwalk!"

Two others shouted a curse at him and walked on down the street.

Wiley straightened his shirt. The man that had shoved him had surprising strength for being so thin. Wiley brushed off his sleeve. This town was rough. As he started to cross the street, a group of riders suddenly galloped around the corner of the restaurant, and Wiley leaped out of their way. The five men yelled and wove their horses around the ore wagons sending cursing passers-by rushing to the boardwalks. Two of the riders stopped, shot their pistols in the air and yelled. The others laughed and hooted, then the group spurred their horses down another side street.

Taking advantage of the thinned crowd, Wiley stepped into the rippling river of frozen mud. He wished he'd worn his jacket as he deftly maneuvered through the crowd and between two wagons. When he reached the boardwalk on the other side of the street, he stood in front of the Silver Heels Bar. Wild piano music, loud shouts and peals of laughter spilled into the street through the full-length batwing doors. Wiley hesitated at the door.

Two miners passed him, and one of them stopped. "Scared to go in there, sonny?" The skinny, ill-smelling codger winked at his companion and added, "Don't be. They're just as likely to eat ya alive out here as they are in there."

Both men laughed raucously as they elbowed their way down the street.

The batwings suddenly flew open. Wiley saw black silhouettes of several men rushing toward him. He counted five men pulling a sixth out the door. As the group shoved past him, one member threw a punch into Wiley's stomach. The blow didn't hurt, but it angered him. He reached out, grabbed the culprit and spun him around.

"Why did you hit me?" Wiley stared into the insolent eyes of a man in his early twenties. Wiley shook him. "I'm waiting!"

The others stopped. An older man walked over and seized Wiley's arm. "Let go'a my boy."

"Not until he explains why he hit me in the stomach."

"Help me!" yelled the man being bullied by the group. "They're gonna kill me!"

The older man turned to his companions. "Shut 'im up!"

Wiley let go of the one he'd grabbed. "What's going on here?" he demanded. "Why are you holding that man?"

"It ain't none'a yer affair," the old man snarled. He pushed the others away from Wiley.

"They're gonna kill me!"

"Should'a thought of that before you ran!" the old man shouted.

"But I didn't do nothin'!" the prisoner whimpered. He suddenly struggled to free himself.

"Grab 'im! Don't let 'im go!" the old man yelled.

The four younger men jumped their captive, forcing him to the ground. The old man kicked the prisoner in the leg.

"Hey!" Wiley leaped at the pile, grabbed the man closest and tossed him to one side. He slammed against the building, head first, and slumped into a heap.

Wiley threw his arms around another, yanked him to his feet, spun him around and threw a solid uppercut to his jaw. He almost laughed as the wiry man stiffened from his punch and toppled over like a felled tree.

The older gent shoved the barrel of his rifle into Wiley's back. "You mind yer business, boy, and leave us be! This here ain't nonna yer affair!"

Instantly, Wiley crouched into a ball, reached back and grabbed the man's ankles. With a quick pull, he jerked the old man off his feet. The rifle boomed, blowing a hole in the top of the building across the street.

Wiley yanked the rifle from the man's hands and pointed it at the scuffling group. "Break it up!"

He jabbed one of them with the barrel. "Get your hands above your heads, and let that man up!"

Sullenly, they stood and raised their hands.

The prisoner struggled to his feet, limped to Wiley's side and brushed himself off. "I'm mighty thankful to you."

"Don't mention it." Wiley shifted his position but kept the rifle pointed at the five men. "Get those two up, and get out of here!"

"We'll be goin', but I'm a-warnin' you, boy," the old man said. "It ain't gonna be safe around here fer you neither."

They pulled their companions to their feet and helped them down the street. The youngest of the group glanced back several times.

Wiley watched them for a few moments, then turned to the man beside him and extended his hand. "My name is...er, Wiley Gray. Let me buy you a drink."

"I'm Jake. Jake Brady." He clasped Wiley's hand with both of his. "I sure could use a drink right now."

Wiley tossed the rifle into the street, smiled and gripped Jake's upper arm. The feel of Jake's rock-hard muscles jolted him. He thought of Max.

Wiley slid his hand to Jake's back as they shoved their way into the bar.

# CHAPTER 9

Inside the brightly lit bar, Wiley gasped when he observed Jake. This man must have stepped out of his own consciousness to become the living, breathing partner he'd dreamed of having since childhood. Suddenly, the image of Grandpa Gray Feather, lying on his deathbed, flashed across Wiley's mind and blotted out everything around him. Grandpa whispered something to him, but Wiley couldn't hear what the dying man said. Just as quickly, the image faded and Wiley again became aware of Jake standing in front of him. For some reason, he felt a strong urge to gather Jake into his powerful arms and protect him from the world. Trying to keep himself from actually doing it, he grasped a chair and squeezed it. What was happening to him? Why had he thought of Grandpa lying on his deathbed? It was like the dream he'd had on the train. His mind reeled.

Jake grabbed Wiley's arm. "You okay?" he asked. Jake squeezed harder and inched closer to the awesome man who'd saved him from the Harrises. He wanted to give Wiley a bear hug of thanks, but he'd most likely get yelled at or hit, or even called a sissy.

The crushing power of Jake's grasp cleared Wiley's head at once. He glanced at the rough, calloused hand gripping his arm, then at Jake's face, and smiled. "I'm fine. I just got...light-headed for a moment." He squeezed the hand holding his arm. "Let's have that drink."

Still stunned by the clear image of Grandpa Gray Feather, Wiley led the way to the bar and ordered a bottle of good bourbon and two glasses. He shoved his way through the crowd to an empty table next to the huge, glowing stove shaped like two barrels, one on top of the other. Several miners snickered as they watched the pair sit at the table nicknamed "The Roaster."

Chilled to the bone, Wiley slid into the chair closest to the stove, grateful for the warmth. After Jake sat opposite him, Wiley smiled and poured each of them a drink. They touched their glasses together. Wiley sipped his drink, but Jake downed his in one swallow.

Wiley took a few minutes to get himself under control, then leaned over the table. "Who were those men outside, Jake?"

Tearing his eyes away from Wiley's chest, Jake met his gaze. "Them're my neighbors from back home. They're aimin' to hang me for gettin' Sara Jean all banged up. They been followin' me from Kentucky for two months." He glanced down at the table, then back
at Wiley. "I'm mighty thankful to you for savin' me. I don't know nobody in this here town."

Wiley flinched at Jake's possible involvement with a woman, knowing full well most men were at some point in their lives. His sudden and powerful attraction to Jake caused him to ask, "Did you...do it to Sara Jean?"

"Hell, no!" Jake stared at the table. "I ain't never even kissed a woman my whole life." He glanced at Wiley for an instant than lowered his eyes back to the table. "Don't know why Sara Jean said I done it. Ever'body in Wilmore knows what I am cuz Pa was always talkin' about it."

"I don't understand," Wiley said. "What are you?"

Jake fingered his empty glass. "Pa was always callin' me one of them damn sissies, but I ain't no sissy. I just hanker after men an' not women." Jake shot Wiley a glance. "That's the way my friend Jesus an' his Pa made me."

Again, Wiley fought for control. The man he'd dreamt about his whole life was like himself! It couldn't be happening! He leaned over the table and whispered, "I...I'm like you, Jake."

Jake looked Wiley straight in the eyes. "You are? You're like me? You're so fine lookin' it don't hardly seem possible."

Wiley chuckled. "I'll take that as a compliment." He cocked his head and eyed Jake closely. "A compliment from the most handsome man I've ever seen in my life." He touched Jake's arm. "Is there anything I can do to help you?"

"Hell, you already done helped by gettin' me away from them Harrises. Don't know what else you can do. They'll likely get me one of these here days, anyway." Jake shook his head. "It ain't like Seth to give up. Even after you saved me, I'm still gonna end up dead."

Jake glanced around. He'd forgotten to watch the door. As he scooted his chair against the wall to have a clear view of the batwings, he realized he hadn't been scared while sitting with Wiley. He'd even forgotten to look for Donny and Sid.

Wiley patted Jake's arm. "I don't think they'll try for you again tonight...at least, while we're together in a crowded bar."

"But, what about later?" Jake asked.

Wiley's face brightened, but before he could say anything, a dozen drunken miners pushed and stumbled into the bar. One of them fell and three others tripped over him, upsetting an empty table and sending two chairs skidding across the floor. The others in the group shouted and laughed as they pulled the four men to their feet and shoved them farther into the room. As the twelve men filtered through the bar, hollering and laughing back and forth, the other patrons were forced to yell to make themselves heard.

Impossible to talk in the din without shouting, Wiley grinned at Jake and shrugged, then glanced around the bar. Craning his neck to see past the stove, he mentally counted thirty-three people in the two big rooms. Even with that number, the bar seemed nearly empty. He noticed every table in the adjoining room held a poker game, and the players seemed calm. Remembering the penny dreadfuls he'd read, Wiley wondered if gunfights over cheating really happened.

He saw two painted-up bar maids hovering near the men with the largest piles of winnings and thought it strange the women needed to sell themselves at all, especially in this town of mostly men.

Wiley glanced back at Jake and saw he was watching the door. For being so big, Jake seemed terrified of the men in black. Suddenly aware of the music, Wiley grinned. He loved ragtime and leaned forward to see around the stove. The man playing the piano wore a green and black striped shirt, black suspenders and a black top hat, just as he'd pictured in his mind. Wiley raised his eyebrows when several men began dancing arm-in-arm beside the piano while onlookers clapped in time with the music.

As Jake stared at the door, he felt his heart pounding. Now that the Harrises had found him, he didn't know how much longer he could stay here. He should saddle Mac and ride out of town in the morning. But where would he go? To Denver? Back home? Anywhere he went, Seth would find him. He'd taken the stage road to Alma and had zigzagged back and forth to scramble his trail. It had taken him five days to get here. How did the Harrises know he was in Alma? Dorsey and Eliott wouldn't have told. They'd helped him escape.

Jake glanced around the bar. He'd been in Alma a week and hadn't seen anything of Donny or Sid. Jake realized Jesus had been sending people all along the way to help him, but none of them seemed to be the special friend he'd asked for when he'd left home. He glanced at Wiley. Only a few minutes ago, this man had saved him from the Harrises. Again, he felt safe sitting near Wiley. Was he the man sent by Jesus? He hoped so. He'd never seen anyone so handsome and strong-looking in his life.

Suddenly, Jake realized he had to pee in the worst way and crossed his legs. Even before the Harrises had rushed into the bar and hauled him outside, he'd needed to make a trip to the outhouse in back. He'd forgotten about it in the scuffle and meeting Wiley. The thought of having to go outside in the dark by himself with the Harrises lurking about made him shudder, but he couldn't hold it in any longer.

In a near panic, Jake leaned across the table and grabbed Wiley's arm. When Wiley leaned forward, Jake whispered, "I gotta pee bad, an' I'm scared them Harrises'll be outside. Will you go with me?"

Wiley looked into Jake's brilliant blue, pleading eyes and felt himself being captured by them. His heart leaped.

"I'd *love* to, Jake...er, of course."

Jake grinned, sprang to his feet and headed toward the back. Slow in getting up, Wiley caught up to Jake as he shoved his way out the door.

Wiley stood in front of the outhouse with his hand on the butt of his gun while Jake took care of business. It seemed colder outside than before, and Wiley wanted to slip into the outhouse and weld Jake to himself with his powerful arms. They could keep each other warm and safe. Wiley shivered a chuckle when he heard Jake sigh inside the structure.

Back in the bar, they found their table still empty and both grabbed the same chairs. As Jake sat down, he heard several coins clinking through a lull in the noise. Searching for the source, he spied a tall, thin man with erect posture standing by himself at the bar. Jake figured he must have come in when he and Wiley were outside. He'd never seen a jacket like the one the man wore. Silver thread, sewn into flowery patterns against a black background, glistened from the lamps in the room. He could almost hear his mother exclaiming over the material. She would have touched it to her face.

Jake noticed the right pocket of the man's jacket bulged and pulsated as he jingled the coins. When the man raised his glass to sip his drink, Jake saw reddish-purple light flash from a jeweled ring on the middle finger of his left hand.

As though the man knew Jake was staring at his back, he turned clear around and looked directly at him. His hawkish, pock-marked face seemed frozen in a permanent smirk. It labored into a smile. Or was it a sneer? Jake looked away.

As Wiley soaked up the heat, he tried to forget his strong desire to enter the outhouse with Jake. To divert his own attention, he began inspecting the main part of the bar. Unlike the Regal Cafe, he knew this building was well constructed. He marveled at the ornately carved, mahogany pillars of the back bar that supported one end of a balcony extending around two walls of the room. Shifting his eyes to the left and looking past Jake, he saw the curved, polished wooden staircase leading up to the gallery and noticed the banister and railing of the balcony were carved in the same spiral as the posts of the back bar. The upstairs held a dozen tables, some with two chairs and others with four, but all had a shaded oil lamp. Wiley saw only two people up there, an attractive woman sitting with a small, piggish man who fiddled nervously with the top of his boot.

Wiley watched as the woman frowned, leaned toward the man across from her and shouted, "I won't sell it to you or anyone!"

Hearing the woman's outburst, Jake noticed the hawk-faced gent with the purple ring turned his head suddenly, looked up at her, then banged his fist on the bar. Jake tapped Wiley on the arm and nodded toward the flashy dresser scowling at the couple upstairs.

Wiley glanced at the man Jake had pointed out, then raised his eyes back to the balcony as the obese man scanned the bar after the woman's outburst. Wiley saw his angry expression turn to fear when he spotted the hawk-faced man staring up at him. The fat man snatched his hand away from his boot, leaned over the table and whispered a few words to the woman, then stood up and scurried toward the stairs. Wiley caught the woman's distaste as she watched him leave.

"Goodnight, Mr. Crain!" the man with the purple ring yelled to the fleeing patron when he reached the door.

Fear again swept across the fat man's face as he glanced over his shoulder. Nodding curtly, he pushed through the batwings into the night.

Jake and Wiley glanced at each other as the hawk-faced man whipped his right hand out of his pocket and grabbed the drink in front of him. With a sly grin, he gracefully ascended the curved staircase. A dazzling yellow jewel on his right ring finger scattered rainbows on the walls and ceiling. After speaking to the woman, he sat in the empty chair at her table, crossed his legs and pointed his toe. Wiley noticed the woman's face tighten.

Jake lost interest in the drama and diverted his attention to the man sitting across from him. He guessed Wiley to be in his mid-twenties. Each strand of his short, black hair seemed to know where it was supposed to be, and a single day's growth of black beard shadowed his square jaw. Wiley's brown eyes seemed to memorize everything, and Jake wondered how he'd gotten the small curved scar on his cheek. He loved the way Wiley's soft leather shirt, with an open V-neck, stretched tight like a second skin over his massive chest and arms. Jake wanted to run his hands over the shirt, feel Wiley's muscles and pull on his black, curly chest-hair fenced by the rawhide lacing.

Jake sneaked a look over the side of the table at Wiley's blue denim pants, and noticed the man's knee-high moccasins. Was he an Indian? He didn't look like a miner. Maybe he was a bounty hunter? The few bounty hunters he'd seen pictures of had dressed like Wiley. But whoever he was, Wiley had saved him from the Harrises.

Wiley felt a flutter in his gut when he caught Jake eyeing him closely. He smiled and began observing Jake with equal vigor. He loved Jake's windblown, blond hair that reached the collar of his flannel shirt. Jake's short beard and moustache, several shades darker than his hair, gave him the appearance of a tough, calloused scrapper who seemed amazingly calm after being accosted by five men. But Wiley wasn't fooled for a minute. He saw a terrified little boy hiding just beneath the surface of that handsome face. Wiley dropped his gaze and noticed Jake's chest pushed open the front of his shirt. His powerful arms and shoulders twisted the black and red checkered pattern into rounded squares.

What a magnificent man, Wiley almost shouted. He drained his glass as he tried, once more, to control the urge to grab Jake and hold him close. What was it about this man that made him feel so out of control? He knew part of it was Jake's handsome face and superb body, but he'd wrestled many men as big as Jake and had never felt this way. Not even around Max. He wanted to get to know Jake but hesitated getting this innocent-looking man embroiled in his affairs.

"Do you live here?" Wiley yelled over the din.

Jake shook his head and started to shout that he'd only been here a week, but the same group of miners who had burst into the bar earlier started hollering that they planned to move on to Mattie's Saloon. As the men searched the bar for more recruits, Jake and Wiley grinned at each other as they declined the slurred invitation from several of them. The two men silently watched the rowdies stumble out into the street. Their departure dropped the bar noise to a tolerable level.

Wiley sighed, then smiled at Jake. "Another drink?"

"Sure." Jake's face became serious. "You here huntin' somebody?" He still had the feeling Wiley might be a bounty hunter.

Stunned by Jake's perception, Wiley found himself completely disarmed by the question. Thinking quickly, he grinned and said, "Maybe I just found him."

Jake flickered a smile and lowered his eyes. "You can tell me why you're here. I won't say nothin'. I don't know nobody."

Wiley slowly poured both of them another glass of whiskey, carefully placed the bottle in the exact center of the table and folded his hands around his glass. Something made him want to tell Jake what he was really doing in Alma, but he decided against it. He couldn't bear the thought of this handsome man leaving so soon, and assumed he would if Jake knew why he was really here.

"I'm...just traveling the West," Wiley finally said.

Jake eyed him. "Where you from?"

"Vermont," Wiley said, out of habit.

Jake felt ashamed for not trusting Wiley, but with the Harrises in town, he had to be careful. "Vermont? What brings you to Col'rado?"

As he gazed into Jake's eyes, Wiley couldn't remember any of the story he'd used so many times to explain his presence in a town. "I...I grew up in Vermont and lived there most of my life. I've always wanted to come out West and...after my folks passed on, I sold our farm, and here I am." Wiley glanced across the room. He could have sworn he'd seen Grandpa Gray Feather standing by the front window, but he wasn't there. How could he be? What was the matter with him? Shaken, his only thought was to shift the conversation away from himself. "This bar is quite an interesting place."

"Here by yerself?" Jake asked. He wanted to know more about this intriguing man who seemed uneasy with the questions. What was he hiding? He didn't completely trust Wiley, but still felt safe having him near.

"Yes, I'm alone." Wiley's voice faltered. "Always have been. I was an only child. I mean, I *am* an only child." He couldn't believe he was having this much trouble talking. Always before, he could flawlessly tell his made-up story of who he was and where he was from, but with Jake, he seemed compelled to tell the truth. At least, as much as he could tell.

Jake leaned closer, urging Wiley to continue.

"Well, let's see. When I was fifteen, my folks sent me to school in Boston. After I returned, I stayed close to home because both my parents were in poor health. I had to work the farm by myself and..."

"Hey, that sounds jest like me," Jake interrupted. He grabbed his drink, downed it, wiped his mouth with the back of his hand then glanced at the bottle. "This stuff ain't bad. Mind if I have another?"

"Help yourself. Here, let me pour it." Wiley poured the bourbon in Jake's glass, stopped, then poured a bit more to fill it to the top. He placed the bottle in the center of the table, picked up his own glass and took a healthy swallow.

Jake took a swig of his drink. "You married or got any women after you?"

Wiley smiled slightly. "No," he replied slowly. "And I'm not married. I told you, I'm like you. I've never seen eye-to-eye with women. I dated a few times in school only because anyone who didn't was suspect." He scowled, drained his glass, and poured another drink. Why was he drinking so much?

"My favorite pastime is tracking animals in the woods," Wiley continued. "Sometimes for days at a time. The last woman I took out told me I ought to grow up and put those childish games behind me. It angered me so much I never asked another woman out and didn't care if anyone said anything about it."

"You sure won't get no fussin' from me about that," Jake said. He shifted in his chair. "Said you're a tracker. Any good?"

Wiley stared at his glass and smiled. If he kept talking about himself, Jake might loosen up and quit glancing at the door. "Ever since I was old enough to walk, I'd spend whatever free time I had tracking animals. My grandfather taught me. My goal was to sneak up on a deer and touch its tail before it spotted me."

Jake sat up straight. "You ever do it?"

Wiley hesitated, then said, "Yes...er...well, almost. I would have succeeded once...if my pants hadn't fallen down." He felt his face turn red. He couldn't believe he'd brought up the incident he'd never told anyone, not even Grandpa Gray Feather.

"This I gotta hear!" Jake yelled.

"Well," Wiley began slowly. He smiled at Jake, suddenly wanting to share the story with him. "I was tracking a deer, and it was the most silent tracking I'd ever done. I followed the deer all morning and covered about two miles of thick brush before I finally got right behind it. I almost had my hand on its tail when my pants fell down. I was so startled, I jerked my head. Naturally, the deer vanished into the woods. My rawhide belt must have come untied in the brush, and my pants went down to my knees."

"Damn, that's the best story I ever heard!" Jake hollered. He slapped the top of the table with his hand so hard the bottle and both glasses lifted into the air.

Wiley grabbed for the bottle, but missed. It bounced off the side of the table and smashed on the floor. Bourbon and glass splattered everywhere.

# CHAPTER 10

"Don't nobody walk in that!" the overweight bartender yelled as he rounded the end of the bar. Holding a short-handled broom and a dust pan, he stopped beside Jake. "Don't you take no mind to that, sonny. Happens all the time 'round here. I'll have this mess cleaned up in a jiffy."

Thankful for the man's kind words, Jake still cringed and hung his head when he noticed everyone looking at him. A man in the next room yelled, "Prob'ly drunk!" and Jake remembered his dead father's raspy voice screaming, "Now you've done it, you damn sissy! You're dumber'n hog shit!"

Wiley saw pain and guilt flash across Jake's face. He reached across the table and grabbed his arm. "It's nothing to worry about, Jake. It happens to all of us. It's only a dollar bottle of whiskey." Wiley leaned closer and whispered, "Besides, the floor needed washing anyway."

Jake raised his head and grinned sheepishly.

As the short, fat bartender bent down to sweep up the scattered pieces of broken glass, Wiley turned toward him. "I'll pay for the mess if there's any charge. And whenever you get to it, we'll need another bottle." Amused by the incident, he found Jake's gregariousness refreshing after living in the East where everyone tried to be more perfect than anyone else. But he wondered about Jake's reaction to such a simple incident.

"Sure thing, sonny," the fat man gasped as he straightened up. "Only you ain't gonna pay fer the next bottle cuz it's good to have laughin' in here. People're too damn ser-yous anymore. You two gents was havin' a good laugh, an' I like that. By the way, my name's Walter, but most folks call me Tubs. I bin called many names and don't know why Tubs stuck." He smiled and pushed his fat stomach toward them.

"I'm Wiley, and this is my good friend, Jake."

"Pleased t'meetcha," Tubs said.

Jake shot a surprised glance at Wiley. Was he really Wiley's good friend, even after he'd knocked the bottle on the floor? Thrilled, he jumped to his feet.

"Let me clean up that there mess, bein' I'm the one that done it."

Tubs shoved Jake back down in his chair. "Now you jest sit tight, Jack." When Jake stayed put, Tubs nodded in satisfaction, grinned, and patted him on the shoulder. "I do this leest once a day. I'll get yur new bottle soonz I finish here." As Tubs bent down to continue sweeping up the glass, he puffed and grunted, and his bald head turned beet red.

Jake squirmed in his chair.

After Tubs successfully chased down the last bit of broken glass, he stood up and sighed, then hollered, "Tiny, get yur ass out here an' mop up this here booze!"

A huge teenage boy bumped through the kitchen door behind the bar. He began cleaning up the spilled bourbon with a filthy, brown mop, but stopped suddenly and stared at Wiley with a twisted grin on his face.

Jake instantly realized Tiny didn't have all his faculties, and he thought of what Jesus said about the "least of brethren" when he looked into Tiny's babyish face. The boy was bigger than both he and Wiley, and his missing front teeth made him look comical. Jake couldn't help smiling at him.

"This here's Tiny," Tubs told them. "He's my son. Takes after his mamma. Tiny, say howdy to these here gents." Tubs pointed to each man in turn. "This here's Jack an' this here's Willy."

Completely ignoring Jake, Tiny touched Wiley's shoulder. "You're sure purdy, mister."

The comment caught Wiley off guard. He glanced at Jake and realized the man was near laughter. Thank God for that!

Tubs whacked Tiny on his back with the small broom. "That's no way'a talkin' to strangers. Where's yur manners? Now get that mess cleaned up 'for I whop yur ass." Tubs turned to the two men. "Sorry, gents. Tiny ain't been right in the head since he fell off his horse as a young'n. He's harmless, but nobody'd better pick a fight with him cuz he's strong as an ox."

"No offence." Wiley gave Tiny a genuine smile.

Tiny's pouting face instantly beamed, and he diligently mopped up the spilled bourbon. Tubs went behind the bar and tossed the broken glass into a barrel. He returned with a fresh bottle just as Tiny finished his chore.

"Like I said, this here bottle's on the house." Tubs clunked the bottle on the table, then spun around and pointed to the kitchen door. "Tiny, stop grinnin' at that man an' get yur ass back inta that kitchen!" He frowned at his son, then returned to his to his station where several men yelled for drinks.

Tiny slowly shuffled toward the bar, dragging the wet mop behind him. He stopped several times to look back at Wiley before he disappeared into the kitchen.

Jake chuckled. "Guess you have a friend for life, *Willy*."

"Thanks a lot, *Jack*," Wiley said, grinning. "Now, I'd like to know something about you." He didn't want a return of Jake's self-torturing mood so he decided not to bring up the five men. "How long ago did you leave Kentucky?"

Jake picked up the fresh bottle and poured Wiley a drink, being overly careful not to upset the table again. He poured himself a shot also, feeling the need for one after the embarrassing incident he'd caused. He set the bottle down with both hands.

"I left home the day after I become twenty-four," Jake said slowly. "That was about two months ago. Reckon I been on the run ever since." He sighed. "One of these here days I'm gonna have to fight it out with them Harrises, but there's five of them an' only one'a me."

"Two," Wiley said. He folded his arms on the table and leaned forward.

"Two what?"

Wiley chuckled. "I'm on your side." He wanted to help Jake with the Harrises and realized the real reason why he was here had to take priority, but felt confident he could do both. "I'll help you any way I can, but I'd like to know the whole story. Why are the Harrises accusing you of getting Sara Jean pregnant?"

Jake cringed. "Sara Jean told her pa I'm the one that done it to her, but it ain't right. Don't know why she's lyin'. Sara Jean an' me was just friends, that's all. My folks' farm borders the Harris land, an' Sara Jean an' me'd walk to the schoolhouse together. But that was before the school got burnt down. Ever'body always thought Stinky did it but couldn't prove it none. Well, after they built the school again Pa wouldn't let me go back sayin' he needed me home. I only went 'til third grade."

Jake braced himself for the usual snicker at his lack of schooling. When it didn't come, he sighed and continued, "I only saw somma the boys from school once in a while after that." His face brightened. "We'd all get in a bunch sometimes, after chores were done, an' sneak about in the woods. We could hide 'most anywhere and nobody could ever find us. 'Ceptin' Sara Jean."

Wiley noticed Jake had a hard time staying on one subject, but felt he would get around to telling the whole story at some point. He enjoyed hearing Jake talk, but cringed as Jake brutalized the English language.

"Sara Jean's a girl, an' this was boy stuff," Jake continued, "so we wouldn't let her come. Sometimes we'd be gone for a few days. After we'd settled down for the night, here she'd come just a-walkin' into camp, scarin' us all to death. An' she'd plop down beside me. The other boys all knowed Sara Jean liked me a lot an' was wastin' her time. They knowed that 'cause Pa was always tellin' ever'body I'm a sissy."

Seeing Jake's pain from his memories, Wiley quickly asked, "Are your parents still alive?"

Glad Wiley had changed the subject, Jake sighed. "No. Ma died when I was twenty. She'd been sick for years an' could only do a few things. But she'd always read to me out of the Good Book. Pa's dead too. One day I come in from plowin' an' he was layin' on the floor, dead. I buried him next to Ma in the birch grove out back of the house."

"My parents are dead, also, Jake. Do you have any brothers or sisters?"

"Ma said I had me a brother, but he left home when I was two. His name is Shed. Ma said he run off to join the war. I never could figger out how Shed could be my brother since Pa married Ma a year before I was born. Pa wouldn't never talk about Shed an' always called him that bad name. Ma never knowed what happened to him 'cause Shed didn't never write or come home. Ever'body said he musta been killed."

"So, just you and your father did all the farming?" Wiley asked. He smiled when he realized Jake had stopped glancing at the door.

Jake raked his hair with his fingers. "Mostly me. Pa'd been gored by one of the Harrises' bulls when I was fifteen. The Harrises blamed Pa for tryin' to steal it, but I knowed better cuz I was there. Pa an' me was tryin' to get the bull back on the Harrises' land when it charged him. One of his horns ripped Pa's leg clean open. Pa like to bled to death, but I got him to town an' he got patched up. He always had to use a walkin' stick after that." Jake lowered his head. "He was a lot meaner, too." Jake downed his drink, poured another and downed it also.

After Jake tossed back his third shot in a row, Wiley grabbed his arm and held it. "Easy on that stuff, Jake."

"It's okay. I had to have me a drink for Ma an' one for Shed even though I never knowed him. An' I had to have me a drink for you, Wiley, cuz I like you lots." Jake smiled at Wiley and quickly lowered his eyes. "But I wish I had me some family now I could turn to for help."

"I'll help any way I can, Jake." Wiley studied him for a long time. He knew he'd already fallen in love with this man of his dreams and wondered how to suggest they become partners.

Suddenly, Jake's face seemed to fade, and Wiley saw nothing except a swirling fog. When it cleared, he found himself sitting cross-legged in a forest next to--*Grandpa Gray Feather*!

"Grandpa!" Wiley shouted. "How can you be here?" He glanced around. "Where *am* I?"

The old Indian smiled. "Great Running Bear, you have finally met your brother, and you must become one in blood."

"Blood brothers?" Wiley asked. "But, Grandpa, we hardly know each other."

Gray Feather shook his head. "You have always known your brother. You must bond with him at once."

"But, Grandpa, the blood ceremony is sacred. I can't do it in a *bar*!"

Gray Feather frowned. "It *must* be done now. You and your brother are in danger. You must bond now and not leave each other's side until the danger passes. If others see the bonding, let them learn the oneness of blood brothers." He touched Wiley's arm. "Now, I will tell you again what I told you as I lay dying. *Never* tell your brother..."

Wiley felt his arm being shaken, and instantly Grandpa Gray Feather vanished. Wiley found himself sitting at the table in the Silver Heels Bar. Jake was shaking his arm and asking, "You okay, Wiley?"

Leaving his right arm in Jake's grasp, Wiley rubbed his eyes with his left hand. "I...I think so, Jake."

"You had your eyes closed, Wiley," Jake said. "I thought you was gettin' sick or somethin'."

Wiley wondered if he'd fallen asleep and had only dreamed about his grandfather. Suddenly, his right arm jerked out of Jake's grip and his hand grabbed his knife and placed it on the table. Wiley stared at the knife as though he'd never seen it before. Something poked his back, hard.

Startled from the nudge, Wiley quickly glanced at the stove behind him then said, "Uh...isn't there an Indian custom of blood brothers?" He wondered if he'd actually said those words. Had Grandpa poked him?

"Sure there is," Jake said, staring at the knife. "But what're you doin'?"

"You...you don't have any family," Wiley said. "And I don't have any family...that I care about anyway. Why don't you and I be family for each other? Let's...become blood brothers."

"But we've only knowed each other for a few minutes!"

"Those were my words, too." Wiley felt another poke in his back, this time harder. "Er...so what?" He composed himself and slid his hand over Jake's wrist. "For some reason, Jake, I've known you all my life, and I think we'd make a great team." He squeezed Jake's arm. "We can help each other. You need help getting away from the Harrises, and I need help...er, just being here. I need to learn this part of the country. Besides, we both like each other. Am I right?" As Wiley looked Jake in the eyes, he was suddenly glad he was going through with it, and hoped Jake would agree.

Jake held Wiley's gaze. He only knew one thing about a blood bond between two men. It lasted forever. Forever with this man? As Jake searched Wiley's handsome face, he thought he felt Jesus' hand on his shoulder, and knew Wiley was the friend he'd asked for. He broke into a grin. "Sure thing, *Willy*." He laughed.

"Give me your right hand," Wiley said.

Jake stuck out his hand and placed it on the table, palm side up. "Cut me," he said, then shut his eyes tight.

Wiley made a small cut on Jake's palm with the knife's razor sharp point and a similar one on his own right palm.

Jake opened his eyes and stared at his hand. "Guess I thought it should'a been bigger."

They looked around the room and saw everyone in the bar watching them in awed silence. The piano player had even stopped. Wiley cringed, hoping no one would recognize him, then shrugged and smiled.

Jake grinned. He realized he was going to have a brother, one who liked him even after he'd spilled the bourbon.

As the two men tightly clasped each other's hand to let the blood mingle, the bar erupted into cheers and yells. The smiling piano player let out a whoop and began pounding out a wedding march. Men laughed, hooted and danced around the bar, and some slapped Jake and Wiley on the back. A few men mocked and derided the new blood brothers, but they were greatly outnumbered.

# CHAPTER 11

From across the room, a pair of cold, black eyes glared at the two men becoming blood brothers. The eyes belonged to a thin, stoop-shouldered man in his late fifties. His gaunt, sallow face resembled a skull rather than a human face of flesh and blood. He drummed his fingers on a small table.

"Goddamn heathens," the man muttered under his breath. He cast his eyes heavenward and in a loud voice yelled, "O Lord, cast them down into the pits of hell and let them burn forever in your wrath! So sayeth the Lord!"

The old man stood up and rushed to the table where Jake and Wiley still clasped each other's right hands.

"Heathens!" he screamed down at them.

He grabbed the bottle of bourbon and doused their clasped hands. "May this wash away the evil of this act, so sayeth the Lord! May you two remember the lesson of Sodom and Gomorrah, so sayeth the Lord!"

"We ain't havin' much luck with the booze tonight, are we, Wiley," Jake said. After twenty-two years living with his father's abuse, he wasn't afraid of this old man. Besides, he could still feel Jesus' hand on his shoulder. A sudden flood of joy, mixed with a little mischief, caused Jake to gently tip the table. The bourbon poured into the old man's shoes.

"My shoes!" the old man shouted. "You will burn in *hell* for this outrage!" He quickly set the empty bottle down, spun around to a man at the bar who mocked his every word, and screeched, "You will *all* burn in the fires of hell for just *being* in this den of iniquity!"

"Then why're you in here, Reverend Quick?" asked a burly miner everyone called Lug. He stood at the bar with one arm around the waist of a barmaid, holding a bottle in his other hand. "If you had a partner you cared for an' who cared for you, maybe you wouldn't be such a mean ol' cuss. Go do yer soul damnin' somewhere else b'fore I toss you outta here."

Lug released the barmaid, walked heavily over to Jake and Wiley's table and slammed down his bottle. "Gents, this is from me. I've never seen anyone become blood brothers my whole life and hope someday it'll happen to me." He turned and stomped back to the bar, grabbed the barmaid and hollered for Tubs.

Many in the bar cheered Lug and raised their glasses to him and the new blood brothers.

With an open mouth and eyes smoldering in contempt, Reverend Quick silently watched the actions of the huge miner. Rather than take on this man, who could easily toss him into the street, he took one more look around, shouted, "Heathens!" and squished out the door.

Shaken by the harsh condemning words of the reverend, Wiley loosened his grip on Jake's hand. The bourbon stung the cut in his palm, and he felt the hell-fire already starting. The memory of his boyhood preacher catching him and Johnny Vanders playing with each other's privates forced its way into his mind. The preacher had whipped them and yelled about fire and damnation for over an hour. Wiley never knew if the preacher had told his folks because they'd neither mentioned it nor treated him any differently. But the deep-seated guilt caused by the minister's condemning words left him skeptical about God, religion and especially ministers. He'd always felt completely drawn toward men and wondered how God could hate him for something that wasn't his fault.

Jake felt Wiley's grip loosen and tightened his. "Don't let the ol' reverend get you to worryin' about your soul, Wiley. My friend Jesus had him twelve men he called brothers, an' he was always talkin' about love. It's Jesus I believe an' not some hateful ol' preacherman who can't rightly figure out how savin' a soul is done. I guess not knowin' nothin' about Jesus an' his Pa makes him mean."

Wiley stared at Jake. He'd never heard anything like that and knew it made sense. He thought of the five men who wanted to hang Jake and made a firm resolve to keep it from happening, even if he had to kill them. Wiley smiled and tightened his grip on Jake's hand. "Thanks, *Jack*."

Almost as if a signal had been given, the two men unclasped their hands. Wiley realized their blood had mingled. They were true blood brothers.

"See there, Wiley," Jake exclaimed. "The ol' reverend couldn't wash it away." He raised his hand to his mouth and licked off the drying blood.

Suddenly, two men walked up to their table and one of them grabbed Jake by the shoulder.

"Jake, when did you get to Alma?"

Jake looked up into Donny's face and smiled. "Donny! I been here a week lookin' for you."

Donny put on a contrite face. "I've been in Leadville helping with a cave-in." He turned to the man standing next to him. "Jake, I want you to meet my new friend. He just arrived in Alma yesterday, and he's going to be staying with me. Stuart, this is Jake. We met in Denver over a month ago."

As Jake shook Stuart's hand, jealousy pricked him until he glanced at Wiley and realized Donny couldn't compare at all with his new blood brother. He grabbed Wiley's arm.

"Donny, this here's my new blood brother, Wiley. He's the friend Jesus found for me."

Donny shook Wiley's hand. "You and Jake make a fine pair. We all watched your little ceremony." He turned to Jake. "Sid's here. He went outside, but he'll be back. Stuart and I are going to Mattie's Saloon before we head back up the mountain. You take care of yourself." Donny winked at Jake, then plowed through the crowd and out the batwing doors with Stuart following behind.

"Donny seems like a nice person," Wiley said. "How did you meet him?"

"I met him in a bar. Him an' Sid helped me lots when I first got to Denver." Jake glanced up and grinned.

Wiley turned to see who Jake was looking at and gasped. The man walking toward them was the largest individual he'd ever seen.

"Jake, good to see you," Sid bellowed. "Get tired of hauling bricks? I can always get you on at the mine." Sid turned to Wiley and held out his huge hand. "I'm Sid Thompson. Saw your little knife trick and approve. This Jake here is a comfortable feeling man." He raised his eyebrows and laughed. "Don't worry. I had him in my arms only once, and it was in the middle of a street in Denver."

"Wiley, he caught me when I slipped in mud after runnin' into him."

Wiley shook Sid's hand. "I'm glad to make your acquaintance. I'm Wiley."

Sid slapped Jake on the back. "You got yourself a fine looking man, Jake. Don't be like Donny. He's a sucker for somebody new in town. He wines and dines them, then leaves them when the stage comes in."

"Bein' blood brothers is forever," Jake said proudly.

"I wish you both well," Sid commented as he glanced around. "Where did Donny and Stuart go?"

"They went to a place called Mattie's," Wiley said. "They left just before you came to our table."

Sid shrugged. "I'd better go up there. I'm supposed to keep Donny from getting drunk again." He grabbed Wiley's shoulder. "You treat Jake right, or you'll have me to answer to." Sid winked at Wiley, then lumbered out the door.

Wiley watched him leave, then raised his eyes to the balcony as the man with the purple ring and the woman left their table. As the couple descended the stairs, Jake turned his head to see what had caught Wiley's attention.

The woman stopped next to Jake and turned to the man behind her. Jake heard every word, but even straining, Wiley caught only bits of their comments to each other.

"Mr...appreciate your...I must decline..."

"You know where I'm...change your mind...room 200...Hotel. I'll be in town...ten in the morning."

"Goodnight." The woman drew her heavy shawl tightly about her and slipped through the batwings.

With a smug expression, the hawk-faced man reached in his jacket pocket and started clinking the coins. He sauntered to the bar and yelled for a brandy.

"Billingsly!" Jake spat out his name.

"*That's* Billings...? Er...do you know him?" Wiley's eyes turned cold as he stared at Billingsly's back. He'd found the man he was looking for.

"No, but that's what the woman called him," Jake said. "He looks like a gambler, an' I'm wonderin' what he's up to. That there woman has somethin' to sell, an' he wants it." Jake shook his head. "He must be somebody 'portant cuz he sure scared the pants off that other gent before he left. You know, the fat little man that has a gun in his boot."

"Why do you say that?" Wiley knew why. He'd used a boot pistol before, but wanted to hear Jake's deduction.

"'Cause he kept fiddlin' with his boot. The strap holster must'a been itchin' somethin' terrible."

"We'll have to keep our eyes open next time we see him." Wiley squinted slightly. "I don't mean to change the subject, but I'd like to know more about what happened with the Harrises." He glanced at Billingsly. The man was staring at them.

"We sure did get sidetracked." Jake rubbed the small cut on his palm and grinned. He stretched, grabbed the bottle and poured himself another drink, downed it, started to pour another one, but stopped and set the bottle down. "Guess I don't want no more tonight." He sat back in the chair and looked straight at Wiley. "If I tell you, will you help me get 'em before they get me?"

"I already told you I would."

"Well, okay then." Jake paused. "After my folks died, I worked the farm for two years. Don't know why I did 'cause I never liked the place after that. Seemed so lonely there with Ma an' Pa gone. But I sure didn't miss Pa yellin' at me for doin' everythin' wrong, like he always done.

"Well, anyway, I didn't see Sara Jean for about five months, an' then one day after I'd finished plowin' down by the river, here she come a-walkin' in the barn an' her stomach was stickin' way out in front. First thing I thought was she got fat. But then I seen her closer an' figured out right quick she was havin' a baby inside there. Well, I said, 'Sara Jean, how'd you get yourself all banged up like that?' Well, know what she told me? She told me it was my doin's."

Jake paused and rubbed his face with his hands. After a short time, he continued. "I knowed that wasn't right an' I told her so, but she just kept sayin' it was my fault an' we'd have to get hitched or her pappy'd come after me. I asked her how her pa knew. She said she'd told him I'd done it to her."

Jake buried his face in his hands again, slowly slid his hands into his hair, then raised his head. "I didn't know what to do, so I told Sara Jean to get off my place 'cause I weren't no party to that, an' I didn't want to get hitched with her neither. She went off a-cryin'. I didn't think no more about it the rest of the day. Then later, all the Harrises, 'cept for Zeke, come ridin' up to my place. That's when Seth said he'd hunt me down an' hang me."

After Jake told Wiley what transpired with Clem and his trip west, he added, "I hightailed it up here to Alma lookin' for Donny. I took a roundabout way, figurin' they wouldn't think a-lookin' here. Got me a room at the Alma Hotel. It's a front room so's I can watch the street."

Jake sighed. "That's about all I been doin' here, just watchin' the street an' not likin' one damn minute of it. I ain't never backed down on a fight in my life. But I know how mean Seth is, an' he done proved he's the best tracker anywhere. He could shoot me down before I could even blink."

Suddenly, Jake stood up. "I think I'm gonna go back to the hotel, Wiley. Just now, I got me a funny feelin' the Harrises are close by again." He started for the door.

"Wait!" Wiley remembered he couldn't let Jake out of his sight and leaped out of his chair. "I'll go with you. I'm staying at the same hotel. We're blood brothers now."

Wiley followed Jake to the door. He nodded to Tubs and noticed Billingsly was watching them leave. The lustful expression on the man's face chilled his blood, but the left corner of Wiley's mouth lifted in a half-smile.

As the new blood brothers trudged through the frosty air toward the hotel, loud music and laughter from the bar followed them. Groups of miners still crowded the street, and the ore wagons continued their endless procession.

Jake glanced around cautiously. As they came to the entrance of a dark alley, Wiley stopped and quickly put his arm in front of

Jake. He whispered into Jake's ear, "I heard someone scraping around in the alley."

The two men hunched down near the corner of the store. Even in the cold, sweat beaded on Jake's forehead and he felt his breath come in short, quick gasps. Then, with a suddenness that nearly caused him to panic, Wiley jumped into the alley, whipped out his gun and cocked it.

"Who's there?" he snarled.

"Meow," came a cry from a pile of rubble. A tiny black kitten with white paws jumped out and began attacking one of Wiley's moccasins.

Jake sighed with relief as he watched Wiley holster his gun, scoop up the kitten and hold it close to his face.

"You little stinker, you almost scared us half to death," Wiley said as he scratched the kitten under its chin. He handed it to Jake. "Can you believe this cute little thing almost got himself shot?"

"Too bad we can't keep 'im," Jake said as he held the playful little animal over his arm. "But we ain't got no home, an' this little tyke prob'ly does."

He put the kitten on the ground. It scampered up the alley into the darkness.

# CHAPTER 12

As they stepped into the hotel lobby, both men noticed the same woman who'd been talking with Billingsly in the Silver Heels Bar sat stiffly in a chair beside the stove in the parlor. She glanced up, then smiled when the two men walked by the door.

Wiley thought the woman had a lovely but somewhat hardened face, as though grief might be her closest neighbor. Unlike women in the East, she wore no make-up, and her brown hair fell naturally over her shoulders. Wiley recognized an Indian symbol woven into her dress, but couldn't read from which tribe it originated. Her heavy woolen shawl was draped neatly over the arm of the chair, and a leather Chatelaine bag leaned against the leg.

"Ma'am." Jake touched his hat as he headed for the stairs.

The woman jumped up. "Sirs?" she said too loud. "Didn't I see the two of you at the Silver Heels a little while ago?"

"Yes ma'am, you sure did," Jake said as he stopped. "You was talkin' to that man called...uh, Billin'sly. You waitin' for 'im?" Feeling slightly off balance, he grabbed Wiley's arm. He knew then he'd had too much to drink.

The woman smiled. "No. I was waiting for either of you gentlemen to come in." She looked at Jake, then started toward them. "I saw you leave earlier and knew you were staying here. After seeing your ceremony in the bar, I want very much to talk with both of you."

Wiley backed up slightly when she reached them.

The woman held out her hand. "Gentlemen, my name is Belinda Castille. I believe you're both new in town and doubt you've heard of me."

Castille? Wiley remembered Mike McGelvy mentioning that name, and he raised his eyebrows. Thank God the woman was looking at Jake and didn't see him do it. He flickered a smile as he shook her hand.

"Since my father died recently," Belinda continued, "I'm now the owner of the Castille Ranch. It's located ten miles south of here." She turned and extended her hand toward the four chairs. "Please sit down, if only for a few minutes." She returned to her chair and sat down.

The two men hesitated and glanced at each other before proceeding across the room. Even holding on to Wiley, Jake weaved slightly. After they sat on either side of her, Jake jumped up again.

"D'you mind if I close these here curtains, Ma'am?" As Jake untied the cords and let the green velvet drapes close, he added, "Don't like bein' looked at by somebody I can't see. 'Specially tonight."

After Jake slid back into his chair, Belinda used a few moments to collect her thoughts. Sitting with two of the most handsome men she'd ever seen didn't make it any easier.

Jake grinned crookedly at Belinda. "Wiley an' me heard you in the bar. That fat little man must want somethin' you got, an'...uh, Bingsly wants it too."

"Billingsly," Belinda corrected. "Mr. Crain owns the Bank of Alma. Both he and Mr. Billingsly were pressuring me to sell my ranch." She clenched her hands. "I'll *never* sell, even though I told Mr. Billingsly I'd think about it. But, like most people in this area, I'm afraid to get him angry. If I do, he'll be sure to take steps to get my ranch, and he won't be kind about it. You see, Mr. Billingsly is a lawyer, and he uses any means to get what he wants. For some reason, he wants my land."

Jake knew then why he didn't like Billingsly. Gambler, lawyer or hardcase gunslick were all the same as far as he knew, and he didn't trust any of them.

"Getting back to why I want to talk to you," Belinda said, "I was hoping you could help me."

Jake raised his eyebrows. "Help you get ridda Binsly?" he slurred. "We ain't gunslinners." He laughed and weaved in his chair.

Wiley touched his right cheek and covered his scar with the tips of his fingers.

Belinda smiled. "You have me all wrong. This may sound strange to you, but I watched you in the Silver Heels, and you seem like the type of men I need on my ranch. To be perfectly frank, I can't work it by myself."

"Do you mean to say your father never hired any staff or range hands to help with the work?" Wiley asked.

"Oh, yes. We had staff and cowboys to run the ranch, but the ones that weren't killed quit after my father died. Now there's only Sa-Ra and I living there."

"Sara!" Jake yelled. He felt a cold chill as the name brought back thoughts of the Harrises.

Belinda eyed Jake curiously. "Sa-Ra was my nanny while I was growing up. Her real name is Soaring Raven. When I was little I couldn't pronounce her name, and I've been calling her Sa-Ra ever since. She and I are quite hard pressed to keep the place up."

"Killed?" Wiley asked. "What do you mean by that? Just how and why did these men get killed?"

"No one knows for sure." Belinda clasped her hands in her lap and stared at the floor. "John Mattock was my father's right-hand man. Actually, he was my father's partner long before they served together in the War Between the States. They remained partners even after Father married my mother. Mother died of smallpox when I was twelve, and Father and John became even closer after that. John was like an uncle to me since I'd known him all my life.

"One morning, about two months ago, John came riding up to the house slumped over in his saddle. He'd been shot twice. As Father and I got to his horse, he fell out of the saddle and died right in front of us." Tears welled up in her eyes. She reached into her bag and fished for a handkerchief. "Father was devastated. I was, too." She bit her quivering lip.

"Did you ever find out who shot him, and why?" Wiley asked.

"Never!" Belinda wept softly into her hanky.

Wiley stared at his hands while she composed herself. Jake appeared ready to burst into tears as well.

Belinda wiped her eyes and dabbed at her nose. "Then, shortly after that, Jason was found shot to death at Walton Spring, one of the waterholes on the ranch." Her lower lip quivered again, and she wiped her eyes. "Jason was like a brother to me. We took him in ten years ago after his parents were killed in a train accident. Even Father grew to love him as the son he'd never had. After Jason was killed, some of the ranch hands searched the area around the spring, but they never found any tracks except his. Then, shortly after that my father died. I think it was too much of a shock for him to have both John and Jason gone."

"Right after my father's funeral," she continued, "all the hands quit. No one would ride the range after Jason was shot, and the cattle have scattered. Sa-Ra and I rounded up a few small herds and pushed them back on my land, but there are just too many. I need someone tough and willing to round up the others.

"I panicked after my father died and sold Mr. Billingsly a strip of land along the Horseshoe River. If my cattle get too far east, they'll be unable to find much water until they get to the river. Many of the new calves haven't been branded, and if they get on Billingsly's land, his men will brand them as their own, calling them strays. I'm asking for your help. I'll pay you each fifty dollars a month and found."

Jake raised his head and squinted. "Found what?"

Belinda smiled. "Found is a term out here meaning lodging and food."

"Oh." Jake grinned crookedly. "Sounds danger-ness, Ma'am. I'm just a farmer from 'Tucky an' don't know nothin' about cowboyin'." He squinted at Wiley with one eye half closed. "Wiley's a mean critter an' good tracker. He'll most likely help you out."

Wiley stiffened. He cleared his throat and shot Jake an icy glance. "I'm in the same situation. All I've ever done is...take care of a small farm in Vermont most of my life. A cattle ranch is a whole different thing entirely. Besides, I'm not even looking for a job. I just arrived today and...want to see what the West has to offer before I settle down to a permanent place." Wiley was intrigued by the idea of being on Belinda's ranch. But, now that he knew who Billingsly was, he wanted to scout the town and plan his strategy.

The front door of the hotel opened, and Billingsly walked into the lobby. When he saw Belinda, he stopped abruptly, then thrust the door shut.

"Miss Castille. If you weren't with these two...*persons*, I'd think you were here to talk business with me. Are you waiting for me?"

"I'm talking to these gentlemen about working on my ranch," she answered timidly.

Billingsly puckered his lips into an amused sneer. "Ah, yes. All your help quit. I did overhear someone speak of that recently." Billingsly's eyes slid to Wiley. His eyebrows flickered as he took in the godlike man, then he scowled when he saw Jake slouched in his chair.

Billingsly stood up straight and half-closed his eyes. "Gentlemen, I am Ed Billingsly. I remember the two of you from the Silver Heels down the street. You both cut yourselves and participated in a heathen custom right in front of everyone." He put his hand on his hip. "I hope you realize you made fools of yourselves and made an enemy of Reverend Quick, a very respected member of this community. I would like..."

"Neither of us care about your opinion," Wiley interrupted. He stood up and stared at Billingsly. "Nor do we care about Reverend Quick." He reached out his hand for Jake. "If you will both excuse us, we've had a long day and need some rest." Wiley turned and nodded to Belinda. "Ma'am." He glanced back at Jake and started toward the stairs.

Jake got up at once. "G'night, ma'am." He grinned at Miss Castille as he staggered after Wiley.

Billingsly watched them climb the stairs. When they were out of sight, he sat down in the chair Jake had vacated. Squinting his eyes at Belinda, he asked, "Who are those two men? Did they tell you what they're doing in town?"

Before she could answer, the front door opened and a man in a long black coat and a wide-brimmed black hat walked in. After he closed the heavy door, he stopped and peered around. When he saw the couple in the next room, he quickly turned his face away and hurried up the stairs.

After watching the man in black disappear from view, Belinda cut her eyes back to Billingsly. "I...I didn't give them much of a chance to say anything. Why do you ask?"

"I don't trust them," Billingsly snapped. "From my office window, I've watched the blond one sitting in his room upstairs looking out the window all day. He's been up there for a week, and now the other one shows up. I think they're wanted men."

After having listened to Billingsly's conniving arguments in the bar, and now hearing his suspicions of Jake and Wiley, Belinda's irritation shoved aside her fear.

"Even if they're not wanted," she snapped, "you'll get them accused of something so you can defend them in court! And naturally, Mr. Billingsly, you'll win! But, I don't think they have any money. Or do you have a room in your mansion already picked out for them?"

From his expression, she realized she'd made the lawyer angry. Belinda stood up and rushed through the door beside the registry counter and down the hall to her room.

As Billingsly sat by himself in the empty lobby, he barely noticed the man in the black coat stealthily descend the stairs and leave the hotel.

"How *dare* that woman speak to me that way," Billingsly snapped out loud. "I've put up with her long enough! I'll get her ranch if it's the last thing I ever do."

He felt her comment about picking out rooms in his house hit below the belt. It was his own business if a few men he employed occasionally shared his four-poster bed. He wondered how many other people in the area knew.

Billingsly stood up. He wasn't tired now, and a brandy would take the edge off Belinda's accusations.

With his hands clasped behind his back, Billingsly headed up the boardwalk toward Mattie's Saloon.

## CHAPTER 13

Jake quickened his steps to catch up with Wiley. When he reached the landing halfway up the stairs, he tripped on the top step, fell into his new blood brother and hung onto Wiley as he tried to regain his balance.

Wiley slid his arm around Jake and helped him up the remaining flight and into the second-floor hallway. Wiley let the fire door swing shut, stuck out his butt to keep it from slamming and steadied Jake at the same time.

"That wazza good move you jes' made, Wiley," Jake said, grinning. "Gettin' away from Binzlee so fast waz zmart." Jake weakly pointed to door 200. "Thaz Binzlee's room. Which'nz yers?"

Wiley stared at Billingsly's door for a few seconds before he nodded to the first door on the other side of the hall. "I'm right here." He tugged on Jake's arm. "Come into my room. Let's talk about tomorrow."

They heard heavy footsteps ascending the stairs.

Wiley gently pushed Jake into his room. When they were both inside he closed the door without a sound.

Jake refused to move further into the room and steadied himself by gripping the doorknob.

Wiley wanted to get Jake away from the door, but there was no time. Right then, the fire door opened and slammed. Heavy boots clomped into the hall and stopped outside their room. Wiley listened to each uncertain footstep slowly double-thump down the bare floor of the hallway, stop in front of each door, continue to the end, then start back. Whoever wore the boots stopped outside their door again and stayed there.

Wiley silently pulled his gun, hoping he could yank Jake out of the way if he needed to use it, then sighed with relief when the fire door opened and the person wearing the boots started down the stairs. Wiley hesitated a moment before holstering his Colt.

"It weren't Blinzy," Jake whispered.

"I don't think it was Billingsly, either," Wiley said. "He was sure lookin' 'round some, though." Wiley caught himself speaking like Jake and laughed. "Jake, you've got me talking like you."

"What?" Jake squinted at Wiley in the dim light.

"I said 'lookin' around,'" Wiley said. "Before you know it, I'll be talkin' *jest like you*" Wiley laughed out loud. He'd never felt so loose. He loved feeling this way, and he loved Jake.

Jake hung onto the doorknob and glared at Wiley with one eye closed. "What'smatter how I talk?"

Wiley laughed. "Nothing, Jake. Nothing at all. I *love* the way you talk, but I'm supposed to have too much education to talk like you."

"What's es-i-kashun got to do with anathin'," Jake slurred hotly. "Jest cuz we're brud blothers, yer laughin' at me fer bein' dumb. What you want fromee anyhow? I ain't smart. Ever'body home calls me dummer'n hog shit Jake!" He closed his eyes and leaned against the door.

"Jake, I'm sorry," Wiley said. "I wasn't saying anything about you being dumb. Where I come from no one talks the way you do. It's refreshing to hear."

Jake turned his head and glared at Wiley. "Jes' go back to Veront an' be es-i-kated!" He opened the door, stumbled into the hall and slammed it behind him.

Stunned that Jake took his comments so personally, Wiley stared at the door. He never expected a reaction like that. He rushed to the door and opened it.

As Wiley stepped out of his room, a door slammed farther down. Street side. It must be Jake's room. He ran to 205, the last door in the hall.

Wiley started to knock, but decided not to. He realized they both had drunk too much, and he'd probably make matters worse trying to apologize. Better to let Jake sleep it off. Wiley sighed, touched Jake's door, then slowly walked back toward his room.

He glanced around twice, hoping to find Jake standing in the hall, but was disappointed each time.

Wiley let himself into his room and quietly shut the door. He stood with his back against it and peered into the semi-darkness.

The room seemed slightly larger than the one he'd rented from Mrs. Gunther in Philadelphia and even with the deep shadows from the wardrobe and dresser, it seemed cheery. The four-poster featherbed took up most of the room. Covered with a brightly colored quilt, it seemed to beckon him. He needed a sound sleep, and his body ached from the cold.

Wiley glanced at the dim spots of light reflected from the white porcelain pitcher on the bedside table. The water he'd used to wash, earlier, had frozen in the bowl.

As he pushed himself away from the door and ambled toward the window, he realized he'd never felt so complete with anyone as he had being with Jake, and the fleeting thought of never seeing Jake again caused him to shudder from a sense of infinite loss.

When he reached the partly open window, Wiley peered through the moving slit between the curtains at the dark street below. After a moment, he distinguished several men standing in a group at the corner of the boarding house across the street. Suddenly, all five men, dressed in long black coats and wide-brimmed black hats, turned and stared at the hotel in the direction of Jake's room.

The Harrises!

Wiley rushed across the room and quietly sprinted down the hall to 205. He opened the door to Jake's room and went part way in, but the darkness hit him like a brick wall and he stopped.

"Jake?" he whispered loudly. "Jake, are you in here?"

No answer.

Wiley dug into his pocket, pulled out a match and lit it. A jumble of blankets revealed an empty bed. He looked behind the door. Nothing. He held the match low and peered under the bed. Jake wasn't there!

Wiley ran back down the hall, turned up the light in his room and tossed his bag on the bed. He pulled out a smaller knife and slipped it into the sheath on the side of his left moccasin, then slid his jacket off the bedpost, shoved his arms into the sleeves and dropped a few pieces of jerky and extra shells into its deep pockets. Wiley touched the butt of his gun and rushed out the door.

Once outside, he stood on the wooden boardwalk in front of the hotel and glanced around. The Harrises were nowhere to be seen in the crowded street. Wild piano music from the Silver Heels, two blocks down, filled the air.

Wiley slipped into the alley between the hotel and the telegraph office. Near the back of the building, he stopped and peered into the darkness. Black, moving shapes about fifty feet away caught his eye, and he could make out several riders milling in a tight group.

He heard some one cry out. It sounded like Jake! Wiley ran toward the shout. A bullet whizzed past his face the instant he heard the blast of a gun. He threw himself to the ground.

The horses suddenly galloped toward Main Street. Wiley heard another yell from Jake, this time from pain.

Wiley remembered the warning Grandpa Gray Feather had given him about staying close to Jake, and he scrambled to his feet and ran after the horses. When he reached Main Street, he paused for a moment to see which way the riders went, then ran a block to the livery he'd seen from the stagecoach window.

Wiley rushed into the building and yelled, "Hostler, I need a horse! *Now!*"

A small groan rose from a pile of hay in the corner of a front stall. The hostler stuck his grass-covered head up and looked around. "Wha?"

"I said, I need a horse!" Wiley ran to a stall that contained a sleek, bay gelding with a black mane and tail and opened the gate. "Five men kidnapped my partner, and they're going to kill him."

"Hold on there!" The stocky hostler bristled as he struggled to his feet. "You can't take that horse! Why, he'll toss you clean through the roof. That there's a mean one, and he'll only let one man ride 'im."

Wiley ignored the warning, grabbed a blanket draped on the rail and threw it over the horse's back, gently positioned the saddle, cinched it, then deftly slipped on the bridle. He grabbed the reins and leaped into the saddle.

The horse gave Wiley an evil-eye and reared. The instant his front hooves touched the ground, he crashed through the partly opened gate and galloped out of the building.

"Well, I'll be danged," the hostler said out loud as he watched the dust settle. "I shore ain't seen the likes of that before." He walked to the door of the building and peered out into the dark street. "If he can stay in that there saddle, he'll catch anybody from around here."

* * *

Seth Harris chuckled to himself as they galloped out of town. They'd captured Jake again, and this time in the dead of night. He doubted anyone would follow and wondered if Aaron had killed the person he'd shot at behind the hotel. No matter. Once they hung Jake, they'd leave this country and return to Kentucky. He glanced behind him, saw Jake leaning precariously, and reined his horse. His four sons nearly ran him down before they slowed to a stop.

Seth moved alongside Jake. He grabbed the drunk and dazed man and yanked him back into the saddle.

"Abe!" Seth shouted. "Gimme that piece'a rope you're always makin' a noose with. I gotta tie Jake to his horse so he don't fall off before we get to that hangin' tree we found."

"It's *my* rope, Pa, and I don't want Jake touchin' it 'til we use it on his neck."

"I'm your pa! You do as you're told!

Reluctantly, Abe tossed the rope to his father. Seth snatched it from the air and secured Jake's hands to the saddle horn.

Seth grabbed the reins of Jake's horse and spurred his own. "Now let's get goin'. We gotta hang Jake quick-like and get gone from here."

Aaron caught up to Seth's horse and whined, "Why can't I just stick my knife in Jake's gut, Pa? That'll kill him just as good as hangin' him. He'll die slower...while he's screamin'."

Seth snapped his head toward Aaron. "I'm tired of yer yappin' about killin' Jake with your knife. You been doin' that since we left home. We're hangin' him, and *that's final*! It's the proper way after what he done to Sara Jean."

"I hear a horse behind us, Pa," Clem whispered.

Zeke turned his horse and glanced behind him, hoping it was the man who'd saved Jake outside the bar. Maybe he could do it again. Even if Jake had gotten Sara Jean knocked up, seeing Jake again had made him realize he couldn't bare the thought of the man he loved hanging from a rope.

Seth cursed. "It's most likely that scum that got Jake away from us before. Clem, you get in them bushes. We'll go on. Shoot him in the back, then catch up."

# CHAPTER 14

Wiley fought for control of the horse as he galloped down Main Street and, with gentle strength, let the horse know he was boss. Even so, at the edge of town, the horse stopped and looked around at the heavy man on his back, challenging him.

Wiley laughed, tousled the horse's mane between its ears and said softly, "You and I have to find Jake. Let's be friends at least until then. How does that sound?"

The horse shook his head, blew once and plunged headlong down the street.

Outside town, Wiley found himself in his favorite element. He had no trouble picking up the tracks of the riders in front of him. The night sky held patchy clouds and a three-quarter moon hung in the south, plenty of light to see the lay of the land. Back in Vermont he could track almost as easily in darkness as broad daylight, and it felt exhilarating to be doing it again.

Since Wiley wasn't the least bit afraid of the horse, it seemed to run with a new-found freedom, and Wiley had his hands full restraining it from galloping too fast. He wanted to travel slow enough to make sure the group didn't split into single riders trying to scramble the trail.

The tracks left the road a short distance out of town and headed northeast up the long slope of Mount Silverheels. One set sunk deeper than the rest and Wiley knew that horse carried a heavier man--Jake. If the Harrises did split up, he'd follow the deeper set of tracks.

As the terrain became steep and forested, scattered clouds passed in front of the moon, but the horse seemed familiar with the area and never faltered in the climb up the sprawling foot of the mountain. Wiley knew the riders were only a short distance in front of him, and even in the dimmer light he could see their tracks.

Wiley spotted a line of bent grass that veered to the left, and realized a single rider had turned off the path while the others had continued up the slope. Out of the corner of his eye, he saw a dark shape moving through the trees not more than twenty feet away. He kept on in the direction of the other riders, but after traveling fifty feet, quickly turned his horse to the left. Wiley slid out of the saddle, tied his mount to a small aspen, and silently stalked the lone rider.

In the deep shadows, Wiley saw a large boulder looming in front of him and saw the rider heading toward it. Wiley crept to the rock and waited. As a dark silhouette approached the other side, Wiley sprang on the rock and sailed over the back of the horse, taking the man with him. Jarred when he hit the ground, Wiley shook his head and quickly pinned the man to the ground. He pulled his knife and drew a tiny speck of blood on the man's neck with the point.

"Where's Jake?"

The man gasped but didn't say anything. Wiley recognized him as the one who had punched him earlier.

"So it's you," Wiley snarled. He cut the man's neck a little deeper.

"Don't kill me!" the man screamed. "I don't rightly know where Jake is. Pa and my brothers is fixin' to hang him from a tree we found up yonder." His face turned hateful. "Yer prob'ly too late, and that scum Jake's most likely daid and swingin' from the tree. Serves 'im right for stickin' it to Sara Jean."

"Jake didn't do it, you ass. *You* probably did. What's your name?" He sunk the knife a hair deeper.

"Clem!" the man screamed. "Don't kill me!"

"Well, Clem, I have a big surprise for you." Wiley lifted the knife and smacked Clem's head with its heavy handle, knocking him out. He slipped a rawhide cord out of his coat pocket, rolled Clem over and tied his arms Indian fashion. His brothers would have to cut the strap to get him loose. After tossing Clem's knife and gun into the brush, he grabbed the reins of the man's horse, tied it to a tree, then ran to his own mount.

Through a break in the clouds, the moon bathed the landscape in silvery light and Wiley found the tracks again without any trouble. He spurred the horse, letting it find its own pace up the steep slope.

Wiley patted the animal on the neck. "I'm naming you Buddy for tonight. So, Buddy, let's go get Jake."

Suddenly, the tracks disappeared. Wiley reined up to look around. "Brushed out," he whispered softly. Expecting an ambush if he dismounted to search the area, he remained in the saddle, drew his gun and began riding a wide circle, glad the spring moon was low in the sky since it accentuated the depressions in the ground. After a few minutes of searching, Wiley spotted the curved shadow of a lone hoof print. He walked Buddy in the direction the other horse had been traveling and found the tracks again. When Wiley raised his head, he saw the outline of five riders topping a ridge a quarter mile away, their shapes black against the moonlit sky.

Wiley spurred Buddy up the slope, taking him higher than the other riders. He wanted to approach the group from above and catch them off guard. Covered with loose stones and fallen trees, the steep terrain appeared impassible, but Buddy seemed to enjoy it as he scrambled up and around a large pinnacle of rock. As they rounded the back of the rock, Wiley saw the five men below riding close to the edge of a black drop-off. He noticed one of the men sat slumped forward in the saddle and knew it must be Jake.

Wiley lost sight of the group as they threaded their horses between a spruce grove and the edge of the black drop-off. He nudged Buddy down a steep slope, staying in moonlight so the horse wouldn't slip on the loose, flat rocks. Wiley soon realized the only way to the others would take him along a ledge hugging a rock wall with a thirty-foot drop on the other side. He noticed elk tracks close to the shelf-like trail and continued on, letting the horse find its own way. At a narrow part of the shelf, Wiley was forced to raise his left leg over the saddle to keep from scraping it on the rock wall. Around a turn, the ledge entered deep shadows.

Wiley stopped the horse and peered into the gloom to see how much farther the ledge went and if it was wide enough to keep going. Too dark to tell, he nudged Buddy forward.

Suddenly, the silence was shattered by long, trailing screams of a man and a horse plunging to their deaths.

# CHAPTER 15

Sitting at his usual table in the corner, Ed Billingsly grimaced as he glanced around Mattie's Saloon. He owned this disgusting hole. He smiled slightly as his mind wandered to Walt Swiller. Poor old Walt. He'd only tried to protect his patrons, and himself, when he'd pointed the shotgun and fired. At such close range, the drunk who'd been shooting up the place had been nearly cut in half.

Billingsly hoped he'd never again see the two ugly strangers he'd paid to testify that Walt had shot the man in cold blood. He smiled broadly when he remembered the brilliant way he'd gotten Walt off the murder charge and the grand show he'd given the town. He'd worn all his rings that day and his purple velvet jacket.

The lawyer nearly laughed when he recalled Walt's face as he'd read the fees for his trial. The only thing Walt had owned was this bar. He'd lived in the back. Billingsly wondered what ever became of him.

He thought again of the tongue lashing Belinda Castille had given him at the hotel. How *dare* that woman talk to him that way. He knew he'd think of a way to get her ranch, but for now stealing her cattle would have to do. As he stared at the amber brandy in his glass, Billingsly failed to notice a big cowboy enter the bar and glance around before settling his eyes on the skinny lawyer.

Whispers could be heard in the room as several patrons indicated to others that Sidewinder had just arrived.

Billingsly's foreman and main hired gun approached the bar and grabbed the beer the bartender quickly shoved in his direction. The cowboy examined the mug carefully, then nodded. He took a long drink, wiped the foam off his lip, then sauntered toward the corner table. With each step, his tight clothes stretched taut over his muscled body. He yanked out the chair across from Billingsly, plopped his big frame into it and slid the mug onto the table.

"What are you doing here this late?" Sidewinder asked his boss. "I thought you needed your beauty sleep." He laughed. "After all this time, shouldn't it start working?"

"Shut up, Winder!" Billingsly snapped. "You interrupted my thoughts." He lowered his voice. "What are you doing back in town? You couldn't have driven all the Castille cattle onto my land in one day."

Winder leaned back in his chair and slid his arm over the back of another. "We had to quit for awhile. Some miners were snooping around Horseshoe River looking for gold. There were about twenty of them, so I figured we'd better make ourselves scarce for awhile. Besides, I forgot to bring any whiskey, and it gets dusty out there."

"I don't pay you to drink! I pay you to do what I..."

"Look!" Winder quickly glanced around, then leaned forward. With a lowered voice, he continued. "You don't pay me enough to get caught stealing cattle. I happen to like my neck the length it is now. And remember one thing. If I get caught, *you* get caught. Savvy?"

"All right, all right. Just get Belinda's cattle on my land by the end of the week." Billingsly sipped his brandy. "And have the men ready to brand the calves as soon as they're weaned."

Winder scowled at Billingsly. "Relax, it'll get done."

"I have good reason to be worried," Billingsly snapped. "Belinda was talking to two men tonight in the hotel lobby. They're both new in town and almost as big as you are. She offered them a job on her ranch." He hit the table with his fist. "Drat! I forgot to ask her if she hired them."

"So what? Two against eleven's no threat. It'd be two against twelve if Jimmy'd ever get off his butt and help."

"You leave Jimmy out of this. I keep him plenty busy around here. Besides, I think he's seeing someone on the sly, and I want to keep my eye on him."

"What makes you think that? There aren't any single women in this town that don't charge." Winder sneered at Billingsly. "As if *you* would know."

"Leave my personal life out of this. If you've never tried it with a man, don't criticize it."

"Well, at least some of your men aren't dick-lickers. And I don't think Jimmy is either." Winder shook his head. "How he can be chummy with them is beyond me, but it doesn't seem to make any difference to him at all."

"Jimmy's the only one I have working for me with any brains." Billingsly frowned at Winder. "Unfortunately, that makes him the most dangerous. I think he's getting suspicious of some of my dealings by the questions he asks. And I don't think he'd take it well if he ever found out for sure. That's why I have to watch him every moment." He glanced around. "I wonder where he is now? He was supposed to bring Sam a bag of money to make change. Sam said he hasn't shown up yet."

Sidewinder grabbed his beer and took a long swig, belched, then said, "Sam sure pours a good beer." He held the mug in front of his face and smiled at it. "Of course, I had to threaten the sucker's life before he learned."

Billingsly stared at his foreman. The man's chiseled features and strong jaw gave him almost a Greek-god look, but Winder's ice-blue eyes overpowered everything and seemed to freeze Billingsly's soul at times. The lawyer let his eyes wander over Winder's body. The man's flexed muscles strained his shirt as he held up the mug. Billingsly sighed. Someday he'd have those arms around him if it was the last thing he ever did. And it very well might be if he somehow managed it.

The rattling of the batwing doors broke into his lusting as Jimmy Ratchett walked in.

"I wonder where he's been?" Billingsly asked.

Winder turned and watched Jimmy hand a small bag to Sam, who snatched it and scowled. Jimmy grinned at the bartender, picked up the beer Sam poured for him and headed toward the corner table.

"Where have you been?" Winder snapped, mimicking Billingsly's nasal, raspy voice. He watched the tall, wiry cowboy with curly brown hair and a handsome sun-browned face swing his leg over the back of a chair and sit down.

"You stay out of this, Winder," Billingsly growled. He glared at Jimmy. "Well? I'm waiting."

Jimmy grinned. "I've been over at Pete's barber shop getting a bath and a rubdown. Why?"

"You were suppose to bring Sam that money three hours ago. He's had to use gold to make change, and I don't like him doing that. Especially when it's *my* gold."

Jimmy ignored Billingsly and turned to Winder. "Did you hear about the two gents who became blood brothers tonight in the Silver Heels? The whole bar cheered them." He shook his head. "Those two sure have guts."

"I was there," Billingsly said. "They're the same two Belinda tried to hire later in the hotel."

Winder chuckled. "Now I *know* we have nothing to worry about. If she does put them to work, we can use them for target practice."

# CHAPTER 16

In the moonlight, Wiley nudged the horse to continue along the narrow, rock ledge. When they entered the deep shadows, Wiley froze when Buddy's hoof dislodged a loose rock that gave way and crashed against boulders far below. The horse scrambled and had just regained his footing when Wiley heard the screams of a man and a horse falling. He heard two thuds, an avalanche of rock, two fainter thuds, more rocks, then a fading hiss followed by silence.

"Oh, God," Wiley groaned out loud, "please don't let that be Jake!"

Wiley tried not to panic as Buddy slowly picked his way along the ledge and sighed with relief when it finally ended. Back on solid ground, Wiley spurred Buddy to a tangle of fallen trees farther down the slope, leaped off the horse and tied him loosely to the exposed root of a blowdown. He descended the slope on foot, then silently wove through the stand of spruce where he'd last seen the riders.

Wiley drew his gun and stepped into the open. He saw three men ten yards in front of him, peering over the side of an abyss, their dark coats and hats clearly visible in the moonlight. Wiley realized two men in the group were missing besides the one he'd knocked out down below, and one of the missing men was Jake.

A horse blew, and Wiley cut his eyes to the left. A few yards away, three riderless horses were grouped together near a horse with a man slumped over in the saddle. Wiley's heart leaped when he recognized Jake. Noiselessly, he ran to the horses and looked up into the face of his blood brother. Jake's eyes were closed, and a streak of dried blood lined the side of his cheek.

Wiley heard a few sobs behind him as he secured the ropes binding Jake's hands to the saddle horn. He glanced back and saw the three Harrises crouched at the edge of the void. He forced down the desire to shoot all of them in the back for wanting to hang Jake, knowing Jake would never forgive him if he killed his neighbors in cold blood.

Without making a sound, Wiley grabbed the reins and leaped onto the horse behind Jake. He pulled his gun and shot twice over the heads of the Harrises. Startled, they fell for cover. Their horses bolted and galloped away into the night.

As Wiley carefully guided the horse around the spruce grove and up the hill to the deadfall, shots fired from below sent bullets whizzing by the two men's heads. Even at the blowdown they were still within range of the Harrises' guns, but a cloud glided across the moon, providing the needed cover of darkness.

Wiley slid off Jake's horse and mounted his own, then grabbed both sets of reins and began searching for a new way back to town, not wanting to take Jake across the narrow ledge. He followed the base of the rock wall and found a game trail that headed west and down the mountain toward town.

Occasionally Jake's horse came alongside Buddy, and Wiley attempted to shake Jake's shoulder, hoping to revive him. Each time he did, Buddy tried to attack Jake's horse and Wiley was forced to keep them apart. Content Jake was alive and away from the Harrises, Wiley assumed his partner was still drunk and possibly dazed from the blow on his head.

After what seemed like an hour, the two men reached Alma. As soon as they rode into the livery, Wiley dismounted and ran to the stall where the hostler slept.

"Wake up! You've got to tell us where we can go to keep out of sight!"

The hostler scrambled to his feet, frowned and rubbed his face. When he saw Wiley, his eyes grew wide.

"You? I thought you'd be dead by now after ridin' that devil of a horse." When he saw the horse, he scratched his head. "You mean to say you're back here all in one piece?" He pointed to Jake. "That your friend?"

"Yes," Wiley said. "One of the kidnappers is dead. He fell off a cliff. The other four will be on our trail once they find their horses, so it may not be until morning. But we have to find a place to stay until Jake feels better. We can't go back to the hotel. Do you have any place in mind?"

The hostler eyed Wiley suspiciously, then pointed at the large hay-filled shelf stretching across the front of the building. "Guess you could hole up there. I usually sleep up there, but lately I've takin' a notion to sleepin' down here." He squinted at Wiley. "But I don't want no shootin' in here! I guard these horses with my life and don't want nothin' to happen to any of 'em!"

Wiley smiled. "There won't be any shooting if those men don't know we're here."

"Guess you're right about that," the man said.

Wiley extended his hand. "Thanks for letting us stay. My name is Wiley, and my partner's name is Jake."

"Name's Bill. Bill Chasteen." The hostler slowly grinned and finally shook Wiley's hand vigorously. "You boys shore look like you've had a night."

A noise caused Wiley to spin around in time to see Jake slide off his horse. As he fell, Jake caught his shoulder on a saddle draped over the top rung of a stall. The saddle, the rail and Jake landed in a heap on the dirt floor.

"Oh my God!" Wiley yelled. "The rope on Jake's hands must have come untied." He ran to his blood brother and lifted the saddle and rail off his stomach. "Jake, are you all right?"

"Wiley?" Jake whispered. He opened his eyes. "Is that you, Wiley?"

"I'm right here, Jake." Wiley bent over him. "Are you all right?"

Jake grabbed Wiley's jacket and pulled him on top of himself, then whispered, "I'm fine, Wiley. Now that you're here."

Wiley felt a flutter in his gut. Saying nothing, he slid his arms around Jake and pulled him close, giving in to the strong desire to shield this man from the world.

Bill hesitated a few moments before walking over to them. "I reckon you boys is pretty dang good partners. But I'd be pleased if you'd get yer asses up that ladder where you'll be safe. There's a stack of blankets up there. And there's some jerky and a box of dried fruit in the corner by the water barrels. Help yerselves." As he watched the two men embracing, he bit his lip and lowered his eyes.

It was no easy task getting Jake up the ladder. Bill climbed up first toting a lantern, then watched as Wiley pushed on Jake's butt with his shoulder. Bill leaned over the edge, grabbed Jake's arm and tried hauling him to the top. Dang, the man weighed a ton! He thought of trying to pull a steer through a chute by its front leg.

Once they got Jake to the loft, Bill climbed down, stripped off the saddles and brushed both horses before leading them to stalls out of sight to newcomers into the building. He figured whoever owned the one Jake rode would surely come looking for it. Bill smiled at the horse Wiley had borrowed. Fancy hadn't acted up the way he usually did while getting brushed.

"Finally, somebody besides me treated you right," Bill muttered softly.

Fancy blew and shook his head.

After Bill replaced the rail Jake knocked down when he fell and repositioned the saddle, he brushed out the few boot tracks before climbing into his blankets.

Wiley was thankful Bill had left the lantern. After making sure Jake wasn't too near the edge, he quickly hollowed a bed in a mound of hay and spread out the grimy blankets. He smiled when Jake's arms became pliable as he helped him strip off his coat.

Jake peered at him through half open eyes. "We gonna get naked?"

"Not tonight. I think we'll stay warmer if we leave our clothes on. Besides, these blankets are so filthy, something might take a bite out of us."

Jake grabbed his crotch. "I ain't undressin'! I don't want no bites outta me!" He crawled to the bed and plopped down on the far side.

Wiley covered both of them with a blanket and mounded hay on top of it. As he lay back, Jake turned and faced him.

"Wiley, can I put my arms around you an' keep you warm? You won't hit me or nothin' will you?"

Wiley grinned, then blew out the lamp. Hesitantly, he touched Jake's arm and felt a tiny spark he somehow knew would be there. As he gathered Jake into his arms, he heard far-off whisperings that seemed to swirl around them in the darkness. He thought he heard Grandpa Gray Feather sigh.

"Let's keep each other warm," Wiley said breathlessly as he pulled Jake closer. He slid his lips across Jake's beard until they found his, then pressed them together. Jake responded instantly, and they nestled together in a crushing embrace. Shortly, Wiley heard Jake snoring softly. He chuckled, then settled his head into the pit of Jake's arm and dropped off to sleep.

# CHAPTER 17

The livery door banged open, and four men dressed in black coats and hats stormed into the building. They split up and began searching the stalls, under piles of hay and behind stacks of lumber for boot tracks or other signs of Jake and Wiley.

Bill jumped to his feet. "Who are you, and what the hell d'you want?"

The morning sunlight, seeping through gaps in the walls, produced golden, dusty slices throughout the building. One of these slivers of light fell on the face of the oldest man. In his late fifties, he appeared older with his weathered face and long gray hair and beard. His steel-gray eyes burned with hate as he glared at Bill.

"I'm Seth Harris. I come all the way from Kentucky with four of my sons. We're lookin' to find the man that got my Sara Jean hit up with child. I aims to kill him since he run and won't get hitched with her." He glanced around the livery. "Last night, one of my sons and his horse was both killed. I'm gonna make Jake pay fer that, too. And I got somethin' special planned fer the skunk that stole Jake away from us last night." He shook his fist at Bill. "*Twice* he done it! We're gonna search this here town 'til we find them. Bein' this here's the first buildin' on the street, we're startin' here."

Jake and Wiley woke instantly when the men entered the barn. They quietly grabbed their guns and crept back into the hay.

"Feel like a fight?" Wiley whispered into Jake's ear.

They froze as someone began climbing the ladder. Zeke had nearly reached the loft before Bill grabbed his rifle. "You men got no right searchin' this here barn!" He aimed the rifle at Zeke. "I'll get the marshal out here with one shot, and that shot'll kill you, sonny. Now get the hell down from that ladder before I split your spine wide open." He cocked the rifle and spread his legs.

"We'll go," Seth finally sneered. "But, if I find you've been a-hidin' Jake and his friend, I'll come back and kill you too." He spat on the ground, turned and started toward the door. "Come on, boys, let's search the rest of this here town."

Zeke climbed down the ladder and fell into single file with his two older brothers as they followed after their father. Bill thought of a mother duck and her chicks, only these men looked more like buzzards.

When Seth reached the door, he turned to face Bill. "You see a big blond man with a beard and a dark-haired man together, you let me know. You hear me, boy?"

"I wouldn't let the likes'a you know *nothin'*! Not even when any of these horses gotta shit." Bill raised the rifle and aimed it at Seth. "Y'all get the hell outta here."

As soon as the four men left the building, Bill crept to the door and looked out. Satisfied they weren't still in the area, he slowly went to his adopted stall and propped his gun against the lower rail. He glanced toward the loft.

"They're gone. You fellers can come on down if you've a mind to. I'm gonna mosey over't the marshal's office and let him know what them men are doin'. Won't mention I've seen you gents, and you can stay up there as long as you like. There's water in them barrels fer washin' up." Bill left without waiting for a reply.

Slowly, Wiley stood up and brushed hay from his head and clothes. "Jake, I think we have a friend in this town."

"He sure did us a good turn just now." Jake crept to the edge of the loft and peered over, making sure no one was in the livery before going to the water barrels. "Think I'm gonna wash up." He took his clothes off and tossed them to the floor.

Wiley carefully examined Jake's thick, muscular body. He'd wrestled scores of men in school and, more recently, in the ghettos of Philadelphia. Some of the men had been so stunning it had caused him embarrassing moments in the ring. But Jake outclassed them all. His solid, work-hardened body seemed to have added bulk from strenuous exercises. Wiley couldn't help wondering what Michaelangelo might have thought. He noticed Jake had no body hair, except around his crotch and a little in his armpits. The thought of feeling Jake all over...wet...made Wiley light-headed. He peeled off his rawhide shirt. "Washing up sounds like a real good idea."

Naked, Wiley approached from behind. He slid his arms under Jake's and grabbed his chest. Pressing himself against Jake's back, Wiley hooked his chin over Jake's shoulder.

"God, Jake, you're the most beautiful man I've ever seen in my life."

Jake's body exploded with tingles at Wiley's touch. After years with no one but the memory of Sergeant Moss to hold him, he nestled against Wiley's naked body and grabbed the strong arms wrapped around him. Wiley, his very own blood brother, held him. And blood brothers were forever. Sergeant Moss seemed only like a fading dream. Jake turned his head until his nose touched Wiley's. "I ain't never had nobody hold me like this before, Wiley. I'm glad it's you doin' it an' not nobody else."

"Me too, Jake." Wiley kissed Jake on the neck and slid his hands over Jake's smooth skin.

Jake twisted around to face Wiley, pulled away to get a better look at him, and smiled when he realized Wiley's body was as big as his own. With his finger, Jake gently traced the furrows of Wiley's massive chest, then grabbed a handful of black hair.

"This'll keep us both warm at night," Jake said.

In the midst of playful splashing out of the top of the water barrels, the barn door opened, then slammed. Bill yelled, "You boys up yet?"

"We're up, Bill. Thanks for what you did for us." Wiley splashed Jake once more and ducked. "We'll be indebted to you forever."

Bill listened to their horsing around for a few minutes before he spoke. "I had me a partner once...fer eleven years."

The men upstairs became silent.

"We went everywhere together and were both stuck on each other." Bill's voice quavered, and he squeezed the ladder. "His name was Chuck. He was kilt back about five years ago." After a brief silence, he continued. "We was ridin' for a rancher down near Buena Vista. One evenin' we was racin' each other back to the ranch, and Chuck's horse got his front hoof caught in a rabbit hole and bowled right over. Chuck got his neck broke...right there in front of me. I weren't right in the head fer a year or so after."

Bill pressed his face against the ladder. "Then one day I told myself I had to find me another partner. I been lookin' ever since. You boys is new at it, I can tell." He cleared his throat. "Sometime you boys can do me a favor for gettin' rid of them men earlier."

"Anythin'," Jake replied. "Just say it."

Bill glanced up at the loft. "Well...I'd like to come up there and take a peek at you boys' naked bodies some time. Don't hafta worry none about me doin' anythin' to you, but I'm a great looker of men. And you two are the most bee-utiful men I ever laid eyes on. It'd do my achin' ol' heart good."

"Come on up." Wiley winked at Jake. "It's the least we can do."

Bill scrambled up the ladder and climbed onto the loft floor. He stopped and stared, then shook his head.

"Lordy, I ain't never seen the likes of you two my whole life. You two deserve each other. Don't neither of you ever get no eyes for nobody else, or you'll be the ones gypped two times over." He started to climb down the ladder but stopped and glanced back. "You fellers can stay here as long as you've a mind to. The marshal and his deputies are checkin' out those men that's after you. You'll be safe up here."

Back on the ground floor, Bill disappeared out the back door and began moving a pile of old lumber out of the corral. Once, he squinted toward the building and shook his head. "Lordy, them two shore are somethin'," he said out loud.

Jake went to Wiley's side. "Will you look at my head where Clem hit me last night?" He bent down and parted his hair with his fingers.

Wiley felt a good-sized lump. Looking closely at it, he saw the skin, barely broken, had already scabbed over. "I think you'll live, but you must have a headache."

Jake straightened up. "When them Harrises come in the barn, I plumb forgot about it. But now, it sure does hurt. With that an' the booze, I feel worser'n a hen with its neck wrung."

Wiley laughed. "Where do you come up with some of your expressions, Jake?"

"Hell, that ain't nothin'. Ol' Pete Claymoore from back home would come up with the best sayin's I ever did hear. He'd most likely say you an' me was close enough to use the same toothpick. An' if he'd meet Bingsly, he'd say he was so crooked he could sit on a damn corkscrew. Pete was always sayin' the hardest work Aaron ever done was take a long squint at the sun an' a short squat in the shade." Jake rattled off more of Pete Claymoore's sayings and kept Wiley laughing as they got dressed.

Wiley had no sooner put his moccasins on when Bill came through the livery door and climbed up the ladder. "I got to thinkin'. I shore won't be surprised if Marshal Cline orders them men outta town before the day's out. He don't take no shit from nobody, not even that dang Billingsly." Bill grinned at the two men. "But even if they leave, you fellers can stay here as long as you've a mind to."

"Thanks, Bill." Wiley put his hand on Bill's shoulder. "It's real kind of you to help us out. We'll repay you one of these days."

"No doubt you will. But just bein' friends with the two of you is payment plenty." He patted Wiley's hand. "I got more work to do out back. Now, before you do anythin' else, you boys eat somethin' to get your strength back from all that drinkin' and ridin' you done last night." He started toward the ladder but turned back and grinned. "And whatever else you two been doin' since you got up here." Bill chuckled to himself as he climbed down the ladder.

After Bill left the barn, Jake stared off into space. Finally he asked, "Wiley, what makes one man good an' kind like Bill, an' another hateful, like Seth...or my pa?"

"Don't sell yourself short, Jake," Wiley said sternly. "After what you told me about preachers last night, I think you already know. From what I've learned about you in this short time, you're more like Bill than even Bill."

"What? Wiley, I ain't ej-a-caded like you. I don't rightly know what you just said. Did you just say I was dumb? Pa was always tellin' me I was dumb. Sometimes he'd say it so I couldn't figger out if he was tellin' me I was dumb or not."

Wiley put his hands on Jake's shoulders and gazed into his sad, hurt eyes. "Jake, I meant you're even kinder than Bill, and I have a feeling you're too big-hearted for what's going on. I know you're not afraid of the Harrises, but because you're such a decent fellow, you won't lift a finger to hurt them, even though they want to kill you. I think your Jesus would want you to protect yourself from those men, whether it meant killing them in self-defense or not." He kissed Jake's nose. "You've probably been sitting in your hotel room all week worrying about having to hurt even one of them. And I'll bet you haven't even considered how you'd protect yourself."

Jake's face mirrored amazement. "How do you know all this about me, Wiley?"

"I feel one with you, Jake. The blood brother ceremony last night was like an awakening for me. Somehow I've always known you and...I feel you've always been part of me." Wiley shook his head. "I can't explain it, Jake, but being your blood brother makes me realize loving another man as much as I love you is still love. Thanks to you, I no longer feel love like ours is bad." He smiled and sat on the blankets.

Jake sat next to him. His bewildered expression softened. "Wiley, will you tell me somethin'?"

"Yes. What?"

"How'd you get me away from them Harrises last night? Where'd you come from?"

"I'll tell you, but first I want to know what happened to you. How did the Harrises get you?"

"Hell, I was so danged drunk an' riled at what you said about me talkin' funny..."

"I'm sorry, Jake," Wiley said. "I drank too much myself to be bringing up something like that. It's just that...I love the way you talk and found myself wanting to talk like you, but I've had so many years of schooling, it's hard for me to do it. Last night in the room it just slipped out. I was actually quite proud of myself for saying a few words like you."

Jake stared at Wiley with a blank expression. He finally muttered, "Let's just forget it. We'll prob'ly both be talkin' like each other before you know it, anyway."

Jake lowered his head. "After I shut my door last night, I felt real bad at gettin' so riled at you. Somehow, I got down the back stairs an' out behind the hotel. I was gonna walk some an' think about the Harrises bein' after me. An' about sayin' I'm sorry to you."

Jake raised his head and looked straight at Wiley. "Then, before I knew it, a bunch-a men ambushed me an' pulled their guns on me. One told me to get on the horse they'd tied nearby. It was Clem, an' I knowed I'd been caught again. I was so damn drunk, weren't nothin' I could do. Somehow I got on the horse like they said, an' they mounted up too. I tried to yell when I thought I heard somebody, but only got a short one out before Clem stuck his gun in my ear. It hurt so bad I shut up. That's when one of 'em shot at somebody, an' we started ridin' off. I tried to yell again, but Clem clouted me on the head with his gun. After that, I just tried like hell to stay in the saddle. I don't know nothin' else that happened 'til I looked up an' saw you bendin' over me."

"It was me they shot at," Wiley said. "I was..."

"You? What was you doin' out there?"

"Looking for *you*." Wiley laughed. "After you left, I went to the window and saw the Harrises in the street. I wanted to warn you so I went to your room, but it was empty." Wiley filled Jake in on the rescue in great detail.

When Wiley mentioned that one of the Harrises had fallen off the cliff, Jake said, "I heard Seth say one of 'em was dead, but I thought he was bluffin'." He hung his head. "Hope it weren't Zeke. Zeke's the only one that ain't crazy. Clem's cruel an' hateful an' kills animals by roastin' them over a fire before they're dead. Likes to hear 'em scream. Jed an' Aaron are the oldest, an' they're the one's that scare the hell outta me. They seem calm an' nice 'til they get rankled...an' they get rankled easy. Then they get like a couple'a devils. When I was little, I saw Jed cut the thumb off one of the boys that used to tease Sara Jean. He cut it off real slow-like. I tried to stop him, but Aaron grabbed me an' made me watch. I couldn't do nothin' to help poor Stinky. He was screamin' an' then passed out. Stinky went kinda crazy hisself after that an' used to start fires an' shit in his pants an' stuff.

"Abe's like us, but he ain't. He ain't got no love in him for men an' uses 'em like things the way he rams his cock in their asses. After he growed up, he started killin' the men he was rammin' to feel 'em squirm an' kick while he was in 'em. Said it made him calm down. A few years back, Abe tried doin' it to me like he done when I was little, but I was too strong for him that time an' I beat the shit outta him good. I can't see no love in doin' that to another man...even without the killin' part."

"How many men has Abe killed?" Wiley asked, shocked at the thought.

"About five, I guess. Anyway, that's all I know about."

"Didn't someone accuse him of murder?"

"One did, an' he was the fifth to die. After that, nobody never said nothin'."

Shouting outside the building caused them to rush to the loft door. Standing in the shadows, they saw the Harrises being escorted out of town by the marshal and his two deputies.

"We'll be back!" Seth yelled as he turned his head and glared at Marshal Cline. "You can bet on it."

"You come back, and we'll toss you in jail!" Cline shouted back. "We don't want killers in this town."

After the Harrises rode out of sight, Jake glanced at Wiley. "I'd better get my gear at the hotel an' get the hell outta here. Seth ain't leavin'. He'll go a-ways an' camp. I'm thinkin' the job at Miss Castille's ranch might be a good way of duckin' out for a while."

"I've been thinking about working for her too, Jake. But first, I'd like to stay around town for a day or so to see it. I just got here yesterday, and I'd like to go back to the bar and visit some of the mines. You've been here for a week, but I'll bet you haven't seen anything except your room, or the bank and the boarding house across from the hotel." Wiley knew he should have already scouted the town, but being with Jake was so enthralling, his job could wait a little longer. At least he knew who Billingsly was. Besides, he couldn't bear the thought of Jake being anywhere near when he took care of the business he'd been paid to do. Also, working on a ranch would further conceal his identity.

"Then, can we work for Miss Castille?" Jake asked. "I been thinkin' I'd like to try my hand at cowboy'n for awhile. This here's wide open country, an' I'd like to ride an' live out in the open for a spell. Ain't nothin' like this in Kentucky."

"That sounds good to me, too. When Miss Castille first brought it up it sounded good, but I didn't want to rush into it. And I don't particularly like the thought of working for a woman. But, after last night, it seems to be the best thing for us to do right now."

"Maybe we can't find her today," Jake said. "Wonder if Bill knows where she's at?"

"I'm sure we can find her. She's probably known all over town. But I think we'd better keep this job a tight secret."

As Jake climbed down the ladder, he stopped and looked at Wiley. "That's a good idea, Wiley, keepin' it a secret. I'll tell Bill right away what we're plannin', an' tell him to keep it a secret, too."

Wiley smiled and raised his eyes to the sky. God, he loved this man.

They found Bill in the rear corral sitting on the fence, smoking a hand-rolled cigarette.

"Smoke?" Bill asked as he saw them approach. "Thought you gents would be comin' out here about now. Saw the marshal toss them killers outta town, did ya?" He scowled at Wiley. "Shut that dang door! That door's gotta stay shut or them dang flies get in and start bitin' the horses. I don't want 'em kickin' the stalls down."

"Sorry, Bill." Wiley smiled and gently shut the door. He noticed Jake watching how he reacted to Bill's scolding. "We did see the Harrises leave, and I'll take you up on that smoke. I haven't had one in two days." Wiley caught the leather bag of fixings.

After rolling his smoke, Wiley offered the bag to Jake.

"Not hardly," Jake said. He climbed on the fence to wait for the two men to enjoy their smokes. "Bill, Wiley an' me thought we'd go out to Miss Castille's ranch an' give her a hand for awhile. We're gonna try ropin' some cows an' stuff."

Bill laughed out loud and slapped his knee. He hadn't realized Jake, and possibly even Wiley, was a greenhorn. But looking at the two, he knew they had a lot of salt in them and could certainly take care of themselves. He'd never seen quite the muscle these men had and wondered how they got that way.

"Workin' for Belinda's a great idea," Bill said. "She shore does need the help, and you two boys'll learn a few things about cows." He laughed again.

"I've knowed Belinda about all her life," Bill continued, "and she's a sweet woman. If you want my opinion, I think it was Billingsly that got ol' John and Jason kilt. He wants that ranch real bad." He shook his head. "I'm real sorry Jason's gone. He was a looker, that one. Used to ride into town, come right in here and set fer a spell just jawin' away about everythin'. And I'd be watchin' him all over. Nothin' ever come of it cuz he was kilt." Pain clouded his face.

"How do we get in touch with Miss Castille?" Wiley asked quickly. "Without anyone knowing it. Jake and I have decided to let only you and Miss Castille know we're out there. We're hoping the Harrises won't track us and cause more trouble." He clenched his teeth, hoping they would.

"She's still in town," Bill said. "Seen her when I went to tell the marshal about them buzzards that's after you. She's stayin' at the Alma Hotel." He snapped his fingers. "Say, I could tell her to meet you gents some place secret so nobody'd know you was talkin' to her. 'Cept me, of course, and you boys know I'm on your side all the way." Bill glowed inside to be part of the two men's lives.

"Sounds good to me." Wiley tossed the butt of his smoke to the ground and rubbed it out with the toe of his boot. "We'll stay right here until you can arrange the meeting."

"Wait a minute," Jake shouted. "What's she like anyway? I've had me a bad happenin' with a woman, an' Wiley an' me're..."

"Don't you go worryin' your backbone about Belinda," Bill interrupted. "She's been out here all her life and knows not to be messin' with most partners like us. Now, I ain't sayin' all partners out here's like us, but lots are. Nobody ever says nothin' about it anyhow. People in the West are mostly good folk and take others as they are. We all got too dang much to do to be gossipin' and judgin' on each other. Besides, Belinda already knows about you cause she spoke about you gents when I seen her in the street. Said she was still hopin' you'd work fer her. She asked me if I'd seen you and told me you was blood brothers. That true?" Bill squint-eyed them.

"Damn right, Bill." Jake grinned at Wiley. He held up his hand and showed Bill the small cut in his right palm. "We're the best blood brothers there ever was." He suddenly felt a tinge of terror that the Harrises might hurt Wiley, and his face turned serious. "Wiley, maybe we should get our stuff an' check outta the hotel while Bill's talkin' to Miss Castille."

"Good idea. Bill, you'll probably be back here before we will, unless she's not in her room."

"She's prob'ly still at the Regal Cafe. I'll go there first and then to her room. Said she needed to get back to the ranch today. I'll see you gents later." He walked out of the corral and started up the side of the livery. Before he reached the street, he turned back and yelled, "You be careful!"

As the two men waved at him, they heard someone in the building and went inside to check. After their eyes adjusted to the darkened interior, they saw Billingsly walking toward them.

White ruffles on the front of the lawyer's silk shirt spilled out the front of his purple velvet jacket, and a diamond stick pin adorned his rose colored cravat. Several jeweled rings sparkled as he passed the many thin shafts of sunlight. Billingsly carried his top hat.

"Wiley, is he goin' to a party in the middle of the day?" Jake asked in a whisper.

"I think he dresses that way all the time," Wiley said in a low voice.

The thin, hawk-faced man walked to the first stall and stood in front of them.

"Where's Bill? And why are you two in here?" Billingsly flicked his wrist. "Up to no good, no doubt."

"What'd we ever do to you?" Jake asked in a flat voice. "We only just met you last night. You ain't got no right in talkin' about us that way." He turned to Wiley. "This here Bingsly sure thinks he's somebody, don't he, Wiley."

"My name is *Billingsly*, and I've already told you who I am." He glared at Jake, puffed up and continued. "To refresh your memory, *gentlemen*, since you were sopped last night, I am Ed Billingsly, lawyer, rancher and wealthy." He lustfully searched every inch of the two men in front of him, then added, "And...I usually get what I want." He forced his eyes away from Wiley's crotch and glanced around the building. "Er...like I said, where's Bill? I need my horse."

"Don't you mean buggy?" Jake snapped.

Ignoring Jake's comment, Billingsly slid his hand across Wiley's chest. "I guess *you* will have to saddle my horse for me."

Wiley grabbed Billingsly's wrist and squeezed until the lawyer's eyes and mouth opened wide, and then released him. He turned and started for the front door. "Jake, let's go."

Billingsly rubbed his wrist as he watched the men disappear out the front door. God, that man was strong. He stomped his foot, then looked around for his horse. His mind searched for the best way to get revenge on those two delectable men. No one treated Alma's most prominent citizen that way and got away with it. And what these hicks up here in Colorado didn't know about him...would probably hurt them. He chuckled at his wit until he realized he'd have to saddle his own horse, and began calling Bill all sorts of vile names. He even yelled that Bill should stick one of the rails in a place that would make it impossible for the hostler to sit down.

Billingsly found his horse in the last stall in the building and cursed Bill for putting it so far from the front door. As he opened the gate to begin the demeaning task, Fancy suddenly reared. When the horse came down, his hoof struck Billingsly's shoulder a crushing blow. It knocked the man to the floor and tore the left sleeve off his velvet jacket and his silk shirt. A line of blood ran down the side of Billingsly's skinny, bare arm.

Sprawled on the ground and dazed, Billingsly finally had the presence of mind to realize the stall gate stood open and his horse pawed the ground, ready to repeat the attack. He leaped to his feet and flung the gate shut.

"You damn horse!" he screamed hysterically. "You tried to kill me!" With a shaking hand, Billingsly pulled out his pearl handled pistol and pointed it at the horse's head. "*You're* the one that's going to be killed!" He cocked the gun.

With a jerk, Billingsly's gun arm was suddenly thrust upwards to the roof as he pulled the trigger, and the bullet added another hole to the already shot-up shingles from past drunks and rowdies.

"I don't allow no shootin' of horses in this barn!" Bill yelled into Billingsly's ear. He drew his own gun and shoved it into the lawyer's side, all the while holding Billingsly's gun arm with an iron grip. "When I let go of yer arm, you'd better put that there gun of yer's away, or I'll blow yer guts clean to Denver." Bill forcibly turned the lawyer so when he lowered his arm, he couldn't shoot anything but the wall or the floor if he pulled the trigger again.

When Billingsly finally holstered his gun, he glared at Bill. "That damn horse tried to kill me!"

"So what? Ain't no crime in that, the way I see it."

"I'd watch my tongue, if I were you," Billingsly snapped. "You could easily lose this filthy thing you call a job." Red in the face, Billingsly pointed to the horse. "I want that horse shot." He glanced at his shoulder, reached down and picked up the two sleeves. They were covered with straw and horse shit and speckled with blood. Billingsly threw down the silk sleeve in a rage. "Ruined!" he screamed. He held out the velvet sleeve. "This jacket came all the way from Paris." He scowled at Bill. "That's in *France.*"

"Don't rightly care where it's from," Bill sneered. "Shouldn't be wearin' such fancy duds in a town like this anyhow. Yer bound to get shit on 'em some time or another around here."

Bill reached into his pocket, pulled out a wad of money, counted out fifty dollars and handed it to Billingsly. "I'm buyin' that horse right here on the spot. He's a devil of a horse, but I'd hate like heck to see him get shot. 'Specially by the likes of you."

Billingsly snatched the money out of Bill's hand and stooped to pick up his hat. After he brushed off the straw and placed it on his head, he pointed his long finger at Bill. "The horse is yours, but if you're smart you'll shoot him. Better yet, why don't you ride him? Then I won't have to deal with you later. And I *will* deal with you later." He turned and walked rapidly toward the front door.

"Thanks for the rag," Bill yelled as he picked up the silk sleeve. As Billingsly turned, Bill blew his nose in the soiled, glistening material.

Billingsly snorted in disgust and slipped out the door at the same time Jake and Wiley approached the livery with their gear. The lawyer stomped past them, without a glance. The men noticed his bare and bloody arm and that he carried the velvet sleeve to his jacket.

The blood brothers piled their things by the front door and walked to the back stall. When they met up with Bill, Wiley asked, "What happened to Billingsly?"

"Had 'im a run-in with his own horse. Said the horse tried to kill 'im. Can't say as I blame the horse any. I'd of liked to kill that foppy a long time ago. Most of the town would, but he's got too many 'floo-enshel people in this town all tied up in his crooked lawyer'n."

Bill grabbed Wiley by the arm. "Bought you a right mean horse. It was Billingsly's horse you took last night. Told you it was a devil of a horse."

Wiley's face lit up. "Thanks, Bill." He walked to the stall and rubbed the horse's nose. "Hear that, Buddy? You and I were meant for each other." Buddy showed his teeth and tried to bite Wiley's arm. The big man laughed and shoved the horse's head away. "I named him Buddy last night. He's as smart as a whip and knew exactly what was going on when we were tracking you, Jake. How much did you pay for him, Bill?"

"Fifty dollars."

Wiley pulled out sixty. "You got him cheap. Here's an extra ten for your effort."

"I don't take no charity from my friends," Bill shouted and handed back a ten. "You'd 'a done the same fer me if you knowed I liked a horse."

Pacing back and forth, Jake finally asked, "Bill, what about the meetin' with Miss Castille?"

"Oops. Almost forgot with all that's happened in here just now. Belinda said she'd meet you gents out by the old Hanson Ranch house. It's about four miles down toward Fairplay and a bit west. There's only one road goin' there, so you'll find it easy. She wants to meet you at one this afternoon and said she'd bring eats. I'd say you'd best get goin'."

The brothers stashed their gear in the loft while Bill saddled their horses. Fancy, renamed Buddy, acted especially docile this time, seemingly pleased with himself.

After getting directions to the Hanson Ranch, the two men waved at Bill and headed south.

## CHAPTER 18

After Bill kicked the Harrises out of the livery, Seth marched his three remaining sons through the field in front of the barn. When they reached the street, they stopped in a tight group at the corner of the Alma Gazette and scanned the town. At six-thirty, most of the townsfolk up at that hour headed for Biglow's Diner across the street from where they stood or the Regal Cafe, two blocks down. Seth led the way toward the center of town, passing the Alma Gazette, Bennie's Tailoring and The Gilded Bootery, all with closed signs in the window.

Zeke hung back as they passed the marshal's office and jail. The word sheriff, hastily written on a flour sack, covered up the word marshal on the wooden sign out front.

"Get your ass a-comin', boy," Seth yelled at him. He pointed to the stone building. "Ain't nothin' his kind can do to us. This here's a family affair."

As they crossed the small side street, Seth studied the building in front of him. The sign said Cummings' Boarding House.

"This here's where we find 'em," Seth announced.

"But Pa," Clem whined, "Jake was in the hotel last night. Why don't we go there?"

"Shut up, boy! Jake's most likely moved outta there. He's still in town. I saw Mac in the livery. Now, get movin'!"

The four men crowded around the front door of the boarding house as Seth flung it open. With guns drawn, they pushed their way in and filled the sitting room. A woman screamed from a chair by the corner window. The owner, a short, skinny man, rushed through the drapes hung in the doorway to the back rooms.

"My name is Cummings. What do you gentlemen want?" The man eyed the Harrises up and down. "There's no money here."

"We ain't lookin' for money," Seth snarled. "We aims to find Jake an' his friend. We're searchin' this here town 'til we do."

"Jake who?" Cummings asked, scanning his register.

"Jake Brady. Now, where's he at?"

"There's no Jake Brady staying here," the man said, trying to appear calm.

"I know he's here." Seth turned to his sons. "We're gonna search this here place top an' bottom. Abe an' Clem, get on upstairs an' look in every room. I'll take Zeke, an' we'll start down here."

"You can't do this," the owner squeaked. "I told you there's no Jake Brady here."

Seth backhanded Cummings across the face, knocking him to the floor, then pushed through the curtains into the back room. Abe and Clem bounded up the stairs.

Zeke started to follow Seth, but stopped and stared at the man on the floor behind the counter. What was happening? Once they'd found Jake in Denver, his father had started acting like a madman. His own growing belief in Jake's innocence fueled a fear for the safety of anyone who crossed his father.

"Get back here and help me, boy!" Seth yelled from beyond.

Zeke shook his head, hesitated longer than he thought he could, then plowed through the curtain.

Dazed, Cummings struggled to his feet. He noticed a few drops of blood on the floor and touched his mouth. His lip was bleeding.

The woman ran to him. "Are you all right, Mr. Cummings?"

"Yes. Can you get the marshal?" he asked weakly as he carefully lowered himself into a chair. He dabbed a handkerchief to his mouth and watched the woman run out the door.

It took only ten minutes for Marshal Cline and his deputies to round up the Harrises and march them to his office. Seth's yelling about it being a family matter fell on deaf ears. When Cline discovered what the four men were doing in town, and why, he began a long process of questions about the night before, especially about Aaron's death. Seth attempted several times to convince the marshal that Aaron had been killed by Wiley, but Cline distrusted the man and everything he said. He had grown up in the mountains of West Virginia and knew well Seth Harris' kind.

What had actually happened to Aaron no one knew, except Abe, and he remained silent through the questioning. He'd been riding behind Aaron last night and had seen him pull his knife. They were all sick of hearing Aaron plead with Seth to let him stab Jake, but Abe never thought his brother would actually defy their father's wishes. Not caring one way or the other how Jake died, Abe had said nothing as Aaron moved his horse alongside Jake's. Abe figured Aaron had been too anxious to stab Jake and hadn't noticed the uneven edge of the cliff.

\* \* \*

Only the diehard drinkers and gamblers haunted Mattie's Saloon this early in the day. At his usual table in the darkest corner of the bar, Billingsly sat toying with his glass. Occasionally, he fingered the padding under the shoulder of his gray, wool jacket where Doc Coulter had bandaged his wound. Unconsciously picking up his glass, he stopped and glared at it. He hated the taste of this rotgut whiskey, but the bar had nothing else until the next shipment of decent liquor arrived from Denver. His shoulder throbbed, and he wanted to get blind drunk. Whenever he gathered enough courage, he held his nose, took a swig of the nasty swill, and spent a few minutes coughing. He hoped this snake-oil would eventually ease the pain, but wondered if it might kill him first.

Billingsly cursed Fancy for attacking him. And what made it worse, selling the horse to Bill Chasteen caused him to get scalped by Reginald Bass when he bought a new one. Three hundred and fifty dollars for a horse and a new saddle was an outrage. But what choice did he have? Colonel Bass raised the finest horses in South Park, and the man hated him. He wondered briefly if one of his men could manage to slip poison into the Colonel's feed bins. That would fix the potbellied old reb.

Billingsly rubbed his shoulder. It wasn't enough Fancy nearly killed him, ruining his favorite jacket, but Bill made fun of him by blowing his nose in the silk shirt sleeve. To top it off, those two handsome men snubbed him on the way out of the livery. Or had he snubbed them? He couldn't remember.

The lawyer closed his eyes, held his nose and threw back the rest of the whiskey in the glass. The liquid burned all the way down this throat. He grabbed his neck, and his eyes filled with tears. Once his coughing subsided, he again thought of Jake and Wiley. Delicious men. He hadn't been able to keep his eyes off them last night in the Silver Heels, but watching them had given rise to smoldering envy. They possessed the two things he'd always wanted...even more than money and power. But he'd always been painfully skinny, and he'd never had a meaningful relationship with anyone. Well, except for Brandon in law school. His eyes teared. He'd loved Brandon, but once the other students had discovered their intimacy, the two of them had been openly ridiculed. Brandon had stayed in school and braved the storm, but he couldn't. He'd changed schools and vowed one day, as a lawyer, he'd get back at the world and use any means to become rich and powerful. He'd show those cretins for making fun of him. Billingsly glanced around the bar and renewed that vow.

Thoughts of Simon caused a twinge of guilt. After he'd received his degree, he'd moved to New Orleans and lived with Simon in his mansion for six months. He'd grown fond of the man despite his being filthy rich and a collector of precious gems. But the relationship became too much to handle, and he found himself torn between feelings for Simon and greed for the gems.

Billingsly tried to imagine Simon's face when he'd returned from New York and found half his gem collection missing along with his housemate. But that was six years ago, and no one had ever searched for him here. He never expected to be caught, certain Simon had moaned the loss of the gems for a week before buying others he would end up liking even better. That's just how Simon was.

Billingsly smiled when he thought of how wisely he'd used the two emeralds from the collection. The Double Dipper mine he'd traded them for still produced large quantities of gold at a time when most mines in the area had already played out.

But he knew owning a gold mine, a bar and a mansion would never be enough. The big money was in beef, and the Castille

Ranch contained some of the best timothy hay around. Everyone knew cattle loved the rich, nourishing grass and rapidly grew meaty on it. After he'd forced Winder to kill John Mattock and Jason Moore, he thought Wade would become disheartened enough to sell. But then Wade up and died, leaving the ranch in the hands of his headstrong daughter. At least he'd purchased a small portion of the ranch from Belinda the day of Wade's funeral, but now the wench refused to sell the rest.

Billingsly thought of Belinda's attempt to hire the two blood brothers to work her ranch and snickered. He crossed Jake off as being a complete idiot, but had a gut feeling there was more about Wiley than met the eye. Much more, in fact, and didn't know if he wanted to find out. Entertaining the two men in his bed crossed his mind again, and he tingled at the thought. But how in hell would he ever accomplish that?

Billingsly's daydreams shattered from the banging of the batwing doors as Jimmy Ratchett shoved his way through. The tall, handsome cowboy glanced around the bar and spied Billingsly. His spurs jingled as he swaggered to the lawyer's table and slid into a chair across from him. Weather lines in Jimmy's rugged face etched a faint smile.

"What's the matter with you?" Billingsly snapped, glaring at him.

Out of habit, Jimmy paused just long enough to irritate his boss. "Just thinking about that old man and his sons."

"What old man? If it's something I should know, tell me." Billingsly rubbed his shoulder, more for sympathy than pain.

"Earlier I saw Marshal Cline and his two deputies escorting four men out of town at gunpoint."

"So what?" Billingsly snapped. "It happens daily in this hole of a town."

The left side of Jimmy's mouth raised in a slight smile. "Yes, but one of the deputies told me these men were after the two newcomers who became blood brothers in the Silver Heels last night." He grinned. "The whole town's talking about those two gents."

Many in the bar turned to listen.

"So what," Billingsly said loud enough for all to hear. "Have a beer and settle down. It doesn't concern me at all."

Billingsly waved at Sam to bring Jimmy a beer. When Sam arrived with the mug, Jimmy grabbed it and gulped the beer right down.

Billingsly frowned and nodded to Sam to bring him another. When Sam returned with the second beer, Billingsly glanced around and saw the others in the room had already resumed their former conversations. The moment Sam left their table, Billingsly leaned over and whispered, "Now, Blabber Mouth, tell me about it and keep your voice down."

"Well," Jimmy said, still quite loud.

"I *said* keep your voice down," Billingsly snarled under his breath.

In a much lower voice, Jimmy began again. "It seems the four men are here from Kentucky hunting the blond brother. It has something to do with him getting the old man's daughter pregnant."

Jimmy took a couple of swallows of beer. He'd always dreamed of having a wife and a baby. But for now, he'd have to put up with Billingsly three more months. This spring, his second working for the lawyer, would be his last. As Billingsly's right hand man, he'd finally realized what Billingsly wanted in this area, and he didn't approve. He suspected the lawyer's involvement in the two murders at the Castille Ranch, but so far had no proof. To make matters worse, several months ago Billingsly had produced a signed work contract solidifying his employment until August. The signature wasn't his, but the forgery looked so genuine he knew no one would believe it. But, since he planned on proposing to Belinda soon, three more months' pay would help build up his nest egg. It wouldn't do for his future wife to own a ranch if he was penniless. And he was shit sure he didn't want Billingsly to find out about his plans. He tried to play the part of the faithful employee as well as he could, and it wasn't easy.

"Go on," Billingsly snapped.

Jimmy took another swig of his beer. "The five men captured the blond last night, but his blood brother saved him. Marshal

Cline's looking for the brothers to ask them some questions since the old man blames them for his son's death."

"What death?" Billingsly asked in a whisper.

After Jimmy explained, he added, "I don't think the marshal believes the old man's story about the son being pushed. Besides, he got real angry about them searching the town. Said he'd jail them on sight if they showed up here again."

Billingsly smiled. He didn't believe for a minute the men from Kentucky had left the area. A vengeful family, especially from that part of the country, rarely gave up trying to get even with someone who had tainted the family honor.

"Jimmy, I want you to find the old man and his sons. When you do, invite them to stay at the house as my guests. I'd hate to think they're uncomfortable sleeping outside when they're so far from home, especially after their tragedy. We have to do our social duty for the good of our fellow men. I'll be waiting for you in the marshal's office."

Jimmy took a swig of his beer and wondered what Billingsly wanted with the men from Kentucky. He hoped it didn't have anything to do with the brothers, but bet it did. He admired the two men for being gutsy enough to become blood brothers in a bar full of people, and felt they were lucky to find each other. If he ever met them, he'd thank them for providing the inspiration he'd needed to finally ask Belinda for her hand.

"Well, what are you waiting for?" Billingsly snarled. "I said go look for them."

"But the marshal ran them out of town. They're probably gone, and I doubt if I can find them."

"I said *when* you find them. Now go find them."

After gulping down the rest of his beer, Jimmy hurried out of the bar.

Billingsly sat in the dim light and stared across the room, seeing nothing. The perfect way to get those brothers under his control just fell into his lap. The men from Kentucky could re-capture the brothers and charge them with murder. His fee for getting the two gorgeous men off would be years of hard labor between his sheets. That would be worth all the gold the Double

Dipper ever produced. Holding his nose, he took two more swallows of whiskey and shuddered violently.

"Sam, when's our next shipment of good liquor due from Denver?" Billingsly asked as he approached the bar.

"Not 'til day after tomorrow," Sam growled, wiping a glass with a towel.

"I'll either have to drink at home or bring my own bottle until then. Sam, use a clean rag, for God's sake! That one looks like you've been wiping your ass with it."

Sam threw the towel into a heap on the floor and grabbed a clean one. "Miners don't mind drinkin' what we got."

"Well, I'm not a filthy miner." Billingsly turned and stomped out to the street. The batwing doors squeaked and rattled shut.

Sam watched him leave and muttered, "You ain't much of anythin', you no-good lawyer crook."

## CHAPTER 19

A quarter mile south of London Junction, Jake and Wiley easily found the old road to the Hanson Ranch. The two ruts, overgrown by grasses and young aspens, had a familiar quality both men picked up on, causing them to remember paths they'd explored in their youth. The road skirted the hills on the west side of the valley. Between tall pine, they caught glimpses of the twisted silver ribbons of Middle Fork of the South Platte River as it meandered into Fairplay.

The road remained in the trees most of the way, providing Jake with a sense of relief. They weren't as easy targets, but he didn't believe for a moment the Harrises had left the area. He figured they'd either holed up somewhere or, at this very moment, tracked them.

Even though it was the first week of May, the aspens had not yet started dropping their catkins. As Belinda would explain later, the residents of South Park claim only two seasons, winter and summer--the latter lasting four and a half months, if they're lucky. The cloudless day was almost hot, much to Wiley's surprise. He'd never experienced such wide fluctuations of temperature and quickly shed his jacket. Jake followed suit.

They rode in silence, speaking only when absolutely necessary to lessen the possibility of being heard by anyone, whether the Harrises or not. The happy titterings of chickadees kept them company as the tiny gray and black birds flitted about keeping up with their friends, the humans. Deep in the woods, scolding squawks of Steller's jays echoed in the vastness. The two men allowed the sounds of nature to wash their minds and become one with them. They knew anything unusual would be quickly announced, either by sudden silence or instant clamor.

The ranch house appeared unexpectedly as they rounded a bend in the road. Paint-peeled, with a leaning barn off behind, the two-story structure seemed to sink beneath the tangle of young aspens springing up in the clearing. Neither could guess how long the house had been empty. Blank windows stared sadly as they approached.

Jake immediately dismounted and led Mac into an old aspen grove on the far side of the house. With his rifle in hand, he walked briskly to the porch.

"Jake, don't be so skittish," Wiley teased. "I don't think we were followed." Wiley dismounted and tied Buddy far enough away from Mac so the two horses wouldn't annoy each other. Jake had told him Mac considered himself human and didn't care much for other horses. Wiley knew from the night before that Buddy didn't like anybody or anything. At least he felt tolerated by his new horse.

When he reached the porch, Wiley saw Jake cautiously eyeing the house. "What's the matter, Jake?"

"I got me a funny feelin' about this here place, Wiley. Like somethin' bad happened here."

"You're quite right, Jake, something tragic did happen here," a woman said.

Both men wheeled around to face Belinda Castille as she stepped out onto the porch.

"Fifteen years ago," she continued, "two brothers from New Mexico brutally murdered the Hansons. They shot Val Hanson, his wife Myrna and their daughter in their foreheads right here on this porch."

Jake gasped and glanced at his feet as though he might be standing on one of the Hansons. Belinda and Wiley smiled as he lifted his feet and did a complete turn.

"The brothers robbed and killed people from Santa Fe up through the San Luis Valley and into South Park," Belinda continued. "They even ambushed several travelers on Red Hill Pass between Fairplay and Como. So, you were right about something bad happening here, Jake." She smiled.

Jake's face flushed, and he stared at his boots. "Guess I always have a funny feelin' like this around somethin' bad."

"I admire that in a man," Belinda said.

Here it comes, Wiley thought as the hair on the back of his neck bristled. She's going to start her charm on Jake. He struggled to remain calm. "You seem to know a lot about this area."

"Having grown up here, I suppose I do," Belinda said. "I was eight when this happened, and the entire region, clear to Leadville, was up in arms. Several vigilante groups combed the area, and they hung one poor man after mistaking him for one of the murderers. As it turned out, he was a businessman on his way home to Leadville."

"They ever catch 'em?" Jake asked.

"After the brothers killed a man near the Hartsel Ranch, a posse shot the youngest one in a canyon south of there. The same posse gunned down the older brother near Trinidad several months later." She turned toward the door. "Gentlemen, please come inside. We can have a bite to eat and discuss the purpose of this secret meeting."

As the two men followed her into the house, Wiley stopped inside the door and looked around at the forlorn surroundings. A dark wooden staircase curved around the cobweb enshrouded entrance hall and disappeared into the gloom of the second floor. Pack rat droppings covered everything, including a buffet that had been shoved in front of a door on their left. It was the only piece of furniture in the hallway.

Jake entered the house right behind Wiley and cringed at the sight. He grabbed Wiley's arm as they entered the parlor.

Piles of old cans made Wiley wonder if squatters had lived in the room at some time in the past. He noticed someone had overturned a makeshift bed in one corner and covered it with old newspapers. A once expensive Persian rug, caked with dried grass and droppings, had a large hole chewed out of the middle, and every scrap of stuffing had been torn off all the chairs. Wiley knew the material lined squirrel or pack rat nests in the area.

Belinda didn't seem to notice any of it. She had dusted three wooden chairs and placed them around a table by the front window. After they all sat down, she unpacked a lunch of dried fruit, bread and the most delicious jerky either man had ever tasted.

Belinda smiled as they wolfed down the food. "Bill said you wanted to talk to me about something in private. I hope it's about working for me."

Wiley pushed his chair back from the table. "As a matter of fact, it is. After last night, we need to disappear for awhile. That's why this meeting is a secret. Only you and Bill know about it."

"What happened last night?" Belinda asked. "Did Billingsly do something to you after we talked?"

"No, not Billingsly, the Harrises. Jake, you'd better tell her your story, from the beginning. Like you told me last night in the bar."

Jake began slowly but seemed to pick up confidence as he got farther into it. He left nothing out. To Wiley's relief, Jake even mentioned he'd never been with a woman, and wouldn't. Wiley saw little in Belinda's face to indicate she cared, and it puzzled him to some degree. But he remembered Bill's words about her and about people in the West being accepting of everyone. Everyone, except Indians.

Wiley picked up the story when it came to the events of the previous night on the slopes of Mount Silverheels.

"No one but Bill and I will know you're working for me," Belinda said. "My ranch is large, and there are plenty of places for you to hide if you need to. As far as I know, no one's been around since the rest of my help left. At least, I haven't seen anyone and neither has Sa-Ra, so you should be reasonably safe."

"If the Harrises find out we're stayin' at your ranch, you won't be safe," Jake cautioned. "I know 'em. They'll stop at nothin' 'til they get me or they're dead their ownselves."

Belinda smiled at him. "I'll let you two decide if you want to stay in the bunkhouse. Also, there's several line cabins scattered around the ranch. You can stay in one of them or build your own. When the ranch was in full operation, some of the hands lived in these cabins and reported to John once a week. When you get there, look around and make up your mind then.

"The ranch is a half day's ride from here. Where the train tracks curve eastward from Fairplay, a road veers to the south. In the distance you'll see Bristlecone Peak. It's a two-humped mountain in the middle of low hills. The ranch house is three miles southwest of it. I will expect you sometime tomorrow."

Wiley balked at this initial order from his new woman boss. "Let's see, today is Thursday," he remarked flippantly. "I just got here yesterday, and I want to spend at least one or two days looking around town. Then, we want to spend another day at some of the mines and get the lay of the land. And we'll probably take a long way around to get to your ranch because I don't want the Harrises to follow us." He glanced at Jake. "Should we be at Miss Castille's ranch a week from today?"

"A week sounds good to me," Jake answered. "An' Wiley's right, you don't want them Harrises snoopin' around your ranch." He grinned at Wiley.

Somewhat peeved at Wiley's attitude, Belinda said dryly, "Well, I guess that is a wise plan. I suppose I'll see you when I see you."

She quickly gathered up the remains of the lunch. "I must leave now. It's a long ride home, and I've left Sa-Ra alone too long as it is. Please be careful, and thank you for coming to work for me. The ranch needs all the help it can get, no matter what you can or can't do. Good-bye."

Belinda walked swiftly to the front door, her split riding dress swished in the stillness. Once outside, she seemed to vanish. After a few moments, the men heard a horse galloping down the road.

Jake glanced around and shuddered. "Wiley, let's get outta here!" He rushed outside to the porch, with Wiley close behind.

After mounting up, Wiley spurred Buddy farther into the aspen grove beside the house. Jake followed him with a puzzled look on his face.

Shortly, Wiley reined to a stop. "Let's not take the road back to Alma. On our way here, I spotted a trail higher up the side of this mountain. It might be a game trail or an old Indian path. Let's take it as far as we can."

* * *

Being ushered out of town at gunpoint did nothing to squelch Seth's desire for Jake's death. He burned inside to watch Jake and his friend swing from a tree until their faces turned black and had no intentions of leaving the area until he accomplished it. He knew at least two of his remaining sons shared his desire.

They made camp a mile south of town in an aspen grove on the banks of Middle Fork. At once, Clem plunged into the woods to hunt any small game they could eat. While Abe carefully unpacked their things, Seth grabbed Zeke by the collar and shoved him to the ground.

"What's the meanin' of you hangin' back all the time? You ain't gettin' soft on Jake are you, boy?"

"Pa, I've thought lots about Jake gettin' Sara Jean banged up an' I..." He lowered his head.

"An' you what, boy?" Seth demanded.

"An' I...I don't think he's the one that done it. Ever'body knows how Jake is, an' he...well, he wouldn't do nothin' like that to Sara Jean."

Seth backhanded Zeke across the face. "That's crazy talk, boy! Sara Jean said he done it!" He hit Zeke again. Blood oozed from the young man's nose. "I don't want no more talk like that from you! You hear me, boy?" Seth left Zeke on the ground and stomped into the trees to find firewood.

A gunshot sounded close by. Clem had found something.

Holding his shirt sleeve against his nose to stop the bleeding, Zeke's mind flooded with thoughts of Jake. He still loved the handsome man who had befriended him. None of his older brothers had ever taken time to teach him how to fish or hunt, or anything. But Jake had taught him lots of things. In fact, almost everything he knew he'd learned from Jake, including the Union Army's training exercises, which he'd used to become a smaller version of Jake.

He and Jake had started fooling around with each other in the Brady barn a little over a year ago. While it had been a glorious experience for him, he knew Jake thought of Sergeant Moss whenever they had done anything. A stab of jealousy stung him as he wondered if Jake and his new friend fooled around with each other.

Another gunshot pierced the stillness, and shortly Clem shoved through the brush holding two rabbits.

An hour later, having just finished eating, Seth and Abe leapt to their feet and grabbed their rifles.

"Howdy the camp!" came a voice from the bushes. Jimmy Ratchett walked his horse into the clearing. He balked when he saw the guns pointed at him and raised his hands. "I'm not here to cause trouble. I came to tell you my boss is offering to let you stay at his house." Not liking the looks of these men, Jimmy wished he hadn't even tried to find them.

"Git down off'a that horse, boy, an' keep yer hands off'a yer gun!" Seth snarled.

Jimmy dismounted and stuck his hands in the air.

"Who's yer boss, an' what does he want with us?" Seth demanded.

While Jimmy related the reason for Billingsly's invitation, Zeke wandered to the river to wash off the dried blood still caked inside his nose. As he stooped beside the water, movement caught his eye halfway up the side of a mountain. Two riders were crossing a clearing on their way to Alma. Despite the distance, Zeke instantly recognized Jake riding Mac. He gasped and turned to see if his father or any of his brothers noticed. To his dismay, he saw Seth watching him.

Seth squinted at the side of the mountain and caught a glimpse of the riders before they re-entered the forest. He broke into a wicked smile and turned to Jimmy. "Tell yer boss we'll be there in an hour. We got some family business to do before we can leave here."

"That'll be fine," Jimmy commented nervously. He sprang onto his horse and galloped north without looking back. As he rode toward Alma, he thought of ways to keep away from Billingsly's mansion for the time these men would be there. He shuddered when he remembered one of the brothers, the oldest he'd guessed, had leered at him constantly. Working for Billingsly, Jimmy knew what that look meant.

As soon as Jimmy disappeared from view, Seth turned to Clem. "Zeke and I seen Jake up on that there hill, ridin' toward town. It's a mite far, but seein' you're the best shot, try and plug Jake when we see 'em again. I'd rather hang 'em, but this late in the year, shootin' 'em in the head'll do. We gotta be gettin' home soon."

"You can't be sure it was them, Pa," Zeke protested. "They was too far away."

Seth glared at Zeke. "By the look on yer face, you're sure. Ain't you, boy! Now, let's get goin'."

They quickly packed their gear and rode north along Middle Fork, keeping to the banks of the river where large rock outcroppings and aspen groves provided the best cover. When they approached a rounded cone-shaped boulder with a balanced rock on top, Clem saw the two men through thinly scattered trees. He leaped from his horse, braced his arm against the rock, sighted the man on the red horse and shot. Clem saw both men disappear.

After the riders vanished, Clem leaned against the rock and scanned the hillside. Suddenly, a bullet hit his rifle. It flew out of his hand and sailed behind him. The impact jarred Clem's arm. He fell to the ground, rolled around and screamed in pain.

"Get up, you damn fool!" Seth snarled. "That's what you get for missin' him an' leavin' yourself in sight. Now, get off'a the ground an' stop yer bellyachin'!"

Seth watched the hillside a few moments longer. Not seeing any movement, he decided they were too far away to get off another shot and to move closer would put them out in the open. Satisfied Jake was still in the area, he decided to continue on to Billingsly's house.

Clem struggled to his horse. He followed the others, slumped forward in the saddle and holding his arm against his body. Despite what his pa had said, he was convinced he'd shot Jake in the head, and if he'd killed Jake, his friend would be gunning for them.

Later, in the heavily wooded hills above Alma, Seth discovered a small clearing overlooking the town. He dismounted, stood on the rise and scanned the area for several minutes.

"This'll do just fine," Seth muttered under his breath.

# CHAPTER 20

After Billingsly left Mattie's Saloon, he walked briskly up the crowded street toward the marshal's office. He scowled at the townsfolk in tattered clothes and shuddered. Somehow he'd own the Castille Ranch and reap the benefits. San Francisco beckoned. It was a wild town, but at least it had sophistication. But until then, having the two blood brothers under his control would keep him going. When he reached the stone building that housed both the marshal's office and the jail, he peered through the window and saw Marshal Cline sitting at his desk sipping coffee as he shuffled through a stack of wanted posters.

Billingsly's abrupt entrance into the office startled the marshal, and he dumped hot coffee down the front of his shirt. "Dammit!" Cline wiped his shirt. "Ed, can't you knock like a gentleman?"

"I've got to talk to you, Wes," Billingsly said, ignoring the question. He walked to the stove, picked up the pot and poured himself a cup of coffee. Billingsly winced. It looked and smelled like burnt mud. He took a sip anyway, then quickly set the cup down.

"Wes, your coffee's undrinkable. I'm going to send you some real coffee from Mattie's before this stuff turns you to stone."

The sheriff scowled at Billingsly. "I like it that way, and the more you drink, the less I'll have. What the hell do you want?"

Wes Cline knew all too well of the conniving streak in Ed Billingsly and smelled a trap. Shortly after the lawyer had arrived in town, he'd hired him to defend him on a murder charge. Billingsly won the case, but for the next two years, he'd forked over a big chunk of his meager salary to the lawyer, choosing payment in cash rather than the "four-poster" way Ed really wanted. Hell, he wasn't prudish about that form of payment. He preferred women, but had fooled around with men quite a bit since he'd been here. What other choice did a man have in this town?

The few women either charged or simply weren't available. Besides, he liked being held by a man as strong as himself once in awhile. While having sex with a man, he didn't have to squelch any roughness to accommodate the woman. However, being the law, he had to keep scandals away from his door, and Billingsly would have bragged to everyone if the two of them had gone at it. Besides, Billingsly was too skinny for his taste in men, and lately a number of uppity people from the East made an issue out of men sleeping together. He figured they were in positions now where they couldn't do it anymore and wanted to make sure no one else could either.

Cline still kicked himself for not realizing the murder charge against him had been one of Billingsly's schemes. No one in town had accused him of killing Herb, the town drunk, on purpose, except Thomas Crain. Old Herb had already scared the shit out of several people that evening the way he'd pointed his bottle at them like a gun. Later, there had been two killings over cards, and even though he was the marshal, the murders had made him jumpy. Then, while making his rounds, Old Herb had pointed that damn bottle at him in the dark and, well...it had happened too fast. He'd learned only a few months ago from Jimmy Ratchett that Billingsly had paid Thomas Crain to demand the murder trial.

Cline wiped his wet shirt again and watched the lawyer slip delicately into the armchair across from him.

Billingsly crossed his legs, pointed his toe and looked the marshal up and down, wondering what it would be like to have this tough, wiry man with wavy brown hair and a handlebar moustache lying next to him in bed. He pondered the marshal's strong hand that held a wanted poster, then said, "I've decided to offer my hospitality to those men from Kentucky who are searching for that scoundrel who got that poor girl pregnant." Billingsly shook his head. "It's terrible the baby's father ran off like that."

"What would *you* know of such things," Wes snapped. "Anyway, you're too late. I ordered those men out of town at gunpoint early this morning and told them not to come back. My deputies have orders to jail them on sight if they show up again.

They're nothing but outright killers." Wes glared at the lawyer and asked, "What do *you* want with them?"

Billingsly flinched. "Want with them? Why, nothing. Nothing at all." The sides of Billingsly's mouth twitched. "I feel sorry for them being so far from home and losing one of their own last--"

"How did you find out about that?" Wes demanded.

"I have my ways." Billingsly cleared his throat. "As I was saying, I want to help them out of their misery by letting them sleep in beds rather than on the cold ground. And, of course, give them a nice hot meal or two."

Cline studied Billingsly intently. "Ed, I don't believe a word of it. Either you want those men for your personal pleasure, or you have something in mind they can do for you. Now, which is it?"

Billingsly inspected the fingernails on his left hand. "Wes, you underestimate me. I'm merely trying to be kind. I'm only telling you this so you and your deputies won't arrest my guests. Besides, your jurisdiction as marshal stops at the town limit, and I live outside that area." He looked up and smiled sweetly.

Wes grinned. "Not since yesterday. Yesterday in Fairplay I was made a sheriff of Park County." Realizing Billingsly's surprise, the newly appointed sheriff laughed. "If you weren't so busy thinking up schemes, you might have time to read the Gazette once in awhile." Cline took a sip of coffee. "As of yesterday, this entire region is now under my jurisdiction." He pulled himself up in his chair and leaned toward the lawyer. "You watch your step from now on. And keep in mind, I am *not* your friend."

Billingsly's mouth dropped open, then snapped shut. "Well, Marshal...er, I mean, Sheriff, I...I still want those men as my guests." He whipped out his handkerchief and dabbed his forehead. "I'll take full responsibility for their actions."

"You damnsite better believe you will, Ed Billingsly!" Wes shouted. "I'll hold you totally responsible they don't hunt down and kill those two men they're after. The two men, I might add, who have this town in an uproar. Reverend Quick stormed in here early this morning shouting he wanted me to arrest those blood brothers for being heathens. Can you imagine anything so stupid?

I haven't even seen those two yet and want to ask them some questions about the man killed on Crazywoman Cliff."

Jimmy sauntered into the office. "I found them," he said to Billingsly. "They'll be at the house in an hour."

"Good, good." Billingsly rose to his feet. He smiled at Sheriff Cline. "If you'll remember our little agreement about my guests, I'll try to find the two brothers you're looking for and bring them in for questioning."

The sheriff glared at the lawyer. "Ed Billingsly, you tend to your own business of feeding those killers, and let me tend to mine!"

After the door banged shut, Cline stared at it. "So *that's* what he's after," he said out loud. He decided to do everything he could to protect the blood brothers from Ed Billingsly. Whoever they were.

Billingsly pushed Jimmy out of the sheriff's office and slammed the door. They walked the three blocks to Mattie's Saloon in silence. At the hitching post in front of the bar, Jimmy watched Billingsly untie the reins of a flea-bitten gray horse with bluish spots and a shovel-shaped head.

"That's not your horse."

"Well, it is now!" Billingsly snapped. "Fancy tried to kill me this morning. Almost tore my arm off. And that despicable old reb charged me a fortune for this one."

Jimmy stared at his boss, thinking it would have been nice if Fancy had succeeded. The lawyer's new horse was the ugliest horse he'd ever seen. He could see Colonel Bass yanking Billingsly past his prized horses and forcing him to buy one he'd cut off his big toe before selling to anyone else.

As they rode out of Alma toward Buckskin Joe, Jimmy thought of that rapidly dying mining town, once billed as the most prosperous town in South Park. But once most of the mines played out, people started leaving the town in droves. He'd come here from Missouri to find gold and had worked in the Sweetheart mine on Mount Buckskin for a year. After the Sweetheart had closed, he'd hired on with Billingsly, but still had a fondness for Buckskin Joe, nestled in the hills four miles west of Alma. Buckskin was now barely holding its own.

They arrived at the mansion Billingsly had obtained in another court battle. Sitting halfway between the two towns, the lawyer's home presented an imposing sight beside the road.

As the two men entered the house, Xu, Billingsly's cook, met them just inside the door. He chattered rapidly in Chinese and bowed as he handed the lawyer a grocery list.

"Get, or no fixee dinner." Xu bowed again and returned to the kitchen, still chattering and waving his arms.

Billingsly handed the list to Jimmy. "Go back into town and get these things."

"Aw, come on. I haven't had anything to eat today, and it's already past three."

Billingsly flipped a dollar at him. "Eat a bite in town. But don't be gone long."

Back in Alma, as Jimmy rode by the livery on his way to the meat market, he saw Bill Chasteen sitting out front whittling. He knew the men from Kentucky had searched the building earlier and decided to see if Bill knew anything about the blood brothers. He turned his horse into the field in front of the barn.

"Howdy, Bill," Jimmy said as he slid off his horse near the hostler. "Fine day, isn't it?"

Bill raised an eyebrow and squinted against the bright sun. "And just what do you want?"

"Have you seen the two men who became blood brothers last night in the Silver Heels?"

"Mebbe I have, and mebbe I haven't. What business is it of yours, anyhow?"

Jimmy flinched. "Just wanted to know, that's all. I haven't met them. But I'd like to."

Bill put down his knife and the whistle, stood up and glared at Billingsly's employee. "I wouldn't tell you nothin' about them two gents, even if I knowed where they's at. Now get yer tight ass outta here before I do somethin' to you I oughtn't do."

"Okay, okay." Jimmy backed up a step. "But if you see them, tell them something for me. Tell them Billingsly invited those men from Kentucky to stay with him. He and the marshal are looking for them for questioning." Jimmy started to leave, but turned back and said in a low voice, "I like those brothers even though I don't know who they are. I'm hoping Billingsly and those men from Kentucky never get them." He leaped into the saddle and trotted his horse toward the street.

"Well, I'll be danged," Bill muttered. He sat down and picked up the knife and whistle. "That Jimmy shore is full of surprises. Here all this time I thought he was just like that dang Billingsly."

Jimmy suddenly turned his horse, galloped back to the barn, and stopped his mount in front of Bill. A cloud of dust engulfed the hostler.

Bill leaped to his feet coughing and sputtering, ready to give Jimmy a piece of his mind.

Without dismounting, Jimmy said, "I forgot to tell you. I think Billingsly plans to use those men from Kentucky to find and capture the brothers. My guess is he wants to get them into court on a murder charge and then get them off. I think you know what for. You've got to warn them. And please don't tell anyone I told you this." He turned his horse and galloped across the open lot and down the street toward the meat market.

Bill felt like he'd spent the day in a flour mill. He coughed, spat and dusted himself off, creating another cloud.

"Dang!" he yelled, swatting his pants with his hat. "Them two boys better watch their step on the way to see Belinda. When they get back, I'll hafta tell 'em to watch their back trail real close." He peered around to see if anyone heard him talking out loud. Not seeing anyone close by, Bill repositioned himself in his hand-carved chair, complete with fitted buttock indentations, wide arms and a spinal-curved back, and continued putting the finishing touches on his sixth whistle that day.

\* \* \*

On their way back from the deserted Hanson ranch, Jake and Wiley pointed their horses up the side of the heavily forested slope. After riding a quarter mile, they came to an Indian trail. Realizing the path hadn't been used recently, Wiley remembered a conversation he'd overheard on the train from Denver about the Utes being forced out of South Park several years before.

"Jake, I think this is an Indian trail. Do you want to take it back to Alma?"

Jake stared at the deeply etched path. "Damn! This is a real Indian trail?" He nudged Mac onto the pathway and slowly looked around. Tall aspen trees lined the trail, and their branches met high above in a green arch.

"Wiley, this is like ridin' in a church," Jake whispered.

The trail hugged the slope of the mountains, much of it in tree cover, and Jake relaxed. "I feel safe on this trail, Wiley. Guess it's cuz I always liked Indians an' their ways."

Wiley shrugged. "So have I, Jake. My grandfather was an Iroquois brave, but I don't think we should tell anyone. On the train from Denver, I overheard someone mention how the people of South Park threw rocks and bottles at the Utes as the army led them out of this area." He lowered his eyes, realizing that was nothing compared to the slaughter at Sand Creek, but an insult nonetheless. He wanted to tell Jake he felt the white race was descended from Cain because of its hatred of other races, but decided not to.

"Damn!" Jake yelled. "You're part Indian? No wonder you're such a good tracker. I reckon you already knew about blood brother stuff, didn't you?"

"Yes." Wiley thought of Grandpa Gray Feather. "But I wanted to make sure you knew before we did anything like that."

Jake grinned. "Guess the only one's I'd ever talk to about Indians would be Bill and Miss Castille."

"Belinda? Why her?"

Jake smiled. "She seems to like us, Wiley. An' she's kind."

Wiley felt a chill in the pit of his stomach. He wanted to tell Jake to stay away from Belinda, but fought down the fear that she might win Jake away from him, telling himself it was only his imagination. Jake had indicated he never wanted to marry Sara Jean, but he had to know how Jake really felt about Belinda. "You like Miss Castille a lot, don't you, Jake?" He couldn't control the shakiness in his voice.

Jake smiled. "She's a real nice lady, an' I like her a lot."

Wiley's gut turned to ice.

Something flicked the brim of Jake's hat as it whizzed by. A few seconds later the sound of a gunshot pierced the stillness.

Both men grabbed their rifles, fell out of their saddles and hit the ground running for the cover of a large spruce. They dove into the needles at the base of the tree. The shot had come from the valley some five hundred yards away. Their shoulders touched as they peered through the dense branches of the blue spruce. Neither moved or said a word for several minutes as they scanned the terrain.

Wiley broke the silence. "I wonder if it's the Harrises."

"Nobody I know, 'cept Clem, can shoot like that from so far away." Jake pointed. "Look, there they are. See, by that rock lookin' like a woman's tit."

A woman's tit? Wiley's fear turned to irritation. Jake still must be thinking of Belinda. But he saw the rock and had to agree with Jake's description. He noticed a thin line of light next to the rock. Slowly, Wiley took high aim with his Winchester and fired. They watched a silver streak fly into the air.

"You hit the damn rifle!" Jake yelled, staring at Wiley with awe. "Damn! That's better'n three hundred yards!"

Wiley grinned. "Don't cuss, Jack."

A short time later, they saw movement. Four riders walked their horses away from the cone-shaped boulder with a small rock balanced on top. The man trailing behind sat slumped over the saddle and held his arms around his body. All wearing black coats and hats, the men rode toward Alma.

"Sure is them Harrises," Jake said. "You either got Clem in the gut, or his hand an' arm is mighty sore from you hittin' the rifle. That sure was some shootin', Wiley."

"I did it for Belinda," Wiley said, then regretted he'd even opened his mouth.

"Miss Castille? What're you talkin' about, Wiley? What's Miss Castille got to do with this?"

Ashamed of letting his jealousy get the best of him, Wiley was slow in answering. He didn't want Jake to get angry. Jokingly, he said, "Well, Belinda seems to like you, and she'd be sad if you got shot."

"Miss Castille likes *both* of us, Wiley. What are you drivin' at?" Jake stared at Wiley for a moment, then stood up in the middle of the spruce tree and got tangled in the low branches. They fluttered and swayed wildly.

"Get down!" Wiley yelled. "They'll see you moving the branches." He grabbed Jake's pants and pulled him to the ground. No shots came as they lay still for a few moments, both breathing heavily.

Jake turned his head toward Wiley. Their noses touched. "You tell me what you mean."

Wiley smiled. He couldn't help but smile at Jake. "I have to tell the truth. I worry about Belinda getting you away from me. Sometimes when she looks at you I feel she's flirting, and I get tied in knots. What I said before was just my fear coming out. I've never loved...er, had a partner before, and feeling jealous is new for me."

Jake stared at him, speechless for a moment, then he shouted, "Miss Castille's a *woman*, Wiley! I don't want me no woman! I got you. I might sometime trade you for a horse, but never for no woman."

Wiley laughed. He grabbed Jake and rolled him on top of himself. They began playfully wrestling under the spruce tree.

While the two men rolled on top of one another, they failed to see an old Indian standing in the shadows watching them. Weathered and wrinkled from countless ages, his face mirrored great wisdom, yet mirth and youth filled his eyes. Clad in brown buckskin garb, richly adorned with multicolored beads, he stood with his arms folded. Two white braids hung over his chest, and a single golden feather wove itself into the tip of each one. The feathers glowed with a light of their own.

The Indian smiled as he watched the men wrestle in the needles, but the moment the blood brothers helped each other up, his image faded into mist and disappeared with the slight breeze.

Breathing hard and laughing, Jake and Wiley brushed each other off, swung into their saddles and cautiously rode back to Alma.

## CHAPTER 21

As Jake and Wiley rode into Alma, they saw Bill Chasteen sitting outside the livery with wood chips curled at his feet like fallen leaves.

When the partners came within earshot, Bill yelled, "Glad yer back. It's been kinda lonesome 'round here with you fellers gone."

"Good ol' Bill," Jake said softly. "Wiley, let's take him to the Regal Cafe later an' pay for his food."

"That's a good idea. Maybe he'll show us the town's night life."

After they said their greetings, Bill related the news about the Harrises staying with Billingsly. Wiley mentioned the shot fired at them. Silent during the exchange, Jake's expression mirrored his dread that the Harrises were still around, and now Billingsly was involved.

Quick to realize Jake's concern, Wiley walked up behind Jake, slid his arm around his partner and pulled him close. "We'll be fine, Jake. At least the Harrises won't be coming into town anytime soon."

Jake relaxed into Wiley's body. The world's most handsome man held him tight, and Wiley's reassuring words made him feel safe. He grinned, spun around and grabbed Wiley around his waist, hugged him as hard as he could, then lifted him off the ground.

"Arrugh!" Wiley groaned. "Jake, you're crushing me!"

Jake laughed and let him down. "Hell, Wiley, you make me feel so happy I couldn't help it." He patted Wiley's chest. "An' I ain't nearly strong enough to crush you."

Bill shook his head. "You two sound like a couple'a dang love birds, if y'ask me. It's disgustin'." He glanced at their shocked faces and broke out laughing. Both men punched him on the arm.

As Bill led the horses into the livery, Jake spied the pile of whistles. He picked one up and began tooting an Irish jig.

"That's wonderful, Jake," Wiley said, amazed how well he played. Wiley clapped in time with the ditty and laughed. "I'm going to buy you that whistle so you can play it all the time." He laughed again as Jake started dancing to his own music.

Bill ran outside. "Dang!" He picked up two whistles and tossed one to Wiley. "If y'can't play, just blow."

Bill piped the same tune as Jake, but a tad slower. Wiley tried, but failed miserably, so he played only one note at a time. After a moment of watching Jake's footwork, both men tried their skill at dancing. Soon clouds of dust billowed up in front of the livery.

Several wagons rumbled by, each containing a dozen miners on their way to a hot bath or the Regal Cafe. One by one, the wagons stopped and miners spilled out. They formed a half circle around the dancing men and began to cheer and clap to the music. A red-haired gent in the crowd sang the words to the tune Jake and Bill played, and a few who could jig, danced close to Jake. Soon, curious townsfolk also gathered, and a half dozen children pushed to the front.

"How much for the whistles, Bill?" a tall miner asked. He saw longing in the young faces.

"Two bits apiece," Bill yelled between bars.

Within minutes, six whistles disappeared into eager little hands. Five silver quarters and one gold dollar took their place in the dirt. Wiley readily gave up his whistle. Bill finally did.

Jake stopped dancing and closed his eyes. He appeared unaware of anything but his own playing. When the crowd grew silent, he finished a couple more bars of a tune then glanced down. At his feet stood a tiny girl, her soft brown eyes locked on his. She held up a coin for his whistle.

"This here's my whistle," Jake said as he towered over her. "It ain't for sale." He closed his eyes again and continued playing a variety of tunes. From the way he puckered his lips, everyone knew he tried hard not to smile.

"You're a mean ol' codger!" one miner yelled at Jake. Everyone laughed.

After treating the crowd to "The Yellow Rose of Texas," a popular Civil War song, Jake opened his eyes again, stopped playing and peered down at the girl. She hadn't moved. Then, she smiled.

"Hell, you shouldn't a'done that," Jake drawled, grinning. The crowd broke into laughter and applause as Jake placed the whistle into her outstretched hand.

Once the last whistle sold, the music stopped and the crowd slowly broke up. Whistles could be heard in all parts of town.

As the dust cleared, two husky miners, their clothes and faces covered with grime, ambled over to the three men. The taller of the two stuck out his hand to Jake.

"Let me shake the hand of a musician and a gentleman. Name's Matt Conway, and this is my partner, Frank Waters."

Jake shook his hand. "I'm Jake. Jake Brady." He extended his hand toward Wiley. "This here's Wiley, my partner an' blood brother." He suddenly looked puzzled. "Er...Wiley, what'd you say your last name was?"

They all laughed.

"You must not have been partners too long," Matt said, slapping Jake on the back.

"Say, are you the blood brothers from the Silver Heels the whole town's talkin' about?" Frank asked as he shook Wiley's hand.

"That's us," Wiley said, thinking it seemed ages since he and Jake had become blood brothers.

Already good friends with Bill, Matt and Frank included themselves in the plans to meet later at the Regal Cafe.

As they walked away, Frank suddenly wheeled around. "Oh, Bill, I'll ask Harry to come too. That okay with you?"

"You know dang well it is, you young punk," Bill yelled. A grin brightened his face.

The two miners smiled and waved as they disappeared around the Alma Gazette.

Jake eyed Bill. "Who's this here Harry?"

"Somehow, I knowed you was gonna ask that." Bill raised his eyebrows and hooked his thumbs in his belt. "Harry jest might be my new partner. 'Course he don't know it yet."

Bill counted the coins as he picked them out of the dirt. "Two bucks fifty. I ain't ever sold so many whistles in one day. You're shore a good salesman, Jake. And where'd you learn to play like that?"

"Mr. Pritcher taught me. He was always right nice to me. Nicer'n Pa ever was."

Wiley caught the bitterness in Jake's voice.

Later in the loft, the two men stripped naked and quickly washed with cold water from the barrels. After drying each other, Wiley positioned himself in front of a jagged piece of mirror and shaved with his knife.

Since Jake's two pair of underwear smelled like the hogs back home, he decided not to wear any. He frowned as he held up his only clean pair of pants and shirt. Both too small, in his haste while packing in Kentucky, he'd grabbed them by mistake. Reluctantly, he pulled on the faded Kentucky Jeans, hoping the last two months had thinned him down some. Not quite as skin tight in the thighs and crotch as they'd been, he knew he'd still have trouble closing the fly. Jake slipped on the unbleached cotton shirt, made years ago by his mother. It would button only half way. Sucking in, he finally fastened the pants, but had to unbutton them again to lace up his boots.

Wiley wore a pair of Levis he'd purchased from the Daniels and Fisher Store in Denver, and the white, billowy shirt with the open front Nathan had picked out for him. He remembered how lonely he'd been the last time he'd worn the shirt. He grinned when he realized wearing his boots made him the same height as Jake.

After the partners climbed down the ladder, they found Bill standing naked, washing up from a barrel of water in the back of an empty stall.

Watching Bill, Jake nudged Wiley and grinned. "He ain't bad lookin' for an old man."

"Old man!" Bill snapped. "I'm only forty, and I work hard."
He faced them and flexed his work-hardened muscles. "I'll have
you know I can still hold my own."

Gray streaked Bill's short brown hair and moustache. Jake
thought it made him look fatherly.

Wiley took in the hostler's lean and tightly muscled body, the
kind built from years of grueling work. Reading Bill's face, he
saw the grief and loneliness Bill endured after his partner had been
killed. He glanced at Jake and could almost feel a similar loss if
anything ever happened to him.

"And don't you be callin' me old 'round Harry!" Bill shouted,
drying himself off.

When the three left the barn, Bill tugged at his vest. "This
dang thing don't fit right."

Wiley helped him straighten the back. "It's a little small, but
you look good in it."

Jake watched his own crotch as he walked and noticed
everything he had was perfectly outlined. "Wiley, these here pants
are too damn tight. I better put some others on before I pop them
buttons."

"You don't have any other clean pants, Jake." Wiley eyed
Jake up and down. "Besides, you look wonderful." He had to quit
looking at Jake before he got more stirred up than he was already.

"I'll say!" Bill exclaimed. "And you'd best stay away from
Harry." He grinned and pointed at Wiley adjusting himself. "And
him, too."

When they walked into the crowded restaurant, Bill spotted
Matt and Frank at a table in the far corner and started toward
them. He wondered why Harry wasn't there.

Most of the people in the cafe spoke to Bill. As Jake and
Wiley followed him through the small spaces between the tables,
the eyes of men and women alike searched every inch of them.
One woman turned her head and stared directly at Jake's bulging
crotch as he inched by.

"Oh, my!" she exclaimed, dropping her fork. She fanned
herself with her napkin and caught her husband swallowing hard
when Jake passed him.

Bill stopped at a table occupied by two older men. When he loudly introduced Jake and Wiley, saying they'd become blood brothers in the Silver Heels the night before, many excited whispers buzzed throughout the room.

Shortly after their introduction, Wiley excused himself and gently pulled Jake toward Matt and Frank's table. As the miners stood up to greet them, Wiley smiled at how different they looked freshly scrubbed.

Wiley took in Matt's long face and square jaw with a slight cleft in the center of his chin. He sported the beginnings of a fine beard and had pulled his shoulder-length brown hair back and tied it in a short tail. He noticed Matt's green shirt, similar to his own, exposed his wooly chest.

Jake liked the looks of Matt, but considered Wiley much more handsome. He was proud to be Wiley's blood brother.

Frank's shorter stature did nothing to take away his imposing appearance. Wiley thought he might be Mexican or Indian, but the man's brilliant green eyes and lighter skin indicated some European ancestry. He wished Jake's face held the calm, jovial expression that Frank's did.

Seeing Frank dressed only in jeans and a sleeveless poncho vest, exposing his hairless chest and arms, Jake thought of Sampson, Mr. Pritcher's ox. "Ain't you got no shirt?" Jake asked him.

Frank laughed.

Matt felt his partner's huge arm. "Frank has so many muscles, he never gets cold."

Before they sat down, the four shook hands around and examined each other closely. Three pair of eyes became glued to Jake's crotch.

Red in the face, Jake dropped into his chair. "Wiley, I told you I should'a changed pants."

"Nonsense," Matt said, sitting down with the others. "I think all men should wear tight pants, especially men that look like you, Jake. You'll give this town something to talk about for weeks."

"I ain't movin' outta this chair all night."

"Guess you'll miss the fun we'll have at the bars, later," Frank commented. He winked at Wiley. "And everybody else'll miss seein' what they ain't gonna get their hands on."

Wiley felt sorry for Jake getting razzed, but found it difficult to keep from manhandling him. "Where's Harry?" he asked, trying to change the subject of Jake's crotch.

"He'll be late," Frank said. "Told us to start eatin' without him. Had an errand to run, but he jumped at the chance to see 'ol Bill, though."

"Now don't *you* start callin' me old," Bill snapped as he slid into his chair. "I made these here brothers promise they'd keep their traps shut about that around Harry. You two dang-well better do the same."

"Harry ain't no spring chicken hisself," Frank said. "Fact is, you look like two beans on a tin plate. Maybe you ought'a go through the blood brother ceremony tonight in the bar your ownselves." He winked at Jake and Wiley.

"Never you mind," Bill snapped. "These things take time."

"Right," Frank quipped. "Just ask Jake an' Wiley how much time it takes."

Everyone laughed, except for Bill who flagged down the waitress and ordered beer and dinner for everyone.

For some reason neither could explain, the blood brothers felt shy in the presence of the three outspoken men who continually razzed each other. They remained quiet even though they laughed freely. Under the table, they gave each other a reassuring squeeze on the leg.

In the room's din, the men heard a loud voice yell, "Over here, Harry!" Bill wheeled around in his chair to see Harry being flagged down by the same two men he'd chatted with earlier. Wiley saw Harry clearly. Jake had to crane his neck to see around Bill.

Wiley felt Frank's expression "two beans on a tin plate" was accurate. Bill and Harry looked enough alike to be natural brothers. Harry had lighter hair and a ruddier face, plus he was clean shaven, but Wiley would have mistaken them for twins if he'd seen them in the street.

Soon, but not soon enough for Bill from his expression, Harry made his way to the table where the five men waited. He approached Bill from behind and placed a hand on his shoulder while he greeted Frank and Matt. When his eyes fell on Jake and Wiley, he exclaimed, "Lordy. Who are you gents?" Without waiting for an answer, he introduced himself. "I'm Harry Windslow." Closest to Wiley, he extended his hand first to him.

"I'm Wiley...Gray," Wiley said, shaking the man's hand.

When Harry wouldn't let go of Wiley's hand, Bill punched him in the side. "The other gent's name is Jake. By the way, Jake, what's yer last name?"

"Brady," Jake answered. His face turned crimson as Harry shook his hand, hard.

Wiley reached under the table and squeezed Jake's leg.

"Glad to meet you, gents," Harry said. "Where are you from?"

Wiley told the same story about himself he'd used on Jake, and briefly told where Jake came from. Not knowing if he could trust Bill's friends, he left out their encounters with Billingsly and the Harrises. Jake gave Wiley a grin for sparing him the ordeal of having to say anything right then.

The beer and food arrived, and the men fell silent as they filled their plates from the huge bowls of steaming beef, potatoes and Indian corn.

As soon as every scrap of food had disappeared, Frank turned to Harry. "Jake an' Wiley are the famous blood brothers from the Silver Heels last night."

"No kidding?" Harry examined the blood brothers. "You fellows sure know how to upset a town." He nudged Bill. "Well, what are we waiting for? If these young bucks can do it, why can't we become partners?"

Bill swallowed hard. "Ain't it rushin' it a bit?"

"Rushing it! After a year of talking about it, I'd hardly call that rushing. You're still glubbering about your dead partner, and you know it. I think it's time to stop that and start living again."

Puzzled, Jake asked, "Bill, why'd you say Harry was gonna be your partner, but he didn't know it yet?"

"He told you that?" Harry yelled. He turned to Bill and frowned. "Why, you old dog! Just for that, I'm gonna make *you* wait for another year." He threw his head back and laughed. The others joined him, including red-faced Bill.

To everyone's astonishment, Wiley paid for the entire meal. They decided to wander over to the Silver Heels Bar and later take in a few other drinking places.

All heads turned again as the six men left the cafe.

# CHAPTER 22

As the group approached the Silver Heels Bar, the crush of men in the building spilled through the batwings into the street. Familiar with the crowds, Matt and Frank didn't hesitate and shoved their way inside. They knew almost everyone in town and, while greeting their friends, skillfully edged deeper into the mass of people. Bill and Harry slipped into the brief path the two miners carved.

Jake and Wiley stopped abruptly as the teeming humanity swallowed up their companions.

Wiley glanced at Jake and smiled at his pensive expression. "Let's stay close so we don't get separated." Realizing Jake didn't hear him, he said, "Jake?" Wiley lurched forward as someone plowed into him from behind.

"Get out of the damn doorway, Mack!"

Wiley ignored the man. "Jake?" He grabbed his partner's arm and shook it.

Jake looked straight at him. "Wiley, what if I get in there an' hafta pee?"

Wiley bit his lower lip and turned toward the crowd. After he'd controlled his silent laughter, he spun back around. "Maybe...maybe you should run to the back now, before we go in. I'll wait here."

Jake pushed his way down the boardwalk and disappeared around the side of the building.

After waiting longer than he thought Jake needed, Wiley saw him stiffly turn the corner. "Jake, what happened? Did someone jump you?"

"Hell, Wiley, my pants wouldn't button back up. I had to lay in the dirt while I was suckin' in. I should'a wore dirty pants."

Wiley gasped when he glanced at Jake's crotch. It was even more pronounced than before, and Jake had stuffed himself in a different way. Wiley swallowed hard, tore his eyes away from Jake's crotch and grabbed his shoulders. "You stay close to me. Let's go." He turned and plowed into the wall of people.

Wondering about Wiley's expression when he'd looked at his pants, Jake glanced down at them. When he raised his head, Wiley had disappeared.

Jake inched his way past the initial throngs and apologized when he stepped on toes. Nobody noticed. He couldn't see Wiley anywhere but kept sliding his body sideways through the crowd. Shocked at a firm grab at his butt, Jake spun around and glared at the back of a man's head.

"Down here!" a high-pitched voice yelled.

Jake didn't see anyone, but through a break in the crush of men, he spotted a short, toothless old man in a greasy black hat grinning up at him.

"You the one grabbin' me in the butt?" Jake asked.

"Shore am. Want 'nother?"

"Not hardly." The man looked so comical, Jake smiled and gave his gray beard a tug.

"Better get used to gettin' grabbed, sonny," the old man said. "Some'a these boys been waitin' all their lives to touch a man like you." He cackled. "Me included!" He squeezed Jake's butt again, rolled his eyes and scurried into the crowd without a backward glance.

Jake stood on tip-toes to see where the old man went, but he'd already lost himself in the press of bodies. Before pushing on toward the bar, Jake snuck a peek at his rear end to see what had enticed the man. A black, claw-like hand print marked the spot where he'd been grabbed.

A brawny cowboy, charging through the bar and shoving people out of his way, slammed into Jake and knocked him backwards into the crowd. Much bigger than either Wiley or himself, the man's chiseled face reminded Jake of Sergeant Moss. He gasped and stared.

The cowboy gave Jake a sneering once-over. He reached down and grabbed Jake in the crotch, then yelled, "Well, looky here! It's a damn dick-licker!"

Stunned, Jake stared deep into the handsome cowboy's mocking, ice-blue eyes. Then, something snapped inside him. After having bottled his feelings all his life trying to cope with his father's insults and name-calling, he'd had enough. He felt a deadly rage take control.

"Keep yer damn hands off'a me!" Jake yelled. He grabbed the man's groping arm above the elbow and jerked it over his head. Jake slipped his fingers around the cowboy's belt with his other hand, growled, then hefted the man above his head and tossed him like a bale of hay. Five miners fell down as the cowboy slammed into them. The bar erupted into cheers and yells. The men closest to the scuffle pushed everyone back to give Jake more room.

Wiley had no idea what had happened but saw Jake standing in the middle of a widening circle. He couldn't force his way through the masses to get to him, so he flung people aside.

When the cowboy got to his feet, he faced Jake and Wiley, standing side-by-side. Towering over them, the man snarled and reached for his gun. The crowd gasped, and a few faint-hearted fell to the floor in panic. After the cowboy cleared leather, Wiley kicked the gun into the air. A hand reached out of the crowd and deftly caught the pistol before it hit the floor.

Jake grabbed the surprised cowboy by his shirt, hauled back and bashed the man's nose with his mule-kick punch. Blood splattered into the crowd. When Jake let go of his shirt, the man fell flat on his back. Everyone stared down at two hundred-forty pounds of mean cowboy, out cold.

The bar fell silent until someone yelled, "Do you know who that is you jest knocked out? That's Sidewinder, Billingsly's foreman. You gotta be crazy fer hittin' him cuz now you're a dead man." Several others agreed, but most cheered the sudden defeat of the town bully.

Wiley leaned over and whispered, "Jake, maybe we'd better leave."

"I need me a drink first, Wiley." Jake inspected his bloody fist, bent down and wiped it on Winder's shirt, then stepped over him and headed toward the bar. An aisle parted as everyone got out of his way.

Wiley followed, grinning. He knew a giant had suddenly awakened inside Jake...at least for tonight.

Bill finally made it to the bar and stood beside Jake. "You shore can hit! I reckon that's the first time that big bully's been knocked out cold his whole life! And with only one punch, too!"

Wiley came up behind and rested his arm across Jake's shoulders. "How's your hand?"

"Fine, Wiley. Jest fine." Jake looked at Wiley with smoldering eyes. "He grabbed me in the nuts, Wiley, an' called me some name I never heard before, so I let him have it. Now I got more'n the Harrises wantin' to kill me." He grabbed Wiley's arm. "But we'll get 'em, won't we, Wiley?"

Wiley's face lit up. "You're right, Jake." He squeezed Jake's wrist, knowing they would fight for each other. Always.

Tubs wiped his hands on a towel, selected a bottle from the back bar and planted it in front of the blood brothers.

"You gents do liven things up when you come in here. As usual, this here booze is on the house." Tubs peered through the crowd, quickly snatched back the bottle and put it under the bar. "I'll jist keep this here fer later. Looks like you ain't gonna be needin' it jist yet."

The brothers spun around and saw five mean-looking cowboys and six grizzled miners surrounding them.

Wiley turned toward Jake and lightly punched him on the arm. "Brother Jake," he joked, "I think you an' me're jist about ready to show this here town a thing'r two about fightin'." He smiled and bowed.

Jake stared at him, then broke into a wide grin. He felt closer to Wiley at that moment then he ever thought possible. Wiley made him feel fearless. He turned his head and noticed Frank and Matt positioning themselves behind Billingsly's thugs. Harry appeared beside Bill and casually pulled on a pair of black gloves. Everything seemed to be happening in slow motion, and Jake felt mischief creep up inside him. He grinned at Wiley, then turned slowly and faced the ring of men a few feet away.

"So, yer all workin' for that no-good Bingsly," Jake shouted. Several bystanders laughed. "Brother Wiley, I think these here men need a damn head doctor." He grabbed the two closest cowboys by their necks, slammed their heads together and shoved them backward. They slid onto a table, which collapsed under their weight. Dazed, the pair groaned and rolled their eyes.

Everyone cheered, then pandemonium broke out.

A man close to Jake threw a punch. Jake turned his body, took it on the shoulder and was knocked into Bill.

"Hey, watch that!" Bill yelled as he lunged forward and hit the man in the face. Jake backed away and let Bill go at it.

The biggest miner swung at Wiley, but he ducked and the man's punch went wild. Wiley grabbed him in the crotch, reached up and got a choke hold, lifted him off the floor and hurled him at two others rushing toward him. The tossed miner hit the men at chest level and the trio hit the floor and rolled into the onlookers.

"Say, that sure was somethin' you just done, Brother Wiley," Jake shouted.

"I had a good teacher," Wiley said. They laughed, shook hands once and dived back into the fight.

One cowhand pinned Harry against the bar, holding his arms down while another man punched him in the face. The man holding Harry suddenly felt cold and looked down. Harry had unbuttoned his pants, they'd fallen to the floor and the cowhand stood bare-ass naked from the waist down. In horror, he let go of Harry's arms to retrieve his pants. Instantly, Harry's uppercut to his jaw flung him on his back amid the screaming crowd. His family jewels flopped around for all to see.

Sid Thompson pushed his huge frame through the throng, picked up the half-naked cowboy and slung him over his shoulder, patted the man's bare bottom and said, "Thanks, boys." He shoved his way out the front door.

With blood dripping from his nose, Harry planted a right, then a left into the face of the cowboy who'd used him for a punching bag. The man slumped to the floor.

Frank and Matt took on two miners they had fought with before. It became a grudge fight since the two men continually taunted the partners in front of the other miners. The fact they worked for Billingsly made their jeers even more irritating. As the four men punched it out, Matt and Frank clearly had the upper hand since Billingsly's other miners were too busy at the moment to intervene the way they usually did.

Some of the men in the crowd suddenly lurched to the side as Tiny pushed his way through from the kitchen. Everyone heard a loud clang as he bashed a cowboy on the head with an iron skillet, flattening the man's hat and knocking him to the floor. Tiny grinned as onlookers laughed and slapped him on the back.

Tubs grabbed his son and pulled him behind the bar. His scolding was drowned out by the din.

Jake took a breather after a slug match with one of the men he'd first attacked, now out cold, and watched Bill put the finishing touches on the teeth of the other. He raised his eyebrows at the forty-year-old tiger. The next thing Jake knew, a fist smashed into the side of his head, dropping him to his knees. When his head cleared, Jake raised up and saw Sidewinder standing over him, his face smeared with blood. Murder burned in the man's eyes, and he kicked Jake in the side. As Jake doubled over in pain, Winder kicked him again.

Billingsly's foreman grabbed a chair and swung it over his head but when he tried to slam it down on Jake's back, it wouldn't move. He jerked his head around and saw a hand holding one of the rungs. Suddenly, a strong arm closed around his neck, and he felt the chair being ripped out of his hand.

"My turn!" Wiley yelled into Sidewinder's ear. With the man still in his powerful choke hold, Wiley charged the bar, bashed Winder's head against it, then shoved him to the floor.

Winder slowly picked himself up and wiped the blood out of his eyes. He growled and flung himself at Wiley, taking him to the floor. While the two powerful men rolled around, Wiley tried a few wrestling holds to the bigger man's head, but his smeared blood made him too slippery. Sidewinder braced his foot against the bar and flung Wiley on his back, pinned his arms with his knees and started punching him in the face. Wiley growled, raised his legs and caught Winder around the head with his boots, then yanked him backward and slammed his head against the floor. Once again, Billingsly's foreman plunged into the black void.

Wiley pushed the cowboy to one side, staggered to his feet and walked into the fist of the same miner he'd tossed earlier. The force of the blow shoved Wiley into the wall of onlookers, and they heaved him back into the fight. Wiley dodged the miner's left, danced around to confuse the burly man, then jabbed his right into the miner's nose. The man fell against the stove, wrenching the chimney out of the ceiling. Soot poured out the hole and covered the miner, Wiley and several men in the crowd. Wiley's final punch laid the man out on the floor.

Jake slowly got to his feet, holding his side where Winder had kicked him. Before he regained his balance, one of Billingsly's miners jumped him and they both fell to the floor. Jake growled and tossed the man to the side. He struggled to his knees, sat on the miner's chest and bashed his face, once. The man didn't get up.

No one wanted to see the brawl end, but none of Billingsly's men were left standing. Many in the bar yelled it had been the best fight in the town's history, and the heros were Jake and Wiley.

As the blood brothers surveyed the scene, they saw Bill with a cut on his face standing beside Harry holding his broken nose. Frank and Matt were uninjured, except for Frank's shredded vest. Frank calmly removed the vest and tossed it to the floor amid shouts of approval as he exposed his hard-packed muscles.

Jake went to Wiley's side, put a hand on his shoulder and looked into Wiley's soot-blackened face. "You're sure a sight, Wiley. I didn't know you took up minin'."

An older man with graying temples and rimless spectacles pushed his way toward Jake and Wiley. "Are you two responsible for this?"

"Sure am." Jake pointed to the men on the floor. "Them're Bingsly's men. It don't matter."

"Well, it matters to me! I'm Doc Colter. *I'm* the one that's going to have to patch these men up. You must think I *like* working constantly. Who are you, anyway?"

They introduced themselves to the doctor, and Jake added they were blood brothers.

The doctor inspected them carefully, then grinned, leaned close and whispered, "Frankly, I'm glad you boys beat the crap out of this scum." He spun around, pointed to various onlookers, and shouted, "You, you and you! Get these men over to my office. Some of the rest of you can help, too. Now, get going!"

After Billingsly's bashed and bloodied men had been dragged out of the bar, Doc Colter yelled, "Tubs, I need a drink. Give these six men drinks, too. On me. They deserve it."

Tubs plunked Jake and Wiley's bottle in front of them. "See, I knowed you gents wouldn't need this here booze 'til now." He lined up seven glasses, then leaned close to Wiley. "It's a good thing that stove weren't goin' yet." He laughed at Wiley's black face.

Doc Colter poured himself a shot of whiskey, downed it, then turned to Harry and examined his broken nose. Before anyone could blink, he jerked the nose sharply and set it.

"Yeow!" Harry yelled. He held up his cupped hands to catch the dripping blood.

Doc Colter reached over the bar and grabbed a clean cloth, ripped off one end, then tore the small piece in half. He rolled each one into a small wad and carefully stuffed them up Harry's nostrils. "Come over to my office in the morning if it's not better." He poured another shot and downed it. "Gentlemen, I have to leave, but let me again congratulate you on your accomplishment. I never thought I'd see the day when we had to drag Sidewinder out of here--when he wasn't dead drunk."

Doc Colter turned and pushed his way toward the door. When he reached the landing, he bumped into Sheriff Cline shoving his way inside. Doc Colter smiled at the handsome sheriff. "Congrats on your promotion, Wes."

"Thanks, Doc." Sheriff Cline smiled at the doctor, looked around at the milling crowd and his face changed to a scowl. "Guess there's been a fight in here again. Heard it was some of Billingsly's men that got beat up. That true?"

"It's true, and that Sidewinder snake got the worst of it."

"Winder? Who had the balls to beat him up?"

"The blood brothers the whole damn town's talking about," Doc Colter said. "I congratulated them, in case you want to know. They knocked Sidewinder out colder than my wife's feet in the dead of winter. *Twice*, mind you. They also messed up his pretty-boy face. It looks like raw meat."

"No shit?" Cline tried to suppress a grin. "Guess I'll have to get a full report. Where are these blood brothers?"

Doc Colter pointed to the six men. "There, at the bar with Bill Chasteen and his friends. Now you'll have to excuse me. I have an all night patch-up job on a dozen men."

"A *dozen*...?" The sheriff's words dropped off as he spied Jake and Wiley. Wes stared at them. He couldn't remember ever seeing two more handsome and rugged men. "Er...g'night Doc," he said and elbowed his way toward the bar.

Doc Colter smiled, shook his head and left.

Sheriff Cline shoved his way over to Harry. "You look terrible, Harry, but I'd hate to see the other guy." Wes placed a hand on Bill's shoulder. "Howdy, Bill." After nodding at Frank and Matt, he scanned Frank's body and grinned. "Don't you own any shirts, Frank?"

The four men smiled at Cline, but no one said anything. Their no-nonsense sheriff had just taken over.

Sheriff Cline turned to Jake and Wiley. "Well, I finally meet the famous blood brothers. Can't stay out of trouble, can you!" He searched Wiley's soot-blackened face, lowered his eyes to the man's ragged shirt that exposed his chest and shoulders, scanned his body from top to bottom, then looked him in the eye.

After he "undressed" Jake in the same manner, his eyes stopped at Jake's crotch. One of the buttons on Jake's tight pants was missing, and Cline could see flesh pushing out the gap. He sucked in air.

Jake looked down and immediately covered his crotch with his hand. His face flushed.

Wes Cline wiped his forehead with his sleeve. "Let's grab...a...a table in the other room and have a little chat. *All* of you."

The sheriff plowed through the bar, shouting threats to a few men who didn't move out of his way fast enough. He broke up a poker game in the next room and sent the cursing men stomping through the bar yelling they'd get even for interrupting their gambling.

"Your drinks are on me!" Cline hollered back.

The sheriff secured seven chairs, pushed them around the table then motioned for Jake, Wiley and the others to sit.

"Now, gents, I want to know what happened here tonight. And I want the truth, because tomorrow, Ed Billingsly's going to be crawling on my back like ticks on a dog."

"That there Winder grabbed me in the nuts, Sheriff, an' called me a damn licker-dicker," Jake said. "Nobody does that to me an' gets away with it."

"I see," Sheriff Cline said, covering a smile with his hand. Winder had a reputation for doing that to anyone he suspected of liking men rather than women. Problem was, no one dared stop him or they'd be flat on the floor in seconds.

"What did you do then?" the sheriff asked.

Jake frowned. "I picked 'im up an' tossed 'im."

"You picked him up and *tossed* him?" The sheriff shook his head, glad he'd resisted grabbing Jake's crotch a few minutes earlier.

"That's right, Sheriff," Wiley chimed in. "When Winder or Sidewinder, whatever his name is, got up, he pulled his gun, and I managed to kick it out of his hand. Then, Jake knocked him out with one punch." Wiley smiled at Jake and patted his arm.

The rest of the men at the table picked up on the sheriff's amazement and began giving him a blow-by-blow account of the fight until Wes couldn't hold it in any longer and burst out laughing.

"Damn! I wish I'd been here. Sounds like the best fight this town's seen for a long time."

Several men close to the table heard the sheriff's comment and cheered Jake and Wiley, the town heros.

Cline wanted Jake and Wiley's version of Aaron's death, whether Jake *was* the father of Seth's unborn grandchild, and what the two men planned to do.

The brothers filled him in on what they knew, except their plans to work for Belinda Castille. Wiley said they might travel toward Breckenridge in a day or two.

"Better ride out tomorrow," Sheriff Cline stated. "Billingsly will be after your hides. Plus, he has those killers living with him, and I'll put money on it he's planning to use them to trap you. Don't go anywhere near them. I'll do everything possible to keep them off your tail, but I'm only one man and I can't be everywhere. Just remember, leave on the sly some time tomorrow...and watch your back trail." He got up, nodded to the men at the table, snuck one last glance at Frank's bare chest and strode toward the door.

The six men stared at the retreating sheriff. Jake turned and grinned at Wiley's blackened face. He had rubbed his eyes, causing elongated streaks in the soot out to points on each side of his face. Two lighter stripes crossed each cheek where his thumbs had touched.

Jake pointed at him. "Hell, Wiley, you look like you been doin' a war dance."

Everyone laughed.

Wiley chuckled, hoping the soot covered his scar so the sheriff hadn't recognized him. He leaned over and pointed at Jake's partly opened fly. The men at the table laughed again.

After passing the bottle around until it was empty, they made plans to meet for breakfast the next morning at the Regal Cafe, then left the bar together.

Frank and Matt said their farewells and trudged to their cabin on the hill behind the Silver Heels Bar. In the cold air, steam rose from Frank's sweaty, half-naked body. The others watched, wondering how he kept from getting pneumonia.

Bill and Harry, dying to hear the gossip of the fight in Billingsly's own bar, went off together to have a nightcap in Mattie's Saloon.

Wiley put his arm over Jake's shoulder, and the blood brothers walked quietly down the street to the livery. After they climbed up to the loft, Wiley lit the lantern, stripped off his ragged shirt and washed the black soot off his face. While drying himself, he noticed Jake standing close to the loft door looking out at the town. Silvery moonlight fell on Jake's face and shoulders. Wiley watched him for a moment, then blew out the lamp and walked up behind him. He slipped his arms around Jake's waist and drew him close.

"I love you, Jake," he whispered into Jake's ear.

Jake turned and faced him. "Wiley, I don't want nothin' to happen to you an' if you stay with me, you'll get hurt...or killed. I'm goin' back to Kentucky an' get hitched with Sara Jean. Then, you'll be safe."

"What?" Wiley pulled back. "Jake, what's the matter with you? I thought we'd settled that. We're blood brothers, partners. I won't *let* you marry that liar. You said you don't want to marry her, so what's gotten into you? If you want to go back to Kentucky, I'll go with you. But I *won't* let you marry Sara Jean."

Jake searched Wiley's face and knew he meant what he said. He rested his forehead on Wiley's shoulder, glad Wiley still wanted him even if the Harrises were after him, and especially after the fight in the bar.

Wiley slid his arms around Jake and pressed his face against Jake's neck. They held each other for a long time.

Later, naked under the blankets, they finally fell asleep, locked in a sweaty embrace.

# CHAPTER 23

The morning sky was pale turquoise, dotted with crimson-orange puffball clouds. Wiley dug into his pocket for the thumbnail-size piece of turquoise he'd bought from an Indian in the Denver train station and held it up in front of his face. Pretty close...the sky had more blue. Lowering his eyes, he took in the blacksmith shop next to Biglow's Diner across Main Street and became aware of the clanging of the smithy's hammer. Funny...he hadn't noticed it before. Alma was already awake, or maybe it never slept at all. Wiley scanned the sky again, but couldn't tell the time. According to the shadows, he calculated the sun's warming rays, still obscured by the sprawling foot of Mount Silverheels, would reach the town in an hour.

Breathing deeply, he wondered why, after being here only two days, he didn't feel the cold as much as that first night. The search for Jake on the mountain had something to do with it because he'd completely forgotten the cold while up there.

He turned away from the loft door and glanced at the pile of hay. Jake's elbow peeked out from tightly wrapped blankets. Wiley felt a surge of arousal as he remembered their love-making last night. The mere touch of Jake's naked body against his own had sent him into instant ecstasy. And it wasn't only Jake's body. He'd never known anyone like this farmer from Kentucky...so much a man, but still a boy needing nurturing and support. And so funny. He chuckled. Jake's simplest statements and actions made him laugh. How had he carried on this long without him? Wiley thought back to the night he'd seen the vision of Grandpa Gray Feather in the bar and realized his grandfather had been right. He'd felt Jake's presence all his life and had even dreamed about him.

Quickly, Wiley bundled up all his and Jake's smelly clothes and tied them in one of his shirts. He found Bill in back of the barn scraping horse shit in the corral.

"You're up early, Bill."

"Dang jaw ached and couldn't sleep," Bill mumbled, reminding Wiley his did also.

Wiley asked directions to the nearest laundry, then trudged through town with the load of clothes flung over his shoulder.

To Wiley's relief, the Chinese woman promised the clothes would be ready at noon. She gave him a genuine smile, showing off perfect white teeth. The woman's smile faded into a frown as she smelled the clothes, then laughed at Wiley's guilty expression.

Turning right when he left the laundry, Wiley passed the Regal Cafe on his way to Mercer's General Store. He scrutinized every shirt and pair of pants in the store before settling on the right ones for Jake. Mrs. Mercer beamed at his diligence, and Wiley thanked her for having pre-washed the Levis.

With the paper-wrapped bundle tucked under his arm, Wiley peered through the front window of the Regal Cafe again as he went by. After crossing the street and walking a block and a half to the telegraph office, he hesitated at the door. Being with Jake made him want to forget the real reason he was here. He'd finally met the man he wanted to live with forever in the wilderness, and the job he'd been paid to do suddenly seemed distasteful.

Half-heartedly, Wiley entered the office, quickly wrote out a message and handed it to the man behind the counter.

The operator read it to himself.

Bristol Campion
Boston University
Boston, Massachusetts

Billingsly STOP Lawyer, flamboyant, jewels STOP Thin, hawk face, 6 ft STOP Will check back STOP Wiley

After Blake read the message, he gave Wiley an evil frown and opened his mouth to say something.

Wiley grabbed his arm. "If you say *anything* to Billingsly about this, I will *personally* see to it you never again see the light of day." He jerked the man closer. "Send it, *now.*"

Blake's expression changed from a sneer to one of terror. He swallowed hard. "Yes, sir."

Wiley folded his arms and leaned against the counter. "I'll wait!"

Beads of sweat formed on Blake's balding head as he sent the message. His hand shook.

Suddenly, Wiley yelled, "Wait! That's a Y, not an I in flamboyant!"

Blake snapped his head around, amazed this man could read Morse Code. "Yes, sir," he stammered. He re-sent the word and finished the message without a hitch.

Wiley paid him, started to leave, then stopped. He turned slowly and faced Blake. "Remember what I said. I *don't* joke." He touched the butt of his gun.

"Yes, sir," Blake said, trembling.

* * *

Jake threw back the blankets in a panic. Wiley wasn't next to him! He leaped to his feet and ran to the wall where they'd kept their clothes. There *weren't* any clothes. At all! *Everything* was gone, except the saddle bags.

He was freezing. Jake grabbed a blanket, wrapped it around himself and plopped into the hay. What had he done to make Wiley leave? He thought of the fight. His ribs ached where Winder had kicked him. Was Wiley angry about him starting the fight? But he couldn't help tossing Winder into the crowd.

Jake touched his left ear, the one Wiley had whispered in that he loved him, then rested his head on his knees. Sergeant Moss was nothing like Wiley. He'd waited his entire life for last night. Jake remembered lying face-to-face with Wiley, naked, with Wiley's hairy chest tickling him all over, the glorious smell of Wiley's body, and his strong arms holding him tight. Within minutes, his fingers had dug into Wiley's back as a lifetime of frustration and longing rushed out in a flood. He'd almost passed out, but clearly remembered Wiley's body had lurched at the same time his had.

Jake sobbed silently. So, why had Wiley left, taking even his clothes? Jake snapped his head up and looked around. Maybe the Harrises took Wiley? Clem was nasty enough to take his clothes and leave him naked and alone. Or maybe Zeke?

Jake jumped to his feet.

When Wiley approached the livery, he heard Jake hollering that the Harrises had kidnapped his partner and stole all his clothes. He entered the building, looked up at the loft and saw Jake standing near the edge, stark naked.

When Jake saw him he yelled, "Wiley, you're here! Wiley, somebody stole all our clothes!"

"I took them to the laundry," Wiley said calmly, trying not to laugh.

"What am I gonna wear for breakfast?"

"Calm down, Jake." Wiley climbed the ladder. "I bought you a new pair of pants and a new shirt. Here, try them on." He stepped onto the loft floor, gave the package to Jake and sat down to watch him open it.

Jake ripped open the brown wrapper and held up the pants. "Levis!" He hugged them. "I ain't never had a real pair of Levis my whole life."

The clothes fit perfectly, and Jake strutted around. "Wiley, how'd you know my size?"

"It's the same as mine. Just looking at you I could tell. You know what that means, don't you?"

"What?" Jake's eyes widened.

"We can wear each other's clothes." Wiley smiled and squinted his eyes. "I'm dying to try on those pants you wore last night."

"No! I won't let you, Wiley. Somebody'll grab you like Winder..." Jake grinned. "Guess you could put 'em on so *I* could grab you like that."

"That was my very thought."

They laughed and started playing grabbies-if-you-can.

Bill slammed the back door. When he got below the loft, he yelled up, "We're gonna be late fer eats if you two don't stop yellin' and horsin' around up there. I ain't never *seen* the likes!"

When they arrived at the Regal Cafe, they saw Harry sitting by himself at the same table they'd all occupied the night before. Both his eyes had already turned black, and Jake thought his nose looked like a sweet potato.

"You look terrible, Harry," Wiley commented as they approached. "I'll buy your breakfast. Yours too, Bill. Neither of you were obligated to help us last night. But we sure needed it."

"Didn't either," Harry quipped, sounding like he had a bad cold. "You gents would have done just fine without us helping you at all."

"Hell, I wouldn't a missed it fer all the balls in Bang-kok...wherever the hell that is," Bill said. "Besides, you gents are friends, and we all speak the same language, if you get my drift."

Jake noticed the empty chairs. "Where's Matt and Frank?"

"Who knows?" Harry said. "You know how their mining jobs are. They were probably in here at the crack of dawn and now are up on some mountain...or in some hole. My job's bad enough. I just can't see how they can work so hard."

"What do you do?" Wiley asked.

"I work for Pete, the barber. I fill up the tubs in the back room when the gents need a bath. I also give rubdowns to miners and cowboys with aching muscles." Harry grabbed his head. "Speaking of aching!"

"Your job sounds hard," Jake said.

"Usually." Harry grinned. "But if not, I make it hard."

Wiley raised his eyebrows.

"Why make it harder'n it is?" Jake asked.

Harry suddenly realized Jake had no idea what he was talking about, and decided to lead this gorgeous man-child on. "Who wants a soft one? All that happens with a soft job is you get hair between your teeth."

"What?" Jake wrinkled his nose.

"Dang it, Harry, be nice!" Bill snapped.

"Wiley, what's goin' on?" Jake asked. His eyes suddenly filled with hurt. "Is he tellin' me I'm dumb...like Pa used to?"

"Jake, no one is saying you're dumb," Wiley said. "Forget about your father telling you things like that. You're *not* dumb. You haven't been around a lot of people, and some men have different ways of explaining what they do when they're together."

Jake's comment and Wiley's reply cut through Harry like a knife. What damaged innocence! A tender spot opened up inside him for the two men, and he decided to help Wiley protect the child-like innocence in Jake, yet somehow make him aware of the real world. "Jake," Harry said, "what I was trying to say was, I--"

Billingsly burst his way into the cafe and slammed the door behind him.

Everyone in the Regal watched the lawyer search the room. As Billingsly swept his eyes past the table where the four friends sat, Wiley detected a split second of terror when he first recognized them.

After composing himself, Billingsly stormed across the room to their table. "What was the meaning of you cretins beating up Winder and my men last night?"

To everyone's amazement, Jake pushed back his chair and stood up. "Jest so you know, Mr...Bingsly, I--"

"*Billingsly*!" the lawyer screamed.

Jake smiled but balled his fists. "Like I was sayin', Mr...*Bingsly*, I was the first one to knock Winder flat."

Billingsly turned red in the face.

"He grabbed me in the nuts," Jake yelled, "so I tossed him away! *Nobody* grabs my nuts...'cept Wiley!"

Wiley covered his face with his hands.

Snickers could be heard from various parts of the room. Billingsly wheeled around and glared at the guilty persons. They lowered their eyes to their plates and continued eating in silence.

Billingsly knew Jake could break him in half like a match stick. He'd heard about the fight in great detail, but couldn't let this ignorant moron get the best of him.

"Since when does a grope in the balls give you the right to beat up my foreman?"

"Since now!" Jake started around the table toward him.

All the color drained from Billingsly's face. He backed up a few steps and stretched his arm in front of him. "You stay away from me, or I'll have you arrested for attacking a defenseless man!"

Jake ignored him and continued on, holding his white-knuckled fists at chest level.

"He's right, Jake," Wiley said as he casually leaned his arm on the back of Jake's empty chair. "He can have you tossed in jail if you lay a hand on him." Wiley worked at a poker face.

Jake stopped and stared at Wiley. "What about last night? Can he arrest me for that, too?"

"No. Last night you were provoked. We were *all* provoked. That's the way the law is stated." Wiley's cold brown eyes bore a hole through Billingsly. "Isn't it!"

Billingsly's jaw dropped as an icy hand clutched his spine. Who *is* this man? When he snapped out of the grip of fear, he screeched, "I'll even up the score with all of you. Soon!" He turned on his heel and tried desperately not to run out of the cafe.

While the men ate a leisurely breakfast of fried steak, potatoes and eggs, Bill and Harry talked at length about Billingsly. Neither one knew where he'd come from, only that the lawyer had appeared one day and opened his office on the second floor of the bank building. In great detail, Harry filled them in on Billingsly's past dealings. They also mentioned the hard cases he employed, Sidewinder being only one of them. Jake half listened, but Wiley cataloged every word.

The conversation shifted to the plans of the blood brothers. Bill swore Harry to secrecy about the intent of the two men to work for Bellinda Castille.

"That's an excellent idea," Harry said. "A team of oxen couldn't pull it out of me."

"You ought'a start out as if you're goin' to Breckenridge," Bill said. "And just before goin' over Hoosier Pass, cut to the east and circle around toward Como. There's a Ute trail high up the slopes of Mount Silverheels. It'll take you on that same route. You can follow it or cut your own trail. Jest remember, after you cross the train tracks goin' over Boreas Mountain, you'll want to head south down the slopes to Como. Keep on goin' south and a bit west 'til you see Bristlecone Peak. It's about fifteen miles from Como to Belinda's ranch."

They left the Regal Cafe at eight-thirty. Harry went back to work, and Bill trudged off to do a few errands. With four hours to kill before they could pick up their laundry, Jake and Wiley crossed the side street and headed to Mercer's General Store.

They found the store empty of people except for Mrs. Mercer, wiping down the shelves inside the candy counter. They introduced themselves to the older woman. Mrs. Mercer remembered Wiley from earlier that morning, but when she found out from Jake they were the famous blood brothers, she raised her eyebrows and smiled.

"Well, my heavens! So you're the two that have this town in such a tizzy. Why, just yesterday Reverend Quick came in here screaming about what heathens you are." She shook her head. "He's such a horrible old fool. I think most of the town's on your side. I know I am. Now, what can I get you boys?"

Wiley shrugged and smiled weakly. "The sheriff advised us to leave town today. We need some traveling supplies and clothes."

"You boys just help yourselves. If I don't have what you need, I don't think the Montgomery Wards catalog would do you much good." Mrs. Mercer laughed, stuck her head inside the cabinet and continued scrubbing a purple spot.

Wiley went first to the ammunition cabinet. Amazed at the large selection of shells, he grabbed four boxes of .45s, two for his brand new Model 1886 Winchester and the other two for Jake's handsome double action Colt revolver. He wondered where Jake had gotten it. Wiley also selected two boxes of .38 longs for his Navy Colt and two boxes of .32 extra longs for Jake's Ballard rifle.

At the bins, Jake bagged several pounds of coffee, dried fruit, a dozen potatoes, and five pounds of flour.

Wiley grabbed a pouch of tobacco and a pack of papers. He didn't smoke much but enjoyed one now and then.

While Jake tried on boots, Wiley held up shirts to his back for the proper fit for both of them. He had a struggle doing it after Jake began hopping on one foot trying to get a too-small boot off his foot. On one of his bigger hops, Jake's gun flew out of his holster. Wiley caught it in mid-air, then grabbed Jake before he upset the pickle barrel.

Mrs. Mercer bumped her head inside the candy counter laughing at Jake's antics. After struggling out from the tight quarters she said, "You boys sure are good partners. I haven't seen two men get on so well with each other for many a year. Don't let anything ruin your friendship, because if you do, you'll both be sad to your graves you let it happen." She turned suddenly and hurried into the back room.

Jake stopped hopping when Mrs. Mercer spoke, and the two men smiled at each other. Bill's words the day before had a similar message.

When Mrs. Mercer returned, she held a gingham bag with a white string tie. "Here's a treat for you boys for after your supper." She opened the bulging bag.

"Doughnuts!" Jake yelled. He reached in the bag, pulled one out and stuffed the whole thing in his mouth. When he realized he couldn't chew with his mouth so full, he started laughing, then choking. He grabbed at his throat. As he reached in his mouth and pulled out some of the doughnut, Mrs. Mercer ran to the back room to get him some water. Wiley pounded on his back.

The front door opened, and Reverend Quick walked in. He frowned at Jake. "Choking on your sins, I see."

Ignoring the reverend, Mrs. Mercer ran to Jake's side and held out the tin cup. "Take a drink of this water and wash it down."

"Mrs. Mercer!" the reverend snapped. "How *dare* you give a cup of water to a heathen!" He snatched the cup out of her hand and drank the water himself.

Wiley clenched his fists and would have knocked the reverend to Kingdom Come if Jake hadn't stood up straight and coughed the last bit of doughnut into the old man's face. Reverend Quick's surprised look turned to one of hideous rage.

"You spit on one of God's *chosen*!" the reverend shrieked. "This is *blasphemy*! God will strike you *dead*!" He took out his handkerchief and wiped his face.

Jake finally stopped coughing and glanced at Wiley. Without warning, he grabbed Reverend Quick by the arm and pushed him toward the door. Still in his stocking feet, he gently shoved the old man to the boardwalk.

"This is for yer own good, Reverend. Wiley's ready to beat you to a pulp. Can't say I blame him none. Only thing holy in you is your butt." Still holding on to the reverend's arm, Jake asked, "Ain't you never read the Good Book, Reverend? You should. It's all about my friend Jesus an' his Pa. If you read it you might learn somethin'."

"Let go of me, you *heathen*!"

"You just stay out here 'til Wiley an' me are gone, then you can come in the store." Jake let go of the reverend's arm and walked back into the building.

Reverend Quick shook his fist at the store and shriked about fire and brimstone, then stomped down the street toward the sheriff's office.

Inside, Wiley gathered up the supplies and stuffed them into a large flour sack Mrs. Mercer had given him. Jake put on the boots he wanted and also selected several pair of socks and a leather hat. Across the store, he picked out a couple bulbs of garlic, a package of salt and a few dried chilies. From a battered tin bowl on top of the main counter, Jake grabbed three shriveled apples, chuckling a little. Crossing to the other side of the store, he chose a stew pot and a set of metal plates with matching mugs. He passed up a skillet since he already had one.

As Jake dumped all the items into the flour sack, Wiley returned with five pounds of jerky, enough bacon for a week and a box of hardtack.

Mrs. Mercer appeared from the back room with a bottle of whiskey. "You might need this. It's good for keeping you warm or disinfecting the cuts and scrapes you're bound to get."

Both men smiled. Just like a mother.

After they settled up the bill and said good-bye to the woman, Jake wanted to leave by the back door.

Always one to confront things head-on, Wiley hated sneaking around. Hiding from the Harrises at the Castille Ranch grated on him, but Jake took priority now. He reluctantly agreed, and they slipped down the back alley to the livery.

They spent the next hour sorting and packing their gear into Jake's saddle bags and into the worn set Bill gave Wiley.

A few minutes past noon, Wiley walked to the laundry and picked up their clothes. On the way back, he crossed the street and casually passed the telegraph office. As he peered through the window, he saw Blake talking to Billingsly. Blake recognized Wiley, and his face froze in terror. Billingsly spun around and gave Wiley a hateful glare.

Wiley did a slash movement across his neck with his finger and smiled wickedly at Blake. He slowly turned and continued walking down the boardwalk. After he crossed the muddy street, he stopped, turned completely around and looked back at the telegraph office. Billingsly and Blake stood on the boardwalk watching him. Wiley chuckled, thinking the two men seemed quite distressed...especially Blake.

After the brothers finished packing their clothes, they discovered Bill had already saddled their horses.

Bill walked with them out the back door of the building. When they reached the side gate, he pointed up the gradual slope of Mount Silverheels. "Up yonder on that there mountain is the old Ute trail. There's some mines between Mount Silverheels and Iron Mountain, but if you stay on the trail you'll be higher up and nobody'll see you. 'Member what I said, after you get to Como, Belinda's ranch is south an' a bit west. It's three miles southwest of Bristlecone Peak. You can't miss it."

Bill grabbed each partner and hugged him. "I'll miss you gents. I'll mislead everyone as to yer where-bouts."

Wiley patted Bill on the shoulder. "We'll keep in touch, Bill. We may have to come into town for supplies."

"You just stay away from here fer now. Do yer shoppin' in Fairplay. It'll be closer, anyhow. Belinda only comes clear up here cuz Wade liked Alma better." He watched them swing into their saddles. "Harry and me know where you are. You'll be fine as long as you don't go wanderin' off somewhere and get yourselves lost."

"We ain't gonna get lost," Jake said. He glanced at Wiley then back to Bill. "But we might get shot."

The partners thanked Bill for everything and waved as they started up the foot of the mountain. If they would have looked back, they might have seen four men, sitting on a hill overlooking the town, watching them leave. When Jake and Wiley were out of sight, the four men in black mounted up and spurred their horses in the same direction.

Bill watched the blood brothers disappear over the top of the swell, then something caught his eye higher up on the mountain. He shaded his eyes and thought he saw the lone figure of an Indian standing on an outcropping of rock.

Bill gasped, spun on his heel, rushed into the livery and slammed the door behind him.

# CHAPTER 24

Jake sighed with relief when they discovered the Ute trail, but the hair on the back of his neck bristled when he saw where it headed.

"Wiley, lookit that there forest. You think it's haunted?"

They felt a cold blast of air. It got stronger as they approached the ragged edge of the dark woods.

"Let's not talk about that, Jake." Above the growing wind, Wiley yelled, "I've never seen anything like this in my life. Those trees grow sideways...like they're reaching for the one in front of it." He buttoned his jacket and secured his hat.

"The wind done it." Jake grabbed his own hat and pulled it down until his ears stuck out. "Leastways, that's what Tully said. He's Stinky's older brother. Tully come out here an' mined for a few years but went back home with nothin'. Course he didn't have nothin' before, neither." Jake tilted his head against the rush of air spilling over the ridge. "He'd always say the wind up on these mountains blew so hard it'd make the trees try runnin'."

"That's a good description." Wiley flipped up the collar of his jacket as they entered the dark green wall. "Jake, let's stay close to each other."

As the trail sunk deep into the ancient tangle of gnarled bristlecone pines, Wiley felt the trees had twisted into frozen screams from the constant lashing of the wind. Long claw-like branches with puffy, green fingers grabbed at them from damp shadows as the trees bent closer to the ground in the raging wind. Both horses became increasingly spooked, and Jake began singing softly to calm Mac as he side-stepped when branches slapped and poked at him. Buddy seemed a little more relaxed, and Wiley wondered if he'd been here before. If so, it must have been before Billingsly bought him.

Mac reared as a branch blew across the trail in front of his nose. After Jake regained control, he turned around in the saddle.

"This here place is givin' Mac an' me the jitters, Wiley. Let's get outta here." He nudged Mac into a trot.

Dodging branches and protruding rocks, they maneuvered the horses along the worn path as it descended the side of the mountain. As though a curtain opened, the bristlecones gave way to a wide meadow thickly carpeted with a new growth of grass. Clusters of leafless aspens followed a tiny stream through the middle. They slowed the horses to a walk. When the path widened enough for the men to ride abreast, Wiley spurred Buddy alongside his partner. He noticed Jake's worried face.

"We're out of the forest, the wind has stopped and the horses have settled down. Now what's wrong, Jake?"

Jake stared at Mac's mane, then said, "Wiley, I gotta funny feelin' bein' away from town. Them Harrises are sure to be trackin' us, an' I don't want nothin' to happen to you. This ain't your fight, an' it ain't right you gettin' mixed up in it. Besides, I don't want to get killed neither. 'Specially now that I met you." Jake paused and looked at Wiley full-face. "An' I been wonderin' what'll happen when we meet up with them Harrises. I ain't never shot nobody before. Have you?"

"Yes, Jake, I have." Wiley's face showed no emotion. "Someone drew on me once, and I had to kill him. I...don't feel good about it, but it was him or me. And I was faster." Wiley decided to relate only one incident.

"Damn! When was this, Wiley? An' where?"

"Uh...two years ago. It happened...inside a tavern in a small town in Vermont, near my folks' farm. I'd stopped in for a drink one evening and recognized a...a former classmate of mine standing at the bar." Wiley wondered if Jake realized he was completely changing the story. "He was...wanted for murder. As soon as he saw me, he drew his gun. I had to shoot him."

"You were faster?" Jake stared at Wiley. "How fast a draw are you?"

"Faster than he was." Wiley wanted to change the subject and quickly said, "Jake, it's only natural to be scared when someone's after you. But this is my fight too, remember? We're brothers now, and will be until we die." He smiled. "I wouldn't have it any other way."

As they entered the trees on the opposite edge of the clearing, the trail narrowed. Not wanting to leave Jake's side, Wiley edged Buddy closer to Mac. He slid his arm around Jake's back for reassurance.

Neither horse liked this turn of events. In unison they reared and flipped the two men out of their saddles. The blood brothers tumbled into the brush.

After Jake untangled himself from the dense undergrowth, he sat up and rubbed his right shoulder. Wiley groaned and inspected a scraped knee. A few feet away, both horses stood side-by-side, smugly looking down on them. They liked each other from that moment on.

Dazed, the two men carefully looked around. Jake pointed to the horses, and they burst out laughing, covering their mouths so they wouldn't make too much noise. Not once did either man let down his guard of listening or watching for anyone who might be near. Jake knew Mac would alert them if anyone tried sneaking up.

But the men, and even the horses, missed seeing an old Indian standing motionless in the shadow of a twisted, half-dead bristlecone pine. His brownish-gray, nearly translucent ceremonial garb, speckled with beads in a rainbow of bright colors, didn't move from the wind gusts buffeting the area. Glistening specks of light flashed from each golden feather at the ends of his long white braids. He nodded and smiled at the two men, once more covered with pine needles. Then, just as suddenly as he appeared, the Indian vanished.

The partners helped each other up and walked arm-in-arm to their horses. Jake shook the needles out of his hair and put on his new leather hat. His blond hair stuck out all the way around.

Wiley chuckled. "Jake, you look like a scarecrow with your hair like that."

Jake stuck his arms out, tilted his head to the side and crossed his eyes.

Wiley laughed out loud, then quickly checked himself and peered around. Quietly, he walked to Jake's side and gave him the hug he wasn't able to finish before they'd been tossed out of their saddles. "Friendliest scarecrow I ever met." His voice softened. "We'll make it okay."

Jake squeezed him. "Thanks, Wiley."

After he mounted up, Jake watched Wiley brush out any signs where they'd fallen.

"Ain't gonna do no good. They'll find us no matter what we do."

"Well, at least we can make them work for it," Wiley muttered.

With an hour of daylight left, they began searching for a suitable campsite for the approaching night, and since they didn't want to risk a fire after dark, they would have to eat soon. As they topped the ridge of the high saddle between Mount Silverheels and Iron Mountain, the panorama of snowcapped peaks of the Continental Divide stretched to the northwest. Quandary Peak was the most prominent.

Wiley pointed at it. "Jake, that mountain looks like the back of a huge elephant. See how it looks to the west with its ears out?"

"It sure does, Wiley. An' it's like that there statue I seen pichers of in school. You know, the one in the desert called the 'Stinks'."

Wiley almost laughed. He clapped his hand over his mouth and quickly turned Buddy away from Jake. Even so, a few short bursts of air escaped through his fingers, making squeaking sounds.

"You're laughin' at me!" Jake yelled. "Now what'd I say? You're always laughin' at how I talk!"

Wiley laughed out loud for a moment, then checked it as best he could. "Because you're funny, Jake. You can make people laugh faster than anyone I ever knew."

"I can *not*!" Jake yelled. "I don't want to make people laugh at me!"

"Do you want to make them cry?" Wiley tried harder to keep from laughing.

"*Yes*!" Jake thought it over. "Well, not cry...but not laugh."

Wiley tried desperately to compose himself. "Jake, do you remember what Tubs said the first night we met? He said not enough people laugh. Well, you can make people laugh, and that's why they like you."

"Like me, shit!" Jake yelled. "People're tryin' to kill me! Maybe you're stalkin' me, too." He pulled his gun and pointed it at Wiley. "Hands up, Wiley, or whoever you are. I don't trust nobody no more."

"The gun's not loaded, Jake," Wiley said flatly. "I noticed it wasn't loaded when I caught it while you were trying on boots. Why isn't it loaded?"

Jake glanced at his pistol for a moment, clumsily put it back in his holster and smiled sheepishly. "I never load it while I'm gonna be ridin'. I'm afraid it'll go off, an' I'll shoot my foot off."

Wiley nearly bit through his lower lip. When he could, he said, "Put only five bullets in your gun, and place the hammer over the empty cylinder."

Jake glanced down at his Colt again, then at Wiley. "I wouldn't a shot you, Wiley. Guess I just lost my head for a minute. Pa was all-the-time laughin' at me, tellin' me I was dummer'n hog shit. An' there ain't nothin' worser'n hog shit. I always think people are laughin' at me 'cause I ain't ej-a-caded."

"Forget your father, Jake. He didn't know a good person when he saw one. You're *not* dumb. God made you to make people laugh. Besides, education doesn't make most people smart. It only makes them think they are."

"Jesus made me for makin' people laugh?" Jake asked. "Wiley, he never said nothin' about that to me."

"Well...he told me to tell you."

"He did?"

"Yes. And he told me to tell you that you can't go through life expecting everyone to be like your father, because they aren't. You have a great sense of humor. It's a *gift* from God. I wish I had a sense of humor, but I'm so straight-laced I can't ever think of anything funny to say. People in the East are brought up to have good speech and manners. But compared to you, Jake, people back there are boring."

Wiley squinted at the sky. "I think we'd better find a secure campsite soon. The sun's already behind the mountains." He turned Buddy away from the trail and entered the dense growth of centuries-old bristlecone pine.

Deep in thought, Jake followed.

Not subjected to the constant wind, the trees grew upright and closer together. As the brothers pointed their horses through the heavy undergrowth, they came to a clearing made from a huge blowdown almost twenty feet across. The tangle of branches and uplifted roots of the fallen trees was a perfect place to camp. No one could get near them without a great deal of noise.

They unsaddled their horses and rubbed them down with bunches of dry grass then picketed them inside part of the deadfall that formed a corral. An abundance of stalk-dried grass from the previous year carpeted the area. Jake moved a few downed trees so the corral enclosed a bend in a tiny stream trickling down from a patch of snow higher up on the mountain. With a flat rock, he dug a pot-size hole in the stream and watched as it filled. Later, when the silt settled, he knew it would provide the horses with plenty of water.

Wiley rearranged some dead trees in the center for their camp and made a single pathway, one they had to twist and turn their bodies through the stiff branches to get in or out. It made for slow going until they tried it a few times.

"Nobody'll ever get through this without gettin' hisself in big trouble," Jake said as he touched a branch sticking out at crotch level in the passageway. "I just hope it ain't us that gets poked with this one."

They cut pine boughs and wove them into the deadfall to obscure the center area, positioning the branches in and around the fallen trees, making them appear as natural low-growing shrubs. Jake made a hole through the branches from the center campsite to the horses, one they could crawl through in case they needed a rapid exit.

After the camp was hidden, Jake built a small fire and began frying bacon and a few potatoes. He seasoned the potatoes with some of the garlic and chilies he'd picked up at the general store. Since it was rapidly getting dark and he wanted to get the meal cooked fast, he didn't notice Wiley changing into his moccasins.

"Jake, I'll be back shortly. I just want to take a look around." Wiley slipped off so silently, when Jake glanced up, he'd already disappeared.

"Damn!" Jake turned his head in the direction he thought Wiley had gone. "Ol' Wiley sure is a slippery one. Just might be a better tracker than them Harrises."

Wiley silently ran back the way they had come. He ran like a deer through the brush, keeping the Ute trail fifty feet to his right. After traveling a half mile, he stopped suddenly and blended into a thicket of cinquefoil and current bushes.

The nearly full moon hung in the eastern sky, and Wiley knew it would be a bright night.

After listening for anything out of the ordinary from normal forest sounds, Wiley crept toward the trail. Ten feet from the path, he stopped frozen in his tracks when a horse whinnied in the shadows a dozen yards away. He crouched behind the cover of a low-growing pine next to a large spruce tree and checked his position. Not liking the spot, he hoped it would do until the rider went on by. As Wiley drew his big hunting knife, the only weapon he'd brought with him, he could now hear the low clopping of several horses coming up the trail.

"Pa, it's gettin' too dark. We'll never find em' at night. Jake's like a fox." Zeke wanted to go back to Kentucky, hoping distance might ease the hurt inside from Wiley's presence. He wanted to be the one riding with Jake. But not if Jake really did put it to Sara Jean.

"You couldn't find 'im even in daylight, you dumb kid." Clem sneered. "Jest 'cause you can't, or *won't* find 'im, don't mean we can't."

"Hush," Seth sneered. He sniffed the air and suddenly reined his horse less than five feet from where Wiley crouched. With a sly grin, he said, "We'll camp here tonight. We're only a mite distant from 'em now, and they have a big surprise a-comin'."

They dismounted and began stripping the gear and saddles from their horses.

Dismayed they'd camped right in front of his hiding place, Wiley watched the three brothers unpack their bedrolls and spread them around the clearing. For a group of men who Jake said were such good trackers, he felt they'd picked a strange spot to camp. The only cover consisted of several current bushes on one side and a stand of scrubby pine near an outcropping of rocks beside the forest wall.

Wiley watched the youngest son build a small fire. He assumed it was Zeke and could see why Jake had fooled around with him. Suddenly, Wiley realized Seth was gone. He knew the man probably slipped off to look for any signs of his and Jake's presence, but had no idea which direction he went. Wiley hoped he'd gone up the trail to see if he could find any tracks. He knew there wouldn't be any since they hadn't followed the trail along here. But would he see Jake's fire?

Wiley thought of his back cover, knowing he was only partly concealed from behind by some low branches of the spruce tree. Barely breathing, he listened for any noise. Beads of sweat broke out on his forehead when he became acutely aware of the strong musty odor of his own body, a telltale giveaway of his presence.

Wiley suddenly felt the cold muzzle of a gun press against the back of his neck.

"Get up, boy, before I blow yer haid clean off," Seth sneered as he stood behind Wiley. "And toss that there knife down."

Wiley stood up, tossed his knife to the ground and put his hands into the air. He silently cursed himself for getting caught. Once again, he'd forgotten Grandpa Gray Feather's warning not to leave Jake's side.

"Who's that, Pa?" Zeke asked.

"This here's the man that stole Jake away from us twice before. I smelled 'im when we rode up. We're gonna find Jake from this here scum. Ain't we, boy!" Seth shoved the barrel of the rifle into Wiley's neck so hard he was pushed into the clearing. Wiley stood in front of the three brothers, all eyeing him with varying expressions.

Clem stared at Wiley with his jaws clenched and remembered the two times Wiley had knocked him out. He wanted to kill

Wiley slowly over a fire like he'd done so many times with opossums and squirrels.

Abe undressed Wiley with his eyes, lusted after the man's muscular body and intended to feel this beefy man squirm and kick under him as he raped and killed him.

Standing closest to Wiley, Zeke gazed at the big man with a mixture of awe and jealousy. He trembled from the masculine aroma caused by Wiley's recent running. Jake's stories about Sergeant Moss flooded his mind, and Zeke wondered if this man looked like him. He couldn't help smiling at Wiley.

Hoping for an ally among these vengeful men, Wiley smiled back.

"We got no fight with him, Pa," Zeke said, still holding Wiley's gaze. "He weren't no place near Aaron when he fell."

"I say we kill 'im slow, like an animal," Clem yelled. He lunged at Wiley and hit him across the side of the head. "That there's payin' you back for my two sore haids you gave me."

Wiley jerked sideways from the blow, causing the barrel of Seth's gun to be roughly shoved away from the back of his neck.

Seth quickly stuck the gun into Wiley's back. "Tie 'im up, Abe."

Abe walked slowly to his neatly stacked gear. When he grabbed the rope next to his things, the log rolled a bit and all his belongings fell into a pile on the ground. Angered by this, he beat the log with the rope and cursed. When he approached Wiley from behind, Abe roughly grabbed Wiley's arms and tied them high up behind his back. As he touched Wiley, Abe again resolved to kill this man while he raped him. He was so agitated now he didn't know how long he could wait.

Once he tied the last knot, Abe picked up Wiley's knife and slipped it into his own belt. He pushed Wiley into the center of the clearing, growled, "Sit down here," then glanced at Seth for a nod of approval. It didn't come.

Clem walked over and kicked Wiley in the back. Wiley fell on his face, groaning in pain.

"That there's payin' you back fer shootin' my gun outta my hands yesterday. I know it was you. Jake ain't that good a shot."

"Don't hurt him yet!" Abe yelled. He wanted Wiley to fully experience what he had in store for him. Abe grabbed Clem by the shoulders and tossed his younger brother to the ground. "I don't want 'im half dead before I have him!"

"You damn pervert," Clem yelled at Abe. "Someday I'm gonna cut your whanger off an' feed it to the hogs."

"That's enough!" Seth hollered. He usually enjoyed seeing his boys fight among themselves. It made them seem more like men rather than the whimpering dogs they really were. But not tonight. "Tie his feet, an' leave that cuss there. We got things to do."

Abe tied Wiley's feet, then followed Seth and Clem as they walked into the surrounding forest.

Lying on his side, the pain in Wiley's back began to subside. In the deep twilight, he saw the three men moving about on the edge of the clearing like ghosts. After Zeke built up the fire, Wiley could see them more clearly and realized they were laying traps around the camp, probably hoping to snare Jake if he came to his rescue. For some reason, he didn't think Jake would fall for it.

Wiley decided to say nothing, fearing whatever he said might enrage one or all of them and his chances of escape, or rescue, could be shortened considerably. He strained his arms and ankles against the ropes but couldn't get anywhere with them. He could only watch and hope Jake would come after him...and be careful if he did.

Occasionally, Wiley saw Zeke looking at him, but the young man was unwilling to help. He felt sorry for Zeke because he seemed torn between his own desires and those of his father.

Full darkness came long before the Harrises finished setting their traps. They returned to the fire at the same time Zeke's three rabbits were ready to eat. Seth untied Wiley's feet and made him sit away from the fire while they ate. None of the men offered him food. Hunger gnawed at Wiley from the aroma of the cooked meat, but he said nothing.

After eating, the Harrises sat around the fire drinking coffee. No one spoke.

Clem continually threw sticks on the small fire to make it blaze brightly. Suddenly, he forced Wiley to sit closer to the group. "Make a move, and I'll plug you."

From where he sat, Wiley could see Seth's face glaring into the flames as though his hateful thoughts made the fire burn brighter. Sparks popped into the air. Clem sat with his back to the fire, staring into the woods. Wiley couldn't see Zeke, but could feel his eyes on him.

As they sat in dead silence, Abe began twitching and wiping his forehead with the back of his hand. Suddenly, he sprang up, dumped the remains of the coffee pot on the fire and scattered the coals with his boot. In the unexpected darkness, he lunged past Clem and grabbed Wiley by the collar of his jacket. He pulled Wiley to his feet and roughly shoved him into the woods.

Abe yelled back, "Anybody that follows me gets killed."

"No!" Zeke screamed. He realized what Abe was going to do. He sprang to his feet and started to run after the two men, but Seth grabbed his leg and pulled him to the ground.

"Leave him be," Seth growled. "It'll take care of one of 'em right quick. And it'll calm Abe down a mite, too. He's been too damn jumpy lately."

It took both Seth and Clem to hold Zeke down.

Wiley couldn't see much for the first few yards until his night vision allowed him to distinguish the moon's light. Even though Abe held him by the collar, he fell a couple of times, quickly turning his body to land on his shoulder. Each time he went down, Abe roughly pulled him to his feet. Wiley heard the man breathing hard.

After they went fifty yards, they came to a small clearing. Abe shoved Wiley, and he fell face down into the tall grass. Abe pounced on him and flipped him over on his back, pinning Wiley's tied arms under his body.

As Abe straddled Wiley, he unbuckled his own belt and ripped open his pants. His long poker sprang out and stood up, the top half bending to the left. He grabbed Wiley's rawhide shirt and tried to rip it down the front but the leather wouldn't tear. Angered, he banged Wiley's head on the ground and grunted like a wild pig.

Wiley tried to lift his feet up to grab Abe around the neck like he'd done in the bar to Winder, but Abe sat too far down and he couldn't move his legs.

Abe ripped open the buttons on Wiley's pants and pulled them below his balls, then flipped Wiley back over on his stomach. He grabbed his bent whanger and rammed it into Wiley's ass. Wiley groaned in pain. Abe leaned forward, put his fingers around Wiley's throat and began choking him as he thrust his body violently.

Wiley nearly passed out from the pain in his butt. He felt the man's fingers gripping his throat, and he lurched back and forth with his whole body trying to wrestle free.

This angered Abe even more. He let go of Wiley's neck and hit him across the back of the head with his fist several times. Once again, he grabbed Wiley around the throat and squeezed.

Wiley struggled, but suddenly his mind went blank.

# CHAPTER 25

Jake poked a stick at the fire. Where was Wiley? He checked the skillet again. The potatoes had started falling apart ten minutes ago. Now they were cooking to death on a hot rock next to the glowing coals. Fully dark, he'd been feeding just enough sticks to keep a few flames, hoping Wiley would be able to find the camp.

After an hour, Jake grabbed the skillet. "Wiley can fix his own damn food," he muttered out loud. He ate all the bacon and crusted potatoes, then cleaned the skillet by rubbing it with dry grass. He poured himself a cup of coffee, leaned back and stared into the fire.

Suddenly, Jake sat straight up. "Damn! Wiley could be in trouble!" He slid a stick through the handle of the coffee pot, pulled it away from the fire and maneuvered the pot onto the flat rock he'd used to keep the food warm. After Jake loaded his gun, he spun the cylinder and holstered it. He tossed only enough dirt on the fire to smother the flames, leaving the glowing coals. In the darkness, he had to wait until the glow of the firelight in his eyes faded and his night vision kicked in before he could start searching for Wiley.

Carefully, Jake wove his way through the deadfall and ran swiftly back down the trail. He didn't know which direction Wiley went, but assumed his partner would go back the way they'd come. He stayed on the Ute trail to make better time, to where he didn't know, but didn't believe Wiley was anywhere close by.

Behind a thin veil of clouds, the moon's light was adequate for Jake to see the lay of the land. The Harrises could be anywhere, and if they'd captured Wiley, they could probably locate him as well, especially since he wasn't being as silent as he should. But his thoughts centered on Wiley in the hands of those treacherous men.

After running almost a half mile, Jake stopped and crouched behind a bush to catch his breath. A slight breeze blowing into his face carried a whiff of cooked rabbit. The Harrises! He sprang to his feet, left the trail and sprinted in a wide circle to his right, staying in the deepest shadows. After he'd gone fifty yards, he saw the wink of a camp fire to his left and stopped dead.

Jake wondered if the fire really came from the Harris' camp. Would they ever build a fire after dark? Suddenly, an incident from his youth flashed into his mind. He'd been with his father, the Harrises and two other men from town as part of a search for a horse thief who'd been stealing from the local farmers. Only ten at the time, he'd begged his father to let him help since his favorite colt had been stolen. He'd gotten to go and when their group settled down for the night, Seth, Aaron and Abe spent the evening setting traps in the woods around the camp then built a big fire. Seth had been positive the thief would investigate and be snared in the traps. At first, the others had tried to stop them, but Seth swore by this method of catching the culprit, and after he and his boys caused a fuss, the rest of the group finally went along with it just to shut them up.

Jake shook his head when he remembered the thief had been caught that same night, a mile away, by another group camped in total darkness. Later, even after the rustler had admitted shying away from the blazing fire, Seth had blamed the members of his group for making too much noise.

Irritated the Harrises might be trying to lure him by the same method, Jake whispered, "Who do they think I am, some damn greenhorn." After he silently asked his friend Jesus for help, he became convinced Wiley had been captured and resolved to save his blood brother no matter what the cost.

Rather than get closer to Seth's possible traps, Jake continued his wide circle, always keeping the fire in sight. Almost back to the Ute trail south of the Harris' campsite, Jake saw the fire suddenly wink out. He thought of the terrifying camping trip when he, Abe and Clem had gone together to celebrate his own thirteenth birthday. Jake shuddered when he remembered that Abe had stared at him all funny-like while they ate. Later, Abe had doused the fire, then lunged at him and ripped the shirt off his back. Clem hollered and came running, but Abe backhanded him across the face and sent him sprawling on the ground. Abe yelled at Clem to get lost or he'd beat him to death.

Jake clenched his teeth. He could still feel the pain of Abe raping him and was glad he hadn't started killing his victims yet. He'd beaten the shit out of Abe a few years ago after he'd tried it again.

Before Jake could figure out what to do, he heard heavy footsteps approaching from the direction of the camp. By the loud rustling of the brush, he could tell the men coming his way weren't being cautious. One of them even seemed to be stumbling occasionally. Jake kept to the dense shadows until he found a spruce tree. He crouched behind it and drew his gun.

The men stopped their advance thirty yards away and Jake carefully inched closer. He heard grunts and a few agonized groans of someone in pain, then a few slaps. After a loud curse, Jake recognized Abe's voice and started running toward them. He saw the black shape of a man sitting on the ground, reaching out to something in front of him. Without knowing what Abe was doing, Jake clouted him over the head with his gun. After Abe toppled over unconscious, Jake saw the prone figure of a man lying face down on the ground, his pants pulled below his firm white buttocks. Jake flung Abe to the side and rolled the man over on his back. It was Wiley! He looked dead!

Jake slid his arms around Wiley, crushed him to his chest and began shaking in convulsive sorrow.

"Oh Wiley, Wiley," he cried softly. "I knew you shouldn't a been with me."

Jake lowered his blood brother and kissed his dirt-streaked face, then squeezed him to his chest again.

"You can't take him, Jesus!"

Once more, Jake cradled Wiley in his arms and kissed him.

Suddenly, Wiley's limp body jerked violently, and Jake heard a gasp from his mouth. "Wha...where am I?" He gulped air. "Jake, where's Jake?"

"Wiley! You're alive! I'm here, Wiley. Thank you, Jesus, for givin' my Wiley back!" Jake squeezed Wiley and sobbed.

"Jake, untie my arms," Wiley gasped. He could barely breathe with his face pressed into Jake's coat.

Still sobbing, Jake wiped his eyes, pulled out his knife and carefully cut the ropes binding Wiley's arms.

Wiley grabbed Jake and pulled him on top of himself. "Jake, I thought I was dead for sure." His voice quavered from the terrible realization of how close to death he'd really been.

The blood brothers clung to each other in the moonlight, both sobbing softly. Jake kissed Wiley's face again and again, but suddenly composed himself.

"Wiley, can you walk? We gotta get the hell outta here before Seth starts missin' Abe."

"I think so." Wiley tried to stand. After getting to his knees, he became light-headed and sat back down on his feet. "Better tie Abe up," Wiley said as he waited for the dizziness to pass. He wanted to kill Abe but knew Jake would never forgive him if he did.

After Jake tied Abe's hands and feet, he helped Wiley stand. Wiley groaned from the pain in his back where Clem had kicked him, and his butt ached, deep inside.

Jake gently brushed away the dirt and pine needles stuck to Wiley's privates, pulled up his pants and held on to him while the groggy man buttoned them up. Wiley put his arm over Jake's shoulders and walked slowly at first until he got back full confidence in his legs.

When they reached their camp, Jake grabbed his saddle bags and found the hardtack. He also unwraped the jerky and dried fruit and made Wiley eat some. The coffee was still warm, and they both had a cup.

"Wiley, I thought you'd been gone too long an' got rankled an' ate all the food." Jake grinned sheepishly. "I ain't never gonna do that again."

"I don't care, Jake," Wiley said softly. "I'm just glad you were there." Still stunned from the ordeal, Wiley tried to ignore the pain in his butt from being raped. He remembered suddenly awakening from blankness, and shuddered.

Neither felt like traveling, but they packed their gear, saddled the horses and rode north, wanting to put some distance between them and the Harrises. They stayed on the Ute trail and saw the lights of the Benson and Monterey mines below. As Bill had mentioned, the trail curved to the east and followed the southern slope of Iron Mountain. As the eastern horizon began to glow, they crossed a set of train tracks. A short time later, they saw the dim lights of Como to the south.

Cold and hungry from riding all night, they stopped behind a stand of Englemann spruce and tied their horses. Jake cleared a space on the ground and built a small fire to take the chill off their bodies.

Sitting on a log with their shoulders touching, they shared a bite to eat and watched the new day begin.

## CHAPTER 26

Pyramids of flaming pink-gold surrounded the still shadowed basin of South Park as the rising sun lit up the Sangre de Cristos to the south and the Collegiates and Buffalo Peaks to the southwest. The golden slopes of Mount Silverheels blocked any view of the Mosquito Range, farther west, as they also received the early morning glory.

Jake tore his eyes away from the vistas and glanced at the handsome man next to him. He slid his arm between Wiley's legs and squeezed his thigh. "Wiley, the way this here day's openin' up...I ain't never seen nothin' so beaut'ful my whole life." He choked back a sob from being able to witness it with Wiley, the only person he'd ever truly loved his whole life, and had almost lost.

Wiley slid his arm over Jake's shoulders and pulled him closer. He felt calmer now that the terrible night had disappeared and a new day brightened.

"I love it here, Jake," Wiley said. "For some reason, despite last night, I feel like I'm finally home." He gazed out at the vast panorama. "This seems like such a wild and struggling land."

"It shore is that, sonny," cackled a high-pitched voice behind them.

In one fluid motion, Wiley sprang to his feet, wheeled around and drew his gun faster than the eye could see.

Startled by the voice and Wiley's instant response, Jake gasped, turned his head and saw the barrel of a rifle pointing at them. When he saw it wasn't one of the Harrises holding it, he stood up and rested his hand on the butt of his gun.

"Now jest hold on there, gents," the man warned, shocked at how fast Wiley's gun appeared. "I ain't no scorpion crawlin' down yer neck. Thunder Joe's my handle, an' I'm usually travelin' these parts. What're you gents doin' here?" He lowered his rifle and half smiled at them. His face wrinkled like a dried apple.

Open-mouthed, the brothers stared at the man in greasy buckskins. Clumps of matted gray hair, mashed down by a filthy leather hat, stuck to the collar of his rawhide jacket. Two beady eyes peered from a brown crinkled face, partially hidden behind a straggly tobacco-stained beard. A head shorter than the brothers and skinny as a fence post, the man made Jake think of the last scarecrow he'd made. He couldn't guess the man's age but knew he was old.

Jake took an instant liking to the mountain man and extended his hand. "I'm Jake, an' this here's Wiley. I heard about you a couple times in Alma, an' now I get to meet you."

Thunder Joe gripped Jake's hand and shook it once.

Wiley hesitated before he holstered his gun. While he shook Thunder Joe's hand, he remarked, "You certainly snuck up on us quietly."

"Quietly!" Joe shouted. "While you two was gawkin' at the sunrise, I jest walked right up. Out in these here parts, you gotta do yer gawkin' and yer listenin' at the same time or yer dead." He grinned and the brothers noticed many of his teeth were missing. "An' you can't stare inta the flames of a fire, like you did last night, sonny."

Shocked, Jake asked, "You was watchin' me last night?"

Joe grinned wider. "Shore was. Had to stay a might distance away so you wouldn't smell me. Hee, hee, hee."

The blood brothers knew exactly what he was referring to. They both had flinched at the terrible odor of the old man and now shifted to a position upwind from him.

"What does them loonies want with you gents, anyhow?" Joe asked.

"They want me dead," Jake replied flatly.

"They're accusing Jake of getting a girl in their family pregnant," Wiley broke in. "Since I'm Jake's blood brother, they want me dead also."

"So yer them blood brothers folks been waggin' about in town." Thunder Joe observed them carefully, then nodded his head. "You'll do." He cocked his head at Wiley. "But you can't pull more'a them stunts like you done last night. Got yerself caught, didn't you. Much of a tracker, are you?"

Shocked the old man knew about that, also, Wiley let his irritation show that his skill as a tracker had been questioned.

"Don't mean to rankle you cuz I knows yer good," Joe said. "Why, I had a son-of-a-time tryin' to keep up with you last night. Even lost you a time'r two. But out here, you gotta remember smells carry far an' fast. You was up wind from them, an' ol' Pappy smelled you right off. You was right, though, not sayin' nothin' to any of 'em. Three'a them loonies would'a plugged you sure."

"But how was you in both places at once?" Jake asked.

Joe cackled at the thought. "I weren't," he finally said. "I first come on you fellers when you was makin' yer camp. Mighty fine job you did, too." He nodded at Wiley. "When you started runnin', I follered an' watched you get caught.

"Now, it ain't my way to butt into other people's affairs, but if they was gonna kill you right off, I would'a stepped in. When I seed them loonies makin' traps in the woods, I run back to warn yer friend." Joe shook his head. "Makin' them traps and keepin' that dang fire goin' was the dumbest thing I ever did see."

Joe looked at Jake. "Got back to yer camp an' saw you starin' inta the fire. Can't do that cuz you get blinded to the dark. If you'd a sat there any longer clearin' yer eyes of them flames, I reckon yer friend here'd be dead."

"I was wonderin' where Wiley was," Jake said.

"Shore you was. An' if you hadn't gotten the idea in yer head to go lookin' for 'im, I'd a skeered the pants off'a you. Hee, hee, hee." Thunder Joe slapped his leg. "You done some mighty good figurin' where yer brother was, though." He put his wrinkled old hand on Wiley's shoulder. "If it would'a been me, I'd a kilt that big one right there on the spot!"

"We couldn't outright kill him!" Jake yelled.

Wiley's face remained impassive but his jaws tightened.

"I admire yer ree-spect fer life, sonny," Joe said, "but sometimes the odds need narrowin'. He was rammin' an' chokin' yer brother. Don't that mean nothin'?"

"Yes, but..." Jake stammered. "They're my neighbors from back in Kentucky. I can't *kill* 'em."

"Where you been, anyhow?" Joe asked, glaring at Jake. "You been sittin' on yer momma's knee readin' the Good Book all yer life? Now, I ain't sayin' nothin' agin the Good Book, mind you. Read it myself when I run across Father Dyer. But our Maker don't 'spect us to be yeller bellies. Gotta look out for yerselves, gents, an' I mean jest that." Joe lifted his rifle and put it over his left forearm. "Now we best find us some cover, cuz we gots company. It's yer neighbors." Joe pointed in the direction Jake and Wiley had traveled earlier. "See? They're comin' round that mountain over yonder." They saw Seth in the lead, followed by Clem and Zeke. Closing up the back, the sullen hulk of Abe rode with his head down and his hat pulled over his eyes. Wiley hoped he had a ferocious headache.

The three men faded into the brush on both sides of the trail, Wiley down the slope and Jake and Joe higher up on the opposite side. Their horses were well hidden behind a nearby spruce grove.

Jake turned to Joe and whispered, "Why you helpin' us now?"

"Didn't know who you was last night. Like I said, it ain't my way to be buttin' in where I ain't needed. I don't reckon you boys need help now, but if it's killin' they's after, it appears the only one that's gonna give it to them is me." Joe shook his head. "An' a couple of 'em shore needs killin'."

"Not Zeke," Jake said, quickly. "He's the one in the green shirt. He ain't like the rest of 'em, an' we used to go huntin' together. Fooled around some, too." Jake glanced at Joe.

Joe grinned.

As the four riders approached, Thunder Joe shouted, "Hold up there! Who are you, an' what're you doin' in these here parts? I got you covered, so put yer hands up an' state yer business!" He cocked his rifle and leveled it at Seth as he stepped onto the trail.

Seth yanked his horse to a stop and yelled, "Ain't nonna your affair who we are and what we're doin'!" He scowled at Thunder Joe standing in the middle of the trail.

"If yer thinkin' of killin' them two brothers yer after, yer askin' fer a heap of trouble neighbor," Joe cackled.

"So you've seen 'em," Seth sneered. "We ain't got no troubles with you. Jest tell us where they are, and we'll let you alone. Jake got my Sara Jean all knocked up with child and won't marry her. That's a killin' offense where I come from, so you stay out of it."

"Ain't nobody gonna do no killin' here, 'cept maybe me," Joe said. "B'sides, how d'you know Jake done it? Was you watchin'?"

"No, I weren't watchin'!" Seth shouted. "Sara Jean told me Jake done it."

"She's most likely lyin'," Joe said. "Mebby it was that big dumb lookin' one in the back that done it. He'd most likely stick his thing in anythin' that even looked like a hole."

Abe's head snapped up, and he growled, "I'll kill you fer that!" He spurred his horse around the others. Seth held out his arm to stop him, but Abe shoved it, pointed his gun at the old mountain man and fired. The bullet whizzed above Joe's head.

When Joe saw Abe coming, he shifted his rifle from Seth to the oncoming rider and pulled the trigger just after Abe's bullet went by.

Seth yelled, "No! Don't shoot!"

But it was too late. Joe's bullet caught Abe right between the eyes, blowing out the back of his head. His body slid off the horse, rolled down the hill and stopped, face up, a few feet from where Wiley crouched. Stunned for a moment seeing Abe's open eyes staring up at nothing, Wiley glanced up the hill as Seth and Clem raised their rifles. Zeke had already leaped off his horse and found cover behind a large pine tree.

Wiley suddenly heard a shot from up the hill. Clem's rifle flew out of his hands, and he screamed in pain. Wiley sighted his own rifle and shot the Sharps out of Seth's hands. He knew neither man was seriously hurt by the impact, but it would be a few hours before they could use their hands. Both their rifles had been rendered useless.

Holding his arms in pain and gritting his teeth, Seth growled, "You had no cause to kill Abe."

"Ain't no law in these parts sayin' I can't defend myself agin some loonie tryin' to kill me," Joe snapped. "You fellers shore are the dumbest bunch'a scoundrels I ever did see. Settin' them traps last night with a full fire goin' proved it right off. I've a mind to kill y'all right here an' be done with it."

Jake and Wiley approached the riders from either side. As Jake came into view, Clem glared at him hatefully and gritted his teeth in pain. "I'll kill you, Jake, if it's the last thing I ever do."

"But I didn't do nothin' to Sara Jean. She's lyin' about me. I ain't never even kissed her. Not even once."

"She must be powerful ugly," Joe quipped.

Jake frowned at Thunder Joe. "She ain't ugly. I just never wanted to kiss no woman. 'Specially not Sara Jean. An' since the time I saw Clem kissin' her, I thought--"

"You lie!" Clem screamed. "I ain't never kissed Sara Jean! Honest, Pa!" He squirmed in his saddle.

"Right," Wiley broke in. "But who's going to believe you if Sara Jean's baby looks like you?"

"Hee, hee, hee," Thunder Joe hooted, keeping his rifle pointed at Seth's chest.

Wiley smiled, realizing he'd made a funny comment.

"Enough!" Seth yelled. "I don't want to hear no more of them lies from you two. Jake, I'll blame you for Sara Jean's baby 'til the day I die. An' it's your fault Aaron and Abe're dead."

"Don't you go blamin' Jake fer that last one!" Thunder Joe shouted. "I kilt him, an' you damn well better give me the credit. Now you'd best be gettin' back to where you come from an' see who that baby looks like before you go blamin' Jake." He glanced up at Clem still squirming in his saddle. "Sittin' on a burr there, sonny?" Joe pointed his rifle back at Seth. "Now, get yer boy that's hidin' in them trees and get the hell outta here."

"We're gonna bury Abe before we leave," Seth snapped.

"Well, get to it then, before I change my mind an' jest shoot y'all."

Seth called Zeke, and the three remaining Harrises climbed down the hill covered at gunpoint by the others. Since neither Seth or Clem could hold a shovel, Jake and Zeke took turns digging. Before placing the body in the hole, Wiley retrieved his own knife from Abe's belt. He helped Jake fill in the hole with black dirt and pile rocks over the mound to keep animals from digging up the body. Seth said a few words over the grave, and all six men stood a few moments with their heads bowed. The silence was broken by a few sniffles from Zeke.

Zeke suddenly turned to Jake. His tear-streaked face mirrored the shock of Abe's death and also of Jake's comment about Clem kissing Sara Jean. "Jake, why'd you say you seen Clem kissin' Sara Jean? I think you're lyin'."

Jake smiled at Zeke. "I ain't the one lyin', Zeke." He looked at Clem. "Now I know you done it, Clem. Never gave it much thought before, but since I seen you kissin' Sara Jean out by Hooter's Pond, then seein' you squirmin' in your saddle up there on the hill, I sure do think you're the guilty one. An' I know why you an' Sara Jean are blamin' me. You don't want your own Pa to shoot you dead."

"You lie!" Clem screamed. "I'm gonna kill you slow over a fire like an animal, so's I can hear you scream. I never done nothin' to Sara Jean! Honest, Pa!" He searched Seth's face with terror filled eyes.

Seth glared at Jake first, then at Clem. "I believe you, boy. For now."

Zeke stared at Clem for a moment, then turned and gave Jake a slight smile. After glancing at Wiley, he turned and trudged up the hill to his horse. Seth and Clem followed.

As the Harrises mounted up, Joe raised his rifle and pointed it at them. "My advice is to get outta these here parts before I come huntin' you like rats!"

The three men headed their horses back down the trail toward Iron Mountain, but after riding a couple hundred yards they stopped. Expecting this, Joe sighted his rifle and shot a hole through the top of Seth's black hat. The Harrises spurred their horses into a gallop and disappeared from view.

While Joe and Wiley went to get the horses, Jake squatted on a flat rock beside the path and stared down the slope at Abe's grave. When the others returned, he jumped to his feet. "I sure am obliged to you, Joe, for helpin' us. But it don't hardly seem possible Abe's dead."

Joe laughed. "You gents didn't need help, but if it weren't fer me, that big loonie'd still be runnin' loose. Sort'a evens the odds."

Jake dug a little hole in the path with the toe of his boot. "I'm sorry about Abe bein' dead, but after what he done to Wiley last night, an' all them others he killed, ain't nothin' else could'a been done with him."

"You're right about that," Wiley said. He tousled Jake's hair. "Let's get going. We have a long way to go."

"An' jest where you two goin' sa-dang fast?" Joe asked. "We jest met, an' now you're traipsin' off like a couple rabbits with a dang coyote after 'em."

"We can't tell nobody where we're goin'," Jake said. "'Ceptin' Bill an' Miss Castille. She knows 'cause we're workin' for her now."

"Jake!" Wiley yelled.

"Hee, hee, hee." Joe slapped his leg. "I ain't heered nobody spill beans so innocent-like my whole life."

Jake instantly got pouty-faced. "Now, what'd I say?"

"Hee, hee, hee."

Wiley tried not to laugh. "Jake, you just gave away where we're going."

"I did not! I only said we was work..." Jake's face turned crimson, and he poked at the hole in the path with his boot. "Hell, Wiley, I didn't know what I was sayin'."

"Mighty fine woman, that Belinda," Thunder Joe said as he climbed into his saddle. "I shore won't tell nobody yer there. Mount up, gents, an I'll show the way. I'm passin' by there anyhow goin' to Ben Harrington's Ranch. There's some big doin's down at Ben's, an' I always stop at the Castille Ranch on my way there fer the best eats this side the Miss'ippi River. That Soarin' Raven shore can cook, but don't get her riled or you'll be the next thing fer dinner."

As they descended Boreas Mountain, the rolling hills of South Park stretched fifty miles in front of them. The surrounding snowcapped peaks, now in full sunlight, ringed the park on all sides.

Jake stopped Mac. "Wiley, lookit them mountains all around an' them little mountains in the middle. Kind'a makes me hungry."

"Hungry? Jake, I don't understand."

Jake pointed at the low hills in the center of South Park. "Them small mountains look like the apple bumps in Ma's pies, an' them big mountains all around are like the crust bumps on the edges."

"Dang if you ain't right, Jake," Joe cackled. "Jest you wait 'til we get to Belinda's. Soarin' Raven makes the best gol-durn apple pie you ever tasted. Ol' Jawbone here'll stand on his head fer a piece'a that pie." Joe patted his horse on the neck.

After riding through the outskirts of Como, the men followed Crooked Creek south. Rather than using Red Hill Pass, they crossed a spine-like range farther south. When they reached the banks of Bristol Lakes, they stopped and dismounted.

After stripping the gear and saddles off their horses and rubbing them down, Jake pulled out the three shriveled apples he'd bought at Mercer's general store. He gave one to Mac and one to Buddy. The third apple he tossed in the air, caught it and gave it to Jawbone.

In unison, the blood brothers pulled off their clothes and dived naked into the brackish water of the smallest of the three lakes. They swam around, played grab-ass and splashed each other like two kids. Propped against a large rock on the bank, Thunder Joe watched them, chuckling to himself.

"Ain't you gonna bathe?" Jake yelled at Joe.

"Hell no!" Joe replied. "I already done took my spring bath over a month ago. Ain't due for another one 'til June'er Joo-ly. Can't be takin' too many of them baths. Rots yer skin right off the bone, water does."

Jake and Wiley grinned at each other. They charged up the slope, grabbed the kicking, screaming and cussing old mountain man and dragged him into the water, buckskins and all. As they gave him a good scrubbing, a brown scummy film began coating the top of the water a short distance out from the thrashing trio. It took the two younger men an hour of holding Joe down and washing him before he smelled any better at all.

"Them buckskins have soaked up years'a stink!" Jake yelled. "They ought'a be taken off yer body an' burnt up. Wiley, we ain't never gonna get all the stink out of 'em."

"I'll cut yer dang balls off an' feed 'em to the damn coyotes!" Joe screeched as he bobbed up and down in the water. He cussed and sputtered through the whole ordeal.

Finally, the brothers relented and let go of Joe. He scrambled out of the chest-deep water and flung himself on the bank, gasping for breath.

Wiley pointed at the water. The brown scum rapidly approached them. "Jake, let's get out of here before that stuff rots *our* skin." They laughed and scrambled out of the fouled lake.

As they dressed, Jake and Wiley ignored Joe's stream of cussing. As soon as Jake pulled out the gingham bag of doughnuts and the bottle of whiskey, the old mountain man stopped shouting and his eyes bulged.

"Bear sign!" Joe yelled.

"What?" Jake crinkled his nose and looked at Wiley.

Joe grabbed a doughnut out of the bag and held it up. "Bear sign." He took a big bite.

"Why're they called that?" Jake asked.

With his mouth full, Joe held the doughnut up again. "Jest look at it an' you'll know why." He reached for the bottle. "Gimme a swig or two outta that bottle an' all's fergiven."

Jake examined a doughnut. The simple twist of dough made him think of a turd. He absentmindedly handed the bottle to the old mountain man.

Joe took a healthy swig, rolled his eyes back and sat down with a thump. "Ah! You boys shore know how to make a tortured ol' man feel better." He took another swig and handed the bottle to Wiley.

After they ate all the "bear sign" and drained the bottle, the three men began laughing and singing on the banks of the small lake with brown, scummy water.

# CHAPTER 27

The noon sun blazed in a cloudless sky as the three men saddled their horses. Still damp, Thunder Joe's buckskins seemed several shades lighter. As they dried, their rank odor diminished. They walked the horses through the shallow water of the Horseshoe River for five miles to erase their tracks, but upon reaching the hills, the river became so twisty they left it and traveled on higher ground.

Jake drank in the vastness. Riding with Wiley and Thunder Joe, he felt safe even though they were out in the open. Occasionally, Jake allowed Mac to lag behind and he watched Wiley. Every time he did, he felt prickles over his entire body. He could hardly believe this handsome man had wanted to be his blood brother. Jake loved the way Wiley sat in the saddle, so straight, and with every step Buddy took, Wiley's clothes strained against his muscles. Jake thanked Jesus for sending him the perfect friend, at just the right time, and for letting Wiley keep his life last night.

Wiley scanned the terrain in awe. He wished Hector could see this. It seemed so long ago that the two of them would sit up late in the dorm lounge talking...about everything. Hector usually brought up geology. Wiley chuckled silently. The friendly arguments they'd gotten into were most often about land formations and evolution. Hector firmly believed the writings of Lyell and Darwin, that it took millions of years for any change to occur. Wiley never knew why, but he just couldn't buy into that. He believed it even less now. This land seemed raw.

Deep in his bones, Wiley sensed that a monumental event had shaped the entire region. Once heaved and broken, time not only had scoured the rocks but also had softened and rounded the lower hills. But not a million years' worth. He noticed only the tops of the hills had trees, and wondered if this had been an inland sea and the salt had leached out of the soil only halfway down the slopes. No trees grew anywhere on the soft, rippled plains that reminded him of olive-colored velvet. From everything he'd gleaned from Hector or read on his own, Wiley settled on ten thousand years since this uplift happened. But geology had been Hector's major, not his.

Wiley realized that ages ago the Horseshoe River must have been fifty yards wide and gouged deep into the terrain. It was barely five yards wide now, and resembled a silver snake as it twisted back on itself, or meandered in graceful curves through the lush hay that carpeted the ancient bed. Clumps of dark brown cinquefoil shrubs gave the illusion of miniature grazing cattle. Glancing at Jake, he saw his partner grinning at him. He loved Jake, and he loved this country.

Jake swept his arm out to his side. "Wiley, lookit all the tall grass along this here stream. It's all standin' up dry jest waitin' for them cows to munch on it. Bingsly sure got the best land away from Miss Castille."

"Hee, hee, hee."

Jake snapped his head to the other side and glared at Thunder Joe. "Now, what'd I say?"

"Dang if you ain't the funniest jasper I ever did see. Bingsly is it? Hee, hee, hee." Joe slapped his leg. "That name shore-the-hell fits."

Later, riding forty yards ahead of the others, Joe reined his horse at the base of a hill. When the partners caught up, he pointed. A herd of cattle had planted themselves in the waist-high grass next to the water. At first, the men only saw full grown animals, but as they rode closer, many three-week-old calves began bawling.

"These're Belinda's cattle," Joe said. "We jest as well move 'em back on her land so Billingsly's men don't get 'em. Them calves ain't branded, and he's likely to grab 'em once they're weaned." He spurred his horse toward the herd, yelling in a high-pitched, raspy squeal.

"Titty-yi-yi-yi! Get along, you doggies!"

Jake laughed out loud when the cattle didn't move one inch. Content where they were, most of them turned toward Joe and cow-eyed him. Tall, rich timothy hay and plenty of clear, cold water--this was heaven, and they weren't budging.

Wiley rode up the bank of the river to a high point overlooking the area. He scanned the horizon and examined every rock and clump of sage. Satisfied no one was close by, he drew his gun, spurred Buddy down the slope toward the herd and shot twice in the air. This got the cattle's attention, and they began moving slowly toward the southwest. Wiley shot a few more times, and the cattle began running.

"Don't shoot no more!" Joe yelled. "Them young'uns can't go much faster in this here grass. "

Buddy knew what was happening more than Wiley did. The horse darted back and forth, keeping the cattle bunched on the right, and several times Wiley almost flew out of his saddle. By carefully observing the cattle's actions and how Buddy responded, he soon got a fair idea what to do.

Jake did an excellent job keeping the cattle bunched on the left. Joe and Wiley occasionally watched him in amazement. He could catch and turn any of the wayward cattle he rode after, and from all appearances enjoyed doing it. But Wiley knew it was Joe who kept the cattle moving forward. It seemed Joe knew every inclination of the cattle long before they knew it themselves. It was obvious he'd done this many times before with Jawbone. The two of them moved with the grace of dancers, wooing the herd forward. This, plus the raspy way Thunder Joe sang to the cattle in his high-pitched voice, so impressed Wiley that he suddenly realized a man could obtain a master's degree even in the wilderness.

After driving the cattle up the banks, they spotted a small cone-shaped mountain a mile away. From that distance, the steep sides appeared black from the thick growth of pine. On its top, jagged pillars of pinkish-tan rock thrust forty feet into the air. Wiley thought of the castles of Europe.

"Let's run 'em to Pinnacle Rock," Joe yelled as he pointed to the mountain. He turned herd toward it.

Thick, blinding dust billowed up from the cattle as they moved across the gently sloping basin between the Horseshoe River and Pinnacle Rock. The three men were hard pressed to keep the young ones from slipping away in the choking clouds.

At one point, Jake appeared out of nowhere and rode up to Wiley. His hair and beard were covered with a fine tan dust. Shocked to see him like this, Wiley realized Jake would still be a strikingly handsome man at fifty.

"Wiley, I sure do like the way you look with that there beard, even bein' it's almost white." Jake grinned and rode back to his side of the herd.

Wiley put his hand to his face, rubbed the stubble, and smiled. Why not? He'd never considered wearing a beard back East. But here in the West, a beard represented the whole concept of what he was doing now. Best of all, Jake liked it.

After they drove the cattle by the eastern side of Pinnacle Rock, they turned the herd southwest toward Walton Spring.

Walton Spring? Wiley remembered the name. Belinda said Jason Moore had been shot to death there. He looked around and realized there wasn't a tree for a mile in any direction to offer any cover, except on the slopes of Pinnacle Rock. The small mountain could be seen from everywhere, and the rocks on the top were sure to have hiding places. Wiley calculated Pinnacle Rock to be six hundred yards from Walton Spring. A considerable distance, but someone with a good rifle, say a Sharps Buffalo gun or a Springfield, could pick a man off his horse. Considering this possibility, he wondered how carefully the Castille crew searched for Jason's murderer.

Once they reached Walton Spring, the men bunched the cattle and circled the herd until they settled down. Wet and swampy from the seepage of water, new grass had already grown six inches tall, and an abundance of dry hay from the year before provided the cattle with conditions similar to where they were before. Mothers and babies seemed content.

After rubbing their horses down with bunches of dry grass, the trio sat on a small rock outcropping to rest. Wiley dug into his pocket, pulled out the fixings for a cigarette and began rolling one. "Smoke?" he asked Joe.

"Shore do." Thunder Joe caught the pouch. After he rolled his smoke, he offered the bag to Jake who turned it down.

Staring at the old mountain man, Jake finally asked, "Why're you named Thunder Joe since you hate water so bad?"

"Ain't got nothin' to do with a dang lightnin' storm. Got me that name in El Paso years ago. Ate me a whole plate of them Mexican beans, and fer two days I was fartin' like I never heard before. Folks tried to run me outta town fer the noise, but I managed to stay around outta hearin' distance. Only the bartender in Josie's Cantina knowed my real name, so folks jest started callin' me Thunder Joe. I kind'a took to it."

Jake's face turned serious. "Now I know what that brown stuff was on the water, back when we was scrubbin' you."

Joe hooted and hollered and slapped his legs in laughter.

Chuckling himself, Wiley said, "See, Jake. You make people laugh."

Jake's smile reached his bright blue eyes, and Wiley realized it was the first time he'd seen him smile that genuinely. Great emotion welled up inside him seeing Jake so pleased with himself. He jumped to his feet and walked away so the others wouldn't see his misty eyes. After he calmed down, Wiley rejoined the others and Joe decided to get moving.

While the men ran the cattle, the sun had sunk within a half hour of setting behind the Mosquito Range. They decided to camp in the area rather than ride on to the Castille ranch. Mounting up, they rode west toward the eastern slope of Bristlecone Peak, a little over two miles from Pinnacle Rock. Jake thought Bristlecone Peak was two mountains since the northern cone was separated from the rocky, southern peak by a low saddle.

Joe headed for a long ridge stretching out from the base of the southern end of Bristlecone Peak. As they approached the long finger of land, Jake pointed to a huge rock at the end of a closer ridge that ended abruptly with a fifteen-foot cliff.

"Wiley, lookit that big rock. It's like them rocks on the top of that Pinkle Rock we just rode by."

"Pinnacle Rock, Jake. It's the same kind of granite."

Joe rode out onto the flat ledge that formed the cliff and dismounted. "I've camped here more'n once."

"Damn! This sure is a perfect spot to camp," Jake said. "Wiley, we could live here."

"We sure could, but I don't see any water close by."

"A spring runs outta the cliff down below," Joe said. "That's why I camp here."

After they unsaddled and picketed their horses in an aspen grove close by, Thunder Joe showed them how to climb the huge boulders that commanded a view of the entire region. On top of the rocks, they found a basin-shaped depression deep enough to hold a considerable amount of water. Joe pointed out the various kinds of animal droppings scattered nearby. Wiley recognized squirrel, weasel and pack rat droppings and wondered how a porcupine could get up there.

Gazing into the vastness, Jake thought of his mother. She would have liked Wiley and would have liked them being blood brothers. All the while he was growing up, she had told him not to listen to his father's hateful remarks about him liking men. "Making you that way is part of God's plan," she'd say. "Jesus wants us all to rest our heads on his breast the way John did. Most women have no trouble doing it, but men do. Only men like you know how, Jake."

Awed by the vast expanse of South Park, Wiley wondered again if this area was the bed of an ancient sea, some thirty miles wide and fifty miles long, completely surrounded on all sides by high mountains. He glanced behind him at Bristlecone Peak and wondered if the mountain might have been a volcano that long ago blew its top, littering the area with a radiating jumble of enormous boulders. Now, covered with soil and trees, the base of the mountain from this vantage point resembled a series of finger-like ridges of an out- spread hand.

Since Bristlecone Peak was the tallest peak in the center of this huge area of flat plains and low rounded hills, Wiley assumed the mountain would have provided the Ute Indians with an unbroken view of their territory. His stomach tightened when he remembered snatches of conversations he'd overheard on the train from Denver. One group boasted of the cruel treatment of the Utes by miners and later by ranchers, who had all claimed this land as their own. Amid the chatter in the dining car, Wiley had zeroed in on a woman talking about Chief Eagle Rising's demise in trying to save his tribe from being forced out of this land forever. The woman had said the chief died of a broken heart after learning the United States government had no intention of letting the Utes stay, even though they had signed a treaty stating they could. Wiley wished he'd known Chief Eagle Rising, and he suddenly missed Grandpa Gray Feather.

The purple sky of late evening made the distant mountains seem like black cardboard cutouts. As the brothers sat wrapped in thoughts, Joe stretched out his arm and pointed to the nearby ridge fingering its way toward the southwest. "Beyond that ridge, six miles'er so, is Belinda's ranch," he said softly.

"Joe, did you know Chief Eagle Rising?" Wiley asked.

Joe snapped his head around. "Where'd you hear'a him?"

"Someone on the train from Denver mentioned him. Was he a Ute chief?"

"Shore was," Joe said. "A fine feller he was, too. I knowed him ever since I come here. He died in Leadville some years back. Folks say they still see 'im wanderin' the woods around Alma and Mount Silverheels. I was hopin' to run across 'im when I first seen you gents makin' your camp. Some folks in Alma said they'd seen 'im that same day standin' high up on the mountain. Soarin' Raven--you'll meet her tomorrow--said she's seen 'im standin' up there on Bristlecone Peak. They say he's wearin' gold feathers in his braids."

"Golden feathers?" Wiley asked.

"That's what they say. Why?"

"There's an ancient Indian legend about golden feathers," Wiley said. "My grandfather told it to me. I haven't thought of it for years."

"Don't you go believin' no Indian legends 'less they come di-rectly from an Indian," Joe said. "The white man don't know nothin' from nothin' when it comes to things like that. 'Cept fer me, a'course."

"My grandfather was an Iroquois brave," Wiley said defensively.

Joe glanced over at Wiley. "Well, that there does make a difference, an' that means you got Indian in you. I'd give my eye teeth to be part Indian. 'Course, I ain't had most'a my teeth fer more years than I kin remember."

After they climbed down the granite chimney, Wiley helped Jake cook a meal of bacon and potatoes. Joe climbed to the bottom of the cliff and filled their canteens from the spring so they could have coffee with their meal.

They ate ravenously.

After a few cups of coffee, Jake and Wiley spread out their bedrolls and within minutes were sound asleep.

Thunder Joe sat in the darkness and pondered the two men and their troubles for a while before he curled up in his blankets. He didn't fall asleep until he flat out decided to help the two likeable men any way he could, even though they had given him an unnecessary scrubbing.

* * *

"Lookit them, Wiley," Jake said, pointing. "Them're like dark fingers crossin' the sky."

Still well below the black Tarryall Mountains on the far eastern border of South Park, the morning sun's radiance spilled between the peaks and flung pointed, tooth-like shadows across the pale blue sky. Scarlet puff-ball clouds also trailed shadows.

"I've never noticed the sky as much as I do here," Wiley said without taking his eyes off the glorious dawn.

Before Joe led them down the slope to inspect the spring, he pointed out an enormous thirty-foot bristlecone pine growing next to the rock pinnacle. From the four-foot thick trunk of the ancient tree, huge gnarled branches twisted and turned fifteen feet out. Some even rested on the ground before growing upward again. Most of the tree was dead.

"That there tree was called Old One by the Utes," Joe said. "They claim it's been here longer'n them."

Jake walked over to the massive trunk and touched it with both hands. A small piece of dead limb, from high above, fell and hit him on the head.

"Hey!" Jake yelled. He picked up the wrist-size piece of wood and held it toward Wiley. "Wiley, this here tree dropped this on my head."

Wiley smiled. "It likes you, Jake. It gave you a gift of itself."

Joe led the way down the steep slope skirting one end of the cliff. He steered them to a large crack in the uneven wall. From a moss-covered opening in the rock, a small spring of pure, cold water gurgled out. The stream flowed down the steep hillside and through an aspen grove farther down.

Enchanted, Wiley followed it into the trees and found foot-high grass dried on the stem. At the farthest edge of the aspens, the stream disappeared into the sandy soil.

Joe filled the coffee pot with water and built a small fire in a natural rock fire-pit a short distance from the spring.

Jake stood in one spot pondering the rock cliff rising in front of him. He suddenly bellowed, "Wiley! Come here!"

Startled, Joe jumped, then fell backwards. His leg kicked out, knocking the coffee pot down the hill.

"Tarnation!" Joe put a hand over his heart. "Don't you ever go skeerin' the holy hell outta me like that again! You do and I'll strap you down and fill yer underwear full'a pine needles!" When Joe realized Jake was paying no attention to him, he watched the big man drag his heel through the dirt. The thought crossed his mind that Jake had gone plumb loco.

After Wiley trudged up the hill, Jake said, "Wiley, we could build us a cabin right here. Look, we can use that cliff as a wall, an' I could make that there stream flow right through the back of the cabin."

Jake had scraped out a square in the dirt about fourteen by fourteen feet with the cliff as the back wall. Wiley stood in the square and looked around. "This is perfect, Jake. No one can see us from down below or up above, unless they're right at the edge of the cliff. And the aspen grove down the hill is a good spot to corral the horses. There's lots of grass and water, plus the cover of the trees." Wiley paused. "Let's do it! I love this place."

"I think it's a damn good spot fer you fellers," Joe said. "'Specially since yer hidin' out." Joe spun halfway around and pointed up the cliff. "And that big rock up there'll make a good lookout."

They ate breakfast in silence as they pondered the site for the cabin. Friendly gray birds flew down and perched a few feet away, hoping for handouts. After Joe tossed one a small piece of hardtack, other birds crowded closer.

"Them birds is called Whiskey Jacks or Camp Robbers," Joe offered. "Friendliest birds I ever seed. But don't go leavin' yer food without one eye peeled or it'll be gone faster'n a cat with its tail a-fire."

They remained in the area most of the morning, planning the cabin and searching the slopes for prospective trees to cut for the walls. They discussed how to attach the logs to the rock face, whether to have one or two windows, and where to build the corral and the outhouse. Joe gleefully listened to the partners design their cabin and got in his two cents every now and then.

Wiley discovered that a family of ravens lived in the rocks jutting out from the long ridge to the west. When all seven of the large black birds swooped down to introduce themselves, Wiley tossed a few pieces of crumbled hardtack toward the tree they had perched in. One by one, the ravens flew down and inspected what Wiley had given them. They weren't the least bit impressed. Wiley laughed and promised the birds he'd bring something more palatable later on.

That afternoon, they mounted up and started out toward the Castille ranch. Joe led the way southwest over a series of forested hills. At the top of the last hill in the narrow chain, they looked out over the barren landscape of bunch grass and sage.

"See there," Joe said, pointing to a snow-covered peak in the distance. "That there mountain's called Buffalo Peaks. See the smaller female buffalo out front and further south? The male's behind and towerin' above. The white man kilt all them buffalo in his greed and thinkin' he's so godlike, but our Maker put that there mountain up as a pointin' finger at what we's ruin't."

The partners were awestruck. The mountain looked exactly like two buffalo.

"Wiley," Jake said, "It's like that there ellerphant mountain we seen the other day."

Wiley silently nodded in agreement. He couldn't take his eyes off the magnificent scene.

# CHAPTER 28

A short ride brought the three men out of the hills and down onto the treeless expanse of the park. Again, Wiley thought of rumpled, olive-green velvet.

Far-off dust told Joe the antelope herd he'd spotted from above had somehow gotten spooked. He swept his arm toward the vastness to the south. "Around that hill off there--the one juttin' out from the others--is the ranch."

The whitewashed house and barn sat with their backs against the forested hills. The empty land in front sloped down for two miles, then back up for another mile before reaching a line of treeless hills that made Wiley think of an immense dinosaur's backbone pushing up from the earth.

Jake pointed to the white picket fence that enclosed the yard in front of the buildings. "Wiley, it looks like that fence is keepin' the house an' barn from bein' swallered into that big hole out there."

As they dismounted at the gate, Belinda Castille appeared from the side of the house. She ran to greet them. The men noticed her riding clothes were powdery with dust.

"Jake! Wiley! I didn't expect you so soon. I'm glad to see you. Thunder Joe, I'm glad to see you, too. There's water on the side of the house if you care to wash up. Sa-Ra has dinner ready. I just arrived myself, and I have a lot of news to tell you, so hurry." She turned abruptly and ran into the house.

Thunder Joe slapped his hat on his legs. Dust from his buckskins billowed out in a cloud. "Dang women!" he growled. "They don't let a body get a word in a-tall."

While the men washed up outside, Belinda rushed through the house, opened windows and prayed for a breeze to keep the odor of Thunder Joe on the move. She wondered why she hadn't smelled him outside.

After the men entered the house, Belinda led them into the dining room and allowed them to sit where they wanted at the table. As Jake gawked at everything, he said, "Wiley, my whole house back home could fit in this here room."

Wiley smiled at him, thinking the house small for such a large ranch, but realized he was used to the mansions of the East.

Belinda stopped from passing out coffee cups and glanced at Wiley. "I heard you and Jake had trouble on the way here."

"How the hell d'you know we had trouble?" Thunder Joe asked.

"You were there, also?" she asked Joe.

"Not the whole time, but enough. How'd you find out s'dang fast?"

She poured the coffee. "I went to Como today to mail some letters and saw Jimmy Ratchett. He told me another one of the Harrises was killed." She set the pot down. "They're blaming you, Jake."

"Damn their hides!" Joe yelled. "*I'm* the one that kilt that loonie, and they're blamin' Jake. I told 'em not to."

"What happened?" Belinda asked.

As the three men chimed in various parts of the story, Belinda's eyes grew wide. When Jake told of finding Wiley almost dead, her face went white.

"You must have blacked out only for seconds, otherwise you probably wouldn't have come to." She sighed with relief that Wiley was still alive.

After bringing her up to date, Jake asked, "Who's this here Jimmy Racket?"

"Jimmy Ratchett," Belinda corrected. "He works for Billingsly. Jimmy hired on about a year ago and soon found out he'd made a grave mistake. When he wanted to quit, Billingsly showed him a work contract he'd signed the day he was hired. Jimmy swore he'd never signed anything, but his signature is on the contract. I've seen it. He still has three months left, and then he's free. Jimmy's a wonderful man and to let you in on a secret, he and I are going to be married in three months. He asked me today, and I accepted." Belinda smiled and blushed. "Jimmy said two people he's never met inspired him to finally ask me, but he wouldn't say who they were."

Both Jake and Wiley sighed with relief at the news. Joe hooted and hollered his delight.

The kitchen door banged open, and a huge woman came into the room laden with platters of beef, antelope, potatoes, corn and bread. She spread the food out in the center of the table, left, came back with a bowl of gravy, and left again.

The men gasped at the mounds of food and immediately dug in. While they wolfed down the meal, Belinda told them the news.

"Billingsly put up posters all over Alma and offered five hundred dollars for capturing both of you alive. The posters remained up for about two hours before Sheriff Cline ripped them down. When the Harrises came back to town with their story of Jake killing Abe, Billingsly put up more posters. Jimmy said this time the reward was a thousand dollars apiece, for each of you...dead or alive.

"Sheriff Cline ripped those down also, but not before several bounty hunters saw them. For some reason, everyone thought you had gone to Breckenridge, and a search party started over Hoosier Pass. According to Jimmy, the Harrises didn't believe you went to Breckenridge since your last encounter with them was on the South Park side of the pass, traveling east."

"Damn them loonies!" Joe yelled. He banged his fist on the table.

Belinda cleared her throat and took a sip of coffee. "I was afraid the Harrises and Billingsly would start snooping around here, so I purchased two one-way train tickets to Denver in both your names."

"That was a wonderful idea!" Wiley said. He suddenly saw this woman in a new light. The fact that she was getting married helped, also. "I'll pay you back for the tickets. How much were they?"

Belinda shook her head. "Never mind that. Let's call it insurance. I'm just glad to have you both here on the ranch." She got up from the table and went to the desk in a corner of the room, picked up a folded piece of paper, then walked to Wiley's side and handed it to him. "You might like to see this."

Wiley opened the paper and discovered it was a reward poster. He read it out loud, including the part accusing Jake of the murder of Aaron and Abe Harris.

Jake stared at his plate. "It don't matter they're blamin' me for everythin'. I ain't done none of them things they say I did, and I know it. I ain't afraid even if they did put a thousan' dollars on my head."

"I knew I should'a kilt them loonies when I had the chance," Joe growled.

Wiley grabbed Jake's shoulder and smiled. "Jake, now that we're worth something, let's make it all the harder for anyone to locate us. From now on we have to be...as cagey as wolves."

Jake's countenance brightened. "Right, Wiley!" He grinned, threw his head back and howled like a wolf.

Joe cackled and chimed in with a howl of his own.

Wiley laughed, then became embarrassed as the two men waited for him to howl. He hesitated, let out a nervous howl, turned red, and glanced at Belinda. Oddly enough, she smiled at them.

The kitchen door banged open, and Soaring Raven filled the room. She stomped over to Thunder Joe. With one hand, the big Ute squaw grabbed the back of Joe's buckskins at the collar, lifted the skinny mountain man out of his chair and turned him around in mid-air to face her.

"You don't sound like wolf!" Soaring Raven yelled. "You sound like cow stuck in cactus!"

Soaring Raven dropped Joe into his chair with a thud, threw her head back and gave a bone-chilling howl. Everyone gasped. Soaring Raven smirked at Joe, then stomped back to the kitchen.

Thunder Joe yelled something filthy in Ute which was followed, from the kitchen, by an even filthier retort.

"Tarnation!" Joe yelled. "Never *can* best that woman!"

Even though this was Soaring Raven's third appearance in the room, Jake and Wiley stared when they saw her this time. Before, she'd been loaded with platters of food, and their hunger gave them eyes only for what she carried. But the full impact of the woman's size made them both feel like dwarves.

"Damn!" Jake yelled. "Who the hell *was* that?"

Belinda smiled. "That's Sa-Ra. She's the reason I'm not afraid to live here alone."

"She ain't only the ugliest woman I ever did see!" Joe snapped, "but she's the meanest, orner'est ol'..."

Holding a steaming apple pie out in front of her, Soaring Raven pushed open the door and marched in. The aroma of the pie wafted through the room as she set the pan in the middle of the table and served each of them a fourth.

As the men fell to eating the pie, Belinda introduced Soaring Raven to Jake and Wiley. With full mouths, they stood up and nodded. The big Ute squaw gave them a disinterested glance and grunted. She went over to Joe and sniffed. "You don't smell like dead something. Why?"

With his mouth full, Joe sputtered, "Cuz these here gents threw me inta one'a them Bristol Lakes! Fer an hour! An' after all I done fer them, too!"

Soaring Raven raised her eyebrows, peered down at the partners and smiled. "You two good medicine. We get on fine." After flinging a scowl at Joe, she gathered up the empty bowls and platters and returned to the kitchen.

"Joe and Soaring Raven hated each other at their first meeting," Belinda said.

"Still do!" Joe yelled. "Never fer-gived her for dumpin' them gol-durn buckets of water over me the first time I ever passed this way!"

Belinda laughed. "That happened twenty years ago, and it was Sa-Ra's first day on the job here. I was only four, but I still remember Joe screaming to high heaven after Sa-Ra dumped the first bucket of water over his head. I stood on the porch and watched him jump up and down. John came running to help Father calm Joe down."

"Then, that dang woman snuck up behind me an' dumped another bucket of water on me!" Joe hollered.

"Hell," Jake said to Belinda, "only two buckets weren't enough. Wiley an' me spent an hour in the middle of the lake, an' he *still* stunk."

Joe pointed his finger at Jake. "Some night you'll find a dang porky-pine in your blankets!"

After the table had been cleared, over coffee Belinda continued talking about Soaring Raven.

"As a young girl," Belinda said, "Sa-Ra was what we call a tom boy. She could ride better and shoot straighter than anyone in her village. Sa-Ra has supplied all our meat since she's been working here. From what I've been told, when she was sixteen she'd already beaten up most of the young braves." Belinda lowered her voice. "She left her village after the council denied her request to go through the Ute rites of manhood. Right after that is when she started working here."

"Damn!" Jake said, under his breath. He glanced toward the kitchen. "The food was good!" he yelled at the closed door.

"Ain't gonna do no good, Jake," Thunder Joe said. "That dang woman either likes you or she don't. An' she *don't* like me!"

Wiley laughed. "I think you're wrong about that, Joe. I think she likes you a lot, but she'd never admit it."

"You're right, Wiley," Belinda said. "Sa-Ra made the buckskins Joe is wearing as a peace offering."

"Damn!" Jake yelled. "You mean them buckskins of Joe's had *twenty years*'a bean farts in 'em?"

Later on the front porch, Belinda pointed out the way to the bunkhouse. Only a hundred yards away, the structure sat out of sight around the foot of an aspen-covered hill. Jake and Wiley lugged their gear down the footpath and stopped in front of the faded red building. Another barn and a larger corral nestled against the hills behind the bunkhouse.

Inside, they found a big open room with ten beds, each with a small chest of drawers beside it. Several lamps hung from the ceiling, and a potbelly stove squatted in the center of the room.

The brothers dropped their gear on the floor inside the door and silently glanced around. Standing behind Jake, Wiley put his hand on his partner's shoulder.

Jake spun around. "Wiley, I feel like I can hear silent laughin' an' talkin' in here."

Wiley slid his arms around Jake and pulled him close. "I couldn't have said it better myself, Jake." He kissed Jake on the nose. "I feel it, too. It must be left over from when this building was teeming with men. Men like you." He grabbed Jake's shirt, pulled it out of his pants and, within minutes, the two men were naked on a bed trying to squeeze their bodies into one.

Later, as Jake pulled on his boots, he said, "Wiley, I can't stay in this here bunkhouse more'n a night or two. Kind'a makes me sad all over cuz all them men're gone."

"I agree. Let's tell Belinda about our plans to build our own cabin. We'll be closer to the cattle anyway over where we found our spot."

Back at the main house, they joined Belinda and Joe on the front porch. Belinda understood why they didn't want to stay in the bunkhouse and agreed to let them build where they wanted. She told them any lumber, tools or nails they needed would be in the barn next to the bunkhouse and for them to help themselves.

"The only request I have," she said, "is that you report to me every three days in case I need something done around here. You can also pick up fresh meat and supplies." Belinda glanced at the star-studded sky. "If you gentlemen will excuse me, I'm going to bed."

The three men stood as she went inside.

In the dull light spilling from the parlor window, Joe turned to the partners. "I was goin' to mosey on down to Ben's, but now I reckon I'll stick around here fer a while an' help you boys with yer cabin. I've built a fair number of cabins in my day an' might be of some help. Might even give you some pointers on runnin' cattle, since I've done my share-a that a time'r two."

Having become fond of the cantankerous old mountain man, Jake and Wiley were overjoyed with Joe's decision.

They stayed around the ranch house for a couple of days doing odd jobs and scouting the barns for things to start work on the cabin. They even found an old wagon Belinda said they could have. On their third day at the ranch, the men hitched Mac to the wagon, loaded it with supplies and headed for the rock cliff with the spring bubbling out the side.

# CHAPTER 29

In the space of five days, the trio rounded up over six hundred head of cattle and drove them into the valley of Walton Spring. Frequent afternoon rains sweeping in from the southwest had drenched the land, greened the bunch grass that carpeted the hills and spurred rapid growth of timothy hay around the spring. Under Joe's guidance, the blood brothers learned much about running cattle and became more confident riding in a twisting saddle. From dawn to sunset, they searched for strays and occasionally found a few head of Billingsly's new herd wearing a Diamond brand. They separated them from Belinda's Lazy C cattle and drove them back to the river.

In the evenings, the blood brothers goaded Joe into telling stories of his past, which he did well once he got going.

Joe shoved his greasy hat back and gave the brothers a nearly toothless grin. "Hell, yes, I rounded up wild longhorns. Did it fer two years durin' the war in the south-a Texas. Them critters was so dang mean they'd run at you an' rip the guts outta yer horse with them horns a their's. I nearly got caught in the leg a time'r two."

"What'd you do with 'em," Jake asked.

"With what, the guts?" Joe kidded.

Jake snickered. "Them wild longhorns."

"Sold 'em to Rebs fer meat. Would'a sold 'em to Yanks, too, if they hadn't been so dang uppity an' thought they knowed everythin'."

"When did you start living as a mountain man?" Wiley asked.

"Hell, I always been one. Inside, anyhow. Come one day I rode up here an' called it home. Been livin' here goin' on twenty-one years."

* * *

On one of the few hot, rainless afternoons while searching for cattle, Wiley crossed the Horseshoe River and headed east into the wooded hills. Earlier, he'd seen Jake take the trail south along the river where it flowed between Johnson Ridge and the Morgan Hills. Not finding any cattle among the trees, Wiley doubled back and started into the canyon after Jake. It would be his first time into it.

Rounding a boulder, the mouth of the canyon yawned in front of him. Wiley stopped Buddy and stared. To his left, Johnson Ridge rose vertically for hundreds of feet, topping out into mammoth spires of crumbly, pinkish granite. Halfway up one of the sheer walls, he noticed a gnarled pine had sunk its thick roots into wide cracks in the rock.

As Wiley walked Buddy down the steep, gravely path, the western side of the wide canyon slowly came into view. When he reached a level spot, he stopped again. The round, forested humps of the Morgan Hills were studded in places with outcroppings of rock and reminded Wiley of natural castles. He wished Hector could see this magnificent scene.

Wiley followed the path into the canyon and found it wove around smooth, water-worn boulders, some so large they dwarfed the Castille ranch house.

Suddenly, above the loud prattling of the river that he couldn't even see at the moment, Wiley heard a horse galloping toward him. Or was it? The hoof beats echoed among the great rocks in the canyon, making it difficult to tell where the rider was or which direction he was going. When the galloping became louder, Wiley pulled his gun, then slumped with relief when he saw Jake on Mac rounding a boulder up ahead.

"Wiley! Come see what I found!" Jake slid Mac to a stop, turned him around and galloped back the way he'd come.

Wiley followed Jake for a mile down the twisting path. Suddenly, Jake slowed Mac and took a hard left through a narrow passage between two rocks. After threading Buddy through the slot, Wiley gasped as he entered an open area surrounded by smooth boulders and tall aspens. On the far side, the rippling water of a pool, fed by a ten-foot waterfall, flung sparkles of sunlight into his eyes before boiling down a steep incline. Wiley stopped his horse and stared. He thought of "The Arabian Nights."

They picketed the horses in the shade of an aspen grove and walked through the wide grassy area to the edge of the pool.

"This is wonderful!" Wiley said. His voice echoed off the rocks. He grabbed at his shirt. "Let's get our clothes off."

Naked, the two men dived into the chilly water.

After swimming across the pool and back, Wiley stuck his head out of the water. Seeing the back of Jake's head, he yelled, "Jake, something grabbed me! Help!" He disappeared into the shimmering depths.

Jake snapped his head around and saw nothing but the widening circles in the water where Wiley had been.

"Wiley? Where are you?" When Wiley didn't surface, Jake yelled, "Wiley, what grabbed you? Wiley?"

Suddenly, Jake felt something furry from behind slip between his legs and nestle into his crotch as two arms encircled his waist from the back.

"Yeow! Wiley, it's got me too! Help!"

Jake reached down and felt something round...with two ears. "Damn! What the--" He stuck his head under water and saw Wiley looking up at him. He could feel Wiley's beard tickling his nuts.

Jake laughed and came up coughing. He lunged behind him, grabbed Wiley in the crotch, and the pair wrestled under water until they ran out of breath.

"Damn, Wiley, you scared the shit right outta me," Jake gasped.

"Where?" Wiley scanned the surface of the water. "I don't see anything floating anywhere."

Jake laughed and dove at Wiley, tackling him. Wiley's body went limp, and Jake dragged him a few feet until they were behind the falls in chest-deep water.

If anyone had been watching, they would have seen the silvery outline of two men locked in a tight embrace behind the glistening curtain of water.

From then on, whenever they could, while Joe snored in the shade at the end of a hot day, the blood brothers raced their horses to the hidden lagoon and splashed around until they turned blue from the cold.

\* \* \*

None of the trio saw anyone the entire two weeks, and Belinda didn't have any news since she hadn't seen Jimmy after his proposal to her. The lack of communication made the blood brothers feel cut off from the rest of the world. This was somewhat disconcerting to Wiley, but Jake loved it.

While they rounded up the Lazy C cattle, no work had been done on the cabin. Exhausted at day's end, after the evening meal Wiley and Joe relaxed in camp on top of the cliff and traded stories.

Used to long hours of grueling labor, Jake busied himself digging a channel at the base of the cliff. Since he had told Wiley and Joe to stay away from the area, they thought it best to leave him alone.

When completed, Jake's channel stretched from the spring where it flowed out of the rock, down through the spot where the cabin would eventually sit and farther on down the hill to the horse corral. Well inside the area they had marked off for the cabin foundation, and next to the cliff, Jake dug a two-foot-deep pit and made the channel go in one side and out the other. He dug a larger trough inside the corral. He knew water would fill it, then flow out the other side and disappear into the sandy soil. Jake carefully lined the channel and both pits with rocks and covered them with the cement he'd found in Belinda's barn.

The evening after the cement hardened, Jake decided to divert the water into his new trench and wanted Wiley and Joe to see it. He trudged up the slope to the camp and silently watched Wiley skin a rabbit while Joe turned one on a spit over the fire.

Jake grinned and cleared his throat. "We're gonna have water runnin' inside the cabin, Wiley. Wanna come see?"

Wiley glanced at him. "*In* the cabin? Jake, we can't have water running inside the cabin."

"Hee, hee, hee," Joe cackled. "You'll be wakin' up with fish bitin' off yer toes."

Crestfallen, Jake ambled down the slope.

Wiley put the half skinned-rabbit on a rock. "Joe, we'd better go see what he's been up to all this time. He hasn't wanted us down there for nearly a week."

When they arrived at the base of the cliff, they found Jake sitting on a log, pouting.

Wiley rested his hand on Jake's shoulder. "Show us what you've done, Jake. Water flowing inside the cabin sounds strange to me."

Jake jumped to his feet. "See, Wiley? The water'll come down this here ditch an' end up in that hole." He pointed to the cement-lined hole inside the square where the cabin would be. "This'll fill up, an' we can get water whenever we want some, an' the water'll go out the other side an' down to the horses."

Wiley squeezed Jake's shoulder. "But Jake, the cabin's floor will cover it up."

Jake scratched his head. "Guess I never thought none about the floor bein' wood. How we gonna get at the water?"

Joe squinted his eyes and rubbed his scraggly beard as he looked over Jake's trench. "Tarnation! That there's a dang good ideer, Jake. All you gotta do is cut a hole in the floor above that pit, an' you can get at the water any dang time you want."

"Damn!" Jake yelled. "See, Wiley, it ain't gonna be in the cabin after all."

They watched as Jake broke the dam he'd made to divert the stream. Water surged down the cement channel, filled the hole inside the proposed cabin, then spilled into the trench on the other side.

Farther down, the water flowed into the cement-lined trough Jake had dug inside the corral. Buddy and Mac watched the pit fill with water. As they jostled each other for the best spot to drink, Jawbone walked up from behind and pushed them both aside.

"It works perfectly, Jake," Wiley exclaimed. "You're a genius." He hugged Jake around the neck.

"Me? Hear that, Joe? Me, a genius?" He threw his head back and laughed. "Never thought nobody'd ever say that about me."

Jake's trench got them excited about the cabin, and the next morning they started work on it. Using the cliff as the back wall, they built the other three walls out of pine logs. They anchored the logs to the rock by driving pointed ends into fissures and secured them with iron spikes or wooden wedges. After they filled the gaps between the logs with cement, they built up a rock and cement skirt around the bottom of the cabin to keep muddy rain water from contaminating the spring water in the trench. Using planks they'd found in the Castille barn, Joe showed them how to tie the foundation together and lay the floor.

Inside the cabin, at waist level, a wide flat shelf had eroded into the rock wall. Directly above the shelf, the rock swept upwards to form a half chimney. Wiley discovered that smoke from a fire built on this shelf swirled up the rock. With Joe's help, they put a trap door in the roof above the rock chimney. An easy climb up the cliff enabled them to close the flap if it rained.

After the roof was completed, the first fire on the shelf burned perfectly. The smoke swirled up the rock and out the opening. Outside, Joe noticed the smoke filtered through the branches of a huge spruce tree, masking it from prying eyes. That night, they discovered a fire in the evening heated the entire rock wall and kept the cabin warm far into the chilly nights.

Wiley chose a spot down the slope and fifty feet west of the cabin for the outhouse. Well into the second day of digging the pit, Wiley stooped at the edge of the five-foot deep hole and watched Jake work. Shirtless, Jake's muscles flexed with each shovel of dirt he tossed into the air.

"Jake, why don't you let me dig once in a while?" Wiley asked. "You've been at it for two hours straight this time."

Jake jammed the shovel into the dirt near his foot and leaned on the handle. His hair stuck to his wet forehead, and rivulets of sweat traced the valleys around the muscles of his heaving chest. Wiley felt light-headed for a moment as Jake's brilliant blue eyes captured his heart again.

"Hell," Jake gasped. "This ain't nothin'." He glanced down at the hole and wiped his forehead with his arm. "I dug three shit-pits back home. They kept fillin' up with water. I hate it when my shit splashes up an' hits me in the nuts."

Wiley laughed and extended his hand. "I'll help you climb out. You should rest. Besides, Joe's got food cooking, and you know how he gets if we aren't there when it's ready."

"Damn!" Jake grabbed Wiley's hand and climbed out of the hole. "If I'd knowed he was cookin', I'd been outta here sooner. I don't want my food fattin' up them ravens again."

Constructed of small aspen logs, the outhouse went up fast. By the end of the next day, it sat proudly on the edge of a cluster of young aspens.

"I'm gonna be first usin' our new shit-house," Jake yelled. He held one of their lamps as he entered the small structure.

"It's daylight," Joe yelled. "What the hell're you doin' with that dang lamp?"

"I made me a mark in the pit, an' I'm gonna see if my shit hits it." Jake grinned and slammed the door.

Wiley took a breather from sawing a plank, turned toward the outhouse, then glanced over at Thunder Joe. "I'm sometimes amazed at some of the things Jake does."

"I shore hope he recollects the dang heat comin' from the chimney when he sticks that lamp down the hole." Joe rocked his body back and forth in the chair he was making to test its stability. The right front leg wobbled.

"Tarnation!" Joe yelled. "I can't get that dang leg to stay put!" He leaped out of the chair, grabbed another rawhide strip and wrapped the loose joint in an X pattern.

"Yeow! Damn!" Jake yelled from inside the outhouse.

Wiley jumped when he heard glass breaking followed by more cursing from Jake. Suddenly, smoke, then flames snaked through the sides of the small building. Jake leaped out the door with his pants down around his ankles. Within seconds, the outhouse was engulfed in flames.

Wiley ran inside the cabin and filled a pan with water from the hole in the floor, then rushed down the hill, but it was too late. Nothing could save the structure. They stood in silence and watched the outhouse burn to the ground.

"Jake, what happened in there?" Wiley finally asked.

"Hell, Wiley, when I tried shovin' the lamp down the hole to see where my shit went, the heat burnt my face off. I dropped the damn lamp, an' it busted on the seat."

The next day, after dousing the smoking embers, Joe discovered Jake's shit didn't hit the mark, but part of the broken lantern did. While rebuilding the outhouse, whenever Thunder Joe and Wiley looked at each other, they'd break out laughing.

"You'da dropped it too if your face got burnt off like mind did!" Jake yelled each time they got the giggles.

During the first days of construction, the three men were occasionally visited by a few chipmunks. After Wiley started feeding them, their numbers grew and they began scampering around the cabin, inside and out, getting into everything.

"In case you fellers don't already know it," Joe said as he scowled at the darting creatures, "one-a my most favoritest eatin' is chipmunk stew." He tried to keep a straight face. "An' them critters would make a nice linin' for my boots, too."

"Forget it, Joe," Wiley said. "I'll stop feeding them."

The next day, Wiley announced, "I think the cabin should be named Chipmunk Rock." He went inside and grabbed a bottle of whiskey Belinda had given them. "Let's christen it now since its almost finished."

After they passed the bottle around until it was empty, Wiley had Jake smash it on the side of the cliff.

When the cabin was completed, the partners tried their hand at making furniture. Wiley helped Jake make a table out of three-inch thick pine boards they'd brought from the ranch. At first, the legs were nearly forty inches high. Since none of them were the same length, it tipped back and forth crazily. After Jake worked on the problem, the table ended up twenty-seven inches high, and still wobbly. Even Joe learned a few new cuss words. Wiley saved the table from becoming firewood by tacking thin wedges under two legs.

Joe made four straight-back chairs and two large armchairs out of wrist-size aspen logs and Jake and Wiley worked together on a frame for the featherbed Belinda had loaned them.

The twenty-sixth day of May broke gray and overcast. When Wiley stepped outside, he met Joe standing with Jawbone's reins in his hand.

"Now that yer cabin's done, it's time fer me to be moseyin' on to Ben's place. Like I said, Ben always has some big doin's goin' on there." After promising the partners he'd return in a couple weeks with news, Joe galloped down the slope and disappeared into the trees.

Later that morning, the blood brothers mounted their horses and explored the immediate area around the cabin. They rode over the saddle between the two summits of Bristlecone Peak, then east toward Pinnacle Rock. Wiley kept a constant lookout at the stone chimneys as they rode by the smaller mountain. When they reached Walton Spring, the clouds opened and spilled out sheets of cold rain. The brothers spurred their horses, arriving at Chipmunk Rock soaked and chilled to the bone.

After rubbing the horses down in the lean-to shelter in the corral, the men scrambled up the hill to the cabin. Wiley built a fire on the ledge, and their snug home became toasty in minutes. They spent the remainder of the day inside, patching leaks in the roof and around the windows.

It rained the entire afternoon, and by nightfall the drops still pounded the roof. After a sumptuous meal of elk steaks and potatoes they'd brought from the ranch house the day before, the men relaxed across from each other in their new armchairs.

Wiley draped one leg over the arm of his chair. "Jake, do you realize this is the first time we've been alone since we left Alma?"

"Hell, Wiley, Joe weren't with us when we'd go to our secret waterfall."

"I know, but we've never had a chance to talk. I'd like to know more about you and your family."

Without hesitation, Jake said, "Pa's folks come from Ireland. They come over to some place called Cumberland Mountains before goin' to Kentucky. Ma's side come from Alle-bama.

"Ma was all'a time sick. But she'd still cook when she could get outta bed. Pa'd always be yellin' at her. He'd yell at ever'body. Ma used to say Pa should'a gone West an' lived on his own. She'd say he felt trapped by bein' married an' havin' to plow an' stuff."

"How often did your father yell at you?" Wiley asked.

"Hell, Wiley, he'd always be yellin' at me. If he weren't callin' me a damn sissy, he'd be sayin' I was dumber'n hog shit." Jake hung his head.

Wiley seethed, wondering how *anyone* could treat such an innocent, beautiful man that way. He changed the subject for his own sake, as well as Jake's. "What was your mother like?"

Jake's face softened. "She was always smilin'...even when she'd be coughin' up green stuff. She'd read to me every mornin' outta the Good Book an' tell me what it meant. She'd always tell me to make friends with Jesus an' tell him ever'thin' I was thinkin'. It got to where Jesus was the only one I'd talk to." He hung his head again. "Guess I ain't been talkin' to him much since I met you."

"How does Jesus feel about you being with me?" Wiley asked.

Jake's head snapped up. "Hell, Wiley, Jesus picked you to be my friend! I asked him for one like you before I left home." He grinned. "Ma'd be happy about me bein' with you. She'd always tell me not to get hitched with a woman if I thought it weren't right for me."

Jake lowered his eyes. "After Ma died, Pa'd barely say anythin' to me. He'd yell 'You damn sissy' when he'd see me an' jest keep on walkin'. I slept in the barn mostly an' stayed away from him. Then one day I found him dead." He cringed with guilt when he remembered his relief at seeing his father dead.

Jake noticed Wiley didn't want to talk about his schooling or what he did for a living, and didn't care. He wanted to know other things.

"Wiley, where'd you get your scar? Was it in a fight?"

Wiley draped his other leg over the arm of the chair and leaned his head against the back. He couldn't tell Jake he'd gotten the scar when he'd fought with Cade Bently during a holdup in Philadelphia's Broad Street Station. Parts of the structure had still been under construction and, as they'd grappled over the money in a supply room, Cade had found a piece of quarter-inch pipe and had jammed it into Wiley's face. Cade Bently had been the first man Wiley killed, and the scar forever reminded him of that night. And it branded him among criminals and lawmen alike.

Wiley sucked in air, shook his head, then blew his breath out in a rush. He glanced over at Jake, saw his blood brother anticipating what he would say about his scar and chuckled. God, he loved Jake. How was it possible that a man like himself, in his line of work, had found the perfect partner? How would he tell about his scar? Taking a stab at an explanation, Wiley said, "My scar was an accident, Jake. I was...horsing around in the dorm at school with a wrestling buddy, and he pinned me against the wall. I cut my face on a...small piece of pipe sticking out through the plaster."

"I like your scar, Wiley. It makes you look mean, but I know you ain't mean." Jake grinned. "Where'd your ma an' pa come from?"

Wiley smiled at the ceiling. "My grandmother's family came to this country from France and settled in upper New York state. My grandmother was swept off her feet by a handsome Iroquois brave."

Wiley turned his body and let his feet hit the floor, then leaned toward Jake and smiled. "They were still madly in love with each other on their deathbeds. Like we're going to be."

Jake laughed.

Wiley sat back. "After they married, they moved to Vermont and started a small farm. That life was hard for my grandfather at first, but he adjusted to it. They had four children. My mother was the youngest. Her name was Lily."

"What was yer grandpa's name, Wiley?"

"Gray Feather. Grandpa Gray Feather. He died when I was thirteen. I still miss him..."

There! It happened again. That subtle stirring of a forgotten memory. It had started on the on the train from Philadelphia. Wiley felt himself being drawn into the past, as though Grandpa Gray Feather was still trying to tell him something from his deathbed. Was it about his present profession?

"Wiley, did he wear war paint?" Jake asked.

"What?" Wiley focused on Jake. He felt like he'd been somewhere else for a split second.

"Did your grandpa wear war paint?"

"Uh...no, Jake. Not for real. He'd paint his face, then mine, and teach me how to track. Sometimes we'd live in the woods for weeks. When we'd get home, my folks would scold him for taking me away from my chores. Then, Grandpa would grumble and sulk in the house I built in the apple tree."

"I built me a tree house, too!" Jake exclaimed. "It's in the old oak tree next to the barn. I could see the whole yard from there. I'd hide up there when Pa was lookin' to beat me for somethin'."

Wiley frowned. "Did he beat you often?"

"Most every day when I was little. Sometimes he'd pick me up an' toss me in hog shit for no reason, then laugh. After the Harris' bull ripped his leg open, he couldn't never catch me no more, but he'd sure be yellin' at me all the time."

"Jake, I don't want to hear any more about your father. It makes me angry." Wiley clenched his teeth, glad the man was already dead.

"Did your pa beat you, Wiley?"

"Only when I needed it. My father was a stern man since he'd been in the French army, but he was always fair and treated me well. His name was Raoul. My mother met him when she visited friends in Quebec. After they married, they lived at my grandparents' farm and took care of them until they died. I did the same for my folks."

Jake shifted in his chair. "Wiley, did you ever have you a partner like me before?"

"No. I always wanted one. I had several offers, but always found fault with them." Wiley grinned. "Until I met you, I'd almost given up ever finding anyone."

Jake's eyes got big. "You gonna find them faults with me sometime?"

Wiley chuckled. "I'm sure we'll discover things about each other that we don't like. But I can't think of anything you could do that would ever make me want to leave you. Not now."

"Not even if I had somebody else before you?"

"Was it Zeke? He's jealous of me, you know."

Jake lowered his head, then looked up at Wiley. "No, before Zeke. You won't hit me if I talk about Sergeant Moss, will you?"

"Sergeant Moss? I'm intrigued, Jake. Tell me about him."

As Jake related the story, his honesty and candor made Wiley's heart swell.

"When I seen Sergeant Moss naked, somethin' happened inside me, Wiley. Then, he smiled an' held out his arms. I don't know how it happened, but I found myself huggin' him. He smelled so sweaty an' good. I couldn't get outta my clothes fast enough an' got a knot in my boot string. Sergeant Moss told me to stop cussin' an' got it undone for me." Jake glanced at Wiley. "We rolled around in the hay all night."

After Jake told Wiley how Sergeant Moss taught him the exercises, he said, "He left in the afternoon. That night, I slept in the same hay we'd rolled in, wishin' he was still there."

Jake looked at his hands. "Next day, Pa told me he'd seen what I'd done an' was gonna teach me a lesson. He paid two men from town to grab me an' drag me into Madame Bovery's place. You know, one'a them houses with women sittin' in a big room with red curtains. They forced me upstairs an' pulled all my clothes off. Then, next thing I knowed, I was pinned down on top of this fat, naked woman. When I started throwin' up on the bed, the woman screamed an' shoved me away. I kicked the two men in the nuts, grabbed my clothes an' boots an' hightailed it down the back stairs." Jake covered his face with his hands. "I hid in the woods for a week before goin' home."

Wiley lifted himself out of the chair and walked across the room. He wrapped his arms around Jake and buried his face in Jake's hair.

Jake's arms found their way around Wiley's waist. He pressed his face into Wiley's shirt and sobbed.

Later, they undressed and snuggled close together in the featherbed. The patter of rain on the roof masked their whispers and soft moans and finally lulled them to sleep.

# CHAPTER 30

Billingsly pounded the top of his dresser. He hated barbarians. From observing Jake, he should have guessed the Harrises would be classic examples of crude, uneducated men. How many times in the past two weeks had he come close to telling Winder to shoot them and be done with it? But the reason he'd invited the Harrises into his home had suddenly changed. Rather than have Wiley and Jake captured so they could share his bed, he wanted them dead.

Every time he thought of Wiley's cold stare in the Regal Cafe the morning after the fight, his spine froze. Who was he? The telegram Wiley had sent gave his name and perfect description. But why had he sent it to Boston University? Unless... No, Simon would never hire someone to hunt him down and kill him for stealing the gems. Still, Simon did have extensive dealings with Boston University. If Simon hired Wiley to kill him, the message would never have been sent to New Orleans.

None of it made any sense, but Billingsly knew Wiley was dangerous. The Harrises *had* to kill him. He guessed Jake didn't have a clue who Wiley actually was.

Shouting in the yard below startled him. Billingsly peered out his bedroom window. He couldn't see anyone, but figured Seth must have gotten Kirby's goat again.

"I'm *not* fixin' fried chicken again, no how!" Kirby yelled from below. "You just stay the hell outta my kitchen! An' another thing, *I ain't no damn boy!*"

Billingsly saw Seth run into the yard. The old man covered his head with his arms as a potato bounced off his back. Billingsly chuckled. He knew how Kirby felt. Ever since they'd moved in, Seth and Clem had been trying to take over. After the first two days of their complaining and meddling in the kitchen, Xu had quit.

Frantic to find another cook to feed his hands, Billingsly had scoured the area around Alma. Everyone seemed to have an excuse not to work for him. Cretins! He'd ridden to Fairplay and asked around, without any luck. But while sipping brandy in the Placer Saloon, a man had come to his table. He'd whispered low and pointed across the room to a man draped over his table, dead drunk, and mentioned that Kirby once held the title of the best cattle-drive cook in Texas and Oklahoma. But that was before he'd started drinking.

While forcing a pot of coffee down Kirby's throat to sober him up, Billingsly had trumped up enough charges against the old geezer to send him to Yuma prison for the rest of his life. Kirby had accepted the job.

During the first couple days, Kirby proved he had more than enough experience to please Billingsly's delicate palate, and even prepared delicious meals the fastidious lawyer had never eaten. But, after Abe's death, Seth and Clem began sitting in the kitchen rather than the parlor. Kirby let them stay as long as they only puffed Billingsly's cigars and nothing else. Once they started meddling in his cooking, he turned as ferocious as the badger he resembled.

Sitting by himself on the veranda, Zeke watched his father run from the barrage of potatoes being heaved at him. He loathed his father and brother now. After Jake's comment about Clem kissing Sara Jean, and the way his brother had squirmed, he was convinced Clem was the baby's father. Zeke wanted to sneak off by himself and find Jake, but knew that was impossible. Every time he'd tried running away before, Seth had always found him. He didn't want to return to Kentucky, so he decided to stay and intervene on Jake and Wiley's behalf...if they were ever captured. It turned him inside-out that Wiley was around and hoped he could win Jake back if he saved him from being hung.

With the exception of the kitchen, Seth and Clem essentially ran the house. The one time Billingsly told Seth they would have to leave, Seth pulled his gun, stuck it against Billingsly's nose and cocked it.

"We took up yer invite, and we're stayin' as long as it takes to find Jake and that friend'a his. You hear me, boy?"

"Well, why aren't you searching for him?" Billingsly asked, his voice trembling. "You've done nothing but sit around my house since your other son was killed."

Seth flattened Billingsly's nose with the gun barrel. "Cuz we're waitin' fer the men that's searchin' over them mountains to come back. We ain't goin' nowhere 'til we know Jake ain't in Broken Ridge. It'll save us a trip."

"Breckenridge!" Billingsly corrected in an unusually high pitch. "I don't know when the bounty hunters will be back. They've been gone for eight days. If they don't find them, they may not come back here. There's plenty of other wanted men roaming these mountains."

Seth holstered his gun. "Yer own men'll come back. They're lookin' for 'em, too. We're waitin' 'til Jimmy comes back from searchin' where we last seen Jake. When they all get back, we'll know."

Late that afternoon, Jimmy Ratchett rode in. He nodded to Zeke as he sprinted up the steps to the veranda.

Zeke turned his head away.

Jimmy shrugged and went inside. He entered Billingsly's first floor office and found the lawyer sulking in his green velvet chair in the corner.

"I found them," Jimmy said. "Or at least where they went."

Billingsly jumped to his feet. "Where?"

Wanting to irritate his boss, Jimmy started from the beginning. "After I followed the Ute trail over to Boreas Mountain, I lost their tracks. All the rain we've had lately has washed even deer and elk tracks away. So, I rode down to Como..."

"Are they in Como?" Billingsly interrupted.

"Let me finish," Jimmy snapped. Billingsly's scowl didn't faze him. "After I had a bite to eat in Como, I decided to check the train station...and what do you think I found out?" He grinned.

Billingsly grabbed Jimmy's arm. "You're playing with me! I *demand* you tell me where they are!"

Jimmy chuckled and yanked his arm from Billingsly's grasp. "They went to Denver."

"Denver! When?"

"The tickets were bought on May twelfth."

"The twelfth! That's over two weeks ago! They could be anywhere by now!"

Billingsly stormed out of his office, through the parlor and shoved open the door into the kitchen. He stomped to the table where Seth and Clem were making card houses and glowered with his arms folded. The men ignored him.

Clem's simple structure suddenly collapsed. "Dammit, Pa! You're always blowin' my houses over."

"Don't you talk to me like that, boy!"

Billingsly scowled. "Gentlemen, I know where Jake and Wiley are." Expecting no reaction, he was surprised when they leaped to their feet.

"Where are they?" Seth demanded.

"They took the train to Denver over two..."

"Clem, get Zeke and let's get packed!" Seth shouted. "We're goin' back to Denver. Jake might'a gone back to workin' on houses!"

Clem dashed outside. Seth started for the back door but stopped and turned back to Billingsly. "You'll haft'a pay fer the tickets. We ain't got no more money. Seein' we're workin' fer you, you can give us spendin' money, too."

Delighted to get them out of his house, Billingsly gladly paid for the trip, giving them extra money for several weeks in Denver. If they had been going to New York, he would have paid.

"You bring them back here alive!" Billingsly shouted as they rode out the front gate. He'd been toying with how Jake and Wiley would die, and he didn't want the Harrises to be a part of it. Maybe the blood brothers could be shot during a mock escape from jail, or they would hang after being found guilty of murdering Aaron and Abe. But he'd prefer it if Winder shot them somewhere away from civilization.

After the Harrises had disappeared down the road, Billingsly sat in a chair on the veranda and stared into space. He wasn't entirely convinced Jake and Wiley went to Denver, but at least it got the Harrises out of his house. For some reason he couldn't put his finger on, Jimmy's message didn't ring true. Something told him Wiley wouldn't have been scared away that easily.

An hour after the Harrises left, Billingsly called Winder into his office. As the big cowboy entered the room, Billingsly saw his foreman was in a foul mood. Understandably so. The man's handsome face was still red and puffy, and his lumpy nose leaned to the right.

Billingsly motioned for Winder to sit in the chair at the end of his desk. He poured the big man a drink.

"Have some brandy, Winder." Billingsly paused. "The Harrises left for Denver to look for Jake and Wiley, but I have a feeling they're still around here somewhere. I have a plan to capture them, if they are."

As Winder slumped into the chair, his shirt pulled taut over his chest, and the buttons of his pants strained against the bulge. "What, more wanted posters?" he asked sullenly, then rubbed his crotch, teasing his boss. "They didn't work the first two times. What makes you think they'll work now?" He downed the brandy in one gulp. Winder's eyes watered, then he started coughing.

Billingsly scowled at him and tried not to look at his crotch. "You fool! Fine brandy should be sipped, not gulped down like rotgut whiskey. It has a habit of kicking back. And, for your information, I *am* going to plaster this town with more posters, but this time they won't be wanted posters." He leaned back in his chair and smiled at the ceiling. "They'll be posters of amnesty. They'll state the Harrises have left town, the reward has been dropped, and the two brothers are free to return." He sat up straight in his chair, picked up an empty penholder and tapped the desk with it. "I think that just might lure them back. If they're camped somewhere, they'll probably be needing supplies by now. Besides, how long can a man sleep in the woods, anyway?"

Winder scowled. "As long as a *man* wants to!"

Billingsly ignored the remark. "I want you to go to Ben Harrington's ranch for his annual wagon race. Scout the area and talk to people. Find out if anyone knows where those two are. Take a few men with you, men you can count on to get the job done if you find them. Play it cagey. Let everyone think you're there only for the race, but I want you to question everyone you can find. The race is in a week, and I want you there a few days before it starts. It's best to be early so you can observe the latecomers as they arrive. You know what those two men look like, don't you?"

"I'll never forget what they look like!" Winder snapped as he rubbed his face. "I hope you don't care if I kill the bastards on the spot!"

"Yes, I do care." Billingsly sipped his brandy. "If they are at the race, watch when they leave and follow them. Kill them far away from any ranch or settlement. I don't want you caught, getting *me* involved. At Ben's place, with all those people there, you wouldn't get away with it. Do I make myself clear?"

"Yah, sure. But if they're there and see me, they'll probably get suspicious and leave."

"So? I told you to follow them!"

Winder shifted in his chair. "What about the wagon race? Questioning everyone will take time. We'll need some time to prepare for the race."

"I don't give a *damn* about the wagon race! The only reason you're going is to find those two men. If you don't get to race, you don't get to race. I'm not paying you to lollygag around. Just remember, this is a job."

Billingsly rose from his chair, strode to the door of his office and opened it. "Now get out of here and start packing. I want you to leave in two days."

Winder slowly got to his feet. "Hell, it won't take *me* two days to get ready." He ambled over to Billingsly and adjusted himself in the crotch. He hated the dick-licker standing in front of him and took every opportunity to tantalize him.

"If I do kill them," Winder sneered, "I'd better be released from my debt to you. I want a ticket to California within a week after I do the job. If I don't get it, I'll go to Sheriff Cline with everything I know. You just remember that!"

As Winder stepped into the hall, he grabbed the brass knob and slammed the door behind him. His heavy footsteps could be heard down the hall, then the front door slammed.

Billingsly returned to his desk, poured himself another brandy and took a sip. He longed for California himself. Once he gained control of the Castille Ranch, he'd be on his way to a real life in San Francisco. He thought of Belinda Castille. The last time he'd seen her was several weeks ago in the Alma Hotel talking to the blood brothers...about a *job*! He slammed his hand on the desk.

"How could I be so stupid!" he yelled. "*That's* where they've been all this time!"

He mentally kicked himself for not listening to the Harrises. Knowing full well the brothers rode toward Breckenridge, the opposite direction of the Castille Ranch, he now realized they could have circled around. His men didn't find any tracks because of the heavy rains in the area, and it would be easy to buy train tickets and not use them. Billingsly chuckled. If that's what Jake and Wiley did, he thanked them for getting the Harrises out of his house.

Billingsly decided to take a ride and pay Belinda a friendly visit. It had to be friendly, or that female brute, Soaring Raven, might tie him on his horse facing backwards again like she'd done once before. He resolved not to say anything this time about buying the ranch. But that presented a problem. Why would he be going there if it wasn't to ask her to sell?

During the ride to the Castille Ranch, Billingsly formulated a bogus story for his visit. Satisfied it would work, he spurred his ugly horse into some sort of a gallop.

Billingsly reached the ranch house at three in the afternoon. He rode cautiously to the gate and dismounted. The place looked deserted, but he assumed Soaring Raven was lurking somewhere, possibly with a shotgun pointed at his head.

He dusted off his clothes with his hat and yelled, "Is anyone here?"

No answer.

Billingsly decided to state his business immediately to avoid confrontation with either woman. He shouted, "I'm here to let you graze your cattle on my land until you can find help to bring them back over here!"

Still, no answer.

A barrel-sized tumbleweed bounced across the front porch of the house, scraping the side of the building. The wind shoved it under the rail and steered it toward the barn.

"Is anyone here?" Billingsly shouted again.

Still no one appeared at the door or any of the windows. He assumed no one was around. Soaring Raven would have fired a shot at him by now if she were here. Irritated he'd ridden all the way out to this barren wasteland for nothing, Billingsly hit the side of his leg with his hat and cursed. As he started to mount up, his eyes caught movement in the trees on the hillside behind the house. Two riders appeared. They walked their horses down a trail that worked its way east toward his own land. When the riders came into full view, he recognized Belinda and Soaring Raven.

Billingsly daintily mounted his horse and spurred it toward them. When the women saw him, they reined to a stop. Soaring Raven frowned and pulled her shotgun out of the saddle boot and leveled it at the lawyer.

When Billingsly came within earshot, he slowed his horse to a walk and yelled, "I've come to let you graze your cattle on my land until you can hire someone to get them off!" He cautiously approached the women and allowed his words to sink in. When he reached them, he stopped his horse and politely tipped his hat.

"Miss Castille, I realize you have more cattle than I do right now, and there's no reason to let all that grass go to waste. You can leave your cattle where they are. All summer if you have to."

"Thank you, Mr. Billingsly, but there's no need for that," Belinda said icily. "Sa-Ra and I have rounded them up by ourselves. If you will excuse us, Mr. Billingsly, after working hard all day we need to clean up and eat."

Without a backward glance, the women rode by him and down the hill.

As she headed for the house, Belinda was thankful she hadn't had anything for Jake and Wiley to do that morning. Shortly after they'd arrived, she and Sa-Ra had ridden back to Chipmunk Rock with them to see the progress on their cabin. Just now returning, Belinda breathed a sigh of relief the partners weren't with them. She glanced at Sa-Ra. The big woman was still scowling.

Billingsly sat on his horse and watched them. The chill in Belinda's voice seemed to freeze the thinning hairs on his head. How *dare* she talk to him that way. He sat straight in his saddle, adjusted his hat, then spurred his horse after them.

"Wait!" he shouted. "I rode all the way out here to be neighborly, and you treat me this way? You could at least give me a bite to eat before I ride back to Alma."

The women stopped their horses and turned them to face him. As Billingsly caught up to them Belinda said, "I'll leave it up to Sa-Ra if she wants to fix you something."

The Indian woman scowled. "I fix you food, but you eat on porch. You no come in house. Thunder Joe stinks it up enough."

Belinda started to turn her horse, then stopped and stared at Billingsly with cold eyes. "I know why you came here. You came to see if I hired the two men I was talking to few weeks ago in the Alma Hotel. Everyone knows you're after them. I must say, Mr. Billingsly, you're not man enough to capture them. Wherever they are."

As Belinda turned her horse toward the house, she wondered how long she'd be living here after insulting the vicious lawyer again. She knew he wouldn't waste time trying to get her land away from her.

Furious, Billingsly spurred his horse north without a backwards glance. How *dare* that wench talk to him that way. He began brooding on how to take possession of her ranch. He didn't know how yet, but he'd think of something. It was a long ride back to Alma, and he had plenty of time.

## CHAPTER 31

Three days later, at eight in the morning, the blood brothers rode toward the Castille Ranch house. They didn't mind checking in with Belinda since it usually meant a meal cooked by Soaring Raven.

"Wonder if Miss Castille has somethin' for us to do today, Wiley?" Jake asked.

"If not, maybe we can ride to our waterfall."

As the partners rounded the last hill, they saw Jawbone tied to the rail outside the fence.

"Joe's here," Jake said. "Wonder what he's doin' back here so soon? Thought he was stayin' at the Harrington place for a couple weeks."

"He may have some news for us." Wiley slid off Buddy and walked him to the rail. He waited for Jake to tie Mac's reins. As they walked to the house, Wiley slid his hand across Jake's firm butt, then squeezed.

Jake grinned. "Our waterfall misses us, Wiley."

The front door opened, and Thunder Joe stepped out. Both men could smell he was up to his stinky self.

"Well, looky who's here," Joe cackled. He smiled, showing his few remaining teeth. "How you boys been doin' since I last seed ya?"

"It's only been five days, Joe." Wiley patted the old man's shoulder. "What brings you back so soon?"

"Gots a pros-pa-sition fer you gents. How'd you like to be in the Harrington's wagon race?" His eyes sparkled slyly. "Winner gets a hunnert an' fifty gold dollars. That'd be enough so's we could split it three ways."

Jake grabbed Wiley's arm. "I'm a good wagon racer, Wiley. I won four years in a row back in Wilmore when we'd have them races there. Mac knows all about them kinds a things cuz I taught him myself." He cut his eyes to Joe. "Are them races for one or two horses?"

"Both," Joe replied. He poked Jake in the ribs. "I shore do think you could beat 'em all down there, Jake. Yer just crazy enough to do it." Joe cackled and slapped his leg. "Belinda already agreed to let you boys take a few days off an' go down there with me. Figgered I'd better ask her first. The boss, you know."

Wiley cringed at hearing that, but shrugged and smiled. "I think the idea is...wonderful. Jake, Joe and I have just elected you as our driver. I'm sure you can beat anyone hands down." He said that more for Jake's self-confidence than out of any conviction he could actually win.

Before Jake could reply, Belinda stepped out the door. "Wiley, Jake, I have something to tell you. Would you mind coming inside? Sa-Ra just took an apple pie out of the oven."

The three men laughed when they all became wedged in the doorway.

As they sat at the huge oak table, Belinda silently gave each one a cup and saucer. By the shaky way she poured half-cups of coffee, Wiley could tell something other than the race was on her mind.

Soaring Raven served the pie. She sniffed the air and frowned at Joe. Jake snickered.

Belinda sipped her coffee. She tried to replace her cup daintily, but at the last moment her hand jerked and the cup smacked the saucer's edge on its way. She glanced at Jake, then at Wiley. Wiley was staring at her. Her eyes dropped back to her cup.

"Billingsly was here three days ago," she said softly. "Sa-Ra and I had just returned from your cabin."

"Bingsly!" Jake yelled. "What'd he want?" He glanced at Wiley.

"Was he by himself?" Wiley asked calmly.

"Yes, I think so. He said he rode out here to tell me I could let my cattle graze on his land as long I wanted. But I really think he wanted to see if you were here."

Jake's fork dropped onto his plate.

"I told him we didn't need his offer of letting the cattle graze on his land. I lied and told him Sa-Ra and I rounded up all the cattle and herded them onto my own land."

"Did he buy it?" Wiley asked. He knew she was holding something back.

"I don't know." Belinda hesitated. "I also told him I knew he was looking for you." Her hand shook slightly as she sipped her coffee. "Then, I told him he wasn't man enough to capture you."

When Joe stopped hooting and slapping the table, Belinda continued, "I've insulted Billingsly twice in the last few weeks. We all know he gets even. I'm afraid he's going to think up some way to get my ranch away from me. And he's the one who can do it." She fumbled nervously with the handle of her cup.

Wiley smiled. "Don't worry about that. Billingsly will never get your ranch. Trust me."

"Why're you so sure, Wiley?" Jake asked. "He's got most'a the stuff he's wanted before, an' nobody's stopped 'im yet."

"He ain't never run across the likes of us, Jake," Wiley said, grinning impishly.

Joe laughed at the way Wiley answered, but Jake eyed him with suspicion.

"We'll git 'im to talk like a normal hoomin' bean in no time," Joe cackled, heaping on the accent. "Done that real good-like, Wiley. Few more'a them lessons, an' you'll talk jist fine."

"Wiley, how come you're so sure?" Jake asked again. "We don't know nothin' about no lawyer stuff."

"I know a little, Jake, and I don't think Billingsly can do anything to get this ranch away from Belinda. After we get back from the race, I'll ride to Alma and visit Billingsly. I'll get him to tell me if he had anything to do with the two murders on this ranch. I'm convinced he was involved. He wants this ranch too much to let murder stand in his way."

"Somebody at the Harrington Ranch might know somethin'," Joe said, "an' they're too skeered to say."

"That's true," Wiley said. "If not, I have a few tricks up my sleeve to take care of Billingsly...and Winder."

Jake stared at Wiley with slitted eyes. How much *did* Wiley know about lawyer stuff, and other kinds...like killin' stuff? Jake's gut tightened. Who was Wiley, really?

After the pie was reduced to miniscule crumbs, the three men rode to Chipmunk Rock, packed a few supplies, hitched Mac to the old wagon and returned to the ranch house. After a huge dinner, followed by a few fingers of whiskey, Jake and Wiley trudged to the bunkhouse for the night. Joe preferred to sleep outside, to the relief of the brothers and the women.

Since all the beds in the bunkhouse were single size, Jake pushed two beds side-by-side and tied the legs together. Wiley built a fire in the stove and stoked it to burn slowly.

They stripped naked, slid under the blankets and into each other's arms.

"I love bein' next to you, Wiley," Jake said as he scooted closer and pressed himself against Wiley's body. "Bein' naked next to you is better'n gettin' in bed with clean sheets. An' there ain't nothin' better'n smellin' you all over." Jake buried his face into Wiley's chest and breathed deeply. He explored Wiley's back with his hands and squeezed his hard butt.

Wiley loved being touched by Jake and knew exactly what he meant. After being on the wrestling team, the most sensuous smell he could think of was a sweaty male body, provided the man bathed often. While wrestling, he'd had to suppress his sexual desires, but when Jake's body pressed against his, he willingly lost control.

Wiley rolled Jake on top of himself and let his hands slide over Jake's smooth skin. God, he loved this man. He wondered what he'd ever done to deserve him. Wiley tightened his arms around Jake, pulled him closer and kissed him. He wanted to protect Jake from everything.

Jake shuddered with joyous pleasure. He felt so safe being squeezed by Wiley. He didn't care who Wiley was. Wiley loved him, and Jesus had sent him to be his partner and blood brother. That's all that mattered. Jake snuggled close to Wiley's ear and whispered, "Wiley...I think I love you." He jerked his head back. "No, wait, I *do* love you." He kissed Wiley.

Waves of ecstasy welded them together even tighter.

Later, Jake relaxed into the pillow and began snoring softly. Wiley fell asleep with his face nestled against Jake's neck.

* * *

They were up, washed--except for Thunder Joe--and gone by six on a bright, cloudless Wednesday morning. Jake and Wiley sat together in the buggy during the trip south. Tied to the back of the rig, Buddy seemed to enjoy running without a saddle on his back.

The road followed a line of forested hills stretching north and south in the middle of the flat, western side of South Park. They traveled eleven miles to the tracks of the Colorado Midland Railway, the northern boundary of the Harrington Ranch. As they rode around the base of a vast land swell, a cluster of buildings appeared in the distance.

"What town's that?" Jake asked.

"Ain't no town," Joe said. "That there's the Harrington ranch. Jest looks like a town."

When they got within a mile, they saw whispy clouds of dust rising from inside a huge circular fence.

Joe pointed to the dust. "That there's the race track. Might be practicin' some cuz the race ain't fer a few days yet. Once we get there, we'll take care of the horses an' you kin meet Ben."

As they approached the main gate, a cowboy waved his arms for them to stop.

"Two bits for camping on the ranch!" the tall lanky man shouted. From the looks of his sweat-soaked shirt, they knew he'd been standing in the hot sun all day.

"We're in the wagon race," Joe yelled back.

The cowboy nodded and waved them in.

At the stable, Jake reined Mac and stopped the wagon. High up on the side of the bunkhouse, a short distance from the barn, he saw a sign and tried to read it.

"Will...will come to the...uh...Har...Harig...Harig tin...uh, I mean, town...uh...ra...ra-nich. Will come to the Harig town ra-nich. Wiley, what's that mean?"

"That's not quite what it says, Jake. But you're close."

"Hell, I can't read nothin'!" Jake hung his head.

"Let me read it to you," Wiley said. "The top line says, Wel-come to the Har-ring-ton Ranch. The next line reads, Wagon Races: Sat-ur-day, June fifth. And the bottom line is, Rodeo: Sun-day, June sixth, eighteen eighty-six."

While reading the sign, Wiley noticed four men below it leaning against the bunkhouse. The tallest, a muscular man with dark brown hair, had his shirt open to his navel. His hat was pulled down to conceal a red, swollen face.

"There's Winder, Jake."

"What's he doin' here?"

"Looking for us." Wiley leaped out of the wagon and untied Buddy. "We may be in for a little more than a race. Let's make sure we're not the one's who start anything."

Thunder Joe rode over to where Winder and his men stood. He wanted to see first-hand who was with Billingsly's foreman, also to see if any of the Harrises had come.

As Jake began unhitching Mac from the wagon, a wizened old cowboy shuffled over and touched his battered felt hat.

"Howdy! Yer new here, ain't ye?"

"Sure are," Jake replied. "Just heard about the race yesterday. Thunder Joe told Wiley an' me about it." He grinned. "I'm gonna be the wagon racer."

"I'm Lonnie," the skinny, bent-over cowboy said in a scratchy voice. He extended his hand to both men. "Said ye know Joe? Where's that stinkin' ol' turd, anyhow?" He waved his arm at the barn, and two men ran to his side. One pulled the wagon toward the parked buggies, and the other grabbed the reins of Jake and Wiley's horses.

Wiley pointed to the bunkhouse. "Joe's over checking out Winder and his men. What's Winder doing here?"

Lonnie spat tobacco juice. "Sez he's gonna race, but that durn side-windin' snake's jist lookin' fer trouble. Bet my ass on it. Stay away from them cuz they's pure trouble."

"Winder's after Wiley an' me," Jake said. "We busted up his face an' beat up ten of his men."

Wiley gave Jake a sharp glance. Jake snapped his mouth shut.

Wiley turned to Lonnie. "We'd appreciate it if you wouldn't say anything about this to anyone. We've been...hiding out for a while until things cool down." He lied and said, "If we'd known Winder was going to be here, we wouldn't have come."

Lonnie chuckled. "Ye boys ain't from 'round here, I kin tell. If ye was, ye'd know ye done the right thing tellin' me 'bout Winder bein' after ye. Ben's the owner o'this here ranch, an' he ain't no friend o'that Billinsee feller. Why, two months ago, Ben wired fer somma them Pink-eeton fellers to come here an' do some checkin' on Billinsee." Lonnie suddenly strode toward the main part of the ranch, then looked back. "See yer boys later."

"Wiley, what's a Pink-eeton?" Jake asked meekly as his eyes followed Lonnie. He still stung from Wiley's warning glance.

"It's Pink-er-ton. They're private detectives." Wiley felt a sharp pain in his stomach and flinched.

Joe rode up, dismounted and handed the reins to a stable hand who'd come out of nowhere. "Winder'n them shore ain't here fer the races," Joe said to the brothers. "Don't see no sign'a them loonies, but they might be sittin' in a hole somewhere. Two'a them with Winder are killers. Nance is wanted in New Mexico fer killin' three or four ranchers an' sellin' their horses. Blackwood hires out as a back shooter."

Wiley studied Winder and the other three men closely. Not wanting to appear conspicuous, he turned away and grabbed Joe by the arm. "Who's Lonnie? Jake accidentally told him Winder's after us. Is that going to cause any problems?" He glanced at Jake staring at the ground.

"You done good, Jake," Joe said. "Ol' Lonnie's the saltiest cowboy you ever did see. If you hadn't told him about Winder bein' after you, I'd a done it my own self. Most likely he's tellin' Ben about it right now. You gents ain't got nothin' to worry about from Winder an' his men as long as yer here. Jest don't go wanderin' off, or they'll most likely tail ya." Joe started walking. "Come on, I'll show you around a mite."

# CHAPTER 32

Joe led the blood brothers to the main house, a sprawling adobe building surrounded by a vine-covered wall. Wiley wondered if the structure had once been a fort. A tall wiry man in his late forties approached them from an arched gate. Brown hair streaked with gray stuck out around the man's hat and framed his weathered face. Wiley noticed his blue eyes matched Jake's in brilliance and sparkle.

When the man reached them, he smiled and held out his hand. "Joe, are these the boys you went to get for the wagon race?"

"Shore are. These two gents're partners an' blood brothers. Name's are Wiley an' Jake."

"I'm Ben Harrington." Ben shook hands with the partners. "Lonnie tells me Winder's after you. Something about you two beating him up?"

"That's right," Wiley answered. "It happened a few weeks ago in the Silver Heels Bar in Alma."

"That's music to my ears, boys. Billingsly and his gang of thugs have been terrorizing this area too long. It's about time someone had the gumption to put them in their place." He scanned the partners from head to toe. "It looks like either of you could pull the claws off a puma. But while you're here, please refrain from fighting."

Ben shaded his eyes and glanced around the area. "I'll send out the word among my hands that Winder and his men are to be watched. Of course, that won't be easy with everything going on. All my men have assigned duties, but I don't put up with any nonsense around here. Especially with so many people on the ranch."

Ben put his arms over the shoulders of the partners. "Come on in the house. You boys are friends of Joe and deserve special treatment. There aren't too many people who can stand to be within fifty yards of the smelly old coot."

"We gived 'im a bath a few weeks back," Jake said. "An' might do it again if we get a chance." He grinned at Joe.

"Tarnation!" Joe yelled. "I'm stayin' clear of you boys fer the de-ration of this here race."

The others laughed.

Ben led them into the adobe house. Upon entering a spacious parlor, they were greeted by woman in her forties. Small in stature, her face held a sweetness that instantly grabbed Jake's attention. Though towering over her, he felt like a little boy again when she singled him out for a smile.

"Boys, this is my wife Rachael," Ben said, sliding an arm around her. "Rachael, this is Jake and Wiley. They recently beat the crap out of Billingsly's foreman and some of his men. By the way, how many others?"

Wiley smiled and lightly shook Rachael's hand. "Nine or ten, I don't remember. But we had help."

"Nine or ten!" Ben and Rachael said in unison.

"What started it?" Rachael asked.

Jake frowned. "Winder grabbed me in the nuts, an' I let him have it."

Wiley cringed and inspected the ceiling beams.

Rachael covered a smile with her hand, thinking Jake looked and talked like her younger brother.

"You sure have a way with words, Jake," Ben said, laughing. "But like I said, it's music to my ears. How long did it take you to finally knock the sucker out?"

"Jake did it with one punch." Wiley winked at Jake.

"One punch?" Ben stared at them. "You boys need a job? I could use you here keeping order this week."

"We can't. We're workin' for Miss Castille an' we..." Jake caught Wiley's stern glance. "Wiley, it just come out! I didn't mean to tell 'em!"

"They's workin' there on the sly," Joe said. "Hidin' out from Billingsly an' some other loonies from Kentucky that want 'em both dead."

Rachael sighed in relief. "I'm so glad Belinda hired you to work for her. I've been worried about her living there alone. Of course she has Soaring Raven, but two women shouldn't be by themselves out in the middle of nowhere. Especially since Mr. Billingsly is trying to get her ranch. We both feel he had something to do with John and Jason's death. Ben took it upon himself and hired some Pinkertons to investigate." She glanced at Ben as though she shouldn't have offered that information.

"It's okay to tell us," Jake added quickly, glad someone else had spilled a few beans. "Lonnie done told us already."

Wiley cleared his throat and cut his eyes to Ben. "Are...the Pinkertons here?"

Jake noticed Wiley seemed a bit nervous, like he'd been when the subject of the Pinkertons came up earlier at the barn. Could they be looking for Wiley, too?

"All I got was a telegram. It said they'd be sending two of their top men. They should be here by now, but I don't know for sure. The wire said they wouldn't make themselves known to anyone until they could solve the murder. If it's Billingsly they're after, I hope they're smarter than he is. The man's a snake-in-the-grass if I've ever seen one. Nobody around here can pin anything on him."

The dinner bell clanged from the back of the house. Rachael grabbed Jake by the arm then reached for Wiley's. "Join us for dinner. You're our honored guests for the time you're here. I can't tell you how relieved I am you're helping Belinda. Come, tell us how you met her over dinner."

As they walked down an arched, adobe corridor with a reddish tile floor, they passed a walled-in courtyard overgrown with vines and wildflowers. Birds drank from a small pool in the center.

Rachael stopped at the courtyard and smiled. "This reminds me of Santa Fe, where I grew up. My three brothers build houses there for a living, and for our wedding present they brought their helpers and put this house up in five months. Ben and I love it."

"Are these here walls made outta cement?" Jake asked as he rapped one with his knuckles.

"It's adobe," Ben said. "Adobe is mud and straw baked into bricks."

"Mud?" Jake knocked on the wall again. "Hell, Wiley, we could'a built us a cabin like this. There's enough mud by Walton Spring for five'a these here houses." Remembering how the mud was at the spring, he glanced at Ben. "Is there cow shit in these here walls, too?"

Still smiling from Jake's question, Rachael led them into a Mexican-style dining room. Brightly patterned wall hangings and large bunches of dried chilies splashed color against the adobe walls. The blood brothers stared at the massive, deeply carved furniture inlaid with hand-painted tiles. Delicious aromas wafted from the nearby kitchen.

During dinner, as Jake told the story of his travels from Kentucky, Wiley watched the three Harrington children listen attentively, amazed they were so well behaved. John, almost sixteen and homely compared to his parents, acted very much a man. Ryan looked about thirteen. Both boys were skinny as the handle of a pitchfork, but likeable.

Jenny, a bright, happy child of five, sat next to Jake and gazed up at him the entire time he talked.

"Jenny, eat your dinner," Rachael scolded. "Jake doesn't want you staring at him like that."

"It's okay, Ma'am," Jake said. "She an' I get along fine."

"We do?" Jenny asked. She giggled and hugged Jake's big arm. "See mommy, Jake's my friend."

Jake smiled at her. "But you gotta do what your ma tells you or I won't be your uncle."

Jenny ate every scrap of food on her plate.

Jake and Wiley accepted the invitation to stay in the guest room rather than in the bunkhouse or outside. Joe stated he would rather camp in the aspen grove where he normally did. Neither Ben nor Rachael tried to change Joe's mind since his odor had permeated the entire house. Clay bowls filled with glowing coals and pinon chips smoked in every room.

Rachael escorted the partners to their quarters and quickly excused herself, saying it was Jenny's bath night.

As the partners opened the massive door, again they gasped in amazement.

"Damn, Wiley," Jake shouted, "two of our cabins could fit inside here!"

One earth-colored wall of the guest room was partly covered by a woven rug in soft blue tones. Other walls displayed paintings in reds, oranges and browns. A high clay pot filled with red, paper poppies flanked a beehive fireplace crackling with fire.

Wiley smiled at Jake and walked to a wall lined with books from floor to ceiling. On his way, he slid his hand along the polished wood arm of one of the chairs on either side of a massive table. A pink glass lamp in the center of the table cast a rosy glow on a wooden bowl spilling with fresh fruit.

Jake wandered around the room in awe, then stopped in front of a huge arched window. He gasped when he realized it was also a door to the outside. Looking out at the deep purple sky of near darkness, he saw the black outline of a mountain shaped like the top fin of a fish.

Wiley scanned the scores of books on the shelves, impressed with the wide variety of titles. After he pulled out a thick volume on law, he turned up the lamp and began thumbing through it. Leaving it open on the table, he pulled out another book from a shelf near the top.

Jake walked over to him. "What're you readin', Wiley?"

Engrossed, Wiley didn't answer.

Jake sighed and ambled to the small bar set up on the top of the long, heavily-carved dresser. He poured himself two fingers of whiskey and drank it in one swallow. After poking the mammoth featherbed, he stretched, then threw himself into the middle of it.

*  *  *

"Miss Castille's got two barns, too, but they ain't that big," Jake commented the next morning as Joe led them on a tour of the ranch compound. "An' Ben's got him a bunkhouse bigger than the boardin' house in Alma."

"He's got twenty-five or thirty men workin' fer 'im," Joe said as he pointed to a few cabins nestled in the trees a quarter-mile away. "Them that are married live out there."

"All the men seem to be excellent workers," Wiley said. "Ben must treat them well."

"Ben brags to ever'body that his boys're the best hands in Park County. They bust their asses to prove him right."

"What's that buildin' over there by the big corral?" Jake asked.

"That there's the blacksmith shop, an' that little buildin' beside is the smoke house. You never et nothin' like Cee-Cee's smoked ham or antelope. Cee-Cee's the cook. Might'a heard her already. She's fat, an' always laughin'."

"Enjoying your tour, boys?" Ben Harrington asked as he walked up behind them.

"You sure have a big spread," Wiley said.

"Seven thousand acres, but it's not the biggest around here. Sam Hartsel's ranch, east of here, is over eight thousand." Ben rubbed his jaw. "Speaking of the Hartsel Ranch, you boys might like to relax in Sam's hot springs pool. It's an indoor pool, and he built a hotel beside it. Actually, his ranch is more like a town. The train stops there, and he's even got a post office and a small general store. People come from all parts of the country to stay in his hotel."

"How far is it?" Wiley asked.

"About six miles. If you want, you can ride in one of our buggies. Whenever I have doings here, I run buggies every hour to get people back and forth to the train."

During the next two days, the blood brothers made three trips to Hartsel. Wiley loved the hot water and sat in the pool or on the edge for several hours at a time. His rugged good looks and muscular body kept the women around the pool in a titter, even though he ignored them.

Jake got dizzy in the hot water after a few minutes and spent most of the time lounging in a chair outside talking with hotel guests. Once, while Wiley soaked in the pool, Jake got a couple carrots from the hotel cook. He tossed them near Wiley and stirred the water.

"I'm gonna have me a big pot'a soup in a few minutes, Wiley."

Wiley laughed, grabbed Jake's leg and pulled him in, clothes and all. This antic got such a laugh from the other bathers, the two men became the talk of the hotel.

During the two days before the wagon race, the partners occasionally ran into Winder and his men. None of them spoke. Jake didn't think anything would happen, but Wiley kept his eyes and ears open. Occasionally, he'd talk to the ranch hands and snoop around a little. Jake didn't mind. He spent much of his time riding Jenny around on his shoulders. But once Jake's curiosity got the best of him when he saw Wiley coming out of the train station in Hartsel.

"What were you doin' in there, Wiley?"

"Just being nosy. If all goes like I planned, there will be a surprise for you on Saturday. Did you find anything in the general store?"

"Picked me up a leather strap." Jake held it out. "I never race without tyin' myself in."

* * *

On Friday afternoon, the south side of the barn, set aside for the racing buggies, teemed with activity. Many participants milled around, checking the wheels, axles and frames of their buggies for defects that could cost them the race--or get them killed. No one noticed Winder and his men standing near Jake and Wiley's wagon.

"Clint, slowly get under their wagon and saw half way through the rear axle," Winder said. "Do the same thing to the shafts in the middle. The rest of us will stand guard." Winder glanced around. "And while you're under there, loosen some of the bolts in the bed."

Once Clint finished his work, they disappeared around the barn and casually walked to a small rise overlooking the corral, out of earshot from anyone.

"Now, boys, we know what Billingsly wants," Winder stated. "He wants both of them dead. The one driving the wagon should get trampled under the horses when the wagon breaks in half and falls apart. I haven't made up my mind how the other one will meet his accidental death, but I'm thinking on it."

Blackwood grinned and displayed his rotten teeth. "I could jest shoot 'im in the back when he wasn't lookin'."

"We've got to make it look like an accident!" Winder snapped. "There's already enough suspicion about us being here. Haven't you noticed Ben's men keeping track of us all the time?" He looked at their blank stares and sighed. "Any more bright ideas?"

Clint, Blackwood and Nance all looked at the ground in silence.

"I picked you three men because I thought you were the smartest. So far, I've been wrong. Now, think! If we do this job well, Billingsly may up our wages."

Winder knew that was a lie. No such agreement had been discussed, but he wanted to spur some kind of intelligent response from them. Like himself, these men drew fighting wages, twice what regular ranch hands made. But the three of them could quit working for the lawyer whenever they wanted. He couldn't leave unless Billingsly consented.

Winder hated working for Billingsly, but ever since the lawyer had caught him in the act of strangling Pops Duran for the miner's sack of gold, that fancy-dressed, dick-licker held the mortgage on his life. How was he supposed to know Billingsly was staying next door to Pops in the Alma Hotel? Those damn paper-thin walls. He'd never forget how viciously Billingsly had laughed when he'd flung open the door and took in the scene of the murder. Even now, thoughts of that laugh chilled his spine.

After being forced to work for the lawyer as his foreman for three years, he'd killed John and Jason on the Castille Ranch, hoping his services would finally end. But Billingsly had only laughed at the suggestion. This time, if he succeeded in killing Jake and Wiley, Billingsly might grant his freedom. At least the lawyer hadn't laughed when he'd brought it up.

"I don't think you know how important it is to kill those two men," Winder snarled. "Clint, got any ideas?"

Before Clint could answer, they noticed several of Ben's men sauntering toward them. They all wore guns.

"Let's go," Winder snarled. "This part of the ranch is getting a little too hot." They turned their backs on the ranch hands and hoofed to their camp on the far edge of the race track.

* * *

At the Friday evening meal with the Harrington family, Jake and Wiley sat across from the two boys. During a lull in the conversation about tomorrow's race, John glanced at the partners and asked, "How did you get such big muscles?"

"John!" Rachael said sharply. "You shouldn't be so personal at the dinner table."

"It's okay, ma'am." Jake said. "I asked the same thing to a soldier when I was a young'n like him." He looked at John and grinned. "I done it by some push-ups an' sit-ups an' stuff like that. Wiley done it by wrestlin' in school."

"What's a push-up?" Ryan asked.

Jake grinned. "One'a these here days I'll show you."

"Show us now!" Ryan yelled. John said the same thing.

"John! Ryan!" Rachael broke in. "Where are your manners? You can wait until after dinner."

"I wanna see now!" Jenny chimed in. She slapped the top of the table. "Uncle Jake, show us now. Please?"

Rachael glanced at Ben for support, but all she got from her husband was a smile.

Ben winked at Jake. "I think this one time we can have a little entertainment at dinner. Jake, do the honors."

Jake rose from his chair, got down on the floor and did fifty push-ups before he stopped and got to his feet. He'd barely worked up a sweat. Even Wiley was impressed. Jake blushed from the big round of applause. Jenny ran to him and hugged his leg.

Ben stood up and shook Jake's hand. "Mighty impressive, Jake. Would you consent to give lessons to my sons after dinner?"

"Sure thing."

As Ben sat down, he said, "I'm going to call all my hands together to watch, and hopefully to participate. Might give them something else to do in their spare time. Wiley, can you show them some of the things you know also?"

"I'd be glad to. Since Jake checked out our wagon early this morning, we don't have anything planned."

Later, outside by the bunk house, Jake and Wiley stripped to the waist and demonstrated exercises and wrestling holds for the Harrington boys and ranch hands. Within a half hour, most of the men had removed their shirts and were doing push-ups, sit-ups, knee-bends and other exercises Jake showed them. Some of the men scrounged the barn for make-shift weights. Others roped off a small ring in which Wiley taught the elements of wrestling and boxing. Lanterns, hung on poles, enabled the men to see after sunset. The lessons continued until ten when the tired and sweaty men ambled off to their beds for a sound sleep before race day.

# CHAPTER 33

Saturday began chilly under a cloudless sky. The rising sun cast long shadows over the Harrington Ranch, already teeming with activity on Wagon Race Day. The half-mile race track, scattered with bunch grass, shrubs and gullies, would prove a challenging course, even for the most skilled drivers.

Ben hooked his heel on the middle rail as he balanced himself on the top rung of the fence that surrounded the outer edge of the track. He waited until Jake, Wiley and Joe joined him, then pointed to several riders walking their horses along the track.

"See out there?" Ben said. "Those men are searching for ground squirrel or rabbit holes. They're the biggest problem. If a hoof gets caught in a hole during the race, the horse's leg can break right off. It happened four years ago. The horse and driver got trampled to death." He shook his head. "Horrible thing."

No one spoke.

"They've been out there since yesterday," Ben continued. "Can't start any earlier or the holes are right back. The men go out in shifts. As long as there's a speck of light, they're out there." Ben faced the others. "It's the hands' own doing. Of course, I back it a hundred percent." He paused, drew in a deep breath and blew it out.

"The man killed in that race was best hand I ever had. Robby. Robby Gorin. Big, handsome man. Looked something like you, Jake."

Wiley glanced at Jake and was shocked at his sad expression. Jake was thinking of Robby and not of his own safety. Before he could say anything, Ben continued.

"Robby could do anything. He was good at taming wild horses, roping, branding, racing. I loved him like a son. We all

did. And he loved everybody. Clay, his partner, went off the deep
end after it happened. He disappeared one night, and no one's
ever seen him again."

Dread gripped Wiley. He touched Jake's arm. "Maybe you
should reconsider."

"What? Wiley, I don't know what you just said."

"Don't race."

"Why?"

"Weren't you listening to Ben?" Wiley asked. "Mac could get
his leg caught in a hole, and then we'd lose you, too. I don't want
that to happen."

"Hell, Wiley, Mac an' me are gonna win. Nothin's gonna stop
us, neither." Jake swung his legs over the rail and dropped to the
ground. "I'm gonna take Mac for a ride. He likes to run a-ways
before a race."

Wiley followed him. "Let's go to Hartsel. It's only six-thirty,
and we can be back before ten."

Joe and Ben watched the blood brothers walk to the barn.
They saw Wiley slip his arm around Jake's waist and pull him
close for a moment.

"Them two shore are the huggin'ist pair I ever did see," Joe
said. "Can't get enough of each other."

"I can't get it out of my head how much Jake looks like
Robby," Ben said. "I can understand Wiley's concern." He stared
at the two men walking to the barn. "Secretly, I suppose I was
trying to change Jake's mind by talking about Robby. I sure hope
he's careful out there."

As the partners dismounted at the Hot Spring Hotel stable,
four men surrounded them. Jake wheeled around with his fists up.

"Hold up there, Jake," Bill Chasteen yelled. "It's just us." He
stood with Harry, Frank and Matt. "We got Wiley's wire to come
down fer the race, and here we are."

"Damn!" Jake yelled. "You gents nearly got yerselves beat
up!" He grinned. "Wiley, is this the surprise you told me about?"

"It sure is." Wiley gave each man a handshake.

"Whoopee! I sure am glad to see you all!" Jake grabbed each
one, giving him a hug and hard pats on the back.

In the changing room, Harry held up his rented swimsuit. It resembled a union suit with the arms cut off at the elbows, the legs reached mid-thigh. "These things cover up everything a man has to show." He eyed Wiley, Frank and Jake. "Well, most men."

Later, as Harry slipped into the water of the hotel pool, cooled to a hundred and ten degrees, he shouted, "This water's going to boil my ass!"

"Harry! There's women about." Bill nodded to four snickering women sitting together on one of the pool-side benches. "Keep yer voice down. This is what the rest of us feel gettin' in *yer* tubs."

"I haven't ever seen anyone's prick get burnt off in my tubs like *mine's* going to get in *here*!" Harry shouted, hoping for another laugh.

"Hey! Pipe down over there!" a white-haired man yelled. His monstrous, pale body sagged over both sides of his lounge chair. "My wife doesn't like that rough talk."

"Hasn't she ever seen a prick?" Harry yelled, turning toward the heckler. Eyeing the obese man, he added, "Looks like she hasn't seen one for a long time. At least the kind I'm talking about."

Even before the snickers died down, the man and his equally fat wife struggled to their feet and left the area in a huff.

"See what you did," Bill snapped. "He's prob'ly some senator, and we'll get thrown outta here."

"Well, if he is a senator," Harry yelled, "I won't vote for him. Looks like those two have been *eating the country!*"

"Harry!" his five companions shouted in unison.

The six men spent an hour in Hartsel, but when the first race started at ten, they were perched on the top rail of the track fence. Jenny ran to Jake, and he lifted her into his lap.

Harry saw her and leaned toward Wiley. "Looks like you've got a little competition going there."

Wiley grinned. "I'd worry if she was twenty years older." He leaned forward, looked past Harry at Jake and watched him put his arm around Jenny and point to the racers. Wiley suddenly had a vision of Jake flying out of a buggy and being trampled. He gasped, stood up on the middle rail and forced himself to erase the thought.

Hundreds of people had camped around the entire length of the track. Since Ben didn't allow anyone in the center area, Wiley could see the far fence. Even though Jake's race wasn't until noon, another pang of terror shot through him as he glanced at the ten buggies lined up into position. Twenty horses fidgeted and stamped the ground.

Wiley couldn't watch. He turned around and scanned the crowd behind him, hoping to spot Winder and his men. Were they going to try something during the race? Not seeing them, he asked Harry to save his spot, climbed down and shoved his way toward the bunkhouse. Wiley spied one of Ben's cowboys leaving the building and hurried over to him.

"Have you seen Winder?" Wiley asked.

"I shore ain't. Afternoon yesterdee, I seen 'em over by the racin' buggies jist standin' around. Didn't see what they was up to. We're 'pose to keep our eyes on 'em, but they might'a left fer all I know. I been ridin' the track all mornin'."

"Well, if you see them, let me know. I'll be sitting over there." Wiley pointed to the only gap on the fence.

"Sure thing. By the way, much obliged fer them lessons last night." The cowboy grinned. "See ya 'round."

A gun blast started the race. Wiley dodged his way back to the fence. He gently pulled down a man trying to take his spot and climbed to the top rail just as the last wagon finished the first turn of the huge oval racetrack. Clouds of dust billowed up from the horses and wagons, completely concealing the rigs in the back.

"Jake, you'll have to stay in front or you won't be able to see anything," Wiley shouted above the clamor of the crowd.

"I sure plan to, Wiley." Jake laughed. "This sure looks fun!"

As the racing teams approached the last quarter of the track, the ground shook from the twenty galloping horses.

"Look!" Jake yelled. "We can see the lead man now. He's doin' a mighty fine job with them horses."

Amid the roars and cheers of the crowd, the lead wagon sped across the finish line. The other racers followed with only inches of space between them. As they slowed to a halt, a thick cloud of choking dust engulfed the screaming onlookers.

When the dust settled, Big Mike Tolbin was named the winner. Foreman of the Dowdle Ranch, located between the Hartsel Ranch and Jefferson, Big Mike was a huge burly man in his thirties. His black hair, beard and clothes had been coated tan.

Matt leaned in front of Frank. "The winner could pass as your older brother, Wiley."

Standing up, Big Mike drove his rig around the track, waving at the cheering crowd. As he completed his victory ride, the left front wheel of his wagon fell off, pitching him to the ground. The crowd gasped. Big Mike slowly got to his feet, dusted himself with his hat, then threw his head back in laughter. Cheers deafened everyone.

Several men ran onto the track. One grabbed the reins of Big Mike's horses and led them out of the circle. Two others ran along beside the wagon holding up the front end, and another man grabbed the wheel laying by the inside fence.

Everyone whistled and cheered again as Ben presented Big Mike with a rawhide bag bulging with one hundred and fifty gold coins. The Dowdle foreman lifted the bag over his head, grinned, then headed into the swarming crowd.

The six companions climbed off the fence and started toward the ranch house. Jenny clung to Jake's hand and skipped along beside him.

Wiley stopped suddenly. "Where's Thunder Joe? I haven't seen him all morning?"

"Thunder Joe?" Frank said with a laugh. "Is that ol' fart here? I'm surprised we ain't smelled 'im before now."

"He's here somewhere," Wiley said. "It isn't like him to miss the race. He's the one who got us to come here in the first place." Wiley veered to his right. "I'm going to his camp to see if he's sleeping off a drunk."

"I'll go with you, Wiley." Jake glanced down at his side. "Jenny, you go up to the house. We'll be back."

Jenny pouted, stamped her foot, then ran toward her adobe home.

"We might as well all go," Bill chimed in. "I ain't seen that ol' coot fer quite a spell."

Reaching Joe's camp, the men found him still in his bedroll. When Wiley pulled the blanket away from Joe's head, he saw a dark streak of dried blood down his face. "Oh, my God!" Wiley knelt down to see if the skinny old man was alive.

"Is he dead, Wiley?" Jake asked.

"He's still breathing, but he's out cold." Wiley picked Joe up and started toward the house. "We'd better get him to Ben's house so he can be looked after. Jake, gather up his bedroll and saddle bags and bring them along."

"Who in the hell would do that to him?" Harry asked. Then added, "Didn't you fellows mention Winder was here? I wonder if he did this?"

"That's what I'm thinking." Wiley scanned the yard as they walked. "I haven't seen Winder all morning. I looked for him just before the race started."

As they reached the house, Rachael ran out the door. "What happened to Joe?"

"Somebody clobbered 'im on the head," Jake replied. "He needs some lookin' after." He cut sly eyes to Wiley. "We gotta get him outta them smelly buckskins an' clean him up while he's still out cold."

Frank snickered.

As Wiley followed Rachael through the house to the family's private bath area, the others tagged along, loudly whispering about everything they saw. Rachael entered a large room, tiled in richly colored, Mexican patterns from the floor to the beamed ceiling.

"Lay him on the rug, Wiley," Rachael said. She started for the door. "I'll get some hot water for a bath."

Wiley laid Joe on the thick rug alongside a polished brass tub. While the others crowded around, the blood brothers breathed through their mouths as they removed Joe's buckskins.

Jake tossed the greasy leather clothes into a heap by the door. "Take them things out an' burn 'em. An' bury the ashes, too. He can wear ord'nary clothes 'til he gets him some new buckskins."

No one moved. They didn't want to get near the things, much less touch them. Finally, the stink got to Bill. He grabbed the clothes, ran outside and pitched them in a heap by the horse corral, then rubbed his hands with dirt.

Bill pushed his way into the barn and asked Lonnie for some kerosene. Together, they returned to the corral, kicked the buckskins away from the fence and doused them. While Joe's clothes burned, belching black smoke, Bill said, "I ain't likely to forget this smell if I live to be a hundred."

After Jake and Wiley bathed Joe in hot water and plenty of soap, they dried him and wrapped him in a blanket. Jake carried Joe to the guest room and put him in their bed. Rachael came in with a bowl of hot broth as Joe opened his eyes.

"Where am I?" Joe asked feebly. He saw Wiley bending over him and the others standing around the bed. "What's goin' on?"

"Someone knocked you over the head while you were in your bedroll," Wiley said. "It must have happened earlier this morning because the blood on your face had dried hard. Do you know who did it?"

"Was prob'ly that there Winder scum. Last night I wandered near their camp to see if I could hear anythin' they was plannin' to do. They must'a smelled me." He sniffed himself. His face turned red. "You boys didn't..."

"We sure did," Jake said with a grin. "Burnt yer clothes up too like we should'a done the first time we gave you a scrubbin'. You'll just hafta wear somethin' else 'til Soaring Raven can make you some new ones."

"*What!*" Joe lifted off the pillow, then dropped back. He grabbed his aching head and groaned. "I'll get even with you coyotes if it's the last thing I ever do."

Rachael moved next to the bed. "Joe, you need to sip some of this broth. It'll give your body back some of the strength it lost."

As Joe sipped the broth, Wiley turned to the others. "We have to find Winder and his men and do something with them. Jake, can you let Ben know what happened? Just before we went to Joe's camp I saw him heading for the barn next to the bunkhouse."

"Sure will, Wiley!" Jake rushed out.

Wiley turned to Joe. "Jake's race starts an hour from now. Can you can make it by then?"

"Tarnation! Wouldn't miss it fer nothin'. I'll be there even if I hafta go nekkid. Jest might go nekkid since you burnt up my duds. You ornery cuss!" Joe grabbed his head.

"You're about the same size as Ryan," Rachael said. "I'll get some of his old clothes for you to wear."

"I'm goin' nekkid!"

"Not on *this* ranch, you aren't," Rachael said sternly. "Now, finish your broth."

"Dang women," Joe muttered. He slurped his broth as loud as he could.

An all-out search of the ranch began for Winder and his men. The few spare hands combed the area around the race track, the barns, even the bunkhouse. None of them turned up anything. One of Ben's cowboys discovered Winder's camp had been deserted.

"Maybe he left," Matt said as he and Frank caught up with Jake and Wiley.

"It's a possibility, but I doubt it." Wiley pulled out his watch and glanced at it. "Jake, we'd better get the wagon hitched and get you to the track. There's only ten minutes left until your race." He grabbed Jake by the arm, pulled him close and whispered, "Jake, are you sure you want to do this? You could get trampled out there."

Jake grinned at him. "I ain't gonna get trampled, Wiley." He held up his long leather strap. "The buggy'd hafta break apart before I'd end up in the dirt."

With the help of Bill and Frank, the partners got Mac hitched to the wagon. After Wiley hugged him, Jake patted Mac on the neck, then leaped into the wagon and drove it toward the starting line.

Bill scratched his head. "That wagon don't look safe fer some reason. It shakes too dang much. You shore you checked it out proper?"

"Jake checked it out early yesterday morning. He said it was in fine whack. I took that to mean it checked out okay." Wiley suddenly remembered what the cowboy had said about seeing Winder and his men lurking about the wagons. Could they have done something to Jake's wagon?

Wiley ran after Jake, shoving his way through the crowd and yelling for him to stop.

When Wiley reached the fence, he tried to climb up between two men. One of them grabbed him by the shirt and shoved him to the ground.

"We were here first!" the man yelled down at him.

Wiley jumped to his feet. As he ran farther down the fence, he tried to look between the milling people for the line-up of buggies on the track. When he spotted the racers, he tried slipping under the fence. He'd gotten only half-way when he felt himself being roughly pulled back. Turning his head he saw two cowboys, each holding one of his legs. They dragged him away from the track.

"Let go of me!" Wiley shouted.

"Sorry, Wiley, Ben's orders," one cowboy said. "No one's allowed on the track but the racers. No matter what."

Wiley struggled free and leaped up, ran to the fence, pulled a man down and climbed it. When he saw Jake he began waving. "Jake! Don't race!"

Eleven buggies had rolled up side-by-side at the starting line. Jake had placed himself third from the inside. He felt lucky to get that spot. It gave him a two-buggy cushion from the fence and put him near the shortest distance around the track. He stood up in the wagon and scanned the crowd. When he spotted Wiley, he waved and grinned, but couldn't hear what Wiley yelled to him.

Jake waved again, then tied himself to the front bar with his six-foot leather strap.

"We're gonna win this one, Mac." Jake knew his horse was eager to race the way he wiggled his butt and swished his tail.

Wiley spotted Ben. Hoping to get him to delay the race until Jake's wagon could be inspected, he shoved his way through the milling people and tried to get closer.

"Racers, get set!" Ben shouted. He pointed his gun into the air.

The gun blasted.

Mac lurched forward, and Jake instantly took the lead. He cracked his whip high over Mac's head. With each snap, the horse galloped faster. Standing up in the wagon, Jake held on as the wheels bounced over the tough clumps of bunch grass. As the track's inner fence became a blur on his left, Jake noticed the screaming onlookers clinging to the outer fence.

"My nuts is gettin' shook off!" Jake yelled to the crowd. He laughed and snapped the whip over Mac's head again.

When Jake approached a pair of red, long-handle underwear hanging from a wire over the track, he knew the halfway point was close. During a brief glance behind him, Jake discovered he was out in front and gaining.

After the gun, Wiley ran to the fence where Bill and the others sat. He climbed up, stood on the middle rail and shaded his eyes. Noticing Wiley's ashen face, Harry nudged him and held out his field glasses. Wiley grabbed them and weakly smiled his thanks.

Wiley kept the glasses trained on Jake's wagon, three horse-lengths out in front. As Jake reached the halfway marker, Wiley saw a black delivery wagon come from behind and move up fast.

Suddenly, out of the clouds of dust obscuring the racers in back, Wiley saw a horse break through the flimsy boards of the track's inner fence. He watched the buggy fly into the air and flip over, tossing the driver out. The man landed on the ground, bounced once and rolled several yards. Ranch hands, stationed in the center area, frantically drove a flatbed wagon toward him.

Wiley swung the glasses back to Jake's wagon. It still held the lead, but not by much. Wiley stood up and nearly lost his balance. "Oh, God! Jake fell out!"

As Jake passed the flapping long johns, he glanced over his shoulder again. A black delivery wagon had just taken over second place and was gaining on him. Suddenly, Jake's wagon hit a dip and lurched into the air. It came down hard, and Jake heard a loud snap under the bed. Before he could look back, another deep rut tossed the rig into the air again. When it hit the ground, the rear wheels flew off and rolled to either side of the track. The back of the wagon slammed into the dirt and snapped in half. Splintered boards flew in all directions. The jolt knocked Jake sideways but the leather strap tightened around his waist, then jerked him under the seat. He smacked his head on the front bar on the way down.

Dazed, it took Jake a few seconds to realize the wagon tilted backwards and the jagged ends of the boards dug into the ground, slowing him down.

The black wagon pulled alongside and began passing.

Jake threw his arm over the front rail and pulled himself to his knees. He leaned forward to tip the wagon and lift the back end out of the dirt. Without the drag, Mac lunged ahead, forcing Jake to lean forward even more to balance the rocking, two-wheeled chariot. Since he'd lost the whip, Jake smacked the horse's rump with the reins.

"Get goin', Mac!"

With another burst of speed, Mac pulled ahead of the other wagon, but only by half a horse-length. Suddenly, the racer next to him veered away, and Jake wondered if the black rig might have lost a wheel. Still trying to balance himself, Jake smacked Mac lightly with the reins. Another bump tossed him back under the seat.

Jake struggled to his knees, but couldn't tell where he was. He glanced around, didn't see anyone behind him and laughed.

"You lost him, Mac! Keep goin'!"

To Wiley, perched on the fence, the crowd's roar kept pace with the racers. Thick dust kicked up by the lead wagons obliterated the track and wagons behind them. Wiley frantically scanned the inner edge of the track and the center area, then trained the glasses back on Jake's rig. He saw an arm reach up and grab the rail. Then, Jake's head popped up from under the seat. Wiley sighed with relief until he realized the back half of the wagon was gone. Jake was driving a two-wheeled pile of broken boards.

Still struggling to keep his balance, Jake couldn't tell where he was on the track. He glanced around and didn't see anyone behind him. It puzzled him when the air began getting dusty up ahead, but he gave Mac another smack and shifted positions to further steady the tipsy wagon.

The dust got thicker. Once again, his rig lurched into the air. When it came down, Jake had one hell of a time trying to keep from falling backwards. The dust became so thick he could barely see, but kept lightly tapping Mac with the reins and yelling.

Suddenly, through the thick clouds, Jake passed a man standing in the track. It was *Wiley*! He was waving his arms. Jake thought he heard him yell, "Stop!"

"What the hell?" Jake pulled on the reins and slowed Mac. When the horse stopped, the two-wheeled wreck lurched forward and dumped Jake onto the ground.

As Wiley ran toward him, Jake yelled, "Wiley get off the track! You'll be trampled!"

"The race is over, Jake," Wiley gasped as he reached his partner. He watched Jake untie himself from the wagon, helped him to his feet, then threw his arms around him. "God, am I glad you're all right."

Jake pulled back. "The race is over? What happened? Who won?"

"You won!" Wiley looked at his dust-covered partner and burst out laughing. "You didn't know the race was over?"

"Hell, Wiley, after the wheels fell off an' the back end broke, I didn't know what else to do 'cept keep goin'."

Ben walked toward them through the clearing dust. "I haven't seen anything like that race since we started this seven years ago. Jake, let me shake your hand. That was a mighty fine piece of driving you just did. But why did you go around the track twice?"

"Twice?" Jake shook his head. "I went around the track twice? I wondered why it was gettin' so damn dusty."

Ben and Wiley laughed, and Ben slid his arm across Jake's shoulders. "Come over to the fence and collect your prize, Jake. You certainly won it."

As they approached the judges' stand, people spilled off the fence and ran toward them. Matt and Frank ran to Jake, grabbed him and lifted him on their shoulders. They inched through the cheering people pressed around them.

"I really won?" Jake asked as he bent over and looked upside-down at Frank and Matt. They sagged a little under his two-hundred-twenty pounds.

Matt laughed. "You sure did. Wildest race I've ever seen. How'd you keep the wagon from tipping over?"

"Hell, that weren't nothin'. I'd practice racin' at home with our ol' broken wagon all the time. Pa wouldn't let me use the good one."

"Ladies and gents!" Ben's loud voice was hardly heard over the din. "Attention, please!" When the yelling died down, Ben proceeded. "Let me say I haven't ever seen a race quite like this one before. Not only did Jake win this race, he won it twice!" The crowd cheered. Ben held up the bag and hollered, "This is awarded to one of the most skilled wagon drivers I've ever seen!" He held out the prize money to Jake still perched on Matt and Frank's shoulders.

Jake smiled and took the bag. He told Matt and Frank to let him down. They gladly did. When his feet touched the ground, Wiley grabbed him in a bear hug. Another cheer went up from the crowd.

* * *

Under piles of hay in the loft of the big barn, four men peered down at the track.

"Damn!" Winder cursed under his breath.

"You kin shore say that again," Blackwood drawled.

"Oh, shut up!" Winder glared at the man crouched next to him. "Now, what are we going to do? You men have bungled this job from the start. First, I want you to make sure the wagon falls apart, and..."

"How were we supposed to know he could drive a two-wheeled wagon?" Clint interrupted.

"...and then I told you to kill that old mountain man for spying on us," Winder continued. "But all he got was knocked cold."

"Hell, I thart he was daid," Nance broke in. "I clubbed 'im wit ma gun like you done tol' me. He was bleedin' when I left 'im."

Winder covered his face with his hands. He knew his men had done exactly what he'd told them to do, but nothing they'd done so far had worked.

"Let's clear out of here," Winder growled, "now, while the crowds are milling around. We'll ride up to the hills above the ranch and watch. When they leave, we'll follow them. After they get far away from any ranch, we'll kill them."

# CHAPTER 34

On the day of the wagon race, Ed Billingsly sat in his plush office above the Bank of Alma and poured himself a brandy. Ledgers and bank documents covered the top of his huge wooden desk. He glanced at them and chuckled. It had been masterful how he'd talked Thomas Crain into giving him the Castille Ranch mortgage papers and Belinda's personal bank statements.

Billingsly despised the weasely banker but had often made good use of him. Getting these records was the best use so far. After telling the greedy man they would become partners in the Castille Ranch once they foreclosed on it, Crain gave him the bank records. After seeing Belinda's books, Billingsly knew they could foreclose within six months. Possibly sooner.

He found all the Castille books in order. Not a single late payment had been posted since Wade Castille took out a second mortgage for operating capital six years ago. But Billingsly knew the Castille Ranch hadn't sold any cattle for over a year. Even though he'd paid Belinda two thousand dollars for the strip of land along the Horseshoe River, her bank statement revealed that she was low on cash. With only enough money to make eight mortgage payments, Billingsly knew the amount would be cut down to five or six since she would need operating and food money. If she hired anyone to brand the calves or make a cattle drive to the railroad, her balance would be depleted even more.

But long before that, he planned to have his men drive her cattle south into the Horseshoe River canyon. Thousands of head could be hidden there among the huge boulders. Since it was well to the north of the Hartsel and Harrington Ranches, he doubted anyone would be nosing around.

He knew the cattle could easily be driven through the canyon to the Colorado Midland Railroad and shipped east. And selling Belinda's cattle wouldn't be a problem. Papers authorizing the sale could be forged. He'd been practicing the woman's handwriting for several months and had it down quite well.

Billingsly finished the last bit of brandy in the glass and closed the ledger. He gathered up the book and loose papers on his desk and headed toward the stairs into the bank.

As the lawyer silently approached Thomas Crain's main floor office, he stopped outside and listened to make sure the banker was alone. Not hearing any talking inside, he opened the door without knocking and stepped into the gloomy room.

Crain looked up from his cluttered desk and scowled. "Don't you ever knock?"

"Why should I?" Billingsly snapped. He slammed the door behind him. "As of this moment, I *own* you." He tossed the ledger and papers down in front of Crain. "In six months I--or rather *we*--will own the Castille Ranch. I *forbid* you to extend any credit to Belinda until my plan is accomplished. *And* I don't want to find you secretly trying to buy the ranch, like you did that night in the Silver Heels Bar!"

Crain said nothing. He watched Billingsly glide to the leather chair against the wall next to the door.

Billingsly picked up a stack of papers in the chair and tossed them on the floor. He seated himself, then crossed legs and pointed his toe. Noticing his rings flash from a small shaft of sunlight finding its way through the painted windows, he moved his hands around in the ray of light to see the stones sparkle.

Beads of sweat dotted Crain's forehead. "What's your plan?" he asked nervously.

Billingsly glanced at him. "Just never mind. Do as I say, and the ranch will be ours before the year is out. *Do* I make myself clear?"

"Very clear," Crain grumbled. "And what if I don't go along with you?"

Billingsly sighed and inspected the fingernails of his right hand. "Thomas, I really don't know why you even bothered to ask that question." He smiled snottily to Crain. "You know full well what will happen to you if you don't. I'll expose all your scams and crooked deals that I've discovered over the past five years. I might even call in the bank examiners from Denver to give your books a thorough going over. I really don't think you're in any position to go against my wishes."

Crain squirmed in his chair. "I see." He fumbled with the top of his boot. "And what happens to me if you suddenly decide you don't need me any more?"

"My dear Thomas, would I do that? Why, just think of it. If we play by my rules, you and I can gain control of this whole area and become very wealthy men. Then, we can leave this filthy burg and live like kings. Anywhere we want. *I* want to get out of this town as soon as possible. Understand?"

"Quite well," Crain said. He knew if he crossed the lawyer, he'd be done for and most likely end up in a federal prison for the rest of his life. He also realized Ed Billingsly had no loyalties beyond himself, and when he no longer needed a person, he'd discard him like a dirty bar rag. The piggish banker didn't like the position he was in.

Billingsly smiled. "I'm glad you see my point of view. I'll keep you informed. Just remember what I said. Give *no credit* or *loans* to Belinda Castille. No matter what!" The lawyer stood, then left the office without further comment, slamming the door behind him.

Crain stared at the closed door for a few minutes, then removed his glasses and dropped them on the papers littering his desk. He covered his face with his hands. He'd been doing well with his own little scams before Billingsly came to town. But even though he hated the lawyer and wanted him dead, he didn't know how to get rid of him without getting caught, or killed. Just as the foppish lawyer had said, Billingsly owned him.

\* \* \*

On the corner of Fifteenth and Wazee in Denver, Seth Harris glanced up and down the street, searching for Jake and Wiley. They'd been in Denver for nearly a week and had turned up nothing.

"I don't reckon they're here, Pa," Clem whined. "We'd 'a seen 'em by now."

"Keep lookin'!" Seth snapped. "This here's a big town, and today we split up. Clem, you look in all the bars. Zeke comes with me, and we'll search all the stores."

"We already done that, Pa," Clem said. "We gotta go back to Alma. Jake ain't here."

"You do what I tell you, boy!" Seth shouted. "We'll give it one more day, and then go back to Alma and start searchin' that whole area. Now, get goin'! We meet back here at two o'clock in the mornin'. You hear me, boy?"

With a half smile, Zeke watched Clem wander up Fifteenth Street with stooped shoulders. He knew Jake and his friend weren't in Denver, but it didn't matter. He enjoyed walking around one of the biggest towns he'd ever seen. The hundreds of people, shops and five-story brick buildings fascinated him. But he'd rather be walking around Denver with Jake, not his father and brother. He wondered if he should hate Jake's friend for taking Jake away from him. But one thing he knew for sure, Jake had never looked as happy as he did with his new friend. Seeing Jake that way made him smile.

"What're you grinnin' at, boy?" Seth snapped. "If I trusted you more, I'd send you off on yer own like I done Clem. But I don't! You stick with me. You hear me, boy?"

"I hear, Pa. But I don't think Jake and his friend are here. I think they're back in Kentucky sellin' Jake's land." He hoped his father would buy this idea so he and Clem would go home. Somehow, he'd manage to escape from his father and brother, return to Alma by himself and hunt for Jake and his friend. They'd protect him from his family.

"That's foolish talk, boy!" Seth yelled. "Jake ain't goin' back home, and neither are we. Jest get that outta yer head. If we don't find 'em tomorrow, we're goin' back to Alma and search again. I ain't gonna rest 'til Jake and his friend are dead. Let's get goin'. It's Saturday. They'll most likely come out tonight."

# CHAPTER 35

While Ben Harrington's men cleared the racetrack of the remains of Jake's wagon, the blood brothers and their companions slowly pushed their way through the cheering crowd. As they neared the outer fence, Jake saw Jenny waving at him. He smiled and held up the bag of coins, then noticed Thunder Joe leaning against the fence beside her. Dressed in clothes Rachael had found, Jake barely recognized the old mountain man.

Jake grabbed Wiley's arm. "Look, Wiley, Thunder Joe sure looks different in them clothes."

"Where is he?" Wiley scanned the fence.

Jake pointed. "Right there, next to..." Jake felt two arms slip around his waist. Glancing down, he saw a painted-up woman with flaming red hair holding him.

"Oooo! You're so strong and handsome," the woman cooed, flashing her eyes at Jake. "I *love* big, handsome men. Don't you want to spend some of your winnings on me? I can show you a real good time, sugar."

Jake cringed and remembered the time his father had paid men to drag him into Madame Bovery's house with the red curtains. He jerked his head toward Wiley. Seeing his blood brother scowling at the woman filled him with joy, and he pointed at Wiley.

"Ma'am, this here's my partner an' blood brother. He don't take kindly to women puttin' their hands on me." Jake felt mischief creep up inside him. "Jest the other day Ben found a woman buried up to her neck in the middle of this here racetrack. Wiley'd seen her hangin' all over me like you're doin'."

Wiley nearly laughed at Jake's statement, but gritted his teeth and twisted his face into a wicked smile. He growled and lunged for the woman with his hands extended like claws. Jake shoved his hand against Wiley's chest and struggled to hold him back.

The woman screamed, let go of Jake and pushed deep into the crowd.

"That was a terrible thing to say, Jake," Wiley said, laughing. "But I'll bet she'll think twice before pulling that again."

"Hell, Wiley, you sure looked like a crazy man jest then. She'll prob'ly have bad dreams after lookin' at you."

"I resent that, but I hope she does. Serves her right putting her arms around you."

When they reached the fence, Wiley peered through at Thunder Joe. "Don't you look like a dandy!"

"Tarnation!" Joe yelled. "You gents give me my share of the winnin's, an' I'll skedaddle. I ain't stickin' around you two no more." He turned his back on them.

As Jake climbed over the fence, several ranch hands saw him leaving and turned instead to Wiley, wanting to know what to do with the broken wagon.

When Jake reached Joe, he put his arm across the old man's bony shoulders.

Joe turned his head. "Mighty fine racin', Jake. Ain't never seen nothin' like it before. But I don't trust you gents no more. I ain't had so many baths at one time in my whole dang life. An' now I gots to wear monkey clothes." He folded his arms across his chest. "You jist leave me be."

Jake smiled at him. "Joe, if you hadn't stunk so bad, Winder wouldn'ta knowed you was there an' you wouldn'ta got conked on the head. Wiley an' me like you lots, but bein' around you is like livin' in a shithouse. You was the one that told us to put ashes down the hole to keep it from stinkin' so bad."

Joe frowned squinty-eyed at Jake. "I knows what yer sayin', but it ain't yer dang right tellin' me what to do! Mebby I *likes* the smell of stink. What's it to yer, anyhow? I ain't me when I'm smellin' like a dang rose! I know my friends by the po-lite way they hold their noses 'round me."

Without a backwards glance, Joe stomped toward the barn.

Stunned, Jake watched him leave.

"What was Joe yelling at you about?" Wiley asked as he climbed over the fence. "He sounded angry."

Jake lowered his eyes. "I think we done hurt Joe somethin' terrible by givin' him them baths. He don't think we're his friends. Said his friends don't care if he stinks or not." Tears came to Jake's eyes. "I feel real sad, Wiley."

Wiley felt a shock of realization through his entire body. By trying to change Joe into something he wasn't, they'd been treating Joe the same way the women he'd dated in school had treated him. Wiley grabbed Jake's shoulder. "We can't leave until we apologize to Joe."

Since their friends had to work on Monday and were eager to see their new cabin, the blood brothers decided to leave that afternoon, giving the four all day Sunday to ride back to Alma.

Lonnie and his crew saddled the men's horses and led them to the tie-bar behind the main house. The Harrington family and fifteen hands gathered to say their farewells to Jake and Wiley.

Standing in the middle of the saddened but laughing group, Jake felt a tug on his pants leg. He glanced down and saw Jenny. After picking her up, he said, "You take care of your ma an' pa like a good girl, Jenny. Wiley an' me'll be back soon."

With teary eyes, Jenny asked, "Uncle Jake, can't you take me with you? I want to be with you always."

"You gotta be lookin' after your family, Jenny. An' Wiley an' me have to help Miss Castille. You don't want nothin' to happen to Miss Castille, do you?"

"No. I like Aunt Belinda." Jenny wiped a tear from her cheek. "Will you come back for my birthday? It's September nineteenth."

"I sure will, Jenny. An' I'll bring you a present, too."

Her face brightened. "Promise?"

"I promise." Jake kissed her cheek and set her down. She ran to her mother and grabbed her hand.

"You men be careful up there," Ben warned. "If I find out anything about the Pinkertons, I'll let you know. They might want to talk to you. And watch your back trail going home. I don't trust Winder. He may be waiting for you to leave. That man carries a grudge and, by the looks of his face, it'll be forever."

After Wiley mounted up, he had to fight Buddy for control. The horse was anxious to get going. "We'll be careful, Ben. Thanks for everything. We'll be in touch. It's good to have friends close by."

Jake put his foot in the stirrup, thankful he'd brought his saddle. Since the wagon was a total loss, he wouldn't have to ride home bareback. He waved at everyone and spurred Mac alongside Buddy.

John watched Jake and Wiley's V-shaped backs as they left, then glanced up at his father. "Can I have a partner some day?"

"Son, you can find a partner or a wife. Just find someone to love." He smiled at Rachael. "Someone who loves you back."

As the men slowly rode through an aspen grove, Jake and Wiley craned their necks to find Joe. Jake finally spotted him halfway to the main gate, sitting next to the road with his back against a tree.

In a low voice, Wiley said, "Jake and I need to talk to Joe in private. We'll meet the rest of you at the gate."

When they reached Joe, the brothers pulled off the road and dismounted. The others continued on.

The partners sat down beside the old mountain man.

"We're sorry, Joe," Jake said. "It weren't right for us to give you them baths. You gotta right to stink if you want."

"Jake's right," Wiley said. "I know how you feel. Back East, women kept trying to change me. I never thought I'd ever do it to someone else. It's taught me a lesson I hope I never forget."

"Where's my gold dollars?" Joe snapped. "It was me that brung you, so pay up! Was you 'spectin' to leave without givin' 'em to me?"

Joe's reaction to their apologies rankled Jake. He dug into his pocket and pulled out the bag of coins. After handing it to Wiley to count out fifty, he yelled, "*Yer* the one that walked off, you ol' skunk! An' don't you go callin' me no cheater!" Jake got to his feet and glared down at Joe. "If you wants to stink, just stink then. My Pa tossed me in hog shit so many times, I can't hardly stand stink no more. But Wiley an' me gived you them baths cuz you needed 'em. Yer damn nuts was so crusted over they could'a fell off."

Joe and Wiley stared at Jake with their mouths open. Without saying a word, Wiley handed Joe the fifty gold coins. He didn't dare laugh and couldn't tell if Joe was angry or not.

"Hee, hee, hee!" Joe slapped his leg. "Jake, that there's the funniest dang thing I ever heard you say! All's forgiven, but you dang-well better never give me another bath or some mornin' you'll find yerselves hangin' by yer feet in a dang tree."

The three men parted company after many pats on the back. Joe promised to visit them after he and Lonnie returned from their hunting trip in the Black Mountain region.

The partners waved at Joe as they caught up with the others at the gate.

# CHAPTER 36

Wiley led the group due north from the ranch, taking the opposite side of the range of hills he, Jake and Joe had followed a few days before. He chose this way back to throw Winder off in case he tailed them. Every so often, one of the men scanned their back trail. Once they reached hills with trees, they entered the forest and traveled through it a few miles, gradually riding to the eastern side of the range. When Wiley spotted the Castille buildings, he kept on until the ranch was out of sight before turning east to Chipmunk Rock. He didn't want anyone who might be following them to know they were connected with Belinda. After they rode completely around Bristlecone Peak, the men finally reached Chipmunk Rock from the south.

\* \* \*

Perched on a hill overlooking the Harrington Ranch, Winder saw a group riding north. He focused his glasses.

"It's them, and they're riding toward Alma. Let's go!"

They skirted the boundary of the Harrington Ranch, then galloped north. Winder decided to stay far to the east of the hills the blood brothers were following. He planned to ambush them at Bristlecone Peak amid the jumble of boulders along its northern flank.

When their horses began foaming at the mouth from exertion, Blackwood yelled, "We gotta rest the horses an' find water fer 'em or we'll be walkin' back to Alma!"

Grumbling, Winder stopped his horse and dismounted. He looked around to get his bearings. Bristlecone Peak loomed in the north a few miles away. He turned to the others and said, "Bently

Gulch is close. Let's go there, water the horses and let them rest. But then we'll have to ride like hell to get to the boulders first."

Bently Gulch, not yet dried up for the summer, had a good flow of water. The men let the horses drink their fill and graze in the lush grass growing at the bottom of the five-foot banks. From where he sat, eating biscuits and jerky, Winder could see the slopes of Bristlecone Peak to the northwest. Suddenly, he saw a group of riders traveling south around the base of the mountain.

"Who the hell is that?" he asked, grabbing his glasses. "It's them! Where the hell are they going?"

"Let's foller 'em," Nance said as he jumped to his feet.

"Get down!" Winder snapped. "They'll see you! We'll let them get out of sight, then sneak up on them. It looks like they're heading for some place in particular. Maybe this is where they've been holed up."

After the riders disappeared, Winder and his men walked their horses toward the southern slopes of Bristlecone Peak. When Blackwood found the tracks, the group followed them until they veered north, up the slope of the mountain.

Winder stopped and dismounted. "You three stay here. I'm going up on foot and see what I can find out."

Winder climbed the steep hillside, using trees and shrubs as cover. When he heard voices, he dropped to the ground and remained motionless, listening. After pinpointing the general area where the voices came from, he surveyed the terrain. To the west, a high ridge stretched south for a half-mile. If they snuck up the back, they'd have a clear shot at anyone below. Silently, Winder returned to the others.

After Billingsly's men rode around the end, they carefully walked their horses up the back of the long spur that stretched out from the base of Bristlecone Peak. Near the top, they dismounted, tied the horses in a sheltered area and inched their way to a large rock outcropping that overlooked the area where Winder had heard the voices.

\* \* \*

When they arrived at the corral, hidden in the aspen grove, Jake, Wiley and their friends from Alma, unsaddled their horses and brushed them. When Jake finished forking hay for the animals, he joined the others leaning on the fence.

"Well, where is it?" Harry asked. "We rode all this way to see a horse corral?"

"Jest look up the hill an' see if you can see the cabin from here," Jake said, grinning proudly.

"We've been doing that since we got here, and none of us see any sign of a cabin," Matt replied. "You must have hidden it pretty well."

"Must'a dug a dang hole, if you ask me," Bill muttered.

"Speaking of a hole," Wiley said with a laugh. "Jake, tell them what happened to you in the..." He doubled over in laughter.

"Damn!" Jake yelled. "Wiley, why'd you have to say that! I ain't gonna tell 'em nothin'!" He climbed over the fence and started up the hill.

"Hey, now wait just a minute, Jake," Harry yelled. "You aren't going to get off that easy. Come on, boys, let's get him and make him tell us what happened."

The four men tackled Jake. After they managed to pin him to the ground, Frank began tickling Jake in the ribs. "I'm gonna keep this up 'til you tell us what happened."

Kicking and laughing hysterically, Jake lurched his body violently and threw off the four men, then leaped to his feet. "I can't stand bein' tickled!" Seeing Wiley still laughing in the corral, he yelled, "I'm gonna get you for this, Wiley!"

Jake cleared the top of the fence and tackled Wiley to the ground. The horses milled uneasily as the two men wrestled in the close confines of the circular pen. Jake had the upper hand since Wiley kept laughing. The more he laughed, the angrier Jake got.

Finally, he'd had enough. Jake grabbed a dry horse apple and shoved it into Wiley's mouth to shut him up.

Wiley stopped laughing, and his eyes switched from surprise to fury in a split second. Jake suddenly felt himself flying off his partner. He landed on his butt a few feet away.

Wiley spat out the horse apple, scrambled to his feet and lunged at Jake, taking him to the ground. He pinned Jake's arms with his knees and sat on top of him so he couldn't move. Wiley scooped up a handful of fresh horse shit, smeared it from one of Jake's ears to the other and from his chin to his forehead.

Wiley threw back his head and laughed, then got to his feet and extended his hand to help Jake up. Jake grabbed it and pulled Wiley face down into the muck. They rolled around in the stinking mess for several minutes, but soon their growling turned to laughter.

At that moment, on the top of the granite pinnacle overlooking Chipmunk Rock, the old Indian appeared. His gray, glistening garb and long white braids, each tipped with a golden feather, remained motionless in the strong breeze that buffeted the area. As the two men hugged each other in the corral and their laughter echoed in the valley, the Indian smiled. He raised his hand over them and spoke in a deep whisper. "Peace and love, my young blood brothers." Then, as suddenly as he appeared, the Indian vanished.

After both agreed they'd had enough wrestling and horse shit for one day, Jake helped Wiley to his feet, and discovered they were alone at the corral.

"Where the hell is ever'body?" Jake asked as he tried to wipe the smelly brown slop from his face and hair. "Wiley, I'm sorry about puttin' that there shit in your mouth. I got rankled at you laughin' at me." Jake grinned. He had horse shit on his teeth.

Covered with the same stinking mess, Wiley chuckled. "It looks like you ate your share."

They climbed over the fence and trudged up the hill. When they reached the cabin, they found the others inside checking out the rock wall.

Without turning around, Harry sniffed the air. "Funny, I didn't think Thunder Joe came with us, but I sure smell him." He spun around and scowled. "Oh, it's you two. Get tired of playing with your food?" He pointed to a bottle of whiskey on the table. "Frank, grab that bottle and let's all go outside while these two, hopefully, clean up."

The four snickered as they filed out the door. Frank held his nose and pointed at the two shit-covered men.

Since the area for washing consisted only of a corner of the room where the floor sloped to the rock wall, Jake let Wiley wash up first.

"It's a good thing this corner is downstream from the basin under the floor," Wiley said as he doused himself with the pan of cold water Jake handed him. After Wiley dipped water for Jake to wash, Wiley put on clean clothes and went outside to join the others.

None of the men spoke as Wiley walked toward them. No one said anything even after he sat on a rock beside Matt. Wiley glanced from one to the other. "What's wrong?"

"Are you gonna tell us what happened to Jake, or are we gonna have to do this all over again?" Bill asked.

"It must be pretty damn funny fer you to laugh, Wiley," Frank said. "You're a real straight-faced kind'a gent."

"I'll tell you," Wiley whispered, "but you have to promise you won't tell Jake. You know how he gets."

"We promise," Harry said softly. "Tell us now, so if we have to laugh, we can get it over with before he comes out."

Wiley quietly told them how Jake burned down the first outhouse. Harry, Matt and Frank covered their mouths with their hands to muffle their laughter. After a few minutes, they noticed Bill wasn't amused.

"What's the matter, Bill?" Harry asked. "Don't you think that's funny?"

"I done the same thing when I was a youngster after my pappy an' me dug a new pit. Only I didn't drop the lantern down it." He closed his eyes and grinned. "An' my shit hit right on the mark."

The others roared with laughter.

"You told 'em what I done, didn't you, Wiley!" Jake hollered from inside the cabin.

"They's laughin' at somethin' I done, Jake!" Bill yelled back. "Come out here, an' I'll tell you!"

Jake walked outside drying his hair with a towel. He wore only his Levis and boots. Beads of water still clung to his massive chest and arms.

"Oh, Lordy!" Harry gasped under his breath as he saw Jake. "And we tried to pin that one down?"

"Wiley's the same size as Jake, in case you haven't noticed," Matt whispered softly. "But I'm sure you have."

They both looked at Wiley's chest pushing out the front of his shirt. Harry rolled his eyes.

"What'd you do, Bill?" Jake asked.

Bill frowned at him. "I've a mind not to tell you since you wouldn't tell us what you did. But seein' it's you, an' I don't mind bein' laughed at, I'll tell you. When my pappy an' me dug a new outhouse pit, I marked the hole to see if my shit would hit the mark."

Jake's eyes opened wide. "You did? That's what I done. Only I dropped the lantern on the seat when I tried to see if mine hit right. The heat burnt my face off." He lowered his eyes. "Burnt the outhouse down, too."

With tear-filled eyes, the other four men pressed their hands over their mouths and shook with laughter.

"Well?" Bill asked, cocking his head. "Did you hit it?"

Jake grinned. "No, but part of the lamp hit it square."

The others rolled backwards off their rocks and howled. Bill and Jake frowned at them.

"Want to see where it hit?" Jake asked Bill.

"Of course."

Jake ran into the cabin and brought out their only other lamp. He and Bill walked to the outhouse.

"Better let Bill hold the lamp, Jake," Harry yelled, then laughed.

While Jake and Bill messed around in the outhouse, Wiley showed the others how they built the cabin.

"That's mighty fine work you did attachin' these logs to the cliff," Bill said.

"I like the hole in the floor and the water so handy," Harry said. He stuck his hand into the basin and swirled the water. "Lordy, that water's cold!"

Matt clasped Wiley's shoulder. "You both did a fine job of building this cabin, Wiley."

"Thunder Joe helped a lot, too."

"You had *Thunder Joe* here while you built this cabin?" Harry asked. "It's no wonder you've taken up wrestling in horse shit."

They heard a muffled crash down the hill, followed by loud cursing.

Wiley sighed. "Well, there goes the second outhouse." When he got to the door, he saw Bill leaping out of the structure holding his face in his hands.

"Dang it to hell!" Bill yelled. "I burnt my face!" He staggered forward. Jake jumped to his side and grabbed his arm to steer him and see if he was hurt.

Harry reached Bill before anyone else. "Take your hands away, and let us look at your face."

Wiley ran to the outhouse and threw open the door. No fire. He peered down the hole and saw sputtering flames blink a few times and go out. The smell nearly knocked him out. Gagging, he ran back to the group.

When Bill finally took his hands away, they saw a soot-blackened face with singed eyebrows.

Bill shook his head. "I plumb forgot about the chimney heat."

"That's what happened to me," Jake said.

After Harry finished wiping Bill's face, he sighed. "Well, other than being covered with soot, your face looks as ugly as ever." He smiled, tweaked Bill's nose and turned to Wiley. "Now you don't have a lamp. I have some candles in my saddle bags you can use until you get a new one."

"What're you doin' with candles in your saddle bags?" Frank asked.

Harry raised his eyebrows a few times. "Never know when I might meet up with a gent who wants a candlelight dinner."

Bill frowned.

* * *

Winder peered around the rocks and saw the cabin and the corral below. He saw the six men gathered outside. Two of them went into the outhouse with a lamp, the others entered the cabin.

Winder pulled back and whispered to the others. "I don't know what's going on down there. Probably some disgusting sex, but we should lay low for a while. They outnumber us, which is no good. Let's set up camp down by the horses and wait. Maybe the others will leave soon."

Winder crawled to a less conspicuous place. "Nance, you stay here and watch," he whispered. "And keep out of sight. After an hour, one of us will relieve you. We'll take turns watching as long as it takes to get them alone."

They made a dry, fireless camp, well out of earshot from the cabin. When it looked like the men from Alma were staying the night, Winder had his men spread out their bedrolls and wait until the next day.

\* \* \*

Jake and Harry built a fire on the rock ledge while Wiley showed the others his rabbit snares. They returned with four fat rabbits. Frank helped Jake skin them, and they cooked a delicious stew.

After dinner, Frank and Matt sat at the table and played cards, trying to lure the others into poker. They finally succeeded and played low stakes.

During one of the hands, Harry noticed Jake sound asleep on the bed. "When did he do that?" he asked.

No one could remember.

An hour later, tired of Matt winning every hand, they decided to turn in. Matt, Frank and Bill found places outside. Harry unrolled his blankets on the floor and groaned as he dropped to his knees.

"If we sleep crosswise, three can fit on the bed," Wiley said, knowing full well the groans were faked.

"Thought you'd never ask."

After rolling Jake across the middle, they sprawled across the bed on either side of him and were asleep within minutes.

\* \* \*

As the morning sun cleared the tops of the Tarryalls, the men had already downed several pots of coffee.

"Wiley, where'd you hear about Billingsly's wanted posters in Alma?" Frank asked.

"Belinda told us. She heard it in Como."

"Well, that dang foppy put up new ones," Bill snarled. "These were sayin' yer free to come back. The reward's been dropped. Billingsly's up to somethin'."

"Sheriff Cline ripped those down, also," Matt said. "The new posters were probably trying to lure you back to town. I think Billingsly's scared of you. By the way, did you know the Harrises went to Denver? For some reason, they're convinced you took the train there."

"Wiley, they took Belinda's bait!" Jake yelled.

"Bait?" Harry asked.

Wiley chuckled. "Belinda bought two tickets to Denver with our names on them while she was in Como. They must have found out. I hope they get lost in the city."

"They'll be back," Jake warned. "An' I been thinkin'. I'm gonna shoot Seth an' Clem when I see 'em."

"No you're not!" everyone yelled at once.

Wiley gave Jake a stern look. "I don't want you killing anyone. Billingsly would have a field day if either of us kills someone."

"That he would," Bill agreed. "Jimmy Ratchett told me about some telegraph message that's got Billingsly lookin' like he wants t'kick a hog. Either you fellers know anythin' about that?" He stared at Wiley.

"What was it about?" Wiley asked, working at his surprised look.

"He didn't know, but it shore got Billingsly's goat."

"Let us know when you find out," Wiley said. "Jake and I will be here or at Belinda's most of the time now that all the cattle are on her land again."

Bill stood up. "Guess we'd best be goin' back. I hate bein' gone from the livery more'n a couple days. By now there's plenty of horse shit fer you two to roll in."

As the four men saddled their horses, they promised to come back in a week or two with any news and to play a little poker.

They rode north, skirting the western slope of Bristlecone Peak, trying to keep hidden in the forest in case anyone was in the area.

Jake and Wiley walked up the hill and watched them disappear into the trees.

\* \* \*

Winder purposefully took the morning watch. He waited until the men from Alma left before he crept back to their camp. He found his men sitting around munching jerky.

"The others pulled out," he said softly. "We'll let them get a couple miles away so they won't hear any gunfire. Then, I want those two down there *dead*."

# CHAPTER 37

After Bill and the others disappeared from view, Wiley took Jake by the arm and hauled him close. They grabbed each other in a bear hug.

"It's good to be alone with you, again," Wiley whispered as he pressed his crotch against Jake's.

"Sure is!" Jake squeezed Wiley, then pulled back and grinned. "Wiley, can we ride to the spring an' see if we can find anythin' of them killers like we said we was gonna do?"

"Uh...of course," Wiley said, then his face brightened. "After that, we can go to our waterfall."

In the cabin, the two men strapped on their guns, grabbed their rifles and trudged down the hill to the corral. They saddled and mounted their horses, then walked them to the grassy valley below. With the sun in their faces and laughing, the blood brothers cantered the three miles to Walton Spring.

* * *

Winder climbed back to the hiding place behind the rocks and looked down on the empty corral.

"They're gone!" he said out loud. "I wonder where the hell they went?"

Winder shaded his eyes toward the east and saw dust blowing from two horses, over a mile away. It had to be them. He scrambled back to the others and yelled, "Mount up! They've given us the slip. We can catch them if we ride now."

The four quickly packed their bedrolls, saddled their horses and galloped down the ridge.

* * *

When Jake and Wiley arrived at Walton Spring, the wind had picked up and began buffeting them with clouds of gritty dust. Holding on to their hats, they rode east for a short distance and found that some of the cattle had spread in that direction, but were still well within the boundaries of the Castille Ranch. Wiley dismounted and scanned the area for a high place where someone could conceal himself and still be within rifle range, and knew Pinnacle Rock had to be it.

Jake searched the ground for anything that might look like a clue. "Ain't nothin' here but cow plops, Wiley." He raised his head and spotted dust from four riders galloping toward them. "Wiley, somebody's comin'. Wonder if it's Bill an' them comin' back?"

Wiley spun around. "I'll bet it's Winder! Let's ride to Pinnacle Rock!"

They leaped on their horses and spurred them toward the cone-shaped mountain with jagged and broken rock chimneys jutting from the top. They rode to the west side, knowing it was the only place they could ride their horses to the base of the rocks, and went as far up as they could. After tying the horses behind a bristlecone pine, they grabbed their rifles and scrambled into the rocks. They climbed to a room-size area near the top they'd been in before.

Surrounded on three sides by huge boulders and jagged spires of crumbling granite, the alcove had a good view below through the many gaps in the rocks. The backside of the shelter, with the exception of a few large boulders, was a cliff that dropped a hundred feet to a jumble of broken rocks. If need be, they could climb down the flat tops of the spires that lined the cliff like stairs. Wiley realized someone could also climb up to them the same way.

The now raging wind picked up sand from below and hurled it at Pinnacle Rock. Wiley shaded his eyes from the stinging grit and peered through a gap between two rocks. He saw the four riders approaching the base of the mountain, and noticed Winder eyeing it as the others scanned the terrain for any signs of them.

He pulled back. "I was right, Jake," he said close to Jake's ear. "It's Winder."

As Jake stood up and peered over a rock to see for himself, the wind blasted his face with sand. "Damn!" he yelled, then flung his arm over his face. Wiley yanked him back.

Clint saw the movement and shouted for the others to split up and surround the mountain. They rode as far as they could, then dismounted. Winder and Clint started up the south side through a boulder field. Nance rode to the east side and began scrambling up the craggy slope. He realized he'd be the first to the top, since the rocks formed a narrow staircase up the sheer wall, but one false move could send him plunging a hundred feet to his death.

Blackwood hung back. He wanted the men to show themselves again so he could shoot them between the eyes, hoping to make a bloody mess on the rocks. Not seeing them, he found a way up between large boulders.

Clint stopped and fired a shot where he'd seen Jake. The bullet hit above Jake's head, and bits of rock showered on him as he crouched low.

The wind on the top blew with such ferocity that a raven, startled by the gunshot, tumbled head over tail in the air before it righted itself and flew away. Jake grabbed his hat before the wind could blast it off his head and fling it over the cliff behind them.

Wiley pulled the brim of his hat over his eyes to ward off the sand. He couldn't hear or see anything. As he scooped sand out of a slot between two rocks for a better view, he uncovered three spent rifle shells and realized they were Springfield cartridges. He dug out the shells and slipped them into his pocket. He decided not to tell Jake. Maybe he would in a week or two.

The partners could only guess the whereabouts of the four killers. Jake peered through a gap between two rocks and saw movement below. He sighted his rifle and fired a shot into the wind and downhill. The bullet hit short.

Wiley held his fire. He didn't want to waste the eleven bullets he had with him. "Don't waste your shots, Jake!" he shouted, not knowing if Jake heard him over the wind.

A sudden burst of gunfire from several spots below showered them with small chunks of rock. Wiley knew the men wanted ricocheting bullets to hit them and some came very close. They were in a bad spot, and he wanted to get Jake out of there.

Wiley leaned toward Jake and yelled above the wind, "Move out to the horses! I'll try to stall them!"

As Jake got to his feet, a man stood up from behind a rock at the same time. Startled, Jake fired his rifle. The bullet plowed through Nance's shoulder and flung him backwards off the cliff. His falling screams rose above the howling wind, then stopped.

Jake froze in horror. He'd shot a man! The man fell over the cliff and was most likely dead!

Wiley knew that look. Jake's first killing. He grabbed his partner, pulled him down and shook him. "Jake! We're fighting for our lives! There was nothing else you could have done! He would have killed both of us!"

Jake slowly turned his eyes away from the spot where Nance had disappeared and stared at Wiley.

Wiley shook him and shouted, "Jake, we're in a bad place! We have to make a break for the horses. We'll talk about this later. We can't do anything in this wind." He desperately wanted to get Jake to safety. With Jake feeling the way he did, he wouldn't be as careful as he should.

They heard another shot from directly below where they crouched. Suddenly, Jake saw movement through a gap between two rocks. Another man was nearly on top of them. He pointed.

Wiley turned just as Blackwood appeared from behind a boulder. The two men stared at each other for a split second before Wiley fired. At such close range, the bullet tore a fist-size hole through Blackwood's chest. He tumbled backward and disappeared among the rocks below.

The wind gained velocity. They could barely breathe. Wiley grabbed Jake's arm and shouted, "Let's go for the horses now!"

Holding onto their hats and rifles, they scrambled into a long gap in the rocks that led to the horses. As they approached the mouth of the fissure, Wiley stopped and listened to the wind's moan as it funnelled through the long, narrow slot. He looked around. Not seeing anyone, he made a dash, hoping the blowing dust would conceal them. Jake hesitated, then followed close behind.

When they got twenty feet from the horses, a shot rang out and Wiley went down. He rolled a short distance and dropped out of sight behind a three-foot cliff.

Jake turned and fired his rifle several times in the direction of the last shot before he scrambled after Wiley. Concealed for the time being, Jake crawled to Wiley's side and saw blood gushing out of Wiley's left leg in two places above his knee.

"Wiley, you're shot!" Jake yelled.

Bullets whizzed over their heads. Jake growled, raised up and fired back.

Wiley gritted his teeth as he tried to get up. "Jake, I'll cover you. Get the horses." He pressed his hand on the two wounds and blood leaked through his fingers. He struggled into position, sighted his rifle at the rocks with one hand and shot several times at movement while Jake ran the few yards and grabbed the reins of both horses.

Trying to keep the horses between him and the rocks, Jake led them behind the huge trunk of a bristlecone pine a few feet from Wiley.

As Wiley dragged himself to Buddy, Jake shot at Winder when he peeked around a rock. He saw Clint, higher up, and fired twice. Both men dodged his whining bullets.

Wiley groaned as he pulled himself onto Buddy and spurred the horse toward the cabin. Jake shoved his rifle into his saddle boot, but kept up the volley with his pistol as he leaped onto Mac. As he galloped after Wiley, Jake heard several shots and one bullet whizzed by his head. In the roaring wind, he finally caught up to Wiley and saw his entire pant leg was red, and blood poured off his boot. Jake remembered his pa had nearly bled to death when he'd been gored by the Harrises' bull and knew Wiley could die soon with the flow that rapid.

Jake grabbed Buddy's reins and stopped both horses. He leaped to the ground, pulled out a shirt from his saddle bag and tied it tightly around Wiley's leg just above the wounds.

A wave of dizziness swept over Wiley. He grasped the saddle horn and shut his eyes while Jake tied the shirt around his leg. The pain made him queasy.

With the bleeding slowed, Jake leaped into his saddle. He turned around, searched the terrain and caught a glimpse of Winder and Clint climbing down the rocks toward their horses. From the time it would take the two men to catch up with them, he knew they could reach the cabin. He glanced at Wiley.

"Tie yourself to the saddle horn, Wiley!" Jake yelled. Again he looked back and saw dust blowing horizontally from the two riders. They were a couple of miles behind.

"They're comin', Wiley! Can you hold on 'til we get home?"

Wiley nodded and kicked Buddy in the ribs. He cursed himself for getting shot, but at least it hadn't been Jake. Another wave of dizziness, this time with nausea, forced him forward. He gripped the horn tighter.

At the cabin, Jake swung down from Mac and helped Wiley dismount. He carried Wiley inside and gently placed him on the bed. Then he ran outside, led the horses to the corral and removed the saddles and bits, letting them fall to the ground. He grabbed both rifles, leaped the fence and scrambled up the hill to the cabin.

Jake slammed the heavy door seconds before Winder and Clint rode up and started shooting. Bullets thudded into the thick log walls. A slug broke one of their precious window panes and showered the inside of the cabin with glass.

"Damn!" Jake yelled. He opened the door a crack and fired his pistol. The second squeeze of the trigger hit on a spent cartridge.

Winder and Clint leaped out of their saddles and ran behind the outhouse for cover. Jake saw them, grabbed Wiley's rifle and fired a few rounds into the structure. Knowing he had them cornered, Jake shifted his position to the broken window and shot a few more times at the outhouse. Bits of wood flew as the bullets ripped through the soft aspen logs.

Jake turned toward the bed. Wiley looked dead. He couldn't tell if the wounds were still bleeding since they were on the side he couldn't see. Not sure what to do, Jake bit his lower lip and sent a couple more rounds into the outhouse, lower this time.

The slugs narrowly missed the two men couched behind the small building.

"We gotta make a run for it to that ridge we was at this mornin'," Clint said. "This outhouse ain't no pertection."

Winder gritted his teeth. "I got one of them in the leg, and I think it's pretty bad."

Another of Jake's bullets plowed through the outhouse. Winder and Clint ran for the ridge, keeping the small building between them and Jake's gun. They made it to an outcropping of rocks before Jake saw them. Jake's slugs whined around the rocks as Winder and Clint dove for cover.

With the men at least a hundred yards away, Jake ran to Wiley and was relieved he was still breathing, but he'd passed out.

"Don't die, Wiley," Jake whimpered.

He rushed to the rock wall and built a small fire. With his knife, Jake cut off the left leg of Wiley's Levis and long underwear just above the wounds. The two holes in the side of Wiley's leg were still bleeding. Blood covered the bed. Jake tightened the shirt around Wiley's thigh, then ran to the window and fired a few rounds at the rocks, wanting the men to think he was staying at the window. He knew they were still there when they both shot back.

Jake put the rifle down, ran to the small fire and stuck his knife blade into the flames to let it get red hot. He rushed to the bed and pulled the moss out of the wounds, bathed them with water and poured whiskey on both of them. Jake gritted his teeth, grabbed the glowing knife and cauterized the wounds. The bleeding stopped instantly. He bandaged Wiley's leg with another shirt.

"Jesus, don't let Wiley bleed no more," Jake whimpered as he loosened the upper shirt. He sighed when the seared scabs held.

Jake ran to the window, peered out and saw movement among the rocks. He sighted his Ballard rifle and shot. He heard a yell of pain, but didn't know who'd been hit.

Wiley groaned.

Jake put the rifle down and ran back to the bed. "Wiley, how're you doin'?" He kissed Wiley's forehead. "The bleedin's stopped. Jest lie still. I've got 'em cornered behind them rocks on the hill, an' think I hit one of 'em."

"I'm okay, Jake," Wiley whispered. "I'm real weak. I'll just lie here and rest for a minute and then help you get them." He closed his eyes and passed out.

Jake gently pulled a blanket over him, ran back to the window and peered out. A slug fired from the rocks shattered another pane of glass. Jake ducked, then aimed at the spot where he saw smoke from the last shot. His bullet whined among the boulders and Winder climbed higher. Jake thought he'd seen him holding his left arm. He fired again, and Winder dived to the ground.

Another volley came from the lower part of the rocks, and the slugs slammed into the logs and door. When Jake fired at a spot below the rising smoke, Clint yelled and climbed to the same sheltered spot Winder had found. Jake shot once more at him. Clint grabbed his leg just as he disappeared behind the rocks.

Jake put the rifle down again and ran to the fire, adding a few sticks. He ladled some of the broth from the leftover rabbit stew into a pan and set it over the flames. If he could make Wiley drink some, he'd be better off than with nothing.

Jake sat by the window until the broth boiled, then pulled the pan away from the fire to let it cool. After his third attempt at waking him, Wiley came around and Jake helped him drink some of the liquid. After he inspected the bandages and saw no fresh blood, Jake covered Wiley and let him sleep.

Both men in the rocks had been hit, but neither wound was serious. Winder's left arm had been grazed, and Jake's last bullet had nicked Clint in the leg. Crouched behind the rocks, they dressed each other's wounds and stopped the bleeding.

"We gotta get outta here, Winder. We can't kill 'em now. They're inside the cabin. They have a clear shot at us no matter which direction we go to get our horses."

"Shut up!" Winder snapped. "We'll wait until tonight, then storm the cabin. There won't be any moon until late, and they can't see us coming in the dark. I want them dead, and I don't care how long it takes to kill them. One of them may already be dead from the looks of the blood on the ground."

He settled back and pulled out his tobacco pouch. "We'll wait."

* * *

For the remainder of the morning, when Jake wasn't bathing Wiley's forehead with a damp cloth, he sat by the window cleaning and reloading all the guns. He fired an occasional shot at the last spot he'd seen the two men. Sometimes they fired back. Jake re-bandaged Wiley's leg with another clean shirt and poured more whiskey on the wounds to fight any infection. But, even after six hours, he felt the sickly red was spreading. He knew if he could disable or kill Winder and Clint, he'd still have to get Wiley to a doctor before infection took control of his body. He already had a fever.

Jake realized he could ride to Belinda's ranch for her wagon, but she and Soaring Raven were probably still in Como. They took the wagon there every Sunday and usually didn't come back until Monday evening. It would be useless to ride there. Wiley needed him here until he could get the wagon. But they both might be dead before then.

As the afternoon sun poured through the west window, Jake closed the shutters to darken the cabin so Winder couldn't see inside. He lit one of the candles Harry had left and cursed himself for breaking both their lamps. Suddenly, he remembered what Thunder Joe had told him about not looking into the flames, and he put the candle behind a wooden box and kept the fire low. Light in the cabin was dim, but he soon got used to it.

Jake tried to eat some stew, but decided he wasn't hungry. For the fifth time, he took stock of his ammunition and checked the guns he'd placed around the cabin. He picked up Wiley's rifle and slowly opened the door. Seeing movement in the rocks, he shot once. Neither man shot back.

Expecting an eventual attack, Jake rearranged the furniture, set a few booby traps, then scattered the coals in the fire and blew out the candle. In the semi-darkness, he felt Wiley's forehead. It seemed warmer than a few minutes ago. Jake plopped into the chair beside the bed, buried his face in the blankets and whispered, "Jesus, you gotta send somebody to help Wiley."

# CHAPTER 38

As Jake sat in the darkened room, he realized the wind had stopped. In the dead silence, it would be easier to hear Winder sneaking up on the cabin. He glanced at the up-ended table he'd shoved against the bed. The three-inch-thick top might not stop a bullet at close range, but it gave Wiley some protection. It gave him some, too, since it hid the entire door from where he sat.

Jake craned his neck and could barely see the rusty cowbell he'd hung on the door to warn of its opening. The wire he'd stretched taut across the lower part of the door frame made him feel a little safer. Clem used to do that to trip his brothers, and it worked every time. Would Winder be the one to trip over the wire? Guilt wracked him when he glanced at the scrap boards he'd scattered on the floor around the door. The nails sticking up from the boards could kill a man if he fell face down on them.

Suddenly remembering the man he'd killed on Pinnacle Rock, Jake held himself and shuddered.

"Sort'a narrows the odds!" he seemed to hear Thunder Joe yelling. "Our Maker don't expect us to be yeller-bellies!"

"Damn!" Jake shouted. He sat up straight. "That's what Joe meant!" He shrugged his shoulders and cocked his head. "Jesus, I'm leavin' them boards there. I gotta pertect Wiley any way I can, an' if somebody gets killed with them nails stickin' up...they have it comin'. Wiley an' me didn't do nothin' to nobody."

In the stillness, he heard Wiley's shallow breathing. Occasionally Wiley would stir and moan, and Jake wondered if he was in pain or having a feverish nightmare.

He kept Wiley's forehead covered with a damp rag and felt his face often, knowing he could still lose his blood brother. Being pinned in the cabin like a trapped animal triggered deep anger inside him. He wanted to sneak up on the two men outside, and... Jake shuddered thinking what he'd like to do to them, but he couldn't leave Wiley unguarded. He hoped Winder attacked soon so he could get Wiley help.

Jake looked at his partner's gaunt face. Only a few hours ago, Wiley was full of life and the most handsome man he'd ever seen, and now he seemed near death. Why couldn't people leave them alone? He dropped his head on the bed and thought back on the five weeks he and Wiley had been blood brothers. They had been the happiest time in his life.

\* \* \*

Jake woke with a start. He hadn't planned on falling asleep. With his head still on the bed, he listened for the slightest noise outside the cabin, but heard nothing. Slowly he raised his head and opened his eyes. In the soft light, he saw Wiley's deathly white face. For a moment he thought his partner was dead, but then saw the blankets move as Wiley breathed.

A sudden terror jolted him. The soft light? He remembered blowing out the candle and sitting in darkness! Jake broke into a cold sweat and fought hard to control his fear as he felt someone else's presence in the cabin. Without taking his eyes off Wiley's face, he slowly slipped his hand to his holster. The instant his fingers touched the butt of his gun, he heard a voice.

"No use gun!" the strange voice commanded. It came from across the room.

Jake snapped his head around and saw an old Indian sitting in one of their armchairs. In the soft golden light, he gazed at the Indian's ageless face, old and wrinkled, but at the same time, young and full of life. The man was beautiful! Jake's eyes were drawn to the white braids that hung over his chest, each one tipped with a single golden feather. The feather in the Indian's right braid glowed brightly. The old man's flowing garb was made from a white glistening material Jake had never seen before. As he stared at the Indian, he realized the light in the room...came from him! Was he dreaming? Strangely, he wasn't afraid.

The Indian raised his right arm. "I am Chief Eagle Rising." The old man's deep voice made Jake think of a howling wind. "I come in peace."

"But," Jake stammered, "Thunder Joe said you was dead."

Raising his head triumphantly, Eagle Rising said, "Only evil ones die. The good live always." His countenance changed. "But even the good are sometimes sorrowful. I am sorrowful. I made treaty with United States to save my people. Now, my people suffer worse than death in barren land where government forced them to live. But this time, I am sent to help you. I have watched you, my young blood brothers. Gray Feather told me of you, and your friend sent me."

As Jake stared with his mouth open, Chief Eagle Rising reached into his robe and pulled out a brown rawhide pouch with a long tie-loop. As the Indian's robes moved, Jake heard the sound of wind rustling through a forest of pine. The Indian tossed the bag toward Jake. The leather pouch landed on the bed near Wiley's injured leg. Jake glanced at the bag, but didn't dare touch it.

Chief Eagle Rising lifted his right braid, carefully plucked the glowing feather from the end and held it in the palm of his hand. The feather floated across the room and settled on the bed near Jake's hand. It pulsated with light for a moment, then the light faded and went out.

"Use what I give to help brother," Chief Eagle Rising said. "Use *only* as I say. Listen!"

The old Indian pointed to the bag. "In bag is sand of the earth. Any sand. Sand from great ages. Drop feather in bag, then hold brother tightly. Soon, Great Wind will come. It will leave you here, but take you far away to strange place. What you have on here, you have on there. In other place, you find Protectors, healing for your brother, and grief in spirit. But, *beware of strange place.*"

Jake cringed, but remained silent.

Eagle Rising continued. "Keep feather in bag. *Always* have bag touching body. If bag or feather lost, you stay in distant place forever, and many sorrows will fall upon you. When time to return, feather in bag will glow brightly. Take feather out and fill bag with sand. Any sand. Then, do as before. If you wish, and they wish, bring Protectors back with you...for a time."

Chief Eagle Rising smiled at Jake and lifted his hand. "Do what I told you in haste. Peace, my blood brothers."

The Indian vanished, and the cabin plunged into darkness.

Jake leaned against the bed and trembled. Not a breath of wind blew outside. The only sound he could hear was Wiley's labored breathing. He glanced briefly at Wiley, then around the cabin. Brilliant lines of sunlight still blazed through the spaces between the shutter boards. Jake shook his head and tried to convince himself he'd just woke up from a dream. When he remembered he had to check Wiley's wounds, he slowly got up from the chair, staggered to the rock wall, found the candle and lit it. As he approached the bed, he saw the leather pouch and feather near Wiley's leg.

"Wiley, they're real! It weren't no dream!"

Jake fell into the chair and plopped the candle holder on the bed. Hesitantly, he reached for the pouch. He touched it. It felt like rawhide. Jake lifted the bag by its string. It was heavy, like it was filled with sand. He set it back on the bed and carefully picked up the feather. At his touch, the feather pulsated again with soft golden light. Startled, Jake dropped it. The feather floated to the blankets, and its light went out.

Jake shivered. He wrapped his arms around himself and turned toward Wiley. "Wiley, what's goin' on?" he asked softly. "I'm scared, Wiley. What should I do?"

Somewhere in the fog of his mind, Wiley felt his body jerk. Had someone touched him? Slowly, he opened his eyes. "Jake? Where are you?"

"I'm here, Wiley." Jake leaned over and kissed Wiley's forehead. "I was talkin' out loud. Didn't figger I'd wake you up. I'm sorry."

Wiley grabbed Jake's hand and squeezed it. "Jake...I dreamed...Chief Eagle Rising was here."

"I think he was, Wiley. Anyway, somebody was. He gave me this here bag an' said it'd help you get better. I'm scared, Wiley. What should I do?"

Wiley's head began to fog again. He stared long and hard at Jake and thought he heard Grandpa Gray Feather urging him on the way he'd always done when he'd been afraid. "Do what he told you, Jake," Wiley said, wondering where the words had actually come from. "Do it now!"

"But what if it don't work? What'll we do then?"

The fog suddenly rushed back and engulfed Wiley. He closed his eyes and felt himself being swept away by it.

Jake stared at Wiley and shivered. He thought he heard someone saying, "What you have on here, you have on there," and remembered Chief Eagle Rising had said it.

Jake sprang out of the chair, grabbed the candle and went to the hole in the floor. He reached in and felt for the small wooden box he'd placed on the ground next to the cement water basin. He pulled the box through the hole and poured the hundred gold coins he'd won from the wagon race into his pockets.

When he remembered the warning about the other place, he rushed to the chair by the bed, grabbed Wiley's gun belt, strapped it around his waist, and shifted the holster so it rested behind his own.

Jake sat on the bed and looked around the cabin for anything else they might need, *if* they were going anywhere.

"Hell," he said out loud. "I might as well do what Chief Eagle Rising told me. Ain't got nothin' else to try."

With shaking hands, Jake untied the bag and opened it. He held the candle close and peered inside. The bag was filled with dirty, brown sand. Cautiously, he picked up the feather and stuffed it into the bag. A puff of smoke curled up from inside. Startled, Jake dropped the bag on the bed.

After the sweet-smelling smoke disappeared, Jake grabbed the bag again and looked in. The sand was gone! So was the feather! He saw nothing in the bag but golden light. Jake held it in front of his face. The bag bulged out and was just as heavy as when filled with sand.

Suddenly, Jake felt a wave of dizziness and saw colored lights dancing before his eyes. He panicked, quickly set the bag down and climbed on the bed. As he did, his knee squashed the bag.

Jake didn't notice the golden feather puff out and float to the floor.

Jake remembered what Chief Eagle Rising said about keeping the bag next to his body. He picked it up and slipped the loop over his head. When the bag hit his chest, it was flat and weighed almost nothing. He grabbed the bag and stared at it in amazement, then stuffed it down the front of his shirt.

Gently lowering himself on top of Wiley, Jake held him with both arms, buried his face into Wiley's neck and closed his eyes.

Nothing else happened.

After a few minutes of waiting, Jake sat up and glanced around the room. He spotted the golden feather on the floor. Chief Eagle Rising said if he lost the bag or the feather, they'd stay in the strange place forever. Jake started to reach down and get the feather when he felt a violent wind blowing inside the cabin. The log walls groaned under its force. He dived onto Wiley, trying to shield him. Jake shut his eyes when the wind grew in intensity. Through his closed lids, he saw a brilliant light flashing on and off rapidly. He squeezed Wiley harder, then everything went black.

* * *

Winder woke up where he'd propped himself against a rock. He shivered in the night air and grabbed his wounded arm. It ached worse now that the temperature had dropped. He cursed his luck. As he glanced around in the darkness, he could tell Clint had dozed off.

Winder reached over, grabbed Clint's shoulder and roughly shook him. "Wake up! We have to get those two shortly, and I want you fully aware of what you're doing."

"I'm awake!" Clint grasped Winder's arm and shoved it away. "You're always gripin' about everybody else doin' stuff wrong, but you never do nothin' right yerself."

"Shut up, or I'll break you in half," Winder snarled. "I picked you to come because you and I think alike. You hate those dick-lickers as much as I do." He shook his head. "A man's not suppose to love another man. It's in the Bible."

"When have *you* ever read the Bible?"

Winder shrugged. "Well, if it doesn't say it in the Bible, it should.

Clint sighed at Winder's comment, then said, "I'm hungry. I'm goin' to my horse an' get somethin' to eat. I can't do no killin' on an empty stomach."

"You're always whining about something! Go ahead, get something to eat if you have to. I don't plan on attacking the cabin for at least an hour. We'll let them think we've left, and they'll drop their guard. We may even catch them asleep."

As Clint got to his feet, Winder said, "As long as you're going, bring me something. Grab that bottle of whiskey out of my saddle bag, and for God's sake, be quiet!"

"Yah, yah, yah," Clint mumbled as he stumbled through the darkness toward their horses.

Winder leaned back against a rock and built a smoke. He'd be glad when this was over. Once he got his freedom from Billingsly, he'd be on his way to the warm beaches of California. He hated the cold of the high country and longed for the night life in San Francisco. He'd heard it was grand. In little over an hour, Jake and Wiley would be dead, and he'd be gone within a week.

Winder smiled in the darkness and took a long drag on his smoke. He thought again of the violent burst of wind that had raged through the valley earlier that afternoon. He'd never experienced anything like it. He shuddered when he remembered how it had stopped as suddenly as it began.

After Clint returned, they ate some jerky and biscuits and passed the bottle back and forth until it was empty.

"It's time," Winder finally said.

Stiff from the cold air, they got up from their crouched positions and slowly picked their way down the rocks, trying not to make any noise. Occasionally, small stones skittered down the slope.

Once they got to the bottom of the ridge, they crept through the small aspen grove to the outhouse. As they crouched behind the structure, Winder whispered into Clint's ear, "You take the left side of the door. On my signal, yank the door open and rush in low. I'll follow right behind."

They crept to the door and positioned themselves on either side. Clint grabbed the handle. On Winder's signal, he yanked the door open. The cowbell flew off the nail, sailed over Clint's head, bounced and clanged down the slope. With their element of surprise ruined, Clint flattened himself against the outside wall.

Both men expected shots from inside at any moment. When none came, Winder crouched low and rushed through the door, guns firing in all directions. When he felt the wire hit his shin, he reached out and frantically tried to grab something to keep from falling, but there was nothing. He turned his body and fell on his side, then let out a blood-curling scream as the nails buried themselves deep into his left arm and leg.

Terrified by Winder's outburst, Clint crept to the open door. When his leg touched the wire, he stopped. Hearing only Winder's agonized cries, Clint stepped over the wire and entered the cabin.

Not knowing what had happened to Winder, Clint yelled, "Don't shoot! Winder's hurt!" He tossed his gun to the floor. "I ain't armed, don't shoot! I gotta see what's happened to Winder!" When his yells got no response, Clint fumbled in his pocket, pulled out a match and struck it on his boot. As the match flared, he saw Winder impaled but trying to get up.

"Oh, my gawd!" Clint yelled.

The match burned his finger. He dropped it, pulled out another and struck it. While the match burned, he saw the candlestick on the bed. Shielding the flame, he rushed over, lit the wick, and held the candle high above his head. He and Winder were the only ones in the cabin!

Clint ran to Winder and helped him to his feet. Several boards remained attached to the man's arm and leg. In a rage, Winder pulled them off with his free hand and threw them against the wall. Clint helped Winder to the empty, bloodied bed seconds before he fainted.

Clint looked around the cabin, dumbfounded the brothers had escaped. To hell with them. He needed to get Winder to the closest town with a doctor. Clint ran out the door, tripped over the wire and fell face-down in the dirt outside the door. He lay on the ground until his head cleared, then staggered down the slope to their horses.

# CHAPTER 39

"I hope you die of lockjaw!" Billingsly screamed as he stood over Winder's bed. "You were around those two men for *days*, and you let them slip through your fingers!"

"I shot the dark-haired one in the leg," Winder rasped. "By the amount of blood I saw on the ground at their cabin, I got him pretty good."

"Not good enough! They escaped!"

Billingsly walked to the window and looked out. "You were the best man for the job! The *only* one I could trust to pull it off, and you bungled it!" He shook his fist in the air. "I suppose I'm going to have to put up with those *idiots* from Kentucky again!" He turned and faced Winder. "But I'm sure they'll have more luck killing those men than anyone *else* I have working for me!" He stomped out of the room and slammed the door.

Outside, Billingsly saw Clint talking to a stable hand. He caught Clint's eye and waved him to the porch.

"Clint, I want you to tell me everything that happened while you were at the race," Billingsly demanded. "And especially after you got to their cabin."

"But I already told you once."

"Tell me again!"

As Clint related the story for the second time, Jimmy Ratchett rode up to the porch and dismounted. When he heard Clint talking about the happenings after the race, he stood behind Billingsly and listened. Hearing that Wiley had been shot and the cabin had been empty, he became alarmed. He had to let Belinda know what happened. When he saw her in Como yesterday, she hadn't known the blood brothers were back from the race.

Jimmy broke into the conversation. "Boss, do you have any errands for me to run while I'm in town?"

His mind taken up by Clint's account, Billingsly spun around and stared vacantly at Jimmy. "No!" He turned back to Clint. "Go on!"

With a half smile, Jimmy mounted his horse and rode toward Alma. When he arrived at the livery, Bill wasn't sitting in front. He ran through the building and called for the hostler, and even climbed to the loft. Bill wasn't anywhere around.

Jimmy leaped on his horse, galloped down Main Street to Pete's Barber Shop. He swung down from his saddle, tied his horse loosely and burst into the shop.

Pete looked up from shaving a lathered face. "Morning, son. It'll be only a few minutes wait. Have a seat."

"Where's Harry?" Jimmy asked.

"In the back, as usual." Pete jerked his head to the side door.

Jimmy ran across the shop, through the door and rushed down the short hall to the back room. He found Harry sitting in a chair with his feet propped on the edge of a tub, reading the newspaper.

Harry glanced up and grinned when Jimmy rushed in. "I hope you need a rubdown."

"Where's Bill Chasteen? I've got to tell him what happened to the blood brothers."

Harry put the paper down and stood up. "What happened? I just saw them yesterday, and they seemed fine to me."

"Winder shot one of them. From the way Clint described the amount of blood around, the wound was serious. Then, when Winder and Clint stormed their cabin to finish them off, the brothers were gone."

"Lordy!" Harry yelled. He ran to the wall and grabbed his gun belt, strapped it on, and put on his hat. "Come on!" He ran down the hall to the barber shop and slid to a comical stop.

"Pete, a friend of mine's been shot. I have to ride out to the Castille Ranch and help find him. I'll be back sometime tomorrow."

"Like hell you will!" Pete shook the soapy razor at Harry. "You leave now, you *stay* gone!"

"Oh, come on, Pete, you know the following I have in town. If you fire me, your shop will close in a week for lack of business." Harry laughed and ran out the door.

Pete glared at the door for a moment, then continued shaving the man in the chair.

"Ouch!" The man yelled. "Watch it, will you?"

"Sorry." Pete grabbed a cloth to wipe the thin line of blood off the man's cheek.

Jimmy ran the block to the sheriff's office. While he informed Sheriff Cline about the shooting and disappearance of Jake and Wiley, Harry ran across the street to the Regal Cafe. He flung open the door and stepped in. Bill sat at their usual table in the corner, sipping coffee. Harry caught Bill's eye and motioned him outside.

As they hurried up the street toward the sheriff's office, Harry filled Bill in on what happened.

Fifteen minutes later, Sheriff Cline, Bill, Harry and Jimmy were riding toward the Castille Ranch. Doc Colter said he would follow after he finished delivering Mrs. Murdock's baby. During the ride, Jimmy told them what he'd overheard from Clint.

"Dang!" Bill shouted. "That shootin' must'a happened just after we left 'em yesterday mornin'."

The men arrived at the Castille Ranch about noon. They stopped only long enough to get Belinda and Soaring Raven before they rode to Chipmunk Rock.

When they arrived at Jake and Wiley's cabin, they found Mac and Buddy still in the corral. The two saddles were lying on the ground in the middle of the fenced area. After dismounting, the group climbed up the slope to the cabin.

The door stood open.

Harry started to rush into the cabin when Sheriff Cline yelled, "Harry! There's a wire across the door!"

Harry stopped in time and saw the stretched wire hanging loosely across the opening. He stepped over it and entered the dark cabin.

As he opened the shutters to let in more light, the others crowded through the door. They stared with open mouths at the disarray. Sheriff Cline inspected the scattered boards on the floor. Many of the protruding nails were coated with dried blood.

"My God!" Belinda gasped when she saw the bloody bed. "Where do you suppose Jake and Wiley are?" She put her hands to her face and turned toward Jimmy.

He pulled her close.

"Their horses are still here," Bill said. "Maybe they went up the slope and are hidin' in the bushes somewhere. I'm goin' outside to look for 'em." He rushed through the door, tripped over the wire and fell flat on his face outside the door.

"Will someone cut that damn wire!" Sheriff Cline yelled. "From the looks of those nails, they did damage to someone."

"It must have been Winder," Jimmy stated.

Amid Bill's cursing, Harry removed the wire, then the pair scrambled up the slope. Sheriff Cline followed after giving the cabin another brief inspection. Jimmy helped Belinda out the door for some fresh air.

Alone, Soaring Raven stood in the middle of the room with her arms folded and carefully looked around. She closed her eyes and began chanting in her native tongue. Suddenly, she opened her eyes and went to the side of the bed, stooped down and picked up the golden feather and held it in front of her face.

When Belinda returned to the cabin, she found Soaring Raven standing by the window with the feather in her hand.

"What's that, Sa-Ra?"

"Big medicine! Brothers not here. They not anywhere where we are. Leave them be, they be home soon."

Soaring Raven walked to the hole in the floor, reached in and felt for the edge of the basin. She placed the feather on the dry ground under the floor, but then grabbed it again.

"Not yet," she mumbled.

"What did you say?" Belinda asked.

"I give feather back to brothers, but not yet. First, I give thanks." Somberly, she walked outside, climbed to the top of the cliff and stood facing south.

Belinda stepped outside the door and watched the Indian woman climb up the hill toward the cliff. She knew enough about

Sa-Ra and her beliefs to realize whatever had happened here was beyond her understanding.

When Jimmy trudged up the hill from the corral, he walked over to Belinda. "You're shaking." He gathered her into his arms. Following her gaze, he saw Soaring Raven. "What's going on with her? Where'd she find that feather?"

Belinda shuddered. "I don't know. She said Jake and Wiley aren't here, but they'll be home soon." She gazed into Jimmy's eyes. "And I believe her."

As the others scrambled down the slope toward the cabin, Harry grabbed Bill and pointed to Soaring Raven, standing at the edge of the cliff. As the woman lifted the feather to the sky, a sudden, violent wind nearly knocked everyone over. Harry, Bill and Sheriff Cline made their way to the door of the cabin where Jimmy held Belinda, both leaning into the continuous blast of air.

High above, seven ravens, soaring into the wind, hovered motionless over the cabin and people below. The largest bird suddenly dived lower, positioned itself in the wind ten feet above Soaring Raven's head and hovered there.

The wind's howling rose to a high pitch. Alone on the cliff, Soaring Raven's long hair streamed behind her as she held the golden feather to the sky, chanting.

## ABOUT THE AUTHOR

Dave Brown is a native of Denver. For the last twenty years, he and his lifetime partner, Jim Bannerman, have split their time between Denver and South Park, Colorado, hoping to make South Park their permanent home.

# ORDER FORM

### Send to:

### GOLDEN FEATHER PRESS
PO BOX 481374
DENVER, CO 80248

NAME_____

ADDRESS_____ APT #_____

CITY_____STATE____ZIP_____

PHONE (Day)_____ (Eve)_____

|  | Qty. | Price | Tax* | Total |
|---|---|---|---|---|
| Bristlecone Peak | _____ | $14.95 | $.45/Book | _____ |

Plus $3.00 shipping and handling per book _____

TOTAL ENCLOSED _____

Please make checks or money orders payable to:

### GOLDEN FEATHER PRESS

Please do not send cash.  Sorry, no credit cards or CODs.

*Colorado residents only

SOON TO BE PUBLISHED


Dave Brown's second and third books of

LEGEND OF THE GOLDEN FEATHER SERIES


THE PROTECTORS

and

HOME TO KENTUCKY